The King's Last Song
or
Kraing Meas

Novels by Geoff Ryman

Unconquered Country
The Child Garden
Was
253
Lust
Air

The King's Last Song
or
Kraing Meas

Geoff Ryman

Small Beer Press
Easthampton, MA

First published in the UK in 2006 by HarperCollins Publishers.
Copyright © 2006 by Geoff Ryman. All rights reserved.
Afterword copyright © 2008 by Geoff Ryman. All rights reserved.
www.ryman-novel.com

Small Beer Press
150 Pleasant Street #306
Easthampton, MA 01027
www.smallbeerpress.com
info@smallbeerpress.com

Distributed to the trade by Consortium.

Library of Congress Cataloging-in-Publication Data

Ryman, Geoff.
  The king's last song, or, Kraing meas / Geoff Ryman.
     p. cm.
  ISBN 978-1-931520-56-0 (trade pbk.)
  1. Jayvarman VII, King of Cambodia, ca. 1120-ca. 1215--Fiction. 2. Angkor Wat (Angkor)--
Fiction. 3. Archaeological thefts--Fiction. 4. Kidnapping--Fiction. 5. Cambodia--Antiquities--
Fiction. I. Title. II. Title: King's last song. III. Title: Kraing meas.
  PR6068.Y74K56 2008
  823'.914--dc22

                                    2008017141

First edition 1 2 3 4 5 6 7 8 9

Printed on 50# Natures Book Natural FSC Mixed 30% PCR paper by Thomson-Shore of Dexter, MI.
Text set in Adobe Caslon Pro 10.4.

Cover photos © Pablo Corral Vega/CORBIS and © Jeremy Horner/Panos Pictures.

dedicated to
Tamara and da boize

"Oh you who are wise, may you come more and more to consider all meritorious acts as your own."

Sanskrit inscription on the temple of Pre Rup, translated by Kamaleswar Bhattacharya

"As wealthy as Cambodia."

Traditional Chinese saying

Awakening

You could very easily meet William.

Maybe you've just got off the boat from Phnom Penh and nobody from your hotel is there to meet you. It's miles from the dock to Siem Reap.

William strides up and pretends to be the free driver to your hotel. Not only that but he organizes a second motorbike to wobble its way round the ruts with your suitcases.

Many Cambodians would try to take you to their brother's guesthouse instead. William not only gets you to the right hotel, but just as though he really does work for it, he charges you nothing.

He also points out that you might need someone to drive you to the baray reservoir or to the monuments. When you step back out into the street after your shower, he's waiting for you, big for a Cambodian, looking happy and friendly.

During the trip, William buys fruit and offers you some, relying on your goodness to pay him back. When you do, he looks not only pleased, but also justified. He has been right to trust you.

If you ask him what his real name is in Cambodian, he might sound urgent and threatened. He doesn't want you think he has not told the truth. Out comes the identity card: Ly William.

He'll tell you the story. His family were killed during the Pol Pot era. His aunty plucked him out of his mother's arms. He has never been told more than that. His uncle and aunt do not want to distress him. His uncle renamed him after a kindly English aid worker in a Thai camp. His personal name really is William. He almost can't pronounce it.

William starts to ask you questions, about everything you know. Some of the questions are odd. Is Israel in Europe? Who was Henry Kissinger? What is the relationship between people in England and people in America?

Then he asks if you know what artificial aperture radar is.

"Are you a student?" you might ask.

William can't go to university. His family backed the wrong faction in the civil war. The high school diplomas given by his side in their border schools are not recognized in Cambodia.

William might tell you he lived a year in Phnom Penh, just so that he could talk to students at the Royal University, to find out what they had learned, what they read. You may have an image of him in your mind, shut out, desperate to learn, sitting on the lawn.

"My uncle want to be monk," he says. "My uncle say to me, you suffer now because you lead bad life in the past. You work now and earn better life. My uncle does not want me to be unhappy."

This is how William lives.

He sleeps in his uncle's house. It's on stilts, built of spare timber. His eldest cousin goes to bed late in a hammock under the house, and the candle he carries sends rays of light fanning up through the floorboards. The floorboards don't meet so that crumbs can be swept through them.

There is a ladder down to the ground. There are outbuildings and sheds in which even poorer relatives sleep. There is a flowerbed, out of which sprouts the spirit house, a tiny dwelling for the animistic spirit of the place.

William and two male cousins sleep on one mattress in a room that is partitioned from the others with plywood and hanging clothes.

William is always the first awake.

He lies in the dark for a few moments listening to the roosters crow. The cries cascade across the whole floodplain, all the way to the mountains, marking how densely populated the landscape is. William is himself in those moments. At every other time of the day he is working.

William looks at the moon through the open shutters. The moonlight on the mosquito net breaks apart into a silver arch. This is his favourite moment; he uses it to think of nothing at all, but just to look.

Then he rolls to his feet.

The house is a clock. Its shivering tells people who has got up and who will be next.

One of his cousins turns over. In the main room, William steps over the girls asleep in a row on the floor. He swings down the ladder into his waiting flip-flops and pads to the kitchen shed. Embers glow in moulded rings that are part of the concrete tabletop. William leans over, blows on the fire, feeds it twigs, and then goes outside to the water pump.

Candles move silently through the trees, people going to check their palm-wine stills or to relieve themselves. A motorcycle putters past; William says hi. He boils water and studies by candlelight.

He has taught himself English and French and enough German to get by. Now he is teaching himself Japanese. He needs these languages to talk to people.

On the same shelf as the pans is an old ring binder. It is stuffed full with different kinds of paper, old school notebooks or napkins taken from restaurants. Each page is about someone: their name, address, e-mail, notes about their family, their work, what they know.

William has learned in his bones that survival takes the form of other people. They must know you, and for that to happen you must know them. Speak with them, charm them, and remember them.

A neighbour turns on her cassette player. Sin Sisimuth purrs a gentle yearning pillow of a song. The working day has begun in earnest. William snaps on the kitchen's fluorescent light, attached to a car battery.

Sometimes at this quiet hour, William is seized by a vision. A vision in which Cambodia is a top country. Like Singapore, it is a place of wealth and discipline. To be that, Cambodia will need different leaders, people who are not corrupt, and who do things well. Who remember other people.

William is possessed of a thought that is common among the poor, but seldom expressed: I know who I am.

And I am as good as anyone.

He discovered that as he hung around the university students. He had one pair of shoes, but they were spotlessly white. He'd sit down with a group and smile and get their names and give them his own. What do you study? they'd ask. Politics, he'd reply. He would find out what books they had to read for their courses.

The university students talked about fashion and machines and motorbikes, just like anyone else. They looked soft and grumpy and made less effort than country people. Some of them made fun of his regional accent and didn't listen to what he said. That's okay, I learn from you, but you won't learn from me. He kept smiling.

There is a grunt and William's cousin Meak stomps into the kitchen. William calls him Rock Star. He has long hair and a torn T-shirt that says WE'RE SO FULL OF HOPE, AND WE'RE SO FULL OF SHIT.

"Hey, coz," Rock Star murmurs.

William makes a joke and passes him his breakfast. Breakfast is a cup of boiled water. Rock Star is always smiling. He plays air guitar at parties, but he is the one family member who truly loves being a farmer. He loves his pigs. He even looks a little like them, smiling, short and bulky.

"I'm going out towards the Phnom for feed this morning. I could go and pay the families out that way for you."

William's uncle and aunt are getting too old to work in the rice fields, so he pays other families a dollar a day to help with the harvest. But he must give them their money all at the same time, or there could be jealousy.

"Cool, cousin, thanks," he says.

Rock Star grins sleepily. "I know you can't wait to get to your foreign friends."

Working for the UN dig team brings in seven dollars a day during tourist season. William has a contract with them; he shows up there first to drive one of them if they need him. That money pays for many things.

Outside, as tall and handsome as William, his cousin Ran goes to wash. He is so proud of his artificial leg. It is one of the best. He goes to wash at the pump wearing only a *kramar* round his waist so that everyone can see that he is not angry at life and very grateful to William. He waves and smiles. William sold all his ten cows to buy the leg.

William must always prove his value to the family.

Aunty comes next. Even first thing in the morning, she does not wear traditional dress. She is a modern woman, with curled hair and lipstick. She smiles at William and takes over in the kitchen. She is as kind and loving to him as if he were her son. William goes back to learning kanji. Outside on a bamboo pole are his clean clothes for the day, washed by his cousin. In his baseball cap, trousers with big pockets, and track shoes, he will look like a teenager in any suburb of the world.

My family, William thinks with fondness and gratitude. Where would I be without my family?

You would meet Map easily as well. Or rather, you would not be able to escape him.

He would scare you at first. Map is forty-four years old and smells of war. His face is scarred, and his smile looks like a brown and broken saw.

But he is wearing a spotlessly clean brown police uniform, and he seems to be patrolling Angkor Wat in some official capacity. As if in passing and wanting nothing from you, he starts explaining the pools to you in good English. The four dry basins you see so high up in Angkor Wat symbolize the four great rivers flowing from Mount Meru.

The information is of better quality than you expected. You smile, say thanks and try to edge away, dreading another request for money.

"You've missed the main bas-reliefs," he warns, again as if in an official capacity. "Come this way." He leads you down steps, to the bas-relief gallery. The stone is polished, the detail amazing. Map explains scenes from the *Mahabharata* and the *Ramayana*. He turns a corner and explains that the roof of this gallery is how all the galleries would have looked.

You might ask him if he is a trained tourist guide. He tells you, "I work for Professor Luc Andrade of the United Nations dig team. I do their Web site."

That throws you for a moment. Who is this guy?

He points to carved soldiers in strange uniforms. "These are mercenaries. Nobody trust those guys," he says. "Like me. I used to be Khmer Rouge, but I changed sides and joined Hun Sen. They made me march in front, to step on landmines."

Then he tells you, smiling, that he guarded a Pol Pot camp. It wasn't a camp; it was a village, in a commune; but Map knows what Westerners expect. He knows he has you hooked.

He takes you on a tour of hell, the long bas-relief of people being tortured. Map lists them all for you.

The frying pan, for people who kill embryos.

Pot baking for trusted people who steal from gurus.

Forest of palm trees for people who cut down trees unduly...

"We need that in Cambodia now," he says and smiles. "People cut down all our forest."

He points to someone hammering nails into people's bones. "I was that guy there," he says.

Howling, for those who are degraded...

Today, April 11, Map gets up later than William does, but then he worked all night. He's a Patrimony Policeman, protecting Angkor from art thieves. He sleeps off and on in a hammock strung across the doorway of the main building.

Then he works all day as well, anything to add to his salary of sixteen dollars a month.

This morning, he has persuaded an adventurous *barang* to sleep alongside him in another hammock. The foreigner, a German, is swathed in mosquito nets and smells of something chemical. He is pink and splotchy and still has on his glasses.

Map rocks him awake. "Come on," Map says in German, "it is time to see the sunrise." The man has paid him ten dollars for the privilege but like all tourists is so scared of theft that he has hidden his tiny digital camera in his underpants. Can you imagine how it smells? Map thinks to himself. I wonder if it's taken any pictures inside there by mistake.

The German sniffs, nods.

Map chuckles. "You never been in a war." The German looks miffed; he thinks he's a tough guy. "You wake up in the morning in a war, pow! Your eyes open, wide, wide, wide, and you are looking, looking, looking." Map laughs uproariously at the idea of the huge German on Highway 6 pulling up his trousers in the line of fire.

In the early morning mist, the five towers of Angkor Wat look magnified, as if the air were a lens. Map leads the German up steps, past scaffolding to the empty pools. He considerately takes hold of his elbow to lead him up onto the next level.

Then come the long staircases to the top. They taper to give the illusion of even greater height, and they are practically vertical, more like ladders than staircases.

"People say these steps are narrow because Cambodians have small feet." Map grins. "We're not monkeys! We don't like pointing our bums at people. These steps make people turn sideways." He shows the German how to walk safely up the steps.

Then, as a joke, Map sends him up a staircase that has worn away at the top to a rounded hump of rock with no steps or handrails.

The German finds himself hugging the stone in panic. From here, the drop looks vertical. Map roars with laughter. The German looks back at him, and his eyes seem to say: this wild man wouldn't care if I fell!

He is not wrong. There is something deranged about Map. He has been shooting people since he was twelve years old.

Map chuckles affectionately and nips around him and up and over the stone on his thick-soled policeman's shoes. He crouches down and pulls the German up.

"You have a lot of fun! You don't want to go up the staircase with a handrail."

"Uh," says the German, just grateful to be alive. He turns and looks down and decides that, after all, he has just been very brave. Adventure was what he wanted. "Not too many old ladies do that!"

Even at this hour, the pavilion around the main towers is full of people. Other Patrimony Policemen greet Map with a nod and a rueful smile at his tourist catch. A large image of the Buddha shelters in the main tower, robed in orange cloth. Black-toothed nuns try to sell the German incense sticks. He buys one and uses that as an excuse to get a series of shots of an old woman with the Buddha.

Map leads the tourist through a window out onto a ledge high up over the courtyard, which is itself above ground level. It is what, a hundred, two hundred feet down to grass?

The ledge is wide—twenty people could easily sit down on it. The German grins and holds his camera out over the edge to take a picture. Over the top of the surrounding wall, trees billow like clouds, full of the sounds of birds and smelling like medicine.

"So," says the German, fiddling with his automatic focus. "There are many bas-reliefs on Hindu themes. Did Cambodians become Buddhist later?"

"There was a king," says Map. The morning is so quiet and bright he wonders if he can be bothered trying to make this foreigner understand who Jayavarman was and what he means to Cambodia.

"When Angkor Wat City is conquered, he takes it back from the foreigners. He make many many new temples. Angkor Thom, Ta Prohm, Neak Pean, Preah Kahn, all those temples. He make Cambodia a Buddhist country. After there is Hindu revolt, but Cambodians still remember him."

Map says the King's name, feeling many complex things: respect, amusement, love. The German asks him to repeat it.

"Jayavarman Seven." Map can feel his smile stretch with sourness.

He thinks about the five-hundred-dollar bribe he paid a few years ago to get a job removing landmines. He bribed the wrong person and didn't get the job. He'd sold his motorbike to get the money. Originally he wanted to use it to pay for his wedding, but he thought the job would be a better investment. His fiancée left him.

He thinks of all the so-called leaders and the tangled, self-serving mess they are making of the country. "Now we need Jayavarman."

The gold leaves have slept for a thousand years.

Two metres down, below the range of ploughs and metal detectors, they lie wrapped in layers of orange linen and pitch.

They were carried at night, hurriedly, jostled under a bridge and plunged down into the mud by the canal to keep them safe. They were cast in imitation of a palm-leaf manuscript, inscribed and inked. The leaves still yearn to speak, though the ink has long since soaked away.

The canal overhead simmered in the heat, then silted up. The water ceased to flow. The soil was parched and inundated by turns for centuries. Rice reached down, but never touched the leaves or their linen wrappings.

Gold does not rust. Insects and rodents do not devour it. Its only enemy is greed.

On April 11, in a version of 2004, something fiercely invasive drives itself into the Book. A corer grinds its way down through five packets of leaves. Then it hoists part of them up and out of the ground.

For the first time in a thousand years, light shines through the soil, linen, and pitch.

The Book is awake again.

Light shines on a torn circle of gold. It shines on writing. The words plainly say in Sanskrit, "I am Jayavarman."

LEAF 1

My name in death will be Parama Saugatapada. In life, I bore a king's title, Victory Shield, Jayavarman. I will be known as Jayavarman the great builder, father of the new city, the wall-builder of Indrapattha. I am lord of the temple that is like no other, the temple that is history in stone, the great Madhyadri. I will be known as the founder of the King's Monastery. I will be known as the son of Holy Victory City, Nagara Jayasri that rose like a flower beside the Lake of Blood. My face will greet those who come to the City for a thousand years. My son calls it my Mango Face, ripe and plump. My Mango Face looks four ways, in the cardinal directions. My face is the four Noble Truths. I am Jayavarman, the bringer of the new way that subsumes the old and surmounts it.

LEAF 2

The Gods themselves listened to the great soul (Buddha) for enlighten-ment. So it is that the new kingship enlightens the old. This new kingship builds walls to protect the City and builds love in the hearts of the people. Love is also a wall to protect the City. I once had the name of Prince Nia, Hereditary Slave. How a prince came to be called Slave is only one reason why I burn to do a new thing. I will turn the eyes of language away from dedications and gods. I turn my gaze towards people, just as I caused my temple the Madhyadri to honor the images of farm girls and merchants and Chinese envoys. I turn the light of my mind to ordinary days. My words will show lost people. My words will show the sunlight of great days now turned to night. My words will show parades and elephants and parasols whose march has long since passed into dust.

APRIL 1136

The Prince was supposed to be asleep with the other children.

The adults were all in their hammocks. Only insects were awake, buzzing in the heat. To fill the silence, the Prince stomped up the wooden steps as loudly as he could.

The King's gallery was empty. The gold-embroidered curtains breathed in and out as if they were asleep. The only other person he could see was a servant girl dusting the floor.

The girl was about four years older than the Prince. Maybe she'd want to play. He broke into a run towards her, but then lost heart. Old palace women with wrinkled faces and broken teeth would pick him up and fuss over him, but pretty young girls with work to do would be told off for it.

The Prince grew shy. "Play with me," he asked, in a soft breathy voice.

The girl bowed and then smiled as if there was nothing more delightful than to be approached by a person of his category. "I must work," she beamed, as if that were a pleasure too.

He was a *sujati*, a well-born person. The girl was bare-chested, some category of worker. A diadem of wooden slats was tied across her forehead, and the stain across her temples was her passport into the royal enclosure. The Prince watched her clean. For a moment it was interesting to see the damp cloth push grains of food through the knotholes and gaps in the floorboards.

Then boredom returned as unrelenting as a headache. Boredom drove him. It was nearly unbearable, the silence, the sameness.

The thin floor rested high off the ground on stilts. The floorboards gave the boy the foot-beat of a giant. He lifted up his bare foot, drove it down hard, and felt the whole house quiver. He giggled and looked back at the girl and then took more high, hammering steps across the floor

The girl paid no attention.

No one wore shoes, so dusty footprints trailed across the red gallery floors where the girl had not yet cleaned.

To the Prince they looked like the tracks of game across a forest floor.

He was a hunter in the woods. He charged forward. "I see you, deer! Whoosh!" He let fly imaginary arrows. "I see you wild pig! Whoosh I get you!"

He looked back at the girl. She still dusted.

Suddenly the footprints looked more like those of enemy troops. He imitated the sounds of battle music: conch-shell moans and the bashing of gongs. He paraded, thumping his feet. He was a Great King. He waved the Sacred Sword over his head and charged.

He thundered back down the length of the gallery, wailing.

The girl still dusted, looking hunched.

He could be naughty, this prince. He had a formal name, but everybody nicknamed him Catch-Him-to-Call-Him, Cap-Pi-Hau.

All right, Cap-Pi-Hau thought, you want to be slow and boring, I will make you play.

He ran back and forth up and down the empty gallery until the entire floor shivered. He shouted like a warrior. He cried like egrets on the Great Lake, surprised by battle and keening up into the sky.

He stalked down the front steps and out into the thinly grassed enclosure. He pummelled his way back into the gallery. He ran in circles around the girl. He bellowed as loudly as he could and jumped boldly, no steps at all, out of the house and fell face down onto the dry ground. He billowed his way back into the gallery, trailing dust behind him.

Each time he ran past her, the little girl bowed in respect, head down.

Most devilish of all, he clambered up the staircase to the forbidden apartments on the storey above. He rumbled all the way to the head of the stairs and spun around, to see if he had succeeded in making her follow him, to chastise him and pull him back down.

Instead the little girl looked mournfully at her floor.

Everywhere she had already cleaned there were footprints and shadow-shapes of white dust.

She dared not look at him, but her mouth swelled out with unhappiness. Abruptly she stood up and took little whisking steps towards the entrance.

Cap-Pi-Hau tumbled out of the door after her to see if he could join in.

She took nipping steps down the front steps to the ground, holding up her beautiful skirt, palace-blue with gold flowers. What was she doing?

"Ha ha!" he said, a harsh imitation of a laugh to show this was good, this could be fun.

She held up her mournful face. She took her cloth to the ceramic water butt and wrung it out.

"What are you doing?" he demanded.

"I will dust the floor again," she said, and turned away from him.

He followed her up the stairs. Suddenly, his feet felt weighed down. He hauled himself back into the gallery and saw the floor patterned with his dusty footprints.

Cap-Pi-Hau only slowly realized that the weight he felt was sadness. He had wanted to make the little girl happy, he had wanted to have fun, and now he had a terrible sense of having destroyed something.

He felt his eyes swell out, as if to burst like fruit into tears. Why did everything turn out bad? Why was fun never possible? Why was it always learning, chanting, sleeping, bowing, and silence?

The girl knelt down and began to dust again. Maybe she would get a scolding or a beating.

Cap-Pi-Hau trundled towards her, softly now. "I have a thought," he said.

Her swollen, sad face still would not look at him.

He had thought of a way to make dusting fun. Gently he coaxed the cloth out of her hands. "I'll show you," he whispered.

He laid the cloth flat on the floor. Then he stepped back, ran at it, and jumped.

The floor had been smoothed by years of cleaning. It had to be free of splinters so that bare feet could walk on it.

Cap-Pi-Hau landed on the cloth, and it slid across the floor, bearing him forward, harvesting dust.

He giggled and turned back to her. "See? See?" he demanded.

A butterfly of a smile fluttered briefly on her lips.

He laughed and applauded to make her smile again. Then he walked all the way back to the edge of the pavilion and ran. It seemed to him that he shook the entire house. When he jumped onto the cloth, physical inertia swept him even farther across the floor.

"I am the Great King who leads his people!" he shouted. "I am the Great King who leads troops in polishing floors!"

The slave girl giggled and hid her mouth.

"You go!" Cap-Pi-Hau insisted. "It will be fine. I will say that I ordered it."

The girl gathered up her skirt. Her ankles looked like twigs. In comparison, her feet looked big, like the heads of buffaloes. She ran and jumped and slid only a moment.

Not enough. She spun and commandeered the cloth, and stepped back and ran again. She was older than the Prince and her coordination was better. She pelted down the floor, leapt, and was swept on. She stood erect, skirts fluttering, and she turned to him and this time her mouth was swollen with a huge, smug grin.

The next day Cap-Pi-Hau asked one of the nannies, "Where do slaves come from?"

The old woman waved her hands. "Oh! Some are the children of people taken in battle. Some are presents given to the King. Many are given to the temples, simply to get rid of them. Most are attached to the land, like cows."

The woman had a face as hard and polished as wood furniture. Taken in battle? Given away? Do they know their families did not want them, did not love them?

The other six- and seven-year-olds were corralled together outside in the shade of the enclosure temple. There was to be a great procession soon, and they would have to learn their parts.

The royal temple of the Aerial Palace, *Vimana-akasha*, rose as a holy mountain in stone and stucco layers. Painted red, black, and gold, the temple baked in the heat. Birds landed on the steps and hopped away back into the air, the stones were so hot. The palace children roasted inside their quilted jackets.

The Prince demanded, "If I wanted to find one of the slave girls, how would I do it?"

"Oh!" The nanny showed her false teeth, which were made of wood. "You are too young for that, young prince. That will come later." She beamed.

"If I want to be friends with one of them now, how would I find her?"

The smile was dropped suddenly like an unleashed drapery. "You have your cousins to be friends with. Your destiny is to lead troops for the King. I should not grow too attached to the slaves of the royal household. You will not always live here. Your family lands are off in the east." She looked suddenly grumpy, and for some reason wiped the whole of her face with her hand.

The children, seated in ranks, stirred slightly with the light breeze of someone else getting into trouble.

The nanny's face swelled. "You will be turned out of this house. You forget your real situation. The time has come to stop being a child."

Before he thought anything else, the Prince said aloud, "Then we are all slaves."

The nanny's jaw dropped. "Oh! To say such a thing!" She gathered her skirts and stood up. "It shows your foolishness, Prince Whoever-you-are. Slaves work, while you sit still in your jacket. You will be at the head of the troops so that the enemy will kill you first, and that is your destiny!"

She started to strut. The thin line of her mouth began to stretch into a smile. "You think you are a slave? We will call you slave, ah? *Khnom!* Or are you a hereditary slave, a *nia*? Shall we call you Prince Hereditary Slave?" Her voice was raised. Some of the Prince's cousins, rivals, giggled. "Children, children, listen."

The nanny grabbed Cap-Pi-Hau's shoulders and pushed him in front of her, presenting him. "This young prince wants to be called Nia. So will we call him Nia? Ah? Yes?"

This was going to be fun. The children chorused, "Nee-ah!"

The Prince tried to shrug her off, but she held him in place.

"Nia! Ni-ah-ha ha!" chuckled the children of other royal wives, other royal uncles, other royal cousins. They had already learned they had to triumph over each other before they could triumph over anything else.

The nanny settled back down onto the ground, full and satisfied, as if she had eaten. The laughter continued.

Cap-Pi-Hau also knew: there are many princes, and I will be nothing if no other princes follow me.

He strode to her and faced her. She was sitting; their faces were level. His gaze was steady and unblinking.

Seated, the woman did a girlish twist and a shrug. What of you?

The Prince felt his face go hard. "I am studying your face to remember you, so that when I am older you will be in trouble."

From a prince of any degree, that was a threat. She faltered slightly.

The Prince turned his back on her. He said to the other children, "This woman is a slave. This is what we do to slaves who mock us."

Then he spun back around and kicked her arm.

"Oh, you little demon!" She grabbed him.

Cap-Pi-Hau sprang forward and began to rain blows about her face. Each time he struck her he called her, accurately, by the name of her own lower category. *"Pual!"* He said it each time he struck her. "Pual! Pual! Know your place!"

"Get this monkey god off me!" she cried.

Perhaps she had also been hard on the other women, because they just chuckled. One of them said, "He is yours to deal with, Mulberry."

Her legs were folded, tying her to the spot. She could hit back, but not too hard, even if this was a prince far from the line of succession.

Finally she called for help. "Guard!"

The bored attendant simply chuckled. "He's a prince."

"Nia! Nia! Nia!" the other children chanted, not knowing if they were insulting him or cheering him on.

The nanny fought her way to her feet. "Oh! You must be disciplined."

"So must you." The young prince turned, and stomped up to the guard. "Your sword."

"Now, now little master…"

Cap-Pi-Hau took it.

The woman called Mulberry knew then the extent of her miscalculation. She had imagined that this quiet child was meek and timid.

"What are you going to do?" she said, backing away.

He charged her.

She turned and ran and he slapped her on her bottom with the flat of the sword. "Help! Help!" she was forced to cry.

The children squealed with laughter.

The tiny prince roared with a tiger-cub voice. "Stop, you pual! Talk to me or I will use the blade."

She yelped and turned, giving him a deep and sincere dip of respect.

"Hold still," he ordered. "Bow."

She did, and he reached up to her face and into her mouth and pulled out her wooden false teeth. He chopped at them with the sword, splintering them.

"These teeth came to you from the household. For hitting a prince, you will never have teeth again."

She dipped and bowed.

"Now," said Prince Hereditary Slave. "I ask again. How do I find a particular slave girl I like?"

"Simply point her out to me," the woman said, with a placating smile. She tinkled her little bell-like voice that she used with anyone of higher rank. "I will bring her to you."

The guard was pleased. He chuckled and shook his head. "He's after girls already," he said to his compatriot.

The next day, Cap-Pi-Hau found the girl for himself.

It was the time of sleep and dusting. He bounced towards her. "We can play slippers!" he said, looking forward to fun.

She turned and lowered her head to the floor.

"Here," said Cap-Pi-Hau and thrust a slipper at her. She had no idea what to do with it. It was made of royal flowered cloth, stitched with gold thread. She glanced nervously about her.

"You do this!" said the Prince. He flicked the slipper so it spun across the floor. "The winner is the one who can throw it farthest." He stomped forward and snatched up the shoe, and propelled it back towards her. She made to throw it underhand.

"No, no, no!" He ran and snatched it from her. "You have to slide it. It has to stay on the floor. That's the game."

She stared at him, panting in fear. Why was she so worried? Maybe she had heard there had been trouble.

Cap-Pi-Hau said to her in a smaller voice, "If you make it go round and round, it goes farther." It was the secret of winning and he gave it to her.

She dipped her head, and glanced about her, and tossed the slipper so that it spun. It twirled, hissing across the wood, passing his. She had beaten him first go, and Cap-Pi-Hau was so delighted to have a worthy adversary that he laughed and clapped his hands. That made her smile.

His turn. He threw it hard and lost.

The second time she threw, she lost the confidence of inexperience and the shoe almost spun on the spot. The Prince experimented, shooting the slipper forward with his foot. So did she. The two of them were soon both giggling and running and jumping with excitement.

He asked her name.

"Fishing Cat," she replied. *Cmâ-kančus.*

The name made him laugh out loud. Fishing cats were small, lean and delicate with huge round eyes. "You look like a fishing cat!" Instead of laughing she hung her head. She thought he was teasing her, so he talked about something else, to please her.

"Do you come attached to the royal house, like a cow?" he asked. Groups of slaves were called *thpal,* the same word used for cattle.

"No, sir. I was given away, sir."

This interested the Prince mightily because he had been given away as well. He pushed close to her. "Why were you given away?"

Her voice went thin, like the sound of wind in reeds. "Because I was pretty."

If she was pretty, he wanted to see. "I can't see you."

She finally looked up, and her eyelids batted to control the tears, and she tried to smile.

"You look unhappy." He could not think why that would be.

"Oh no, Prince. It is a great honor to be in the royal enclosure. To be here is to see what life in heaven must be like."

"Do you miss your mother?"

This seemed to cause her distress. She moved from side to side as if caught between two things. "I don't know, sir."

"You're scared!" he said which was such an absurd thing to be that it amused him. He suddenly thought of a fishing cat on a dock taking off in fear when people approached. "Fishing cats are scared and they run away!"

Her eyes slid sideways and she spoke as if reciting a ritual. "We owe everything to the King. From his intercession, the purified waters flow from the hills. The King is our family."

The Prince said, "He's not my family." Fishing Cat's head spun to see if anyone could hear them. The Prince said, "I miss my family. I have some brothers here, but my mother lives far away in the east."

Cat whispered, "Maybe I miss my mother too." Very suddenly, she looked up, in something like alarm. "And my sisters too. And my house by the river. We lived near the rice fields and the water. And we all slept together each night."

Cap-Pi-Hau saw the house in his mind.

He saw the broad fields of rice moving in waves like the surface of the Great Lake, and long morning shadows, and the buffaloes in the mire, and rows of trees parasolling houses along the waterways.

He saw home.

He himself had been brought from the country, carried in a howdah with nine other distressed, hot, fearful children. He dimly remembered riding through the City, its streets full of people. Since then, he had not been allowed outside the royal enclosure.

Cap-Pi-Hau had only been able to hear people from over the walls. The calls of stall owners, the barking of dogs, the rumbling of ox-cart wheels, and the constant birdlike chorus of chatter. For him, that was the sound of freedom. He kept trying to imagine what the people were like, because he heard them laugh.

Cap-Pi-Hau asked, "What did you like doing best?"

She considered. "I remember my brother taking the buffalo down to the reservoir, to keep cool. It would stay in the water all day, so we could too."

Cap-Pi-Hau thrust himself up onto her lap, and suddenly she was like an older sister, tending the babe for her mother.

"I want to stay in the water all day," he beamed. "I want to drive water buffaloes. Great big buffaloes!" Something in the sound of that phrase, big and hearty, made him explode with giggles.

Finally she did too. "You are a buffalo."

"I'm a big, big buffalo and I smell of poo!" He became a bouncing ball of chuckles. Even she chuckled. Laughter made him fond. He tilted his head and his eyes were twinkly, hungry for something different. He writhed in her grasp. "What else did you do?"

She had to think. "My brother would catch frogs or snakes to eat. He was very brave."

"You hunted snakes and frogs?" Cap-Pi-Hau was fascinated. He could see a boy like himself, skinnier maybe. They would hunt together in the reeds. He mimed slamming frogs. "Bam! Bam!" he grinned. "Flat frog! Yum. I want to eat a flat frog."

She joined in. "I want to eat mashed cricket."

"I want to eat...monkey ears!"

That joke wore out. He asked about her family. She had six brothers and sisters. They were the nias of a lord who lived far away from the perfect city. Their canal branched off from the meeting of the three rivers, far to the south. She could see all of that, but she could not remember the name of the place.

All of her brothers and sisters slept in a tidy row on mats. When one of them was sick, that child slept cradled by their mother. So they all pretended to be sick sometimes. One night, so many of them said they were sick that Mother turned away from them all. Then their mother got sick herself. With no one to work the fields, they had to do something to feed all the children, so Fishing Cat was sent away.

The Prince still wanted fun. "And you never went back, never, never, never." He rocked his head in time to the words. "I never went back either."

Something seemed to come out of them both, like mingled breath.

"What's your name?" she asked, because Cap-Pi-Hau was a nickname.

"Nia!" he said, delighted, and started to chuckle again. "I am Prince Slave!"

"I will give you orders!" she chuckled, something irrepressible bubbling up.

"I will have to dust floors for you," he giggled.

"I will say, you, prince, come here and help me with this thing."
She snapped her fingers.

"You can call me Prince Nia."

She chuckled. "You can call me Princess Nia!"

For some reason the laughter faded.

"I hardly remember my home either," said Cap-Pi-Hau.

Until the day of his marriage, Cap-Pi-Hau called himself Prince
Nia. When people expressed astonishment at the choice, he would
explain. "All princes are hereditary slaves."

The day of the procession arrived.

The Sun King's great new temple was to be consecrated.

Prince Nia stood high on the steps of an elephant platform.
Ahead of him the next batch of hostage children crowded the platform, scowling at the sunlight, flicking their fly whisks.

The Prince had never stood so high off the ground. He was now
level with the upper storey of the Aerial Palace. There were no walls
and all the curtains were raised.

He saw servants scurrying, carrying, airing, beating—taking
advantage of their mistresses' absence to perfect the toilet of the
rooms. Category girls ran with armloads of blackened flowers to
throw them away. They beat cushions against each other. They shifted
low bronze tables so that the floor could be wiped.

In the corners, musical instruments were carefully stood at attention, their wooden bellies gleaming. The lamp hooks screwed into
the pillars were swirling bronze images of smoke or cloud-flowers.
The rooms had handsome water butts of their own, with fired glazed
patterns. The pillars on the upper floor were ornately carved, with
images of celestial maidens, as if the rooms were already high in
heaven.

He could see the lintels and the gables close up. Monsters
called *makara* spewed out fabulous beasts from their mouths. Gods
abducted women. Brahma rode his giant goose; Krishna split a
demon *asura* in two. Regularly recurring shapes of flames or lotus
petals were embedded with glass pieces. And the roof! It was tiled
with metal, armoured like a soldier's breastplate. The metal was dull
grey like a cloudy sky, smooth and streaked from rain. So many
things had been kept from him!

An elephant lumbered towards them. It was old, and the howdah on its back wobbled on its loose skin.

It was not a good elephant. The howdah was functional, no carvings. The beast came close to them and coughed, and its breath smelled of dead mice.

Now the King's elephant! Its tusks would be sheathed in gold, and the howdah would rest on a beautiful big carpet!

The children began to advance one at a time onto the elephant's unsteady back.

And the King himself, is he blue, Nia wondered, like Vishnu? If he is the Sun Shield, is he blinding, like the sun?

Someone shoved Nia from behind, trying to push him aside. Nia thrust back and turned. It was an older, more important prince. "Get out of the way. I am higher rank than you." It was the son of the King's nephew.

"We all climb up and take our turn."

At the top of the steps, a *kamlaa*-category slave herded them. "Okay, come on, press in, as many as possible." He wore only a twist of cloth and was hot, bored, and studded with insect bites. He grabbed hold of the Prince's shoulders and pulled him forward. Nia tossed his shoulders free. He wanted to board the howdah by himself. In the future, I will be a warrior, Nia thought; I will need to be able to do this like a warrior. He saw himself standing with one foot outside the howdah, firing his arrows.

The kamlaa peremptorily scooped him up and half-flung him onto the howdah. Prince Nia stumbled onto a girl's heel; she elbowed him back. Nia's face burned with shame. He heard older boys laugh at him.

Then the kamlaa said, "Okay that's enough, step back."

The King's nephew's son tried to crowd in, but the kamlaa shoved him back. The higher prince fixed Nia with a glare and stuck his thumb through his fingers at him.

The elephant heaved itself forward, turning. Was the procession beginning? Prince Nia craned his neck to see. All he saw was embroidered backs. Nia prised the backs apart and squeezed his way through to the front. Two older boys rammed him in the ribs. "You are taller than me," Nia said. "You should let me see!"

The elephant came to rest, in no shade at all. They waited. Sweat trickled down the Prince's back.

"I need to pee," whispered a little girl.

Adults lay sprawled in the shade under the silk-cottons. Soldiers lay sleeping, wearing what they wore to battle, a twist of cloth and an amulet for protection. Cap-Pi-Hau scowled. Why didn't they dress for the consecration? Their ears were sliced and lengthened, but they wore no earrings.

The musicians were worse. They had propped their standards up against the wall. A great gong slept on the ground. The men squatted, casting ivories as if in a games house. Did they not know that the King created glory through the Gods? That was why their house had a roof made of lead.

The afternoon baked and buzzed and there was not enough room to sit down. Finally someone shouted, "The King goes forth! The King goes forth!"

A Brahmin, his hair bundled up under a cloth tied with pearls, was being trotted forward in a palanquin.

The Brahmin shouted again. "Get ready, stand up! Stop sprawling about the place!" He tried to look very important, which puffed out his cheeks and his beard, as if his nose was going to disappear under hair. The Prince laughed and clapped his hands. "He looks silly!"

Grand ladies stood up and arranged themselves in imitation of the lotus, pink, smiling, and somehow cool. Category girls scurried forward with tapers to light their candles or pluck at and straighten the trains of threaded flower buds that hung down from the royal diadems.

The musicians tucked their ivories into their loincloths next to their genitals for luck. They shouldered up long sweeping poles that bore standards: flags that trailed in the shape of flames, or brass images of dancing Hanuman, the monkey king.

A gong sounded from behind the royal house. A gong somewhere in front replied. The tabla drums, the conches, and the horns began to blare and wail and beat. Everything quickened into one swirling, rousing motion. The procession inflated, unfolded, and caught the sunlight.

The footsoldiers began to march in rows of four, spears raised, feet crunching the ground in unison and sweeping off the first group of musicians along with them. A midget acrobat danced and somersaulted alongside the musicians, and the children in the howdahs applauded.

Then, more graceful, the palace women swayed forward, nursing their candles behind cupped hands.

"Oh hell!" one of the boys yelped. "You stupid little civet, you've pissed all over my feet!"

Prince Nia burst into giggles at the idea of the noble prince having to shake pee-pee from his feet.

The boy was mean and snarled at the little girl. "You've defiled a holy day. The guards will come and peel off your skin. Your whole body will turn into one big scab."

The little girl wailed.

Nia laughed again. "You're just trying to scare her."

Scaring a baby wasn't much fun. Fun was telling a big boy that he was a liar when there wasn't enough space to throw a punch. Nia turned to the little girl. "They won't pull your skin off. We're not important enough. He just thinks his feet are important."

Nia laughed at his own joke and this time, some of the other children joined in. The older boy's eyes went dark, and seemed to withdraw like snails into their shells.

Endure. That was the main task of a royal child.

Suddenly, at last, the elephant lurched forward. They were on their way! The Prince stood up higher, propping his thighs against the railing. He could see everything!

They rocked through the narrow passageway towards the main terrace. Nia finally saw close up the sandstone carvings of heavenly maidens, monsters, and smiling princes with swords.

They were going to leave the royal house. I'm going to see them, thought the Prince; I'm going to see the people outside!

They swayed out into the royal park.

There were the twelve towers of justice, tiny temples that stored the tall parasols. Miscreants were displayed on their steps, to show their missing toes.

The howdah dipped down and the Prince saw the faces of slave women beaming up at them. The women cheered and threw rice and held up their infants to see. No men; their men were all in the parade as soldiers.

Beyond them were their houses—small, firm, and boiled clean in tidy rows. Planks made walkways over puddles. The air smelled of smoke, sweat, and steaming noodles. The Prince tried to peer through the doorways to see what hung from the walls or rested on the floors. Did they sleep in hammocks? What games did the children play?

"What are you looking there for, the tower's over there!" said one of the boys and pointed.

Tuh. Just the Meru, the Bronze Mountain. They could see that any day. Its spire was tall, but everybody said that the King's great new temple was taller.

The road narrowed into shade and they passed into the market. The Prince saw a stall with an awning and a wooden box full of sawdust. Ice! It came all the way from the Himalayas on boats in layers of sawdust. He saw a Chinese man press a chip of it to his forehead. He had a goatee, and was ignorant enough to wear royal flower-cloth. The Khmer stall-wife was smiling secretly at him.

The howdah slumped the other way. The Prince saw sky and branches; he steadied himself, clinging to the rail, and looked down. Beyond the stalls were ragged huts, shaggy with palm-frond panels. A woman bowed before a beehive oven of earth, blowing air into it through a bamboo pipe.

The air smelled now of rotten fruit and latrines. The Prince saw a dog chomp on the spine and head of a fish.

Splat! The little girl squealed in fear. Overripe rambutan had splattered over their shoulders. Overhead, boys grinned from the branches of trees and then swung down. One of the kamlaa took off after them with a stick.

Along the road, other people watched in silence.

One of them gazed back at Nia. His mouth hung open with the baffled sadness of someone mulling over the incomprehensible. How is it, he seemed to ask, that you stand on a elephant in flowered cloth, and my son stands here with no clothes to wear at all?

The man standing next to him was so lean that every strand of muscle showed in lines like combed hair. His gaze turned to follow the howdah, insolent, fierce, and angry.

These were the great people of Kambujadesa? The young prince didn't like them at all. They were ugly, their houses were ugly, and they smelled.

This was Yashodharapura, abode of the Gods, the perfect city. The soldiers should come and take away all such people.

The procession moved on, into the precinct of the holy mountain, Yashodharaparvata.

Here in the old center of the city, everything was better. Wives of temple workers, all of them royal tenants, waved tiny banners. Their hair was held in handsome fittings, and they wore collars of intricate bronze.

Nice people, smiling people. They dipped and bowed and held up their hands for princes, as was fitting.

Their houses stood on firm stilts and were linked by covered walkways. Airy cloth bellied outward from the rooms. The Prince glimpsed the canals beyond, full of boats. Amid fruit trees, carved stone steps led down to small reservoirs.

Prince Nia turned around and saw stone steps going all the way up the miraculous hill of Yashodharaparvata. The trees were hung with celebratory banners, and the gates to the hilltop temple had sprouted poles that supported ladders of colored cloth. From the top of the hill, golden kites swooped and dipped. The kites reflected white sunlight that continued to dapple the inside of the Prince's eyes long after he looked away.

The procession passed into orchards and rice fields and dust began to drift over the howdah like smoke.

Suddenly they came upon a new, raw desert. All the trees had been cleared, their fresh yellow stumps staring out of the earth. Dust blew as if out of a thousand fires, and above rose the new temple, the Vishnuloka.

The Prince was disappointed. The five towers were not that much bigger than the spire of Mount Meru. They were made of raw uncarved stone, unfinished and undecorated blocks that bore down on each other. The towers looked like the toy buildings he himself made out of clay cubes. Some banners trailed limply from the scaffolding.

Ahead of them, pickaxes rose and fell out of a great ditch. Men struggled up the banks, passing baskets of dirt to queues of women and children who swept the baskets away hand-to-hand into the distance. Boys ran back with empty baskets. To the Prince the workers looked like busy termites swarming around their nests.

More banners bobbed on poles that marked where the entrance would be. The elephant passed between them and rocked the children up onto a causeway that crossed the moat. The moat looked like a dry riverbed running due north, sweltering with a few puddles.

The elephant did a slow dance round to join a row of waiting elephants. The Prince saw the puffy faces of other children in howdahs sagging in the sun. They waited again, on a plain of churned earth.

The Prince craned his neck to the right. "I can't see the rest of the parade," he said.

"Aw, poor little baby," said the boy whose feet had been peed on.

Another elephant full of unwanted princes churned up the dust and came to rest beside them. Dust polished the Prince's eyes every time he blinked.

Finally an elephant strode past them, shaded by two heaving parasols. The howdah was carved and balanced on a beautiful rug, and on it stood a high-born warrior. He wore a felt coat and a diadem and a bronze tiara, rising up like an open lotus. He stood holding his arrows in his hand.

That was more like it!

White horses pranced, lifting their feet high, but holding to formation. Their riders rode on their unsaddled backs, hands on hips.

Behind the horsemen came a ballistic elephant, a crossbow on its back. Its protecting infantry marched in rows alongside it.

A third elephant followed, with a solid shell of wood over its back. Resting one foot outside the ornate howdah, a real warrior prince stood in full armour with a crown and a metal breastplate tied across his chest.

Prince Nia squealed in delight, and leaned so far out of the howdah that he nearly fell.

Soldiers trooped past. These were nobles. They wore flower-cloth chemises and their topknots were held in metal tiaras in the shape of totemic beasts: eagles or tigers or deer, which showed that they were fast, or fierce.

More horses wheeled past, white like falling water. The Prince's military heart danced. Then, oh! Their riders stood up and pulled back their bows and let loose flaming arrows. They arched up into the blue sky over the southern moat.

Nia was beside himself. He yelled and shouted and pummelled the shoulders of the bigger boys next to him. Suddenly affectionate, they laughed with him, pleased by his fervour, sharing it.

"Steady, Little Warrior," one of them chuckled.

The other rocked him by the shoulders. "You will have your chance of battle soon enough."

The little prince cried aloud. "We are the soldiers of the world! We are the warriors of the Gods!"

Some of the troops heard him, and they waved and smiled. The sun was in the sky at the same time as a pale daylight moon. Auspicious or what?

The soldiers passed and boring high-rankers followed. Women reclined in carved palanquins. Fly whisks and fans replaced swords. The elephants had a bit more glitter, but who cared? Glitter does not need skill.

One elephant, bigger than the rest, heaved its way through the fog of dust. The howdah was a bit bigger than most too. An old man wearing a temple-tower tiara stood up in the howdah with all the usual stuff. He had a lean, pinched face like an old woman.

It was not until the man had passed with a forest of parasols and nothing further followed that Prince Hereditary Slave realized: that must have been the King. That old man had been Sun Shield, Suryavarman. The King, it seemed, was just another soldier.

The dust settled, but the thought remained.

APRIL 11, 2004

Luc Andrade steps down a little stiffly from a white Toyota pickup.

He feels thin-legged and pot-bellied. Too old really for beige Gap jeans and blue tennis shoes. Out in front of him stretch the plains of Cambodia.

Luc sighs. He loves the heat, the silver sky, and the wild flowers clustering in the shade. The palm trees always remind him of Don Quixote with his lance—tall, stretched thin, and riding off into the blue distance. And perhaps of himself.

In the back of the pickup truck, Map and two of his friends from the Patrimony Police are gathering up tents and rifles. Mr. Yeo Narith steps out of the cab. Luc has spent a lifetime reading Cambodian smiles and Narith's wan, tight smile is still angry.

No one is supposed to excavate anywhere in the precincts of Angkor without an APSARA representative being present. APSARA defends the interests of the artifacts and the monuments. They contend with tourist agencies, art thieves, airways passing too near the monuments, or museums in Phnom Penh—interests of all kinds. The last thing APSARA needs is to find it cannot trust its archaeological partners.

"Allons-y," says Luc. Narith is of the generation who finds it easier to speak French. He nods and extends an arm for Luc to precede him down the bank.

Out in the field, the contractor is guarding his find, next to a motorcycle and William, the spare driver.

Luc skitters a little awkwardly down into the field. Underfoot, the harvested rice crackles like translucent plastic straws.

It's April, the end of the dry season and horribly hot. Luc is Director of the United Nations archaelogical project. Most of his UN dig team have gone home, except for one Canadian excavator and Sangha, the Cambodian dig manager. Work is normally finished by the end of March, but the project might not get financing for next year. Since the JPL/NASA overhead flights four years ago gave them a radar map of the old road and canal system, their trench has uncovered one unremarkable stone yoni and nothing else.

A white sheet is spread out on the ground, and rocks and earth are lined up in order along it. Village children squat, peering at the stones. As Luc approaches, the contractor and William the driver stand up. The children chew the bottoms of their torn T-shirts. The contractor from the university hangs his head and kicks the white dust.

So, thinks Luc, he came out here with William and took a risk. The augur, a long slim white tube a bit like a hunting stick, lies abandoned. The contractor grasps two full lengths of pipe. God knows how he got the augur that deep in all this dry ground. William probably sat on the handles.

The contractor is called Sheridan. He's a microbiologist, out here to identify where he will core in the rainy season. Like Luc, he works at the Australian National University. The UN dig has paid for only four days of his time.

Sheridan launches into his apologies. They sound heartfelt, but Luc shakes his head. "I still don't understand how it happened. You know the rules."

"I knew this was where a bridge crossed a canal. The ground was still very wet, and I thought: why not just do a test, see if this will be wet enough in rainy season..." His voice lowers. "I was trying to save you money."

At least he hasn't laid the gold out on the ground for the village children to see. They walk back towards the pickup to look at the find.

At the top of the embankment, Map guards the truck. Map jokes with someone, an old farmer. The farmer has a face Luc has often seen in Cambodian men of that age. The eyes are sad and insolent all at once. The man glares at Luc over half-moon spectacles and stalks away. Map shakes his head and calls, "Hey, Luc!" then surfs down the embankment on his heavy police boots.

"Oh-ho, is that guy ever unhappy with me. He came and said this is his field and we can't stay." Map strolls companionably alongside Luc. "I told him to go buy a mirror and practise smile. I said that you guys find something that Cambodians can't use—knowledge." Map claps his hands together. "He used to be my CO in the Khmers Rouges, and he didn't like me then either."

Map outrages people. He drives the APSARA guides crazy by stealing their business. He exasperates the Tourist Police by taking elderly foreigners to stay in country farmhouses. A single red cotton thread barricades his wrists with some kind of magic and his long fingernails are a mottled white like the inside of oyster shells. Luc once wondered if Map was an exorcist, a *kru do ompoeu*. Map told him that he uses the fingernails for fighting, "like knife."

But he takes good photographs, speaks French, English, and German, and knows HTML.

Inside the cab of the pickup, away from the village children, Sheridan reaches into his rucksack and takes out a disk about twice the size of a silver dollar, dull yellow with crinkled cookie-cutter edges. Luc sees Sanskrit.

Gold. Writing. From Angkor.

"We've got to excavate as soon as we can," Luc says to Narith. Narith then telephones. They already knew they were going to have to camp out all night to guard the find. Mr. Yeo asks for more police, with guns.

Outside, the old farmer marches up and down the dike. Wind blows dust up around him, Map, all of them, like the smoke of war.

They dig through the long afternoon.

The walls of the tent run with condensed sweat. Luc, two volunteers from the Japanese dig, and Jean-Claude from Toronto are crouched inside a trench, brushing away dirt.

Slowly, rows of packets wrapped in linen are emerging.

"*Meu Deus!*" mutters Jean-Claude. For some reason he always swears in Portuguese. He gestures towards the packets. "There's at least ten packets there," he says to Luc, in French. "Ten to a packet, that's one hundred leaves."

They've found a book. An Angkorean book made of gold.

Map darts from side to side, taking photographs from many angles.

William, the motoboy, leans over the trench, looking forlorn. Luc can't let him leave in case he tells anyone about the find. He's trapped here. He knows that.

Luc pulls himself out of the trench and gets cold Cokes from the chest. He passes one to William.

"What we're trying to do," Luc explains to William in Khmer, "is to get as much information as we can about the earth around the object. See the side of the trench? See, it's in layers, white soil, brown soil, then black soil? That will tell us a lot about when the leaves were buried."

William dips and bows and smiles.

Map intervenes. "Hey, Luc. You think we should take the book out of those packets and photograph it here?"

Luc shakes his head. "No. The packets will have information too. We could photograph what the augur pulled up. The disks."

The ten torn disks are laid out on the ground. The gold is brown, thicker than paper, but not by much. A light slants sideways across their surfaces, to make the incisions clearer.

Luc can read them.

The text comes in torn snatches across the face of the ten disks. Luc's breath feels icy as he reads.

...who conserves perpetuity...

...men seek for heaven and its deliverance...

...the ninth day of the moon...

"We have a *saka* date," Luc announces. The Japanese volunteers stand up to hear. Luc is so skilled at this that he can do the conversion to the European calendar in his head. The text is about a consecration in 1191 AD.

"It's twelfth century. The time of Jayavarman Seven."

"One hundred leaves from the time of Jayavarman?" Even Yeo Narith rocks back on his feet. Map looks up, his face falling.

"*Plus que ça,*" mutters Jean-Claude inside the trench. He holds out his hands as if at a Mass. He has brushed aside all the loam. Inside his trench, lined up in rumpled, pitch-coated linen, are fifteen packets of ten leaves each. "Plus there is one smaller packet to the side," he says.

One hundred and fifty leaves of gold?

Art gets stolen in Cambodia. It gets chopped up, incorporated into fakes, shipped across the world, sold by unscrupulous dealers. If it's gold, it might get melted down.

Luc turns to Yeo Narith. "Who do we trust in the army?"

William can't go home.

It's late at night. The tent glows in the middle of the field like a filament.

Around a campfire, William and Map face each other. Working for the same boss, they should be polite and friendly with each other, but Map won't even look at William.

Many other people sit drinking coffee: Dik Sangha, officials from APSARA, Map's captain from the Patrimony Police, and a friend of Teacher Andrade's from the École Française d'Extrême Orient whose name William keeps trying to catch. Patrimony Police stand guard round the field. They've already stopped people with shovels and metal detectors.

Map cradles his gun. He's been sipping beer all evening and his face is bright red. He grins and tells unsuitable stories.

William is mystified. Teacher Andrade trusts Map and gives him responsibility. Map knows about the Internet and a lot about the monuments. He could teach these things to William, but he won't.

William thinks: when I started to work for Teacher Andrade, you were friendly. Now you won't talk to me or even look at me. I've done nothing to you.

Map is talking in English. "So my older brother and me go to shoot the Vietnamese. They have a big ammo dump behind the Grand Hotel. And my older brother Heng is crazy man. You think I'm crazy, you should see Heng. He strap grenade launcher to his wrist. One launcher on each arm. He fires both at the same time, kapow, kapow. I hear him breaking his wrist. But he keep shooting, shooting. I say, Older Brother, you are a crazy guy. Then all that Vietnamese ammo goes up, huge big fire, and I have to drag Heng home."

Map pauses. His eyes get a wild look to them.

"He died of Sweet Water Disease. Diabetes. Nobody give him insulin."

Another sip of beer, a shaking of the head.

We are not tourists, William thinks. There is nothing you can get from us by telling sad stories, over and over, boasting about your wars.

"I went to look for my parents, all that time. I look all over Cambodia. I have to go AWOL to do it. And it turned out they are dead since the Lon Nol era."

William has noted that Map's sad stories do not add up. He also tells a story in which his uncle tells Map when he is twelve that his parents are dead and Map goes to hide in a haystack. Both cannot be true.

There is something wrong with Map's head.

"Cambodian joke," says Map and grins. He is so ugly, thinks William. He has a big mouthful of brown teeth that push out his jaw, his nose is sunken, and his face is covered in purple lumpy spots.

Map tells a story about a truck driver who has to stay in a farmer's house. He sleeps in the same room as the farmer's daughter. The truck driver gets to do everything he wants to with the daughter. In the morning the farmer asks, did you sleep well? The truck driver says, yes, your daughter is very beautiful, but her hands are so cold! Ah, says the farmer and looks sad, that is because she is awaiting cremation.

Map roars with laughter and pummels his foot on the dust. He looks at Teacher Andrade's frozen smile and laughs even louder.

William shakes his head. He says in Khmer, "That is not a good story to tell someone like Teacher Andrade. What will he think of us?"

"He will think we tell funny stories."

"He will think we are not respectable."

Map still won't look at him. "He knows more than you do."

William shrugs. "He is a great teacher and of course knows more than I do."

"You know nothing." Map lights a cigarette.

William has had some beer too and his tongue is loose. "Why don't you talk respectfully to me? If I have done something wrong, you should tell me what it is, so I can correct it."

Map sneers. "Monks tell you that?" He finally looks at William. "Yes."

"You're so *peaceful*," says Map, smiling slightly. He sits back, inhales and watches. "I do all the fighting, you have all the getting. I march for forty years, you go to school. You have a pretty girlfriend, I have no family."

"My mother and father are dead," says William.

Map is silenced and looks away. His face closes up like a snail going into a shell and he coughs. He says nothing for a very long time.

William believes in connection. It is how he survives, and he is good at it because he practises on people whom no one else can reach.

All right, thinks William. I promise. I promise that you will be my friend. I will have your name and history in my notes, and you will know my family. We will celebrate New Year together.

There is a rumble of trucks in the dark. All the Europeans stand up. The Patrimony Police lift up their rifles. The trucks stop, their brilliant headlights go off, and a full colonel strides down the bank towards them. His lieutenant follows.

The Colonel holds up his hand and greets Yeo Narith as if they are old friends. William's ears prick up; he does not know this colonel. He must be from somewhere other than Siem Reap. The lieutenant is Sinn Rith, a man William knows is far too rich to have earned all his money from soldiering.

Teacher Andrade trusts these people?

In Banteay Chmar, it was the army itself that stole the bas-reliefs.

They enter the light of the fire and Tan Map grins.

"Lieutenant-Colonel Sinn Rith! My old friend!" Map cackles with glee.

Sinn Rith is impassive behind his sunglasses. He mutters in Khmer, thinking the Europeans won't understand. "The Frenchman's brought his dog."

Whew! William has to expel breath. They hate Map. What's he done? Sinn Rith fingers the handle of his pistol. Map's captain looks alarmed, eyes flickering between them.

The Colonel's polite smile does not falter. He ignores Map and greets the scholars, shakes their hands, and says how privileged he feels to be asked to help protect such a treasure. Can they view the find?

Still grinning, Map leaps to his feet. "I am the dig photographer, I do the UN dig Web site," he says, every word directed at Sinn Rith. "It would be an honor, Colonel, to explain the finds."

He is so rude! The man has no shame. He is humiliating everybody, making them look small. Dik Sangha, the Cambodian dig director, is smiling but he's shaking his head. Map swaggers his way in, laughs, and claps Sinn Rith on the shoulder.

Sinn Rith flings off his hand.

Inside the tent, the Colonel has to exclaim over the packets. "So many!"

"We actually think it's written by Jayavarman himself," says Yeo Narith. Luc explains. The Sanskrit text uses first person. It seems to be memoir. By the King himself.

The Colonel shakes his head. "For such a thing to come to the nation now. It is a gift from heaven."

The lamps baste the interior of the tent; it is roasting and airless. Back outside Map sits down and says to William, "Hey motoboy, go get me a beer."

Teacher Andrade says gently to William. "Perhaps the officers would like one as well, William."

It gives William something to do. He sompiahs and makes himself look lively.

Even inside the tent, getting the beers, he listens to the debate.

The army, it seems, want the Book to stay in Siem Reap. William thinks: the generals all own hotels, they want a museum here for the tourists.

The archaeologists say the Book needs to be repaired. It should go to the National Museum in Phnom Penh.

"Is it safe anywhere?" the French archaeologist asks.

Map takes his beer from William without even looking at him. He smiles and says, "The army want to take care of the Book to earn merit to make up for all the people they killed."

It is too much for Sinn Rith. He turns his head with a snap. "Like all the people you murdered?"

Map still smiles. "Everybody knows not even Buddha himself can keep a Khmer Rouge out of hell."

The next day, the army resolves all debate. They send a helicopter to airlift the Book to Siem Reap.

April 1967, April 2004

Luc is sixteen, loves sport, and is planning to study medicine.

He plays football and tennis even in the heat. His shoulders swell, his hips shrink. He is very handsome—long-nosed, thin-lipped, but with a deeply sweet face. He plays outside so often that his brown hair is sun-streaked.

His *cyclopousse* driver has fallen in love with him. Arn is from somewhere in the county, near Kompong Thom. Luc finds him heartbreaking, for Arn lives in his pedal taxi with all his possessions folded under the seat. His bank is a back trouser pocket secured with a safety pin. There is a pouch for his comb and his toothbrush. He washes in public fountains, wearing his kramar around his waist, sleek, muscular, and happy.

Arn is twenty-two, which to Luc is old, in another state across the border into adulthood. Doing anything which earns you a living, and which gives you independence in the city, seems exciting and glamorous. And Arn looks happy. He smiles when he talks about his sister's troubles with a recalcitrant fiancé. He talks of his father and mother and cousins and how rich they are, relatively.

Arn's face seems to melt slightly whenever he sees Luc. The smile goes softer, the eyes narrow and gleam, and dart back and forth between Luc's face and the ground.

"Monsieur. I see you and birds sing," he says.

"Monsieur, I see you and I see the sky, with all the stars."

Taken aback by Arn's grandness of expression, Luc stumbles up onto the front seat. He is flummoxed by his own response, which is a heat around the heart. He always feels tension around Arn, sometimes unpleasant and anxious. Luc is dismayed if chance means he must take another driver's vehicle. It is nonsense, but he feels that he has betrayed Arn. He worries if Arn's feelings will be hurt and calculates when and how he can apologize.

And Luc is aware.

Aware that he looks back as often as he can at Arn's thighs and calves. Aware that his own people—plump, pink, grey, and precise—do not attract him. The female dancers of the Cambodian Royal Ballet are pretty and firm of flesh, but Luc is aware that they earn only his attention and admiration. He does not masturbate thinking about them.

When he masturbates, he thinks of the girdle of lean muscle that joins the stomach muscles to the slim hips of Cambodian men. His heart goes up into his mouth when he passes them washing, glossy as seals, in the public fountains. At times the full meaning of this sinks in and he becomes utterly miserable, staring at the walls of his mother's villa, or watching the lights of the passing traffic on the ceiling, listening to faraway flowering music from the nightclubs of Phnom Penh.

Today, after the lycée, Luc descends to the courtyard with its mango tree. He wears his white tennis shirt, white shorts, and as he expected, Arn waits outside the gate.

"*Le Club, comme d'habitude, Arn,*" he says. It's tennis day.

"Oh, monsieur," says Arn. For once he is not smiling. For once he stares moonfaced and unhappy. He sighs, glances down, and pulls in his lips until they are as thin as Luc's.

"Arn. My friend?" Calling Arn his friend always produces collywobbles. For it is perilously close to the truth.

"Today is New Year. I wanted to do something with you."

Luc knows what his mother would say: the boy only wants money; they need money; if you want to give him money, do so. But don't get too involved. You can't really help him, you know. Unless you turn him into one of us.

His mother has read Luc correctly as being soft-hearted. His mother is an old hand. All her Cambodian friends are rich. They have handsome sons who also go to the lycée. But they don't break Luc's heart by keeping their one pair of trousers folded under the seat of a pedal-driven taxi. Some of them harden Luc's heart by boasting of their houses and cars. He does not think that these middle-class Cambodians might be trying to establish equal grounds for friendship.

Luc, perhaps, wants to pity his friends. In any case, whatever it is that has hold of his heart is far too strong. It grips like a crocodile, no argument possible, only acceptance.

"*D'accord.* It will be nice to spend New Year with you." Luc's tongue stumbles slightly over the words. "I can't think of anyone I'd rather spend it with."

"Pardon?"

Luc has to explain the complicated French. By the time Arn understands, both of them feel awkward and hurt. Arn's smile is not like the sun, but like the moon—wan, faded. "I thought we go to lake. Sit on pier. I have bought a lunch."

The thought of Arn buying him anything causes Luc an anguish of heart. Arn can't afford to buy anything. He has to rent the machine, he hardly eats. "Arn, you shouldn't have done that, please, let me pay you for the lunch."

What can Arn do? He accepts Luc's money, but he looks unhappy, for this has ruined the gesture. Luc knows that he wanted to pay, wanted to pay him back. For what? He wants to make something manifest, but the act is disproportionate. What has Luc done for him? Except be friendly and open and ... and well, yes, something more, but how could he see that?

Luc feels bad, and Arn feels bad that Luc feels bad, but above all just wants ...

... wants them to be, not equals, that would be stupid; nobody is anybody else's equal in Cambodia. Luc knows that Arn just wants them to be who they are with each other. Which is? Friends, friends at least.

More than friends, Luc.

These are the feelings that people sing about in cheap songs. They are real, those cheap feelings. They turn out not to be pretty lies after all. They are demanding realities.

Luc's eyes feel hot. They swell as if about to burst. Dear God, I'm going to cry. I don't like this; I should go and play tennis with that wizened old coach who I don't even like. Arn is whispering. "Maybe you go to tennis."

"No! It is a lovely idea. To celebrate New Year. Let's go to Boeung Kak Lake."

Sometimes genius comes to Luc, as if a powerful, spiny but beautiful flower thrusts itself out of the heart of his life. Luc says, "Let me pedal you."

"Luc!"

"No! I need the exercise. Really. I will pedal."

Arn is smiling again and laughing. Luc stretches back and squeezes the brake. Laughing aloud Arn rises out of his seat and the cyclo wobbles from side to side, tipping slightly. Luc bounds out of the seat and pulls Arn, who is weak with hilarity, forward to the wide, padded bench. "No, no, no!" laughs Arn.

"You are an old grandfather," Luc says in Khmer. "I respect you. You should rest, I will pedal."

Arn shakes his head at his overturning young French friend. He takes hold of Luc's pink hairless biceps and holds them. He swings up onto the seat and looks over the back.

Luc pedals. Shadows of trees flicker across his face. Women saunter past, trays on their heads. And for some reason Luc starts to sing a Françoise Hardy song about looking on while boys and girls love. He bellows as he pedals, grinning at Arn, whose face is turned towards his as steadily as the moon.

His song mingles with one by Sin Sisimuth coming from some passing Dansette. The voice of Sin is warm, the music trills like birds. The sound mingles with the savours of roadside cooking, the gasps of bananas deep-frying on mounds of earth baked into stoves, wafts of satay on skewers dripping over charcoal, and the sticky smell of all that fruit. The song harmonizes with the singing clatter of people speaking and the horse-like clopping of the feet of Luc's own people, strolling in shorts and white shirts, more unbuttoned than they could ever be at home.

The song flowers alongside the modern apartments painted cream, with bougainvillaea purple along the tops of the walls, and the palm trees and the sprinklers and the uniformed children and *librairies* crowded with books in Khmer and French and pootling little Citroen 2CVs peeping horns as sharp and bouncy as Cambodian smiles.

I love it! I love it, thinks Luc as he cycles. I never want to leave; this will be my home. Good-bye medical school, good-bye hospital.

I will become a cyclopousse driver and live under the stars.

Arn laughs and covers his face. "Oh! I cannot afford your fare."

Something comes over Luc and he leans back. "My fare costs everything, but I do not charge money."

My fare is you.

"Oh, monsieur!" and Arn permits himself a florid *khutuy* gesture that would not be conceivable in Kompong Thom. "I fear my purse is not big enough."

Luc doesn't get what he means but something hot and heavy impels him. "Ah, but it's not always the amount, it's the quality that is important. Is it fine stuff?"

"Oh, oh." Arn is leaning forward and shaking his shoulder. "It is the finest stuff. For you. Oh, everyone is looking."

Luc only now registers Arn's embarrassment. "They know we are just having fun," he says gently.

There is a look on Arn's face that Luc has never seen shining out of anyone else's. It is a kind of surrender. Very quickly, as they buzz past buses and women in stalls and lunchtime workers on their way back to the bank or telegraph office, Arn lifts himself up onto his knees, turns around over the back of the seat, and pecks a kiss on Luc's cheek.

He plainly could not help it. Luc doesn't blame him. Arn was overcome. But Luc does not know what to make of it. In the end, he decides to pity. His friend could not help it, he got overexcited, he is from a different culture, and you have to be aware of imposing Western meanings. It was a familial kiss...

No, it wasn't.

Luc feels the dark.

You know what this is, Luc. So does Arn; his expression is full of both love and awareness. It is kindly but not exactly innocent.

Oh God, this is what it is. I am that. That thing.

He looks at Arn, his gently burnished face, and accepts. If it means I get Arn, then yes. Yes, I am. That is me. I am that thing. And right now, nobody can see, and if they can see I don't care.

Suddenly Luc shouts like John Wayne, and drives the pedals even harder and faster, and Arn chuckles and laughs. Luc lifts his feet off the pedals and just for a moment, he is flying.

In those days Boeung Kak Lake was surrounded by a park that

people could stroll around. Luc and Arn arrive and Arn's friends cluster round to laugh and joke about the spectacle of a barang pedalling a cyclopousse. The laughter is good-natured. It's New Year, you get to do crazy things. The two men…boys…are sent on their way with good cheer by the other drivers, who agree to look after Arn's machine. Arn goes to the latrines, but not to relieve himself.

He changes into his white shirt and his perfectly creased khaki slacks.

They head out for the park, full of prostitutes at night but families by day. Halfway to the lake they are pelted with water balloons by a gang of kids. They are nice kids, boys and girls all about fourteen, so Arn and Luc just laugh. They walk along the pier and all the cubicles are taken. Well, they would be full, wouldn't they, it's April 13.

Luc sighs. "We can always go back and sit on the grass."

Except that the very last little cubicle, right at the end of the walkway out over the lake, is empty. Maybe nobody persevered all the way to the end of the pier; maybe a family has just vacated it. But there it is—hammocks and a charcoal stove and a view of the little lake, with its lotus pads and dreamy girls and serious boys in canoes.

Heartbreak time. Arn has bought them lunch, bundled up his kramar. The kramar serves as his pyjamas, his modesty patch, his head-dress, and his shopping bag. He unties it carefully, gently, and there is sticky rice in vine leaves, soup in perfectly tied little bags that have spilled nothing, pork in sauce with vegetables.

Luc tells him it is a wonderful lunch and they sit and talk about the usual things. And Arn becomes overwhelmed. Because his unlikely dream has come true. The huge beautiful kindly barang is his.

"Luc, I want to study," he says as he eats. "Luc, I am so happy. I know life will be just great. Everything in Cambodia good now. We have our Prince. Your people good to us, but the politicians go home, so now we can be friends."

Arn sways from side as if to music as he says, "We all live together and work hard, so Cambodian business, Cambodian factories, Cambodian music, all do very well now. We will become modern country. We join the world as friends."

"Modern country," says Luc and lifts his hand as if raising a toast. "Friends."

It is April 1967 and rice exports have collapsed and the news says that in a place called Samlaut, somewhere near Battambang, the peasants are in revolt. The Prince blames Khieu Samphan and the communists.

For now the song keeps singing in Luc's head. *Lovers*, the lyrics tell him, *don't fear for tomorrow.*

Arn would be fifty-eight now, thinks Luc, waking up in a tent in the dark, reeking of insect repellent. Where is he?

Whenever Luc visits Phnom Penh, he peers at the moto-dops and elderly motoboys. He scans bus windows, taxis, and stalls in the Central Market. Most likely Arn would be using a different name now and his face would be changed. Arn could be bald, fat, or sucked-dry skinny. But most likely…well…

One out of three men died.

Geoff Ryman

LEAF 35

April is when the red hibiscus announces the change of seasons like the musician blowing his conch. April is after the harvest and before the rains. April is when the oxcart falls back, lifting its long neck to sniff the wind. The oxen sleep under the house. Inside it people sleep or dance. Season of rest, season of labour, April is when we hoe the earth to guide the waters like children to their beds, making straight canals to bear new stone. April is when we lay courtyard pavements. The people kneel and drop the stones like eggs. They hoot like birds and bellow like elephants and laugh and start to sing. April is when we bear the temple stones up the ramps and rock them to sleep like uncles. Season of war, April is when the generals make one last effort before the rain to press on with the campaign. April is when we create. April is when we destroy.

April 13, 2004

April is the Time of New Angels, just before New Year.

Old angels will be sent back to heaven. They will be replaced by new angels who take better care of mortals.

On the morning of April 13, 2004, the year of his retirement, King Norodom Sihanouk himself visits Army Headquarters in Siem Reap to view the Golden Book.

He gives the Book its Cambodian name: *Kraing Meas*, which means something like Golden Treasure. Photographs are taken of the King standing in front of a green baize background with leaves from the book balanced against it. He shakes the hand of General Yimsut Vutthy.

The National Museum is determined that the *Kraing Meas* should come to rest in Phnom Penh, but there are high politics involved. Sihanouk has a house in Siem Reap. Prime Minister Hun Sen does not. The King himself has argued that neither APSARA nor the National Museum are secure enough to display such a treasure. Perhaps the Book could be the centerpiece of the much-needed museum in Siem Reap?

The Book would be repaired by none other than the royal jeweller, a man much experienced in gold and in repairing artifacts, including, it must be said, stolen ones.

The Siem Reap regiment would have responsibility for transporting it. They too want the treasure to come back to the town. Most of the regiment's many generals have invested in hotels there.

Most particularly General Yimsut Vutthy.

⤳

So on the last day of New Year, Professor Luc Andrade packs a small overnight bag, pays Mrs. Bou, who runs the Phimeanakas Guesthouse, and tips the staff.

The Phimeanakas security guard helps Luc out with his cases, including a large, empty metal case, usually used to transport film cameras. *National Geographic* has loaned it to Luc in return for favours. It is lined with shock-absorbent black foam.

He gets in a taxi and makes the short drive to the regiment's headquarters, feeling reasonably content. He has told no one about the arrangements, not Map, not William, not his Cambodian dig director. He had tried to tell the Director of APSARA, who just laughed and waved his hands. No, no, don't tell me; I don't want to know.

Luc will be the Book's escort during the flight. It must be because he clearly belongs to no Cambodian faction. Which may be why he was not invited to the royal viewing this morning.

He sees the fine new army HQ. From a distance it looks like a Californian shopping mall in the Mexican style—long, low buildings with red-tiled roofs. Closer up, Luc can see the roofs slope upwards and the tips of the gables reach out like the white necks of swans.

A chain is lowered, the taxi turns crackling into the huge gravelled forecourt. Along the mall, individual offices line up like shops, each with its own door and blue-and-white sign in Khmer and English: Infirmary, Operations Office, Intelligence Office.

One of the doors is open. It does not have a sign, but Luc knows it is the General's office. Soldiers stand crisply to either side of it, and murmuring emerges from it.

Luc walks on, carrying the metal case, accompanied by a soldier.

The General's office runs the depth of the building and is crammed with military men. They throng around canapés and cognac laid out on tables. The seats are huge, heavy wooden benches that look like thrones and make your bottom ache. The wooden floors gleam, and there is a bank of TV and DVD players on shelves.

Right on top of the General's desk is the Book itself, spilling somewhat loosely out of its ancient silk and pitch packaging. Some of the gold leaves are out of order, resting on thumbtacks on the baize. Two days' work, calculates Luc, just to find out where they belong.

The General greets Luc like an old friend and jokes, "In the old days, people would call me a Cheap Charlie for not offering cigars, but now CNN says they are bad for your health."

Luc knows much more about Yimsut Vutthy than the man would care for. Luc knows which hotels he has invested in and who his Thai and Singapore partners are. He knows roughly what percentage he takes from the forty- to sixty-dollar fees tourists pay to enter Angkor Wat, for the General is a protégé of the establishment, someone of whom Sihanouk himself would be wary. Yimsut Vutthy is a compromise candidate.

A player, in other words.

The General introduces a number of army officers and civil service functionaries, all of whom want to be associated with the Book.

"You see," one of them says, "we take the safety of the Book very seriously."

Luc cannot stop himself smiling.

They crowd round to look over Luc's shoulder as he packs away the Book, still in its sections of ten leaves. The measurements were correct and the sections fit with serendipity into the slots, gripped in place by the foam padding.

Then everyone toasts the health of the King and Mr. Hun Sen. Canapés have done little to absorb the alcohol. Hungry and slightly fogged from cognac, Luc glances at his watch, anxious to get going.

Later than he likes, Luc and the General walk out to a waiting Mercedes. It takes two soldiers to load the now heavy case into the boot. The General holds out an expansive arm for Luc to precede him into the car. Luc smells the soft tan leather upholstery and runs his hands over it as he slides into place.

Two motorcycles roar ahead of them. Almost inaudibly, the Mercedes eases out behind them, with an army jeep following. Feeling presidential, Luc settles back with relief as the cavalcade pulls out of the gates.

Conversation with General Yimsut Vutthy soon runs out, but Luc has ready that morning's *Herald Tribune*. Rather gratifyingly, if well into the middle pages, the paper reports the Book's discovery. GOLDEN BOOK HOLDS KEY TO CAMBODIAN HISTORY. An official press photograph shows the General himself displaying the leaves on a wooden table. Luc passes the newspaper to him.

Then very suddenly Luc is sure he has left behind his passport and letter of contract to the Cambodian government.

With a lurch of panic, he reaches down for his belt pouch. He has time to feel his passport and papers securely inside.

The car swerves. In his slightly befuddled state, Luc thinks the veering has come from him.

Tires squeal; metal slams. Inertia keeps Luc traveling forward, folding him against the front seat.

An accident. Luc struggles his way back into his seat. He sees an angry face against the window.

Luc behaves entirely automatically. There's been an accident, someone is upset, so go and see if you can help.

He opens the car door.

The angry man seizes him, pulls him out of the Mercedes, spins him around, and pushes him forward. Luc stumbles ahead in shock.

A silver pickup gleams by the side of the road. New, Luc thinks, and probably rented. Very suddenly, as if a tree trunk had snapped, there is a crackling of gunfire behind him. This is it, he thinks, this is really it. He's absurdly grateful for his belt pouch. He's thinking that it will hide his passport and money. They'll only get the twenty dollars he keeps in his pocket.

The back of the pickup truck is down. Someone shoves him towards it. Other hands grab him, hoist him up, and then slam his head down onto the floor. He hears a ripping sound and he realizes that heavy workman's tape is being wrapped around his head. It blacks out his eyes and covers his mouth. Something like a heavy sack is thrown against him. It groans. Luc recognizes the General's voice. A light, rough covering is thrown over them both; Luc smells cheap plastic sacking.

Someone shouts urgently. A bony butt sits on the most fragile part of his ribcage. The engine revs and the truck jerks forward, bouncing over ruts and slamming the metal floor against his shoulders and head. The truck swings back around onto pavement and accelerates away. Luc assumes it has U-turned back towards town.

The strange things you think when you are in trouble. Luc finds he is worried about the duct tape pulling off his eyebrows and jerking out his hair. He thinks of Mr. Yeo and wants to tell him, see how brave I'm being? He thinks of his mother. See, *Maman*? I don't feel any fear at all. This is bad, this is very bad, but I'm not panicking. He wants someone to be proud of him, to sit up and take notice.

He remembers Tintin. Tintin always remembered how many turns, left or right, and the kind of terrain, and the kind of noises.

So he pretends he is in a Tintin comic book. As they whine along the airport highway he counts to sixty five times. Then they shudder over open ground to the count of sixty times twelve. After a couple of almost vengeful crashes over humps he loses count.

They slow to a stop. He smells dust and something else, metallic and sour, which he realizes is probably blood, his own or the General's.

The back of the truck thumps down. "Out, out," someone says. "Let's go!" Luc shifts, feeling his way out of the pickup. He is seized, hauled out, and thrust forward. Stumbling blindly over the ground he thinks: I will have to learn Braille in case I ever go blind. Why did I wear my good shoes, they'll be all dusty.

Well, *mon cher*, they will look very *branchée* at your funeral. OUCH the stones are like teeth jabbing through the thin soles. Scrub crackles, prickling ankles.

Luc hears the pickup rattle back onto the road behind him.

Then his feet go out from under him and he slides down a dirt slope onto rocks. A wrench and a folding-under and he knows that his ankle is twisted. Someone crouches down on top of him. He hears sirens wail past on the road above them. We're down a ditch, he thinks. A ditch or a channel for floods in the dry season. You'd need to know it was here. These are local people.

The sack is thrown over him again. Some tiny insect nips him. Daylight mosquitoes, they carry dengue fever. He tries to slap it, and realizes that he can't—his hands are tied. He tries experimentally to talk through the tape.

"You say nothing!" The voice is so close to his face that he feels breath on his nose. An insect bites him again.

He tries to count how long they wait, but then Tintin loses his nerve. Very suddenly Tintin wants to go home.

You are local people. I've probably seen your faces. All smiles. Well, Cambodia is smiling now isn't? I can see it grinning at me.

See, Cambodia is saying, you thought you could love us out of ourselves. Well, here it is. This is what everyone else in Cambodia went through. Do you love it now? See how powerful love is? How long did you think you could be in Cambodia and avoid this? How long did you think you could avoid the strong men, the gangs, and the armed ex-soldiers? This is Siem Reap on Highway 6, one of the most dangerous parts of Cambodia for most of the thirty years of conflict.

Your turn, Luc, to be in a war.

April 1142

.

The teacher could not grow a beard.

This was a great sadness for him and probably an embarrassment for his students. The teacher was a Brahmin, originally from India, Kalinga. His people could grow beards. It was a mark of their holiness. This Brahmin wondered if he had sinned in a previous life. Or perhaps his beard refused to come because of his lack of courage. He was too lax with challenging the boys, especially the one who called himself Prince Slave.

For the sake of my beard, the Brahmin promised himself, the next time Nia questions authority, I will put him in his place.

In the class they were discussing the ordering of castes, and Nia sighed and said, "There are no castes of people in Kambujadesa. In Kalinga, I'm sure these things hold firm, but here everyone is either a noble or some kind of slave."

Now, the Brahmin thought, I must act now. "Do you deny the ordering of categories?"

The slave prince said with a sideways smile, "I am sure the categories are orderly in a country where everyone can grow a beard."

The silence in the room was clenched.

Prince Nia continued. "Here everyone keeps telling us to support the ordering of categories and professions, but I can never tell if they are talking about *Varna* or *Jakti*. I don't think they can either."

"Your problem, Prince," said the Brahmin, "is that you think words have no power. You use them too freely."

"I think truth has power. Words have power when they are pushed out of you by truth."

51

"You have no humility."

The young prince paused. "Not enough, it is true."

"You should learn humility, Prince."

"That's true too. From whom should I learn it, guru?"

"From the King!"

"There is no possibility of learning anything other than humility when confronted by a king. I find it more instructive to learn it from slaves."

Like a clam, the jaw of the Brahmin slammed shut. Too, too clever, this slave prince. The Brahmin tried to humiliate him. "You speak of your little friend."

"She is my friend. She sweeps and scrubs and fans and whisks. But she has a loyal heart."

Just lately, the Brahmin had noticed, the children were not laughing at Nia. The other princes hung their heads and looked sullen, hiding something. The Brahmin had a terrible thought. This Nia is recruiting them. Recruiting them to what? The Brahmin had no words, but he felt this overturning prince was an enemy of religion.

"I think you learn pride from her," said the Brahmin.

The cursed boy just looked thoughtful. "There is pride there, for I find her an exceptional person and so I am proud that she has condescended to be my friend."

"Upside-down boy! She is the slave, you are The Prince."

"So I should learn pride, not humility?"

He was a treacherous lake that made the boats unsteady.

"You…you take pride and turn it into humility and then turn it into pride!" The Brahmin knew that he sounded weak and shaken.

A danger, this one. This one is a danger.

Who knows what this danger to the Gods will bring? War? Famine? Drought? Severe lack of observance always brought the wrath of gods.

Even at twelve, this overturning Slave Prince must be brought down.

Shivering with the importance of what he was about to do, the teacher visited Steu Rau, the Master of the King's Fly Whisk.

The Master's family had whisked kings in public for generations. Family members had also been the Guardian of the Royal Sword and the Superintendent of the Pages. They were not Brahmin but they were definitely Varna. The Fly Whisks understood loyalty and the meaning of the categories.

Steu Rau agreed. "Yes, yes, you are right. You have no idea how this friendship unsteadies the palace girls. They keep looking for similar favours. Why, some of them have even offered themselves to me."

"Shameful!"

"In the house of the King!"

The King was supposed to sleep with them, not the officers.

"It is the singling out that is the problem," the teacher said. "The lower categories have to understand that they lack distinction, that they are as alike as cattle. That they earn distinction slowly, life after life, though obedience."

"This girl shoots up like a star!"

"Through the attention of a capsizing prince. So. I think we must remove this attention by separating them. Permanently."

"Yes! Yes! Kill her!"

The Brahmin admired Fly Whisk's energy. But he also thought that perhaps the girl might have offended Fly Whisk. "I do not think the killing of a female nia would earn merit. It *might* have the reverse effect."

"Humph! Well. You are the expert in these matters, guru."

"I think the King will be making donations of land to a temple soon, and that she should be one of the gifts. She should be donated to work in the fields. No serving in the temples. In other words, the attention of this capsizing prince will have resulted in a lowering of her status. It will have taken her even farther from heaven."

The Master enjoyed the idea. "Yes, yes, that would be an object lesson. And a donation will earn merit."

"For all who are part of it." The Brahmin smiled and held up his holy, bestowing hands.

Suryavarman had many names, and would have another name after his death.

He slept each night at the summit of the palace temple. At least that got him away from his wives. Attendants had strung up his hammock and lowered draperies to keep out the night air. In the old days a woman might have been left with him, for the sake of form.

But the Universal King was old now. He did not want women with him. He did not like the way they searched his face and looked at his old body. He was exhausted with the impudent stripping gaze of everyone who saw him. They searched his face for signs of glory and found only a man after all.

And yet, what he had done! He was the Sun King, who had swamped his enemies. Might not a little of that show on his face?

Nowadays, Suryavarman turned might into merit. He had built the biggest temple in the world in honor of Vishnu and all the Gods. Perhaps doubt was the burden that gods lay on kings for coming too close to them.

You sluiced water around a stone, and claimed it was holy. You did not know whether it was or not. You never saw a god, or felt a god. At times you used the Gods strategically, to frighten or threaten or shame your rivals.

Sometimes you wondered if any of it was true.

At night, lying awake and listening to the sounds of insects, you would know: you were tough and strong but sometimes that strength crushed things you wished to keep. You had a mean streak, you had a fearful streak, and you had a mind that always played chess with people's lives. You took pleasure in all the politicking; you promised yourself that you would stop. You tried to convince yourself that you had finally won and could afford to be more forgiving. Something in you prevented it.

Bigger and bigger temples, more and more stones piled high, more exiles, more confiscations, more setting families off against each other. And at night, loneliness.

Something fluttered in the shadows of the candle. It slipped around the draperies, like a gecko.

"I am child," a boy said, and flung himself down onto the stone.

I can see that, thought Suryavarman and sat up. The boy must have avoided the stairs by climbing up the sides of the temple, on the carvings. "Have you ruined the stucco?" the King demanded.

"I took care to avoid doing harm, Great King. I am small and light. I do not come for myself, King, but for another."

The King beadled down on him. "Whose son are you?"

"Yours," said the boy, and then hastened to add, "in spirit I am yours, for I have grown up in your house, but my father is Dharan

Indravarman, who serves you as a small king in the Northeast."

"I know him," rumbled Suryavarman. My cousin, not particularly troublesome, a man of no obvious faults and a Buddhist, so doubly harmless. "You can sit up, I want to see your face."

The boy was a plump little fellow only about twelve years old, with a big round face and thick peasant lips. No matter what he said, his serious, regarding eyes had no trace of real fear.

The King asked him, "What makes you think you are not in a lot of trouble?"

The boy replied, "Because you are a Universal King. A Universal King is brave and has faced terrible danger. Such a king would have no need to frighten me."

"You are troubling my sleep." Like bad dreams.

The little fellow bowed and crawled closer. Determined, wasn't he?

"King. You are generously setting up new temples, and you are to give to these establishments great gifts of land and water and parasols and oil and wax and people."

"Yes?" Dangerous stuff, little fellow, for these gifts are the canals of politics. Gold and silver and obligation flow down them. And blood.

"There is a slave girl. Her name is Fishing Cat. She was honored to be made part of our household when she was five. She is so happy to be here, she has not thought of her village since. She does not even remember its name. But I have checked the records and I see she must have come from the villages near Mount Merit. If…" Here the child faltered, bit his lip, became a child again. "If that is where you are planning a temple, then perhaps if she is sent there, that would be a good thing. She could see her family again."

"Is that all you want?"

"I have been very foolish," said the child in the tiniest possible voice. "I became friends with her. It was easy for me, it was fun. I had no thought of the danger for her. It is my fault, but she is the one being punished."

The King could not help but smile. "You climbed up here for a slave girl?"

The boy sompiahed, yes. "My guru says I must learn humility."

The King chuckled. "A strange way to show humility, to wake up a king with demands." The boy went still and looked down.

Impossible to gauge, little fellow, how much of a danger you will be. But what a heart you have. A brave heart and a good heart, to care so much for a slave girl. "All right. I will order it."

The boy flung himself face-down onto the stone. Then the little imp sat up and made sure the King remembered. "Her name is Fishing Cat. Mount Merit."

The King nodded. He stood up. His chest had sagged, his belly swelled, his calves had shrivelled. He shuffled into his sandals. "Come along, little fellow, I will get you past the guards."

"Don't punish them," said the boy, suddenly alarmed. "I am very small and quiet."

The King had to laugh. The boy's heart is a kingdom; it could contain everyone. He cares for guards! They would kill him at a nod from me.

"I won't punish them," promised the King.

Suryavarman quickly calculated. Little Buddhist, you have ten more years before you become a danger. By then, I will be dead. With all this sudden trouble over my wife's brother in Champa and with the Vietnamese in the north, someone somewhere will betray me soon. And so I know who you are. You are the danger to whoever is my successor. You can be my harrow.

If you love me.

"Can I tell you who you are?" Suryavarman said as they walked. "Your father is my first cousin. Your mother was from Mahidharapura, the same pastures from which my own family came." His hand on the boy's shoulder pressed down hard. "So I am fond of your family, that is why I asked especially for you to be here. Really."

He nearly laughed aloud again; the boy's eyes were so completely unfooled.

"That is why I said you are my father," whispered the boy.

"But now I will remember you as the boy with the good heart. You know the greatest pleasure in being king? It comes when you know you have done something good." Suryavarman mounted his kindly, regal countenance. It was a heaving great effort.

The boy narrowed his eyes and considered. You're not supposed to think, lad, about what the King says. You're supposed to agree.

"Yes," the boy said. "Yes. That must be the greatest pleasure. That would be the whole reason to be king."

"Yes, but bees make honey, only to lose it. Are you good with a sword, young prince?"

The boy seemed to click into place. Good heart or no, he had a man's interest in all things military. "I'm better with a bow. Better with a crossbow on an elephant's back. Swords or arrows, the thing is to have a quiet spirit when you use them."

Oh, yes! thought Suryavarman. You will be my revenge; you will be my scythe. I pity the poor cousin who succeeds me.

"I want to train you specially," said Suryavarman. "In the art of war."

Everyone learned how the beardless Brahmin's scheme had backfired.

Why exactly the King favoured his cousin's son no one knew. A cousin's son was there to be held hostage, ground down, watched and limited. Not raised up.

Instead, the King demanded that the case be taken up by the Son of Divakarapandita himself, who had consecrated three kings. This highest of the Varna was to go to the consecration personally and ensure the foundation was well done, and it was said, ensure that the slave girl had the right to return to her own home.

Some of the Brahmin said, see how the King listens, he is making sure they are separated.

Then why does the King show the boy favours? He gave him a gift of arrows, and sent him to train two years early. And why were the palace women—wives and nannies, cooks and drapers alike—all told to let the boy and the slave girl be friends?

The only one who seemed mutely accepting of these attentions was the Slave Prince himself.

The rumour went round the palace that on the night before the slave's departure, the Prince had called for a meal of fish and rice to be laid on a cloth, and invited the girl Fishing Cat to share it with him.

The girl had knelt down as if to serve.

"No, no," Prince Nia said.

But he could not stop her serving. She laid out a napkin, and a fingerbowl.

He reached up to try to stop her. "No, don't do that."

Cat's sinewy wrists somehow twisted free. Out of his reach, she took the lamp and lit scented wax to sweeten the air and drive away the insects.

"Leave the things."

Fishing Cat looked up with eyes that were bright like sapphires. "I want to do this. I won't have this chance again."

"Don't be sad. We will always be friends," he said. "I will still hear you talking inside my head. I will ask how should a king behave, and you will say, how am I to answer that, baby? And I will say, with the truth. And you will say, the king should not lie like you do. And you will remind me of the time I hid my metal pen and made you look for it. It will be like we are still together."

"But we won't be."

"Huh. You will not even remember the name of the palace or one of its thousand homeless princes."

Both her eyes pointed down. "I will never forget."

The Prince teased her. "You forgot the name of your home village."

"I was a child."

"You are still a child. Like me. We can say we will always be friends and believe it." He smiled at this foolish hope.

Then Nia jumped as if bitten by an insect. "Oh. I have a present." He lifted something off his neck. "Soldiers wear these into battle. See, it is the head of the *Naga*. It means no harm can come to them." He held it up and out for her.

"Oh, no, Nia, if I wear a present from you, I will be a target."

"Ah, but no harm can come anyway."

"It is for a well-born person."

"Like kamlaa warriors, who go to their deaths? Look, there is no protection really. It is just something to have. You don't have to wear it. Just keep it." He folded it into her hands. "When you have it you will think, I had a friend who wished that no harm could come to me, who wanted me to know my parents."

Cat looked down at the present and it was as if he could feel her heart thumping. I wanted to make her happy and now maybe she thinks I have sent her away.

"Fishing Cat," he said, holding on to her hand. "I stand waiting with all those kids who hate each other, and I think of my last day at home. I was being taken away, and I was sad and frightened, but everyone in the house kept smiling. They had to look happy or risk being thought disloyal, but I didn't know that. My mother was allowed to kiss me, once. She whispered in my ear instead and she told me, 'We did not ask for this. We are not sending you away. I will think about you every day. I promise. Just when the sun sets, I will think of you.' So whenever the sun sets, I know my mother thinks of me."

Fishing Cat thinned her mouth, trying to be brave. The Prince said again, "I am not sending you away. I will think of you every day. I promise. Just as the sun sets."

A slave cannot afford unhappiness for long. Cat managed to smile. "I will think of you too, Nia. Whenever the sun sets. I will tell my parents about you, and how you brought me back to them. I will ask them to offer prayers for you."

"And I will hear you in my head," promised the Prince. "Now. Eat."

APRIL 13, APRIL 14, 2004

People heard the shots and thought at first that they were fireworks.

Then sirens streamed out towards the airport and ambulances screamed back. Soldiers had been shot. It was said the King had left his residence, his large dark-windowed car squealing as it pulled out of the drive.

Pirates in the back of pickup trucks drove around the city, their faces covered with kramars. They had guns and took aim at hotel signs. All along the airport road, it was said, every hotel sign had been shot. Tourists walking on Sivutha Street had been screamed at. They turned, and saw a rifle and a deadly grin pointed straight at them.

Cambodians in town for New Year scurried to their cars with suitcases. Traffic began to build. More shots were heard. Buses full of tourists came back from the airport and gathered in the hotels, forlornly asking if they could have their rooms back. At New Year? "I don't know what's goin' on," said an American. "But they closed the airport. No more flights and all these big ugly dudes are stopping all the traffic and checking everybody's bags."

Then the power went. The hotels outlined in Christmas-tree lights, all the blazing karaoke signs, and all the brightly lit forecourts fell dark. In an instant, the music booming out of beer gardens and bars went silent.

People panicked. The last time the Khmers Rouges attacked Siem Reap was in 1993, and it was just like this. They closed the airport and the power station.

Soon the streets leading out of Siem Reap were crowded with

unmoving cars stuffed with plastic bags, aunts, and wide-eyed children. Workers trudged home, holding their good city shoes and walking barefoot. Dust billowed up like a fog. Murky car headlights crept through it. Motorcycles weaved unsteadily around pedestrians. A woman lay on the side of the road, unconscious, bundles scattered, her tummy being plucked by anxious, helpful passersby.

Just outside town, the cars encountered the first roadblocks. Furious-looking soldiers pulled people out of cars and emptied luggage onto the street.

"Our colleagues have been shot and killed!" the soldiers shouted.

People despaired. Was war really still this close? All it took was a few shots, and here they were, repeating history. Evacuating the city.

It's late in the evening at New Year, but the restaurants outside Angkor Wat are dark and silent.

The temple guards are glad.

Normally at New Year, cars stop at the crossroads to beam their headlights on the temple towers. From across the moat, the karaoke drums, the pounding of feet and voices, the revving of engines, the celebratory beeping of car horns and the light-scattering mist of exhaust fumes, all would usually have risen up as a haze of light and noise.

This New Year, poor people keep their privilege of having Angkor Wat to themselves at night. Only moonlight shines on the temple. The towers are ice-blue and streaked with black like solidified ghosts. Bats flit across the moon.

The guards sit on the steps of the main temple entrance, the gopura, at the end of the long causeway. APSARA guides and Patrimony Police relax together. They lean against the wall in shorts or kramars and wish each other Happy New Year in quiet voices that the night swallows up.

Poor people still have to work. Village boys lead their oxen to pasture in the wide grounds of the temple enclosure. Farmers putter past on motorcycles.

The temple guards share a meal of rice and fish from plastic bags. They've pooled together four dollars to buy twelve tins of beer, and they are all tipsy.

"Did you see those City people run? They all came through here going Uhhhhhh!" An APSARA guide waves his hands in mock terror. He sports bicycling shorts with Velcro pockets: his best clothes.

"Oh! Oh! Somebody turned out the lights, it is a disaster!" They mock their richer cousins.

"They all sleep out here tonight."

"Good, let the mosquitoes bite them for a change."

In the hot dry season there are few insects, except in the temple park with its sweltering moats. The guards slap their arms and wipe their legs almost unconsciously. Malaria is as common as a cold. They get sick; they go to bed.

Map sits with them wearing only his underpants. His police uniform is laid out on the steps like shed skin.

Map is about to go to work. He will walk the corridors armed until about midnight. Then he will string his hammock across the main entrance and get some sleep.

Once he caught thieves hauling off a celestial maiden they had hacked out of a wall. Chopping Angkor Wat, what jerks! He opened fire and they ran. Everybody thought that they'd got away with the treasure, but Map knew they couldn't run that fast with a statue. He figured out which way they'd gone, and so he went swimming. Sure enough, they'd hidden her in the moat, to come back for her later. So he camped out by that moat for weeks and got all five of them. Just kids. Man, they'd been in prison for years.

One of the APSARA guides sighs and stretches. "I get to go home and see my wife next week. That will be my New Year."

"New Year is not always such good luck."

"Tooh! That is true."

The guide has a story. "My village is out towards Kompong Thom on Highway 6. Every year they have the party on the road. They don't think that trucks ever come that way anymore."

Map says in his quiet spooked voice, "It used to be dangerous to drive that road."

The guide from Kompong Thom holds his ground and keeps talking. "One year all the kids were out on the road singing, and at midnight a truck came driving through. It just smashed into the kids. It was like the war all over again. Bad, bad luck, all that year, for everybody."

"Then bad luck for us this year as well," says one of the police. The theft of the Golden Book has been big news.

Map's face settles into a lazy, hooded grin. "I drove that road when the army told you not to do it. I wanted to go to Phnom Penh to see this girl, and they said, you go that way those bastards at Kompong Thom will steal our motorcycle."

The guard from Kompong Thom chuckles. "Did we?"

"No. I killed all you guys." More chuckles, heads shaken. Map is always extreme. He sits up and mimes riding a motorcycle one handed, while armed. "I tell you. I had one automatic here. I had my grenade here, my buddy was on the back and he had his grenades too. We had guns like a tiger has teeth. We just drove, man, no lights. We drove full speed across bridges that were just one plank of wood. Nobody touched us."

"What about the girl?"

Map beams. "*She* touched us."

They all laugh. Map shakes his head, with the same sleepy smile. "She was a nice girl, my buddy's sister. Oh, she was beautiful. I thought I would get married to her and then me and my buddy, you know, we'd make a new family for ourselves. He was like me, all his family dead. It was a good thought. A meritorious action." He raises his can of beer up in salute. It's empty. "More bad luck."

A motorcycle coughs its way towards them from the main gate. "Oh man," says Map. He recognizes the sound of this particular bike.

"Bad luck," grunts an APSARA guard.

Map calls out in English. "Mister, you want cold beer?"

The guards murmur laughter. Nobody else treats the Captain this way. Map is so rude.

The causeway is high off the ground and the steps are higher still. Map's boss Captain Prey straddles his bike four metres below them. He shines a torch up at them. "*Ch'nam t'mei*," he says to the men who murmur respectfully back. Then he raises his voice. "Chubby. How can you be wearing even less of your uniform than normal?"

Map's smile is thin, like a snake's. "I could be naked."

"Wild man," says Kompong Thom with something like affection. Map is famous for shunning the police village and camping out in the woods around the temple, as if it were still wartime.

Geoff Ryman

His boss laughs, weary and tough. "I tell you, one day I'll come past here and you will not be modest."

"You can come and guard all night too if you like."

"If I see your bum in this temple, you're fired, okay, no job." Captain Prey sounds mad, but not that mad. It's New Year and Map is at his post. I do my job, thought Map, just in my own way.

"Look, Chubby. I came out here to give you some news. They think whoever stole the Book also got your Frenchman."

"What?" Map flings himself to his feet and exclaims, *"Chhoy mae!"* The expression means, precisely, mother-fuck.

"Chubby, please be more polite." The Captain shifts. "I know this is bad news for you. The army says that Grandfather Frenchman and a general took the *Kraing Meas* with them. One of the army guards says the thieves took them both as well."

Map is shaking his way into his T-shirt and trousers. "More like the army got them."

"Or the Thais," says one of the guides.

"The Thais gave us back a hundred stolen things," Map snaps back. He's fed up, angry, sick at heart. "It's not the Thais, it's our own people, it's just we want to blame the Thais. Captain, I need to go into town. Can you give me a lift back to my bicycle?"

"Chubby. Your job is to guard the temple."

"Who do I value more, Captain—you or Grandfather Frenchman? You can keep your sixteen dollars a month; the Teacher pays me more. Any of you guys want two dollars? I'll pay you two dollars to sleep in my hammock. Here's my gun."

Map holds his gun out to one of the guides. The guide doesn't want to touch it. "You might need it man, the army hate you."

"I won't need it. My dick shoots bullets."

The guides hoot: Map knows no bounds. He squats down and laces up his shoes. "A snake bites me, she curls up and dies. A jungle cat comes to eat me, I eat her."

"Map, Map." Captain Prey shakes his head. "Talking that way is why you sleep in a hut."

"I don't sleep in a hut. Huts give me bad dreams. I sleep like I got used to sleeping for twenty years—on the ground. Gunfire helps me sleep."

"Ghosts like huts," someone says.

Map jumps down from the causeway, three metres to the ground. His short thick legs soak up the shock and he lands like a cat on all fours. "I can walk to my bicycle."

His boss chides him. "Chubby. I'll give you ride."

With an angry sniff, Map kung-fus himself onto the back of the bike. "Okay, let's go."

The Captain revs the bike, then turns to him. "Chubby, the thing that bothers me is that really, under all the rude talk, you are a good man."

"Yeah, I know. I also know that life is shit and I don't see why I shouldn't say so."

"Because," says his boss, looking at him seriously. "It makes it sound like you're shit too."

"You are what you eat," says Map and grins like a corpse.

Map is bicycling alone into Siem Reap.

The Patrimony Police don't have enough money for motorcycles. They keep their men occupied by training. Every day, the Patrimony Police cycle all around the Western Baray or up the main hill of Phnom Bakeng.

Map always has to be the first. He boasts that he can cycle as fast as any motorbike. He certainly can cycle faster than his captain or any of the younger guys. He is the oldest man on the force. He says: from the neck up, there's a face that should have had grown-up sons to work for me. From the neck down, I am my own sons. I have no sons, so my legs are sons for me.

He cycles now with his eyes fixed on the moon. He thinks of the famous stone portrait of Jayavarman. The stone face is white too, and it also glows, with wisdom and love. The face of the moon is the face of the King.

So what is all this about, Great King? How come someone with as many good actions as Ta Barang gets taken by pirates? Explain to me how that can be justice. Tell me how there can be any justice.

There are whole fields of angry spirits, Jayavarman. Am I the only guy who can see them? I see their hands coming out of the ground, all prickly like thistles. All around here, in the ditches, are bones and mud that used to be people. You can put out your tables of food at New Year and Pchum Ben, but these ghosts don't want rice cakes. They want me, Jayavarman, because of what I did. So I just keep laying them down. All those ghosts. The grass in Cambodia is ghosts, the termite nests swarm with them.

And no one remembers. No one talks. They don't want to harm the children by telling the truth. They think the truth is dust that can be raised. The truth is teeth in the air. The truth bites. Truth is thicker around us than mosquitoes.

I know who stole the Golden Book. At New Year? It's us again, isn't it, Jayavarman? It's the Khmers Rouges, *Angka*. We've come back like all those vengeful spirits that don't want to be forgotten. Just when they thought they'd paved us over, built a hotel on top of us, and made themselves rich, we jump up and take their strong man, and the barang who wants to help us. Like the spirits, we come back not because we think we can win. We just want to make this world hell. Like the one we live in.

The road is absolutely dark and still. On the last night of New Year. No one's traveling. They're all scared again, scared in their souls, scared all the way back to the war. Two gunshots and they're like birds flying in panic.

We are so easily knocked down, Jayavarman. We try and try, we work so hard. We maintain our kindnesses. We smile, and help each other, and make life possible for each other. We perform our acts of merit and still our luck doesn't change.

Acts of merit don't work, Jayavarman.

They didn't work for Ta Barang, they don't work for those guides on the stone steps. So I don't do them, Jaya. I don't do good actions. Good actions don't get you anything; good actions have no power. Nothing seems to have any power.

Why doesn't anything change? Why am I stuck on a bicycle? Why are my friends not teaching college instead of swatting flies in the dark? Why do our children give up being smart?

Map imitates the children aloud to the moon. He says in English, in a child's voice, "Sir, you buy cold drink, sir? Something to eat, sir?"

Map wants to weep for his people and their children. They wait all day in the sun to sell the beautiful cloth that is spun on bicycle wheels by people with no legs. They get up at 4:00 A.M. to buy tins of Coke and bottles of water and they carry the ice four kilometres and they are six years old. "If you buy cold drink later, you buy from me. Promise, sir?"

Instead of going to school.

Jayavarman answers, in the person of the moon.

Because, the moon says in a soft voice. *That is the only reason. Just because. You must work very hard now to catch up.*

Yeah, everybody's ahead of us, not just the Americans, but even the Thais. The Thais come here in air-conditioned coaches and won't use the toilets because they are too dirty. They cannot believe we ever built this city or gave them their royal language. The Vietnamese are way ahead of us, making their own motorcycles for profit.

Moonlight reflects on the paved, smooth road as if it were water. The moon on the empty road speaks again.

So. Cycle. Cycle hard, cycle fast, cycle all the way into your old age. The world won't notice.

Work. Work without success. Grind and sweat and cheat with no merit. You are starting from the bottom. You are the lowest in the world.

Because.

"Because," repeats Map.

Excuse me, King. But I know who I am.

I am a smart guy. I am a brave guy. I am a scary guy. I have power inside me, *Jayavarman Chantrea*, Jayavarman Moonlight. I could be anyone. I could be Hun Sen himself. So *Because* is why I am cycling on this road alone? Just Because? Is that all?

The moon inclines his sympathetic head. *No. You are cycling to rescue Ta Barang.*

Yeah, I guess I am.

The moon says, *Under all the bragging, you are a respectable man, Tan Sopheaktea.* Sopheaktea is Map's real name, cruelly inappropriate. It means Gentle Face.

"But I killed children."

The moon purses its lips. *You killed children.*

Everything in Sivutha Street is dark. Even the whorehouse bar is closed.

The gates of the Phimeanakas Guesthouse stand locked and the forecourt lights are off.

Map knows Prak, the Phimeanakas security guard. Like Map, Prak stays awake all night under mosquito nets. Like all of Mrs. Bou's staff, Prak is an honest man, meaning he doesn't steal and tells only harmless lies. Whether he is a good man is another matter. Map has known Prak in other lives, as war followed war.

"Prak! Prak!" he hisses.

Map peers into the courtyard that is crisscrossed with the shadows of tall fencing and palm leaves. "Prak?"

Somewhere in shadow Prak says, "Go away, gunman."

"Prak, this is the policeman, Tan Map. What has happened to Teacher Luc Andrade?"

"I don't know, come back tomorrow."

"Prak, they say he was taken hostage. Do you have any news, do you know anything?"

"What do you mean? I don't know anything about it. Go away!"

"What are Teacher Luc's team doing? Prak, don't be stupid, I'm no thief. The Frenchman is my patron, come on! What are the army doing?"

"Mrs. Bou remembers you, she knows who you are and what you did."

"I remember too, everybody remembers what everybody else did. Everybody did something to stay alive. So did you."

"I am not coming out. I am coming nowhere near that gate."

"What are people saying about what happened?"

"I am not telling the whole street!"

This is getting weird. "Prak, have you seen a ghost or something? I just want to know about my sponsor."

"I don't know anything. The army came and talked to the guests and left. I didn't hear what they said; it was none of my business. Now go away!"

Something clicks, a shutter closing.

Prak was always roostershit; his pants were always full of it.

Okay, Teacher Luc, I am committed to helping you so I must think very hard about what to do.

The Patrimony Police didn't know the Book was being moved, and neither did APSARA; at least the guides didn't know and nobody from APSARA was in the car. So the army would have been in charge.

Map smiles to himself. No gun. He only has a knife. He giggles. Stay out of trouble, Map. Me?

Trouble is my girlfriend; I love Trouble; she comes up to me all slinky and says, you want to have a party? I don't even need a dollar to pay her, Trouble loves me so much.

Okay let's go.

There's no one at the gate of Army HQ.

Map's bicycle crunches its way into the forecourt over the fine gravel. Lights blaze all along the long white veranda. One of the doors is open, full of light and talk.

Oh, my old friends will be so happy to see me. They will have a party with Trouble too. Map sticks his knife into his belt and strolls towards the room.

"Are you all happy?" he says, sticking his head through the door.

A flicking of safety catches and a dragging of chairs; soldiers leap up from around a desk.

One of them is Map's old officer, Lieutenant-Colonel Sinn Rith.

"You?" Rith demands, "What are you doing here?" He looks fatter these days. Meaner too, his face behind mirror sunglasses after midnight. Map thinks: maybe moonlight blinds you, Rith.

Map's smile goes snakelike. "I hear you guys got my mentor kidnapped, so I came here to find out more about it."

Rith makes a light, swift gesture: guns down, hold back. "We think you already know all about it."

Map shakes his head. "No, like I said. I don't know anything. That's why I'm here."

Rith looks grim but amused. "We were just thinking maybe you did it."

"That would not be clever. I kidnap my boss and lose all my money."

Slowly, the guns creep back up. They really are still mad at me, aren't they?

"It's more like this, Private Tan Map. We didn't tell anybody about the car. Nobody knew except the army and the Frenchman. But at the right moment, on the airport road, out come two pickups from those unfinished houses side by side. One stops in front of us, one stops behind. They shoot some of our men. They take

General Yimsut Vutthy and the Director of the UN project, who is an important man we are supposed to protect. We ask ourselves, who else would know when the car was going and what it was carrying? Who else would Grandfather Frenchman know and be stupid enough to trust?"

This is Trouble, all right. Trouble has strung up a hammock for me to stay overnight. All the safety catches are off, and they are all easing up to their feet.

"I have another story," says Map. "You've got some old general over you and nobody is getting any promotion. Who is going to be so fast and good at kidnapping from the army? Some Thai art dealers? Some farmers who only care that the Book is made of gold? How about some guys from the army who want an old general out of the way?"

Rith is smiling and shaking his head. "Oh, I like that story. It's a good story. A good theory, guys? So now we have two good theories. And we have you."

The soldiers come towards Map slowly, like they're digging out clay at the brick factory and their feet are stuck.

Map keeps smiling; he can't help it. Bad as it is, this is his idea of fun. "All those guns, pointing at one little policeman."

They stand around him in an arc, but he's backed into the doorway so they can't surround him.

They really believe this shit. I'm going to get beaten up. I've been beaten up before. Then they'll stick me in some hot little room until they can come up with something for a trial.

Also, they have reasons of their own for wanting to hurt me.

The soldiers start to hustle him backwards out of the doorway.

Aren't we a dump of a country? Other places have spy satellites and missiles; we have angry little men and fists and rooms in the back. Doesn't mean to say it doesn't hurt.

There are certain satisfactions in life. One is not waiting until you are hit first. Another is hitting them hard out here in the motel light, where everybody can see that it's eight to one.

Map kicks the knee of the guy closest to him. The guy sinks. Map head-butts the guy who was trying to sneak around behind him.

Then Map takes off. He runs, but to the right, not to the left towards the gate and his bicycle. He tears away, right, and then around the back of the building.

My legs are my sons. He can hear their shoes on the gravel spurting off in the wrong direction and doubling back. You thought I'd go for my bike, but I'm going where there are no lights and I can make a straight run for the fence. You got razor wire round the top? That's why I'm going for it.

Map is gleeful. It will take them a minute to find the perimeter lights. He sprints blindly in the dark for the fence. He hears shouting and whistling. Dogs. Sure they got dogs, I can outrun dogs and it's a still night, no wind. There's the moon, and he thinks this is fun too; he's grinning down.

This is like the gang wars with the arrows when I was a boy. This is what I'll do when I die. They'll try to send me to hell, and I'll climb up the fence to heaven anyway.

Fingers into mesh, and I hear the paws, the lovely padded paws of dogs. They'll jump at the fence, so scamper Map, scamper like the day they told you Mom was dead and you ran away and forgot that they'd told you that. It's vines, Map; you're climbing vines, back to Mom, back to your brother, back to everybody.

The dogs bark, and here's the wire.

Lightly as possible, as if vaulting on a hot skillet, Map pulls himself over the razors. They tear his hands and legs but he knows there will be leaves on the other side to wipe them clean.

I always shoot better with sliced fingers anyway.

You think I'll stay on the roads for you? You think I'm not a local boy, so I don't know how to keep out of sight?

The dogs are going crazy, they're making hound music, and the big lights have snapped on and maybe you see me in pale light like a ghost, maybe you'll shoot, so I'll just duck behind the old TV station that's empty now, like an empty snail's shell.

The road.

Map starts to laugh. He imagines Lieutenant-Colonel Rith, swearing and stomping up and down. He imagines the guy whom he head-butted holding his bloody nose. Oh man, will they be after my liver after this! I'll be sleeping rough on the moon after this! I'll sleep under the hay! They'll chase me everywhere; I'll just be a ghost.

He darts across the scrub field towards the dry flood canal that roaring waters had gouged so deep.

Overhead the crazy moon laughs. Map laughs too. He's home. Map loves war.

Luc is on a boat.

It's made of overlapping timbers, so water slops and gurgles against the hull with a noise like musical springs. The floor of the hull stinks of fish and is ribbed with joists that aggressively jam against buttocks, kidneys, ankles, and hips. Luc is jammed under the low deck. It's impossible for him to sit up, let alone stand.

Tape covers Luc's mouth and eyes; his legs and wrists are lashed with the sort of bungee cords that hold pigs and hens in place on motorcycles. He can do two things: hear and smell.

Outside, marsh birds warble, whistle, or keen. Frogs make their odd beautiful sound like a cross between a gong and a flute. The boat rocks continually, and he can hear wind in reeds, so they are somewhere on the shores of the Tonlé Sap. Next to him, the General keeps groaning through the tape.

Luc smells cigarettes and fish being kebabed on the deck above. He hears the slosh of drinking water in a bottle; he hears boys making light and friendly chatter. Then one of them hisses and everything goes still.

Another boat putters towards them. The silence is long except for one whispered question. Then a calm voice calls clearly across the lake. The boys chuckle with relief and shout; feet thump onto the deck and there is hearty laughter.

A rough voice barks. "You should have seen it! It was a sight. They all thought the Khmers Rouges had come for them again! The whole town was running away. We shot a few extra bullets here and there to add to the party, and then all the power went, like it does every New Year, and all the women screamed."

"New Year, let them remember New Year!"

"Happy New Year!"

"Well, let's have a look at our prizes. I want to see their eyes."

More feet thumping, and a rough sound of wood sliding. "Whew! You guys stink!"

A padding of feet and a tugging at the tape over Luc's face. Suddenly, with a ripping sound, it's torn away, taking Luc's eyebrows with it. Thank heavens, he thinks, that I keep my hair cut short, number-one buzz cut. Torchlight blazes like sunlight into his eyes. He blinks, dazed. The torchlight becomes beautiful, like a star fallen to earth, surrounded by a corona.

"Welcome to Siem Reap Hilton," someone says in accented English.

Luc squints, dazzled by the light. Don't look at their faces! He turns his head away and sees the General's bloodhound face—heavy and crumpled, with dark, wounded eyes.

The same barking, exuberant voice says, "Hey, General, you must have thought everything was going the way you like it. Welcome back! Make yourself at home here in the hotel. We have everything! Food, water, a comfortable bed. Guns."

The General stares heavily and says nothing.

They're showing us their faces; they don't care if we see them. That's bad. Before he can stop himself, Luc looks up, eyes now adjusted to the light. He sees the face of an older Cambodian man. Luc's eyes dart away, but not before he realizes that he knows the face. From where?

The older man berates him in English. "Barang. Welcome to the real Cambodia. Lots of mosquitoes. No air-conditioning. Real Cambodian cuisine."

Uneremoniously, a whole burnt fish, small and bony, is pushed into his mouth.

The man has a competent face, the face of an old, tough business-man. He looks like he runs a shoe factory. He's wearing half-moon spectacles and Luc tries to remember where he has seen those before. The eyes are wide, merry, glistening, yellow splotched with red. The teeth are brown and broken, framed in a wild smile. It's not a face I've seen smiling. That is why I cannot place it.

Luc feels sadness for the world. This is a world of roses, forests, rivers, and wild animals. It is a world of mothers and children and milk. How do we get so wild-eyed, so anguished, and so cruel?

Luc, you are already a dead man.

"Chew it, barang, the fire's burnt all the bones. They break up in your mouth. It's more than we have to eat most nights. It's New Year. A celebration."

The old man switches to Khmer. "You too, General. Without us, you wouldn't have a job to do. Eat!"

A head appears through the trapdoor and warns, "Lights!"

The smile drops and the face settles into its usual immobility. It looks numb; the mouth swells as if novocained. The staring, round eyes are encircled by flesh. Fish Face, Luc thinks.

Fish Face says, "Ah, make a lot of noise, wave the fish at them, wish them Happy New Year."

With the smile gone, Luc recognizes who it is.

"If they don't go away, shoot them!" Fish Face jabs a casual thumb in Luc's direction. Then he sniffs and pushes the tape back over their mouths. Luc needs to spit out the bones and can't. He can't swallow either. The bones and half-chewed fish plug his mouth.

Fish Face wrenches himself round on his haunches and as if levitating shoots up and out through the trapdoor.

Luc remembers the farmer in whose fields they found the Book.

Luc tries to remember everything Map had told him about the man. He had been Map's CO for a while.

They are in the hands of ex-Khmers Rouges.

Luc hears the chortling of an engine. Fish Face seems to be going. So what's he done with the Book?

That damned Book. I should have left it with the army and walked away. Even if it was stolen, melted down and lost forever, I should have made sure that it was the army who carried the *Kraing Meas*.

Instead, you made sure that you did. From now on, Luc, the Book is number two. You have to be number one.

I wish I had a god that I could pray to. I wish I believed in miracles, or had enough faith to find comfort in eternity. Hell. I want my mother.

My trousers are full of shit, I need a drink of water and my mouth is taped shut. I need to wash, I need a friend nearby, I need more courage than I have.

The only thing you can do, Luc, is regard this as an opportunity.

Luc decides to listen to the birds. They flute and warble as dawn approaches.

Birds and lapping water, so many things, are beyond the reach of guns.

APRIL 1147

Jayarajadevi read books.

This might be harmless. The girl would sit cross-legged on cushions, as perfectly poised as a long-necked samsoan marsh bird.

There was nothing idle about her reading. She clicked the palm leaves over as regularly as an artisan weaving cloth. Indeed, some people said: she reads like a man. She thinks if she reads she will grow a beard and become a Brahmin.

Jayarajadevi was beautiful and of royal stock and would beyond doubt marry a prince. She was a *Rajanga*, a person of the highest degree, and the name Jayarajadevi was also a noble title. For everyday use she had a Khmer name, *Kansri*, which meant Beautiful or Happy.

Jayarajadevi Kansri was an especial devotee of the Buddha. Her mind could flick through the arguments for Buddhism as purposively as her fingers flicked through the leaves of her book. She had the art of presenting these arguments to her teachers while showing no disrespect.

Kansri had caught the attention of the great Divakarapandita, Consecrator of Kings. His title, *Dhuli Jeng*, Dust of the Feet, meant he was the King's deputy, at least in religious matters.

Divakarapandita enjoyed her interrogations. She was not at all frightened of him and he enjoyed the way she listened and responded.

Jayarajadevi would sit with him beside the four pools, high in the upper story of the Vishnuloka. In the shaded gallery, they would debate. Sometimes her even more formidable older sister would join them.

Today, thank heaven, it was just her. The two sisters together were too much even for a Consecrator of Kings.

"It is of course permitted to be a devotee of Gautama," Divakarapandita granted her. "No doubt he passed onto us the greatest possible insight into how to escape the toils of this world. But he is not a god, and devotions to him must be balanced, no not balanced, *outweighed*, by actions of devotion to the Gods."

Jayarajadevi considered this and she was like water dripping from a rock garden, steady and in relaxing rhythms. From all about them came the whisper of brooms sweeping.

"But, Teacher, Gautama was so wise that he taught the Gods themselves how to attain Nibbana. If gods so privilege his teaching, then surely so must we? Especially if he speaks the language of a human and shows us the limits of what humans can achieve."

Kansri made Divakarapandita smile. She is so tenacious! Kansri will always, always argue that the Great Soul is the only true Way. Divakarapandita answered, "His words are notable. Powerful expression is like the wind, it wears down mountains of resistance. In the end. But the Gods do not talk the language of words. They make facts. Due observance of their powers is necessary."

"Oh indeed." Jayarajadevi sat up even straighter, slightly outraged perhaps at the implication that she was saying the overlords, Siva, Vishnu, and Brahma, should be neglected. "Though these powers seem so alien and strange that some of our devotions to them come from terror not from love."

Divakarapandita considered, and smiled. "The Gods are not responsible for the quality of emotion we bring to them. If people approach the Gods with terror in their hearts, then terror will be returned to them. Gods make facts, men only speak words, even the Buddha."

Kansri's answer was ready. "But we need words to explain what is righteous. Without words, we just burn."

Divakarapandita said, "Do not misinterpret this, but I think that is a certain kind of wisdom. It is the wisdom of the feminine principle. To listen and express, to take the hard fact and surround it lovingly. The male principle is the making of facts. In human beings male and female are divided. Only in the Gods are male and female conjoined."

Jayarajadevi scowled. "They why do we split the power of Siva up again, into the yoni and the lingam?"

It was such a pleasure, such a privilege, to see a fine young mind blossom like the lotus. It was a noble thing to find you could discuss the holy significance of the male and female parts with a young woman whose mind was so clear that there was no embarrassment.

"They are split in our realm precisely because *we* are split, and the hard fact of godly power must take different forms when working on us. A woman seeking pregnancy will drink from the lingam. A man seeking a still heart and a calm mind will drink from the yoni."

Jayarajadevi nodded and smiled. Something in that idea pleased her, or solved something for her.

"What we need," she said, "is men who are also partly women."

Divakarapandita smiled to himself. Oh no, he thought looking at her determined face. That is what you need. He thought of how very lucky or very unlucky her husband would be.

"Two great winds blow through our souls," she said. "The winds of war, and the winds of peace. We do not conjoin them."

Mulling it over later, Divakarapandita realized that this girl had said that what they needed was a different kind of king. And he, Kingmaker, Consecrator, at least in part agreed with her. Had not he and the Sun King long ago made Vishnu a new focus of worship for just that reason?

The princesses would gather to watch the training.

It was a piddling annoyance to the old sergeant, but there was very little kamlaa people such as himself could do about it.

If the King's female cousin eight times removed wanted to make a fool of herself, giggling and prodding other girls and looking at handsome young princes wearing only battle dress, who was a category person to tell them no?

It was saddening to see the Lady Jayarajadevi caught up in the craze. It did not matter that she strode across the training ground with the mature elegance of a married woman. It did not matter that she was accompanied by her older sister, the Lady Indradevi, who was just as beautiful and accomplished as she was. They were still reviewing potential husbands, like the King looking at his elephants.

There were crazes for particular princes. The favourite now was

Yashovarman, the son of the King's nephew. He'd already been selected to succeed old Suryavarman, who had no children of his own. The boy then married one of the King's nieces and promptly got himself a son, also lined up for inheritance.

So he wasn't as dull in the court as he was on the battlefield.

Yashovarman had the physical qualities of a bull; he was somewhat short with strength bunched up around his shoulders and springing out of his calves. He had a warlike heart but was impatient and easily distracted. The women liked him though. Many of the princesses threw flowers at him even knowing that he was married.

Other princes found favour, too, all handsome and skilled with sword and shield and bow.

Like the quiet one, the curious favourite on whom the King had also bestowed his love. Some of the girls liked him a lot too.

He had a woman's beautiful face.

He had a moustache.

This was the damnable thing, a hard fact that made even his enemies acknowledge he had the blessing of the Gods. All the great teachers of Kalinga had beards or moustaches. Gods like Yama had moustaches. This prince was only sixteen years old, but he already sported a thick, unmistakable, and unpainted line of facial hair on his upper lip.

He was not perhaps a man's man and certainly was not destined for kingship. He was small, slight in the shoulders, and perhaps also slightly plump.

So he was not strong, but he never made a false move. He would nip up the side of an elephant unassisted, barefoot. He strung and sprung the crossbows, not by brute force, but by knowing how to stroke things into place. He made the weapons work by loving them.

Yes, he was a good soldier.

The old sergeant saw him scamper up a balding beast, finding footholds in the creases of her skin. The old sergeant approved of this lack of wasted motion, for he had served under generals who moved by sheer force. Without this neatness, they sometimes lacked strategy. They would march you into a swamp of blood. You survived, but your comrades had been opened up to the sun, transformed into abandoned corpses that only the floods or scavengers would remove.

The old sergeant saw the Prince tuck himself into the howdah. Again, he did it almost invisibly. If you blinked you would miss him doing it. The old sergeant saw him look up, and under his black lip, his white teeth suddenly glowed. Life warmed the old sergeant's heart, he who had seen so much death. The old sergeant followed his gaze.

Oh, ho ho, it was the Lady Jayarajadevi who had caught his eye. It was a young man's fiery heart seeking what it needed. Oh yes, there was competition among these young hawks, these young elephants.

Still smiling at beauty, the Slave Prince turned, dipped at the knees and pulled his young training partner up into the howdah.

Responsible. That was another thing a commander needed to be. He needed to know where his men were and who they were, who needed help, who needed to be chastised and beaten. His young partner was willing but unsteady. The Slave Prince did not mock him or complain that his partner was dragging him down. His job was to make the most of his young partner, and he did. He pulled his young apprentice up onto the platform and steadied him on it.

And then he glanced again at Jayarajadevi. Oh, he aimed at the stars, that one.

"'Sru, who is the short fat one?" asked Jayarajadevi.

"Oh, you know him," said Indradevi, her sister. Her Khmer name was *Kansru*, which meant Well-Shaped. The sisters nicknamed each other 'Sri and 'Sru.

"No, I don't."

"You do, 'Sri! He is a great favourite of the King. He is the one they call Slave."

"Oh yes. So that is him." Kansri did not quite like the knowing look in her elegant sister's eyes. "'Sru! Careful."

"His father was a Buddhist," said Indradevi. "His father and his brother are now dead, so he is in name a little king. Only, he doesn't seem to be bothered about being consecrated or taking a title."

"Perhaps he is showing indifference to the world." Jayarajadevi Kansri meant to be mildly sarcastic. Indradevi was always looking out for her.

Indradevi pretended to take her seriously. "I was wondering the same thing."

The sisters held each other's gaze and suddenly both started to laugh. "We all must look to our futures," said Indradevi Kansru with a gentle, teasing smile.

"Look after your own! I only asked who he was. I did not recognize him because of the moustache."

"You only *like* him because of the moustache."

Jayarajadevi saw how it looked to her sister. "It does give him the air of a holy man, and it is foolish of me to think that. But then I am young and foolish."

"At least he looks like a man who does NOT regard women as if they were elephants."

"Fortunately some great princes are beyond our ken."

"For…tune…ate…leeee," said Indradevi Kansru and rattled the tips of her fingers on her sister's arm. Between themselves they called some of the highest princes in the land the Oxen. Among them, Yashovarman.

But oh, even the Oxen were beautiful young men. They wore their princely quilted jackets, all gold embroidered flowers, and were finely built and swift of movement. That gave low pleasure but also higher pleasure. If lotus flowers were a symbol of divinity for their color, their form, and their life, then surely the same could be said for beautiful young men?

Though the lotus had the advantage of not trying to be beautiful, or being arrogant about it.

Kansri had indeed heard of the prince who called himself Nia. She wondered why this favourite of the Universal King would do himself such an injury as to be named after the lowest category of slave. He could be consecrated as a little king and take a noble title, but he still called himself Nia, Hereditary Slave.

Jayarajadevi Kansri knew why she would give herself such a name. She would do it to show that the titles of this world were meaningless, that compassion was owed to the lowly.

Was it possible that in this palace of warmongers there was a man who would give himself that name from the same motives? Possible that he would regard slaves as being worthy of attention, simply other souls trapped in samsara? How wonderful it would be to find a man with whom you could talk about such things, who would take such thoughts and manlike turn them into solid facts.

Such a possibility. A dream, like the cloud-flowers that everyone hoped to see and never did.

So this happy prince—and he does smile beautifully—helped his younger comrade up. He was neat and quick; and he explained so patiently to the little boy about the double crossbow on the beast's back.

He pointed out the weapon's thick arms and showed how to pull them back. He made it look easy. He guided his charge's hands and together they pulled back the nearest bow. Then he nipped out of the howdah down into the bamboo cage that clung to the side of the beast.

Jayarajadevi Kansri heard the sergeant cluck his tongue. The old female elephant trotted forward, creased and whiskery like a granny.

The little one in the howdah was having difficulty. He wavered as he pulled back on the bow; he wobbled as he knelt on the platform; he squinted into the sun. The Slave Prince half stood, balancing on the bamboo struts of the cage and encouraging the boy.

The little boy looked cross. The elephant's motion jostled him. The crossbow veered dangerously.

Without warning the bolt sprang forward, as long and heavy as a spear. It plunged deep into the elephant, just where the rounded dome of its head met the hunch of its neck.

The old female screamed, and broke into a charge. The Slave Prince pulled himself back into the howdah.

Some of the Oxen roared with laughter. Jayarajadevi Kansri sent tiny blades out with her eyes: oh it is so funny to see a beast in agony. Oh it is so robust to laugh when someone might be killed!

Bellowing, the old female stumbled into the high fluttering banners, scattering category people. She dropped down onto her knees and shook her head as if saying no, no, no. The sergeants ran to secure her again. The howdah jerked from side to side. The Prince grabbed the boy's hand and turned to jump free. Just as he launched himself, the elephant shrugged and he lost hold of the boy.

The Prince was dumped heavily onto the scrub earth. His knees gave way, but he caught himself with his hands and he scuttled forwards out of the way. He jerked himself to his feet and twisted around, to see the elephant lower herself onto her side. The side basket crackled as her weight crushed it.

The boy clung to the low sides of the howdah. "Jump!" the Prince called up to the boy and held out his arms to catch him. His charge hung back, weeping. The Oxen laughed.

The elephant began to roll onto her back. The little boy screamed and flung himself free, hurtling down onto the Prince, who fumbled him, held him, and staggered backwards, pulling the boy out of harm's way.

The elephant, nearly on her back, kicked her legs and shook her head, trying to scrape the bolt out of her neck. She drove it deeper in. The balustrades of the howdah collapsed under her with a sudden thump.

The keepers edged forward with spears. Ducking and fearful, they tried to grab the harness around her body and shoulders. The bell around her neck clanked and clattered.

There was a gasp from the onlookers. The foolish Prince had run up her ribcage. He looked as though he was climbing rocks in the river, only these rocks shifted underfoot. The Prince grabbed the thick shaft of the spear in the elephant's head. The old beast cawed like a giant crow and kicked and the Prince was swung out over the ground, still holding on. Then the shaft swung back. He found his footing, and hauled out the weapon. He jumped free from the beast and flung it away all in one motion.

The elephant kicked once more and then went still.

The keepers advanced on her with lances.

"No, no, no!" the Prince cried aloud, holding out his hands.

The dazed old elephant lifted up her head. She snorted out breath as if in relief. Very suddenly she kicked herself back onto her feet. She stood still and blinked at her keepers who warily approached.

"The bolt just went into the flesh of her neck," the Prince said. As if treading across thorns, he slowly crept towards her. The old animal lowered her head and shuffled backwards. She associated him with pain. He backed off as well and instead turned to his young charge.

The little boy was standing at stiff attention. His face was dusty and tracked with tears, but he was not crying now. Poor thing, he thinks he will be punished, perhaps even sent back to his mother, who knows?

Jayarajadevi Kansri leaned forward, turning her head sideways to hear, aware that her sister Indradevi was looking at her and not at the Prince.

"You were not strong enough to use the bow," said Prince Nia. "You will get stronger if you work. Will you work?"

"Yes!" said the little boy, nodding hard.

"I will help you get strong," said the Prince and touched the boy's arm. Then he saw the keepers approach again with spears.

"No, no, no!" he commanded them. "She will live. No! She can carry things!"

"Well," said Jayarajadevi, settling back. "He is certainly not one of the Oxen."

As soon as people got wind of the potential attachment, they took sides.

Indradevi Kansru wound her way through the palace routines until she could sidle up to the Slave Prince. "You are a popular man, Prince."

"Am I?" He had a nice open smile.

"Oh indeed. You have found favour in the eyes of a certain lady. You are a lucky man to secure such favour. This is a high-born lady of the greatest beauty and accomplishment."

He beamed in measured pleasure. "That is very pleasant to hear."

"May I tell the lady that?"

"I cannot think which lady it may be, but if she is as you describe then only a fool would not be grateful."

"Hmmm. And I think you are not a fool. I will tell you, ah? Oh, this lady is special; she outshines all others. She is a *friend* of mine. No one knows her as well as I do, and she has such a good heart, such a fine mind. Oh! If only I were so adorned."

"What is her name?"

Indradevi finally whispered it in his ear, carefully gauging the warmth and tenderness of his smile. She was not unpleased.

But another girl came and said, "Oh Prince, everyone speaks well of you, everyone says you have a good heart. I have come to warn you. Oh! There is a certain person who gives herself airs and graces. She knows you have the attention of the King, and seeks to climb your virtues like a monkey climbs a vine. She has a bad reputation that one, for a cool head and a cold heart." Then, in a whisper, "Some say it is the King's bed not yours she seeks."

Nia's loyal friends, who like him were good on the field and well behaved in the Royal House, clustered around him. "Oh! Lucky man, the Lady Jayarajadevi is so beautiful. When are you going to have the courage to present yourself? Oh, you must be quick, such a prize as that will not go unclaimed for long."

The Oxen caught him off guard as he washed. He was nearly naked and defenceless. Yashovarman looked scornfully down at his less bullish body. "You are a small slip of a thing to think that you can claim the attention of high ladies. You should know, before you get into trouble. The Lady Jayarajadevi is spoken for. She is a king's wife, not for semi-peasant like you."

"Prince Nia!" one of the Oxen laughed. "What title will he take, do you think. *Niavarman*, Slave Shield?"

They all laughed. Prince Nia stayed calm. "Until she marries, no one is spoken for. And I think she speaks for herself."

"You cannot speak for her, that is certain."

"Neither can you. You should know, before you get me angry, that she calls you an ox. You are unsubtle and don't know that women do not measure a man's worth by the thickness of his thighs."

"No, but the world gives to the man who takes, and to take one must be strong."

"And smart. And fearless. And not easily led. Oxen are strong and bear the world's burdens, not its prizes. Unless you want a fight now, Ox, I will finish washing myself. You should try washing some time."

Nia had just enough love of war. The strong ox Yashovarman hesitated, and in hesitation made his ground unsteady. "I have warned you!" he said, but retreated.

To his friends, the Prince sighed in disgust as they played checkers. "Oh! I wish everyone would cease this matchmaking. You would think the marriage had been announced."

The friends chuckled. "We will not let you escape. The Lady Jayarajadevi is perfect for you. Not just her beauty. It is a matter of her character." And they laughed at themselves, for they were imitating old village women.

"Uh!" groaned the young prince. "Just leave it, please!"

One night the Prince woke up in his hammock to see Divakarapandita leaning over him.

"Teacher!" he exclaimed in fear and alarm.

"I was seeing how you sleep," said the great religious leader. "I wanted to see the quality of your dreams."

The Prince scrambled to make himself decent.

"No, no, you do not insult me sleeping innocent in your bed. You appear whole and complete with no blemish. Does your penis work, does it produce seed?"

"Yes."

"Hmm. I hear that you have a copious heart and mind."

"I can't judge that."

"I can. That is why I am here. Now that you are awake, please cover yourself, and we will walk out into the night so that we can talk." The other soldiers in the room lay frozen with that particular listening stillness of people who pretend to be asleep.

The Prince swung out of the hammock, twisted a garment around his middle, and joined the great Consecrator of Kings, the Dhuli Jeng.

"What is your view of the Gods?" the Consecrator asked.

"Toh! It is hardly for the likes of me to have a view on the Gods."

"Of the relation of the King to the Gods?"

"Even less so."

"Come, come, courage, you are a favourite of the King. Let us pretend for the moment that no harm can come to you for any view you express. This interview will go better for you if you do."

Insects buzzed about them. You couldn't see the moon, but the high silk-cottons were silver and the light along the leaves joined up as if there were tiny creeks flowing from leaf to leaf.

Nia could not think of much to say. "I suppose I think that the King should pay observance to the Gods. Certainly not anger them." He sighed. "Perhaps invent fewer of them. It seems unlikely to me that one's great aunt can suddenly become one with a god under a new name."

"That is about the Gods and the great aunt, not the King."

"I sometimes wonder if it is enough to make observances."

"Ah! Elaborate, young prince."

The Slave Prince looked at the old man's ordinary face. Despite his beautiful shawl, purple and sewn with gold thread, despite his fine white beard, despite the gold parasol with its ivory handle, which he used now like a walking stick, despite all of that there was nothing special about him.

His face had gone waxy like a candle, and was spotted with age. His teeth were brown and crumbled, his back bowed, his arms stiff and shrivelled, bone-thin but with hanging withered pouches of skin along the lower edge. This was an old man, whose every glance stared ahead at his own death.

The young Prince felt sorrow for him, sorrow for all things that pass.

The Prince said, "I know it takes a lifetime to learn how to make observance. I think it is hard work to parade on an elephant and look like something that talks to gods. Harder still to look like you will become a god when you die. Hard work, but that is not enough."

The old man blinked. "It isn't?"

"I once had a friend. She was a slave, a gift to this house. I saw that her world was as big as our own. I saw that whatever was holy in us was also holy in her. I think we try to climb towards the Gods. We get higher and higher up to the King, and then over the King, to the Gods, and when we look at the Gods, we find ... what? A cycle? Back down to the flies and the fishes. There is no top. Everything is holy."

The old man disapproved. "A radical notion. What do you know of the Buddha?"

"Almost nothing."

"Oh, tush!"

"He was a teacher great enough to be treated almost like a god."

"And what did he teach?"

"Virtue. I am to be a soldier, and I will be a good soldier. I will serve with honor and courage and efficacy." The Slave Prince clenched his fist. "I have no doubt of that. But what I want, if anyone should ask, would be to be a Brahmin."

Divakarapandita chuckled and waved a hand.

"A Brahmin who rides an elephant and fights for his king when the time comes ..."

"Oh ho-ho!"

"And who is *not ignorant*." The words were hot; they made his eyes sting.

Divakarapandita's mouth hung open. "Ignorant?"

"I know nothing!" Then less heated. "Nobody has bothered to teach me."

"Do you think anybody has bothered to teach the Lady Jayarajadevi!" The Consecrator looked appalled. "You have to teach yourself!"

Nia hung his head. "I speak heatedly from shame." He began to see what the interview might be about. Another round of match-making. Who was this Lady to have the Consecrator concern himself with her marriage?

"So you should be ashamed." But the old man seemed to say it from sorrow. He touched the Prince's arm. "You have no ambition to be king?"

"Toh. All these little princes, all dreaming of being king, all making tiger faces at themselves. I want to be a holy warrior."

The old man stopped, shuffled round to face him, took hold of both the Prince's arms, and stared into his eyes. "War is never holy," he said. "War makes kings, and kings perform holy functions. But the two are separate."

Nia felt shame again. He hung his head. "I feel things. But I don't know things."

"Maybe there is someone who will take the time to teach you," said the holy man. "And then you might become what you want to be, a wise man." He drew himself up. "What will you do when the King dies?"

Nia felt alarm, for himself, for his whole life. "The King is ill?"

"Ssh, ssh, no, but he is a man. What will you do when he dies?"

Nia thought. With his protector gone, with the Oxen fighting over kingship, there would be years of violence. He imagined Yashovarman, and found he felt disgust and alienation and fear. "It depends how he dies."

"How do you mean?" The holy man's eyes were narrowed.

"If someone murders the King, then I will seek justice. If he dies in his bed, that's different."

The old man looked up and then back. "There is a war coming," he said. "In Champa and in the lands beyond. You will be sent away and may not come back. You are sixteen and it would be good if you were married. You see, Prince, you are as dear to Suryavarman as the Lady Jayarajadevi is to me. We have discussed a marriage between you and the Lady, the King and I. I have assessed you and find you as the King described."

The Dust of the Feet drew up his robes. "The marriage will proceed," he said.

It was only the marriage of a high lady to a prince whose lack of family was made up for by his own subtleties of person.

But not only the Dhuli Jeng but the King himself were to attend. It was to be held in a pavilion in the royal enclosure. The greatest soldier, Rajaindravarman, General of the Army of the Center, was to be the young Prince's sponsor, as his father was dead.

And since this prince was already in line for a small throne, the Dhuli Jeng was to recognize him at the same time as a little king. He was to take his title.

The princes and the princesses all washed exuberantly around the cisterns. There were to be musicians and dancers. This was a chance for the King to express his love. A general sense of satisfaction emanated from him and was communicated to his loyal court. They were to be joyous before a time of war.

The Slave Prince was married wearing his quilted flowered coat and carrying his shield. A crown of bronze had been wound into his hair. As always, he did without his torque, which gave immunity from harm.

Nia marched with a column of his comrades in arms. His friends looked pleased. They passed through the well-wishers and then climbed the steps to the pavilion.

Torches fluttered in the wind. Pressed around were wives of the King, high courtiers, and a few members of Jayarajadevi's family.

The nephew-in-law of the childless King was there. Prince Nia saw in the eyes of Yashovarman something measured and measuring. He is not an Ox, that one, thought Nia. He may have been one once, but now he simply uses them. How wise he was, to marry the King's niece. The certitude came. He will indeed be Universal King. As he advanced, Nia sompiahed particularly to him. Yashovarman blinked in surprise, and indicated a return of respect.

So that Jayarajadevi could in fact be married to a little king, the title-giving came first. Consecration was too high and holy a word for it. The Universal King would recognize the new title and the Little King be given a chance to swear loyalty.

So the Dhuli Jeng was to give out one more regal honorific. Which was to be?

The Prince smiled. He had thought long and hard about this. Once he took his title, then his bride might have to give up or amend her own if their titles clashed inauspiciously or gave obeisance to different principles. Why should she change her great name? His smile widened as he said, "My name is Jayavarman."

He had taken a name to match his wife's and not the other way around. The onlookers murmured among themselves.

It was a better title than Nia, but Jayavarman was also the honorific of many Great Kings. Did it show ambition? Suryavarman's countenance did not flicker.

Divakarapandita's smile widened a little further. The overturning Prince had overturned again. "You are now Jayavarman of the City of the Eastern Buddha."

Little King Jayavarman beamed as he swore loyalty to the Universal King.

Then he was married.

Indradevi Kansru held up an embroidered cloth so that the Little King could not see the beauty of his bride too soon and then be dazzled speechless or struck blind. Indradevi was so pleased for her sister that a whole night sky seemed to beam out of her eyes.

Divakarapandita himself scattered flowers, and poured water on the stone lingam and yoni. The embroidered cloth still stood between them.

My wife, thought Jayavarman. Behind that cloth is my wife. I shall be a husband, we will be together, we shall make love, we shall be each other's support, and we will have children, brilliant babes.

Divakarapandita beckoned him forward and the Prince knelt and drank water, sign of everything, source of everything, as poured from the yoni. Unusually, making some obscure point, the Dust of the Feet asked him to drink from the lingam as well.

Then the cloth was lowered.

And Nia was dazzled and he was stuck dumb, for there was

Jayarajadevi, his wife, and her smile stretched all the way to the moon.

Her smile was pulled wide by a joy she could not express, and her eyes shone. She was sheathed in gold, jewels, and signs of office, surrounded by fans and fly whisks and parasols, all borne by her friends. The paraphernalia bobbed around her beautiful face like flowers.

Jayavarman stared and could not speak. People chuckled. His mouth hung open. He had a declaration to make and could not make it.

"Lord," reminded Divakarapandita.

Jayavarman restored himself and stumbled rough-voiced and awkward through the words that declared and promised and established and called upon others to witness. His wife's eyes were on him all the time.

There was feasting and dancing. The Little King's friends hugged him, shook him, teased him, and declared that they would marry too, it would give them heart for battle, they had not known until now that wives completed warriors.

The bride's female friends warned him, shaking fingers, that he must treat their friend well or the women would take revenge. It was both a joke and serious.

Indradevi Kansru wove her way towards them, her whole body writhing with happiness. Her eyes shone almost too brightly, and she took her sister's hand, called the Little King "Brother," and said repeatedly how happy she was. It was a good marriage, and they should both count on her always as a friend. She pulled away suddenly and Jayarajadevi started after her. And stopped.

For Yashovarman was upon them. Their other friends drew back. "Little King," he said, "the Universal King does you a great honor."

"He does, oh, he does indeed!" said Jayavarman, still buoyed up with joy like a bobbing raft.

"I wish you well in your marriage, and wish you good heart in the coming war."

"Oh! The same to you, Prince!" Jayavarman was not exactly himself, the words were not appropriate for once, but the force behind them was good hearted.

"We will fight many wars together," said Yashovarman. "I hope I can rely on you?"

What a dangerous question. The waters of joy receded. Swiftly Jayavarman mounted the bank, the bank of politics, princes, rivalries, and himself.

Jayavarman said, "I try to be friends with all men and certainly loyal to all my comrades in arms."

Yashovarman whispered. "What if I am more than that?"

Jayavarman did not have the heart to be anything other than direct. "I think you will be Universal King, Yashovarman, and I intend to serve the King. For me to be loyal to the next king, my Lord Suryavarman, who is beloved by me, must die in his bed, honored, and his ashes kept in his temple with great remembrance. Let us have a pact, Yashovarman, to preserve our Lord so that all can see he died a natural death."

Yashovarman went very still and silent. "Of course," he said without further ceremony or display of feeling. He very suddenly smiled, and flipped the tip of the Little King's nose. "What a little puppy you are." It could almost pass for affection. Yashovarman strode away.

Did Suryavarman see the exchange? It seemed to Jayavarman that the King went out of his way to hold him up to the household. "I give you my trusted right hand, my support in old age, my young and supple Shield of Victory!" the King cried.

There were groans and protests: no, you are not old.

"I give you my cloud-flower of virtue and respect whose name will join the web of stars overhead!"

He hugged Jayavarman's shoulders, and leaned on him. The King's breath smelt of wooden teeth and palm wine. The Little King smiled and thought, this could be dangerous. The King whispered to him, "My harrow after death."

Finally, finally he and his wife were left alone. They walked hand in hand to the household reservoir. It creaked with frogs and crickets. So, the Prince thought, I have a wife as beautiful as the moon, as tuneful as the birds. But I don't really know her. All our friends surround us.

And from somewhere came grief and he found he was crying.

"Husband," said his new wife. "You weep?"

She tried to pull him around. It was not manly to weep. He tried to stop. But suddenly he found he could not stop, and that his legs were giving way under him. He slumped down to the ground.

Gracefully, Jayarajadevi lowered herself next to him. "My Lord, be happy?" she chuckled, her voice also unsteady.

"I don't know why I do this."

He looked up at the leaves, stars, moon, and the temple, black and red and gilded, dancing with torchlight.

"I wish my mother was here," he said, locating the grief. "I wish my father was alive. I wish I'd been with him when he died."

"Ah," she said, like wind in the trees. She sat in her gold-embroidered gown on the dry ground. She took him in her arms. "It is our fate to lose our families."

"I will not see her or my father again. My brothers are taken by the wars. My mother said she did not choose this, that she would always think of me."

"She was a very wise and loving mother to say that."

"I don't know why I do this!" He was so frightened of looking unmanly for his bride.

"You are weeping because you have come home after such a long time." Her own words rocked as if over a bumpy road. She cradled him closer and kissed his forehead. She kissed his closed eyes, for all of their dead. "Your father. My father. Your mother." She looked into his eyes. "What is your name? I don't know your real name."

Jayavarman smiled, embarrassed, and shrugged. He closed his eyes and said his real name. "Kráy."

Jayarajadevi's face froze.

He said, "Kansri, don't tell anyone, please. It is not a name I can live up to!" The name in Old Khmer meant Huge, Powerful, Exceeding—Too Much.

Jayarajadevi asked, "Your father gave you that name?"

"No, my mother." Jayavarman grinned. "She had a vision of me. Mothers do."

Jayarajadevi Kansri sighed. "I won't ever know your parents."

"That's okay, neither do I." He looked smiling, accepting. "They were the reverse of what you expect a man and a woman to be. My mother was brave, strong, and calculating, but also wilder. She saw things. My father, Dharan Indravarman, was sweet and gentle, always saying look, look at the butterflies. Look at the flowers. Maybe the flowers take wing as butterflies. He cried when animals died."

His wife took his hand. "They sound like exceptional people."

The tears came again. "They were. And I hardly knew them."

She made him look at her. "We will make a new family," she promised. "We will people that family with children who will honor and respect you. We will build a house of our own, a great house where all our families can come home."

"And I will learn about the Buddha. My family were Buddhists. Did you know that?"

She smiled. "Everyone knows that, Nia." She shook her head. "That is why we were matched."

The Prince bounced up and down. "Well. We will build a Buddhist capital! We will make a city of compassion." Jayavarman, Victory Shield, clenched his fist. "We will make a precious jewel of a kingdom and keep it safe from thieves and hold it up as a shining star to light the rest of the world!"

His wife, his queen, draped herself across him. "Yes, my Lord, yes," she said. There was a sensation as if they had mounted on the back of a swan. Their world was winging.

Then Jayavarman went away to war.

April 14, 2004

The hatch clunks open.

Luc feels sweet air move on his cheek. He smells sun-baked wood, muddy water, and reeds. Something in that smell tells him it's early morning and he imagines open blue sky and the expanse of the Great Lake.

The boys on the deck grunt. "Ugh! It smells like a pigpen. You. Out here to wash."

Wash! The only thing Luc wants to do now is wash; dust and sweat coat him like a layer of latex. Luc tries to sit up and bashes his forehead on the low ceiling. He inches his way forward on his buttocks. He hears the General being seized by his ankles and hauled backwards across the shallow hull.

No thanks. Luc rolls over onto his hands and knees, and backs his way towards the hatch. He hates not being able to see anything. The joists press into his shins.

Hands grab his arms and pull him up the hatch, peeling off skin from his elbows and ankles.

But the air is as sweet as spun sugar, and the sunlight as warm as a mother's touch. The bungee cords around his wrists are unsprung. He can move! He hears the tape being torn away from the General's face and then the plunge when the other man jumps off the boat. The thought of cool, cleansing water makes Luc chuckle with anticipation.

Then a boy shouts. "He's gone under. There! There! There!" Terrifyingly close to Luc's ear, gunfire slams out towards the reeds. Feet thud on the deck and the water parts with a puff-whoosh as someone dives.

The General is trying to escape.

Luc reacts like a child. I won't get my wash, he thinks. He wants to cry from disappointment. He imagines the General diving under the thick layer of floating plants and slipping away through the reeds. He imagines himself left alone with the kidnappers. Despair comes instantly.

Then a thumping on the deck and a streaming of water. "Get back up here you old roostershit! Move!"

And despite himself, Luc feels relief, a certain warmth around the heart. He will not be left alone.

Something is heaved onto the deck. The General starts to call out but two quick snaps of gunfire cut him off and he keens like a seagull.

They've shot him. The General yelps and squeals as he's hauled across the deck. The boat's tiny engine begins to throb and gurgle.

The boys shout, "Get in! Get in!" The boat moves and turns. Cold wet hands grab Luc and push.

"I'm going, I'm going!" Luc grunts through the tape. He stumbles down through the hatch and the boys club his head with the butt of a rifle or pistol, to beat him down into the hull. He ducks and dives, slamming his forehead.

The boys clamber down after him and cram him up against the General. The General's cold skin twitches and he makes a thin continuous wheedling sound, fighting pain. Tape is ripped around him; he howls in agony as someone lifts his legs, presumably to bungee them together.

The boys leave the General tossing back and forth like a child trying to rock himself to sleep.

The hatch closes. The boat drones on for hours.

William pulls up at the Phimeanakas at 8:00 A.M. and finds the forecourt crammed with foreigners he doesn't know.

They are climbing into the back of the dig's pickup truck. "They say the airport is open again," says an Australian tourist.

"What has happened?" William shouts to him.

"They say one of the archaeologists who is staying here has been kidnapped." The man's mouth sours into an odd mix of the fearful and the exhilarated. "We're heading out."

William tries to find the team's Cambodian director. Prak the security guard stops him, a hand planted on his chest. William is only a motoboy and not allowed even into the forecourt of the Phimeanakas.

Normally Prak has a sweet temper, but not today. He glowers and his breath smells of beer. "Wait outside. If your friends are here they will come out for you."

"What's happened? Who was kidnapped?" William asks.

"I don't know," says Prak and stomps away.

If all the tourists leave, there will be no money. No money for anybody.

One of the other motoboys eyes William. William thinks of himself as a businessman. He lays claim to the patch outside the Phimeanakas. He pays a commission to Mrs. Bou—and all the other Phimeanakas motoboys pay him.

This is Mons. Mons is older than William and doesn't like paying him money or being trapped as a motoboy. He pretends to be friendly, but everything he says has hidden teeth.

"So you have no more UN friends," says Mons.

"Neither have you."

"Oh, I have plenty of business today. I drive people to the airport."

"Do you know who got kidnapped?"

"It is a terrible thing. Grandfather Frenchman. Your mentor!" Mons looks glum but he says it loudly, for everyone to hear. The other motoboys look sullen and confused.

"You can drive a tourist back to the airport only once," William replies in a quiet voice. "And when all the other tourists stay away, you'll see. This is bad for you too."

The other motoboys hang their heads.

William turns to the foreigners, smiles, takes off his baseball cap, dips and bows. He tries his Japanese on some Asian tourists and gets business. He's unsure about some of the Europeans. He tries German; they turn out to be Italian, but they understand "Five dollars, five dollars to airport."

"I have suitcases," says a man in strange English. William organizes two motorcycles for him, ten dollars, but it's still cheaper than a taxi. "I'm sorry," William says. "Today taxis will be hard to find."

The man nods and smiles, grateful for anything. He's from Iran. William gets his name and asks about the government. "Is the religion Islam?" he asks.

He gets business for all the motoboys and pointedly leaves Mons until last.

Luc, he thinks. Of all the people they could have done this to. Those idiots! The foreigners bring money, they come here to help us! Why are they doing this? What will it do to Cambodia?

The US special quota for garments will end soon. The garment industry brings 250,000 jobs and when it goes, what will replace it? All we have is tourism!

William feels the trickle of dreams washing away. I won't get my new bike. I won't be able to help aunty buy her new house. The land we were hoping to sell for development—twelve thousand dollars we were told we would get for it—maybe that won't sell. I won't have the UN archaeologists to talk to, to find out about things.

He remembers one of Luc's students insisting to Mrs. Bou that William was a colleague, not a motoboy. He got William inside the pink marble dining room of the Phimeanakas and up the stairs into the social area. It was large enough to unfold huge photographs of Angkor taken from airplanes.

One photograph covered seven hundred square kilometres. It used a kind of radar to penetrate the ground one dot at a time, and a computer joined up the dots. The signals had bounced off a satellite in space. Luc's student explained geosynchronous orbits to him. William's head jerked back with shock and pleasure. What a wonderful idea.

The machine is always falling, but the ground falls away at the same pace. So it always stays above the same spot of ground.

Who would do things like that for him now?

Luc had bought him a mobile phone. He simply passed it to him one day outside the guesthouse. "This is so we can telephone you whenever we need you."

William had stood in silence, stroking the phone. He didn't want to show strong emotion. He was embarrassed, and fearful of doing something unseemly like crying.

A mobile telephone made him part of the world. His friends could telephone from Japan, from Australia, and say, William, we are coming, please organize a trip. William, we are at the airport, can you come and fetch us?

William was silent for so long, wary of speaking, that Luc had become worried that he'd done something wrong. "I've paid for the sim card and for fifty dollars' worth of calls. But you'll have to show up with your family ID card to collect them."

Finally William had something neutral to say. "I know the people in the shop." He coughed and still did not dare look at Grandfather Luc. He was horribly aware that he had said nothing polite, not a word of thanks. The beautiful numbers were illuminated from within.

Nobody had ever done such a thing for him before. Not unasked, not something so perfect for William. Luc must have known it was perfect for him without having to be told.

William coughed again, trying to find words. Finally he'd said, still not looking up. "This is a very good action. This is a thing that is full of merit."

Then he was able to look up and bow and sompiah respect and thanks. "Luc, I am so lucky that you are my friend. I tell my aunt about you. She says you must be a very good man. I am so unhappy whenever you go away."

Unmanned, he had to thumb water out of his eyes.

Those tears well up again now. What they have stolen from me, what they have taken from Cambodia! Do they even realize?

Sangha, the Cambodian dig director, stands in front of him. He doesn't greet him with the usual, "Are you happy?" He is looking directly into William's sad eyes and sees what is there: grief.

William sompiahs in forlorn respect. Sangha's face goes solemn, his words kindly and formal. "The dig has been closed, William. All the foreigners are going. I telephoned Geneva and they say to use any money to help APSARA with the investigation."

Sangha has a meeting and needs William to drive. William feels better; at least he has work for today.

They go along the river, past the repainted Wat, the Grand Hotel, and the new Foreign Correspondents Club, its white marble luxury now closed. The road narrows. Along the bank, the houses of poor people stand out over the water on stilts. People had been saying no more poor people will live in Siem Reap soon, only rich people and hotels. What will happen now?

APSARA HQ is an old villa behind walled gates, with offices upstairs and a simple meeting room downstairs. Sangha gets off his bike, and William says, "Please, Loak Dik Sangha. May I go to the meeting too? Teacher Luc is my mentor, he did so much to help me, I want to help him."

Motoboys don't go into villas and attend meetings. They wait outside. Guards in three different kinds of uniform—blue, brown, and green—eye them. Sangha says kindly, "I will tell you everything that happens, William. Don't worry, you have a contract with us, I'm sure there will still be work for you to do."

That's not what I meant; that's not why I'm worried.

Sangha smiles and nods and walks off to the meeting.

I am smart; I could do much more to help than you think.

William approaches the guards, offers them cigarettes and asks them all kinds of questions. How was the Book taken? Has anybody written or telephoned to make demands or say why they did such a thing?

"There were shots this morning, out on the Lake," says one of the guards. "Two. One for each of them."

Luc could already be dead. William cannot stop himself spinning on his heel. "When?"

"Very early this morning. So the Lake Police are helping too, looking at all the boats."

The army had roadblocks on all roads, with APSARA's agreement. Within a forty-square-mile area, the investigation was the responsibility of APSARA and therefore of the Patrimony Police who worked for them. Outside the Angkor precinct, federal, provincial, lakeside, and tourist police forces were involved.

The guards tell him all the details. Two stolen pickup trucks were found with blood in the back. Their legal owners spent a bad night locked up in tourist police cells. "Oh well, at least they had a view of the Grand Hotel!" The guards are relaxed enough now to joke with him.

William waits for four hours, plans for action itching inside him. Sangha finally comes out, looking pleased and amused.

"We've got a job for you, William," he says. His smile is crooked. "I don't know if you'll like it."

"I will do anything I can to help," William says, slightly dismayed at the picture Sangha has of him, even now, after all the times they have spoken together, all the intelligent questions William has asked.

Sangha looks at him with pity. "I'm afraid you are going to be Sergeant Tan Map's driver."

William does not miss a beat. "Excellent," he says.

The boat passes a succession of radios playing Vietnamese music.

Finally it shushes to a halt. They wait.

The stench in the hull is terrible. Luc imagines the filthy water getting into the General's wounds. Vutthy writhes continually, lost to the world, occupied by pain.

There's no one else now, Luc. You are responsible for both yourself and the General. If either of you is to survive, it is down to you.

Luc has read somewhere that you survive kidnapping by building alliances with your captors. By talking with them. His mouth is taped. He's unshaven and stinking; he must look like a vagabond. Already, so easy to kill.

The General starts to thump his head against the wall from pain.

Luc tries to mew sympathy at him through the tape.

The General makes a sudden, angry gurgling in his throat. Everything is irrelevant except the agony in his legs.

Luc has never considered himself to be a wise person, but he has a certain kind of faith in people that he attributes to his mother.

At a time when it was not so easy for a woman without a husband, his mother had supported them by herself. She had not told Luc who his father was, but he understood well enough. His father was an important man, who would never be part of their lives, someone very high up. Luc never dared to speculate who, but he did note that whenever the President of the Republic was on the TV news, his mother walked briskly out of the room.

They lived well away from France and any potential scandal. His mother coped with living in a foreign country, working as liaison for the Royal Cambodian Ballet. In practice the job meant liaison with France and sometimes Russia. She had taken the company to perform in Moscow and Japan.

Once she told her son, when he was suffering one of his bouts of adolescent angst, "You have a quality of listening, Luc. That is good.

Because how you listen to people is exactly how they listen to you."

So how, Mama, do I listen to Fish Face?

He imagines a reply in her tone of voice.

Well, perhaps you start by NOT calling him Fish Face. I don't suppose you have a name for him? No. Well, I would call him by the name of someone you like. Try to listen to him as if he were that person.

Nobody I like points a gun in my face.

Exactly. If he likes you perhaps he won't either. I know you like a lot of people, and they are often people who don't like you. It is your most endearing trait, Luc; really, it is most touching sometimes. I would suggest that in these crucial circumstances you ensure that the person concerned also liked you.

He imagines her cool, reassuring voice; her rugged, slightly rueful smile of amusement and acceptance. Already things seem easier to bear.

I'll pretend he's Arn.

I can't help you choose, that is for you to do. Is Arn dead? Don't surround yourself with the Dead. You might find it too easy to join them.

She means herself. She is dead too.

She seems to lean closer. He sees her with her 1966 hair teased high, her jet-age eye makeup, and her arts-administration directness.

You have more chance of survival if you refuse to accept even the possibility of death. You ... will ... live.

I will live.

Another boat shushes to a halt next to them. Luc hears Fish Face's barking voice. Don't think of him as Fish Face. He's Arn.

That's Arn's voice, grim with anger but not harsh, not yelling. Arn is angry with the boys for shooting someone. And perhaps for coming to a place where there are people.

The boat rocks as he steps onto it. The engine coughs to life again and they begin to move.

More hours in the heat and the dark. Sealed in tape, Vutthy is sobbing.

Finally the boat stops, one hour, two hours later. The hatch at last is opened and sweet air pours into the hull.

The old man says, "This is not bearable, we can't stay on this boat with this stench. Untie the barang, and bring him out here."

Luc tells himself: this is Arn, helping me. The cords spring free again. Luc lifts his knees and is immediately disabled by cramps running up his calves, deep into the muscles of his thighs. He groans.

The tape is peeled away again from his head. His cheeks stink from having been sealed for a day.

Luc flounders his way like a walrus along the floor and grasps the edge of the hatch. The boy's voices are clenched as if they are going to be sick. They don't want to touch him. He pulls himself up and it's sunset, a beautiful sunset, wonderful blue-grey clouds on fire along the edges. The satin-surfaced water reflects it. Everything is cooler, grey, gold, and blue. On the very tip of a reed, a tiny bird bobs.

Fish Face—no, Arn—*Arn* glares at Luc and down at his filthy clothes. One of the boys covers his mouth and nose. Arn says, "Barang, you're filthy. Get out of those clothes."

Luc feels fat, grey, and clumsy. His hands quiver with fatigue and fear. He finds that he is near tears. Clothes are protection in front of these young, healthy men. He doesn't want to be seen stripped and old, his sagging chest furred over with white hair.

Arn takes his shirt from him with the barrel of the AK-47 and flings it away from the boat. "Go on, get in. Wash." Luc shivers his way out of his clinging trousers. Arn looks amused. *Maybe he is just pleased I can go for a swim.*

Luc doesn't care how deep the water might be or if there are hidden bamboo stakes or even crocodiles. He plunges in and the water bubbles up and over him, as delicious and cool as champagne. Something in his chest shudders with relief. He cleans himself as thoroughly as he can, but the cleaner he gets, the worse he seems to smell. *We are just animals. We must pity the animal self, who aspires so. Aspires always to the celestial. Is that why water is holy?*

"I'm just moving away from my clothes, to wash better," he warns them, in his mild, and frightened voice.

He washes over and over again. He wants to sink into the dark water and never come up, swim to a secret mermaid realm. Captain Nemo and his submarine.

He can't pull himself back into the boat and so is hauled in like a particularly awkward fish. He's naked, and covers his privates with his hands. The boys mock him.

"Some good clothes, barang?" says the old man, smirking. He holds out something.

This is Arn, with a present. This is Arn giving me a gift.

It's a kramar, the mystifying cloth that Cambodians can twist into a pair of shorts or a shopping bag. It is a test, a joke. Okay, barang, this is how we dress. Just how stupid will you look, trying to dress like us?

"You can wrap a kramar, can't you?" the old man asks, eyes twinkling.

Talk, Luc.

"*Aw kuun*, thank you," he says and takes the red-checked cloth.

Luc remembers a love-hotel long ago, outside town by the river. The room was high up on the top floor, and flooded with light. The sheets and shower were clean, and the hotel towels had been embroidered with hearts.

He and Arn had stood naked side by side and looked at each other in the mirror, startled at how much taller Luc was. Then gently, shyly, Arn had shown him how to wrap the kramar.

Help me now, Arn.

Luc imagines gentle Arn, squatting down beside him to guide his hands. The old man sniffs a laugh as Luc fumbles for the tail of the cloth. Arn had laughed as well; he had covered his mouth in glee to see Luc trying to put on the kramar. The boys laugh now. These are just merry boys, Luc tells himself; they are just having fun. He even manages to smile himself.

Warm morning air had moved, like Arn's fingers. Arn pulled the kramar tighter about him, like a pencil skirt. How did it go? Like tying a Windsor knot in a tie, there is always a moment of remembering. Luc pulls the tail of the cloth up between his legs to make a pouch, and eases the cloth up into two leggings. His pale, limp fifty-year-old tummy overhangs it.

Luc looks up, finished, and tries to see Arn in the old man's hard face. He doesn't see Arn, but he does see reflected back at him in the spectacles what is so funny. It is not so much him as the kramar—the cloth is evidently far too small.

"You barang are all fat," says one of the boys. He looks like a hard-working, decent boy. His smile not all that different from all the smiles in hotels.

The old man's eyebrows flick. The joke is over; the barang has shown he can tie a kramar. The old man reaches forward, and jerks the end of the kramar tighter. He passes Luc his shirt. It has been fished out of the brown water, but somehow, miraculously, it is clean, smelling of fields and sunshine.

An imagined voice comes with the cat's-paw over the lake.

Just remember, says his mother, *that he is not Arn. Watch him. He has no kindness, he thinks of himself as a series of disciplines and links and duties to other people. He only has good behaviour and bad behaviour. And both are equal to him.*

"The General is still bleeding," says Luc quickly. "He will get infected."

The old man shrugs. That's nothing to him. He passes Luc a yellow plastic bucket with dried concrete in the bottom. "If you care about it, clean out the hull." He gives Luc a heavy brush thick with fish scales.

Luc almost cannot bear to go back into the hull. He can smell it; he can taste it in the back of his mouth. Disgust feels like a physical wall, stopping him.

But, he thinks, they have left me untaped to do it.

He folds himself back down under the deck. The air is clotted with the smells of shit and blood. Luc gapes at the General's wounds; they gape back like two exploded oranges. The General has been kneecapped.

"I am cleaning up in here," Luc tells the General in Khmer. "We will get it clean. Maybe that will stop infection."

The General sags as if to say: what difference will that make now?

"It will be better than leaving it dirty." Luc scrubs and rinses and retches. The light is going; he has to work quickly. He stands straight up through the hatch and dumps the water over the side.

"Don't do it that way," says the old man. "People will see you. Boys, take the bucket."

Arn, that's Arn wanting to help me. Luc finds himself smiling and nodding thanks to the old man.

A boy, his face wrenched in disgust, takes the next bucket. "*Somtoh,*" says Luc, meaning excuse me. "We don't like making a mess."

He ducks back down, crab-crawling.

His mother's voice says: *You look afraid. Move neatly, quickly. Look at how they do it.*

The next trip up Luc says to the boys and the old man, "The lake is beautiful. Maybe we move away from here and fish. Get away from this filthy water."

"Maybe," says the old man.

Each time he goes down, Luc says something to the General. "I will ask if we can boil water and try to clean up your legs."

Back up with the bucket, he says to the old man, "The General is still bleeding badly. I can clean up, but all that blood will be dirty too."

The old man sighs. "Stupid children." He flicks Luc out of his way, and swings down into the hull. He blows out air with exasperation. "Why did you do this!" he barks at the boys.

Angrily he scoops up the General's legs. The General trumpets like an elephant. Brusquely, the old man wraps duct tape with ferociously hard jerks around each leg.

"That will stop the bleeding, yes?" Luc asks.

Still angry, the old man does not answer.

"I'm sorry, Vutthy," says Luc. The General, still blind and dumb, nods in acknowledgement.

Luc practises moving along the low hull. This is exercise, he tells himself.

Move with confidence, his mother says. *Imagine you are a doctor in a coal mine.*

When he pops up again, he sees the boys are boiling water on the boat's concrete stove.

Luc asks them, "If you are boiling water, can I use some of it here?" The boys stare back at him. Luc keeps on. "I can scrub in here with boiling water, that would make it really clean."

The chief calls out from inside the hull. "Give it to him." He moves Luc away from the hatch and climbs out. "Barangs like things clean," he says, almost with satisfaction.

Luc keeps bailing out the hull. The next time he surfaces, he sees that the chief seems to be boiling his shirt.

"I think they're making a bandage for you," Luc tells the General.

By now it's dark. The old man thrusts his way into the hull with steaming strips of boiled shirt. Behind him, one of the boys peers

Geoff Ryman

into the hull holding both a lamp and a rifle. The chief unwraps the General's wounds. The kneecaps weep clear fluid. Luc feels an answering sting of heat around his eyes.

The old man wraps sterile strips around each of the General's knees. The General groans in the explosive, repetitive rhythm of a cough. Luc takes the General's hand. The General grips ferociously and holds on, jiggling from pain.

The old man works none too gently, briskly moving the legs. That's Arn, Luc tells himself, helping a fellow driver in an accident. He makes a perfect field dressing.

"Thank you," says Luc. The old man looks up directly into Luc's eyes.

Then he turns and springs up and out. The hatch slams shut and the motor snarls to life. "The barang is still loose," says one of the boys.

"So sit on the hatch," says the old man.

Luc crouches next to the General in the dark. The General still has hold of his hand.

Luc's mother whispers, *Learn the boys' names.*

William finishes driving Sangha for the day.

At the gates of the Phimeanakas, he shakes hands and agrees to meet Sangha and Map early the next day.

Then he goes directly to his two adopted sisters who run the hat and handbag shop.

They are sophisticated ladies. They design handbags, not for tourists but for Cambodian women who live in the villas and who want to look modern.

William expounds. "*Kraing Meas* was written by Jayavarman himself, it is a message from the great king to us now. This book has been stolen and Teacher Luc Andrade and the General taken with it. The army are ashamed because they were in charge, and so they blame the Teacher's man, Tan Map."

One of the ladies wrinkles her nose. "Oh, I know Tan Map, he is not a good character."

William bows. "He is not someone who tells people what he thinks they want to hear. But the Teacher trusted him, and everyone says the Teacher is a man of good character."

106

"So they go for the wrong man, and the ones who took the Book go free."

"Tuh! It could be the army themselves who took it!"

"That's right. So everyone else should look as well," says William.

The ladies are enrolled. "Oh! Yes, we should. You should go and tell everyone, Will."

They will keep their eyes open and ask anybody they meet. If they find anything out they will go to the APSARA main building.

Next William goes to Bopha, his adopted sister who sells gas by the roadside.

These adopted sisters are good friends who lack families. They come to his aunt's house at New Year and Pchum Ben, and find ways to help about the house. They help William find work.

William tells Bopha about the *Kraing Meas*, and the kidnapping. Does her older brother want to help? They need people to look. Could he show up by the police village tomorrow?

William goes to the old man who roasts corn and pork on the roadside, who has been his friend for years. He used to call William "nephew" until he unexpectedly found a real one. William and his nephew are now *samlaing*, good buddies.

William explains excitedly to both of them the great wrong that has been done.

"Ah," says the old man. "The men in the villas are the thieves. They will profit whatever happens."

"Well, this time there is the Patrimony Police to investigate, and they have guns."

"And only sixteen dollars a month. Who says they didn't take it?"

"Because Ta Barang has won their hearts. He has awakened their love of Cambodia and our great kings."

The old man jokes. "Oh yes, and how much money did he pay them?"

"Oh, plenty of money too!" They all laugh.

Did the nephew want to help? Could he come tomorrow to Angkor Wat police village and await orders? The nephew glances at his uncle; his uncle nods yes.

William drives out towards the Phnom to all the people he paid to help in his uncle's fields. He drinks tea, and tells them how the voice of Jayavarman has been returned in a book, how the Teacher has been kidnapped, and how the Patrimony Police need everyone to look for clues. Does anyone remember anything?

One old granny remembers seeing on New Year Day a long, low boat go down the Siem Reap River through the town. The punter did not wear a kramar or a *yuon* straw hat, and got stuck going under the town bridge. So he is not local, and did not know the river.

Do their sons and brothers want to help? Could they come tomorrow?

One of the fathers says, "My son Ea is just out of the army. He rents out his pickup truck. Maybe he could drive people there?"

"That is a very good suggestion, Grandfather. Ea could help us look too."

The family are poor, their house perches on the dike out towards the lake. They sleep directly on the ground. "Yes. It is time all this kind of thing stopped. We lose everything with all this thievery and violence!" The old man has a lot to be fed up about.

"Where is Ea now?"

Hands are flung vaguely out towards the town. The bars, the lot where the pickups are parked—who knows?

So William goes to the pickup lot past the New Market along Highway 6. No tourists here, but a huge unpaved space full of footstools, bowls of noodles, dust, flicking headlights, and pickups stuffed with baskets and people swinging back out towards Sisophon or Kompong Thom.

Ea looks wind-burnt and bleary, still in his army fatigues, eating pork and staring ahead. He has been driving for twenty-four hours straight.

William bounces up, looking lively, to make the night more fun. He brings beer, and talks about car batteries and who is selling them cheap. Then he pitches. Could Ea do him a favour and pick up some lads? He can't pay, but maybe APSARA would. He talks about the Book, he gets Ea angry, and then gives him something to do about it. William gets two pickup trucks in the end, Ea and his mate who also drives.

William has been talking to his old forester friends, and he knows where they've abandoned some rough-cut timber. Maybe they could all go and take some.

They load William's bike on the back of the pickup and fetch the timber. Ea drives William and his plank back to the beginning of the track to his house. He even guards the fresh-smelling red wood while William goes to get his cousin Meak to help. William and Meak carry the plank back balanced between two motorbikes, weaving around tree trunks.

Why not have a party? Ea goes for more beer. They all sit in the kitchen with its strip light. The neighbours come by to hear the news and filch a beer. The price is simple. Their sons go to Angkor tomorrow.

It's past midnight when William goes out again to tell everyone where to meet the trucks in the morning.

It is dark, airless, and hot inside the hull of the boat.

The General still writhes, hissing through the tape that will not let him breathe.

Luc has been taped up and trussed again, so he cannot help. He drifts in and out of sleep, listening to the noises the General makes. He calms himself by thinking of Arn, imagining that life had let them be together.

In that life Luc does not go back to France or move to Australia. He buys an apartment near the National Museum in Phnom Penh. Arn lives with him for a little while. His French improves, speaking it every day with Luc. Arn takes the civil service exam and passes. Arn becomes a functionary, in a crisp white shirt and tie. He has to marry. His wife is sweet and kind; his family have stopped asking questions; and Arn, instead of beginning to sleep around with new men, falls on Luc twice a month with love and gratitude.

The Americans decide to get out of Vietnam earlier. Nixon and Kissinger do not bomb eastern Cambodia, nor do they support a coup to remove the legitimate head of state. Sihanouk stays president.

There are no Khmers Rouges, only scattered powerless cadres in provincial towns.

Phnom Penh stays beautiful. There is no exile to turn Luc away from a study of medicine towards exploring the culture and history of a land that is his secret home. Luc studies medicine in Phnom Penh. He and Arn make love during the long lunch hours. They exchange cards and gifts. Arn has children and makes Luc their godfather.

Nike invests heavily in its Cambodian operation. Honda opens up a huge motorcycle factory. It is the duty of loyal Cambodians

Geoff Ryman

to buy from their own factories. Unlike Vietnam, Cambodia is not war-torn and Communist. Phnom Penh is not an ex-R&R destination for American marines, full of drugs and whores like Bangkok. It is untouched by the West or by the Communists. Phnom Penh's reputation as the most unspoiled city in Southeast Asia spreads.

John Paul Getty moves there for its beauty. The Rolling Stones buy a villa on the river. John Lennon moves there and decides to stay, and so he is not shot in 1980. He records an album with Sin Sisimuth, who is also, in this life, alive. Derrida and Baudrillard come regularly every winter to teach. Phnom Penh becomes the place to be.

When Arn and Luc celebrate the fourteenth anniversary of what Arn calls My Other Marriage, a small company called Apple opens up a manufacturing center there. Something happens. Luc is inspired. He joins Apple as a liaison officer. He also learns programming. He sees this as the way ahead for Cambodia.

Alongside his day job, he begins to train as many Cambodians as he can in the art of programming. They began to author beautiful and jewellike applications.

Luc persuades Apple to set up a 24/7 programming operation. Cambodians continue to author programs while America sleeps.

Phnom Penh becomes a world center of computing. Cheap Apple programs on inexpensively produced Cambodian Apple hardware mount a viable challenge to Microsoft.

Luc is received by Prince Sihanouk in honor of his accomplishments. He comes with Arn and his wife and children. It is the right kind of Sunday so they all wear something red. The Prince beams and shakes their hands. Luc sees Arn's face at forty, and it is as real as his own—handsome, creased, and distinguished. Merrily in Arn's eyes amusement dances, and love.

For a while trussed and helpless in a stinking boat, Luc is happy.

The trapdoor opens. His mouth is untaped, and one of the boys shoves more burnt fish into it.

"Curse that dog of yours," says the General in Khmer.

"I do not understand," says Luc.

The General snorts. "You told Map about the Book. We wouldn't be here except for him!"

Why, wondered Luc, after all this time, does the army still hate Map?

April 1988, April 1989, April 1990

All through the early 1980s, Map tried to find his family.

The Vietnamese drove the Khmers Rouges out of Cambodia into Thailand. Map's only brother died and Map was truly alone. How could he look for his parents, trapped in border refugee camps or hiding out in enemy territory?

Map deserted the Khmers Rouges in 1983.

His gun came with him. The Vietnamese-backed government trusted defectors more if they bore weapons away from the Khmers Rouges.

The government classified Map as a Misled Person. It was not his fault that he was a mass murderer. The government needed Cambodians to fight alongside the Vietnamese. Map found himself an ally of the hated yuon, whom he had once pledged to drive from his country.

Map changed uniforms and went back to a soldier's life, trooping along roadways or through minefields. He lived on one bowl of rice a day. Or less.

By then the Khmers Rouges had renamed themselves in English, the NADK. They renounced Communism, denounced the Vietnamese, and were supported by China and America against Russia and Vietnam. War by proxy. Map fought it.

1985 was the worst year of his life. The Vietnamese had decided to build a wall around Cambodia. They set up labour camps deep in the forests and sent Map to guard the Cambodian conscripts. Map had not found his family, and he was now as far from being able to search as he had ever been.

He met and befriended another guard in the camp. His name was Nim Veasna and, like Map, he was an NADK defector. Like Map, he too was looking for his family.

He and Map deserted again. In the prevailing disorder, no one noticed. Veasna and Map joined another government regiment in Siem Reap. They began to help each other find their families.

They had to go AWOL to do it. They took turns pedalling a push bike from village to village. Sometimes they walked, or hitched a lift with an army vehicle.

They had fun.

Twenty years later, Map still tells stories about Nim Veasna. He gets them wrong. He says that because of thieves and guerillas, he and Nim rode a motorcycle at night without lights. Veasna drove without stopping across bridges that were only a plank of wood.

Nobody in Cambodia had motorcyles in 1985. But that's what Map remembers now.

Muddling his stories softens them.

They'd cling to the sides of a five-wheel truck, and the wind would wuther past the upright barrels of their guns. The sun would come up; it would be cool and clear; and Map or Veasna might let off a round in sheer high spirits.

From around a reservoir, a flock of egrets might take off all in unison. The trees in dry season were leafless blackened stumps as if there had been a fire.

"Nobody stops us, man!" Veasna yelled. Veasna looked like a movie star. He had oiled, carefully combed hair and shades he had taken from a dead yuon soldier. He hated the Vietnamese, even if they were allies, and he kept making fun of them. He had a character he called Ying Ying who was an effeminate screeching yuon who was always trying to steal everything. *Oh, you have cigarette? I Vietnamese, now you don't. Hey, you want to fuck my sister? Oh! You have a hundred dollar, oh, you fuck me instead!* Veasna would wail Vietnamese songs in the same way he shot his gun, out of fun and hatred.

They asked the same set of questions of everyone they met. Cambodian names are so flexible they would start with a place instead. Veasna would ask, "I'm looking for some people from near Battambang, in Banian District? Commune Chheuteal, deDon village? The family might be called Nim? The wife would be called Mrs. Hing?"

Everybody was trying to find someone, and people asked similar questions back: Do you know anybody taking care of a little boy from Wat Bo? Maybe called Dara? Maybe he is still with his brother Chann?

Map would think back over all the families he knew—soldiers in his regiment, girls in roadside stalls, or friends of friends. Whenever he met someone new, he would ask them where they were from and what their family members were called. He would try to bolt down in his memory the names of as many people as possible. How else was the country to fix itself?

They had false alarms. A woman sitting on a roadside platform who sold potatoes said, "I did meet a family from Banian when I was in Preah Vihear. A widow woman. Might she have been called Heng instead? No? Oh, I am sorry for you."

Once a soldier back from leave to Sihanoukville ran up to them to say, "Hey Map, any chance people might pronounce your family name Tang? I found this guy called Tang Heng, maybe he's your brother?"

"My brother's dead," Map said quietly.

Then one day in April 1988, they were lounging around Siem Reap, and they talked to a stall owner who had once been a schoolteacher from Battambang. He'd dug dikes for years and now he was selling combs and lighters on the street. He looked up at Veasna and said, "Yeah, I know a Mrs. Hing in Battambang. She moved in from deDon village with her cousin, a woman called Ary."

Veasna went very still. Did he know this woman Ary's family name?

"Khim," the vendor said. "I think she was from Chheuteal commune."

A silent chuckle seemed to shake Veasna and he ran a hand over his forehead.

"Any chance?" the schoolteacher asked, looking hopeful.

Veasna started to smile. "I think so, yes."

The schoolteacher was overjoyed for him. "Oh, I hope it is your mother. Oh, I hope it is true!"

Veasna suddenly laughed aloud. He even bought one of the guy's lighters.

Map shook his head and said, "All we need now is cigarettes."

Over the next few months, Battambang became their destination.

Whenever they could escape their army duties, they would find someone taking a boat across the Great Lake and up the river.

Each time, the boat would edge its way into one of scores of channels through the reeds. The fisherman or trader would get frightened and turn off his engine and Map and Veasna would jump into the cool water. They would pull the boat in silence for hours.

Those were the happiest times Map could remember. They were screened by overgrowth with only their heads and arms above water, so they were hard to spot. The poor old boatman would be shaking with fear but Map and Veasna felt somehow immune.

They saw purple herons, cormorants, jacuna, and even kingfishers darting among the plants. Watersnakes churned the water to get away from them. They'd spear striped catfish for lunch. Overhead, fish-eagles would turn in the wind. Sure there were leeches, but they'd found a good use for that cigarette lighter—singeing them off.

Map felt peaceful.

They'd climb back into the boat and putter into Battambang. The town was flat, colonial, crumbling and stark, stripped of the palm trees that used to crowd around it. It was such a sleepy place that they would sometimes shoot their guns into the air just to see the confusion. Once they squelched in boots that were still wet out to the Central Market, and, for no reason at all, they strafed the vaulted ceiling. The stall owners screamed and ran.

Map laughed and slapped Veasna with his hat. "That was dumb! We could have asked them about your mother!"

"Oh! This is a country full of ducks!" said Veasna. "Quack, quack, quack!"

A bureau had been set up in Battambang, registering families who were looking for relatives. Not many people had applied. Saying who you really were had caused people trouble in the past.

But on the day they shot up the market, the bureau said that they had found Mrs. Hing. They had an address, meaning a quarter of the city. Veasna's map was his mouth; they asked all day where the house could be found.

A woman scolded them. "You are the pirates who shot up the market, so I should not tell you, but I know Mrs. Hing. She is a decent woman and maybe she can make a decent son of you."

Mrs. Hing lived behind a laundry near the art-deco bus station. Veasna saw a skinny kid emptying grey water out of a tub. "Yeha?" he asked. It was his little brother. Yeha hardly recognized him. He led Veasna around grey peeling walls to a courtyard that smelled of drains. A woman looked up from a water trough. She was as scrawny and tough as an old scrub tree growing out of a termite's nest.

Big, slick, mean Veasna collapsed against his mother, heaving with sobs. She had a man's face, hard and folded in on itself. She did not cry. Veasna asked her, "How are you? How are you, Mama?"

"I work. I eat." Her teeth and fingernails were black. She glared at Map. "Who is that?"

Veasna looked around at Map and said, "This is my best friend, Map."

Mrs. Hing stood with her arms folded, her eyes narrow. "You have enough brothers to support. Do you have any money? Do you know where Thom is? Tula?"

Whenever Mrs. Hing spoke to Veasna, her voice came in sharp slivers like flint. If anyone else showed up other than her son, she used a different sweet little voice, which was as horrible as rancid oil. Her son saw her dark face. Veasna kept landing his boat on the rocky island shore that was his mother. That island never grew flowers.

"You fight with the yuon," she said. "You are all traitors."

She said, "You look for this Map's family, why don't you make more efforts to find your own?"

She said, "I don't want hugs, I want cash."

Going to Battambang was not fun. Veasna and Map went back to looking for the Tan family. They had to keep going to Kompong Thom province, as dangerous as it was. Map's family had lived there when all this had started, back in 1970. Map could not remember where the house was.

He did remember that it had a wooden roof with a tiny Kompong Thom spire on the roof beam, and there was a causeway across a reservoir to it, so it must have been a grand house. Map liked to think maybe they had been rich. They had an ox for the cart, he remembered. He remembered washing it in the big reservoir. He remembered carrying water. He remembered his older brother cuffing his ears. A palm-lined track went down a hill into the cluster of fruit trees that shaded the village. He remembered sitting in the oxcart coming home from the town. That hill, that group of trees, always signalled they had come home.

One day, Map and Veasna got a lift with a five-wheeler going all the way to the town. The driver was smuggling rice, so they left in the dark. He drove so fast that the truck bounded up and down and finally ruined its suspension.

The driver tried to rig up something with his belt. Map and Veasna stood watch, safety catches off. It was later than they wanted to be on this stretch of road. Everything was blue-grey, enough light to be seen by guerrillas or dacoits.

Map was staring down a track that ran along a flat plain through a few trees. Very suddenly the track came into focus. He felt his breath catch and a fist seize his heart. Was that it? Was this little slope his big hill?

"I'm going down there," he said.

Their sergeant would have said this was a dumb thing to do. Since the Vietnamese had bombed all their border camps, the guerrillas had moved into the interior.

Map and Veasna walked along the track. They saw fire through the trees as if there was a sunrise in the wrong place. What looked like ground mist clung to the lower valley. They smelled smoke. The people were burning straw or scrub.

The village was less than a hamlet and had fallen in on itself like an old person's cheeks. Some of the huts lay flat on the ground.

Map saw his spire, tipped sideways, grey. The straw roof had been gnawed thin, and the causeway over the reservoir was no more than a plank two metres long across a stinking black ditch.

An old woman crouched in the raised doorway. For just one stabbing instant, Map thought it might be his mother. She had always squatted in that doorway to signal that she wanted company.

An old man with a round face like a mango rolled his way down the ladder. He wore a skullcap. These were Chams, the Muslim minority.

Out of another house crept a young mother with a babe, a white scarf wrapped around her head and pinned under her chin.

Under that house, he and his older brother Heng had played with the dogs and the roosters, and swung together in one hammock. There had been a huge carved table on which the family and guests had sat to share rice and fish paste and sometimes vegetables. All gone.

Map made sure they saw his gun. He waited for them to sompiah an army man, but they were all older than he was. The family looked in complete unison at the guns. Veasna jerked his up and down to cock it.

Angka had killed Muslims, unless they renounced their religion, any religion. The Organization said they did the same to Buddhists, except everyone knew that Angka disliked anything that was not Cambodian.

Map asked his question. Had a woman from this village called Koy Da come asking after her husband, Tan Phirum? A slim, older woman? A round-faced man, about forty-five?

No, no, the Cham families chorused, nobody called Tan. Isn't that so? They looked to each other and called each other by both names, Haji Brahim or Toun Abdul. These people were not related. They had simply formed a new kind of family. Ash from the fires flecked their wary faces.

Map asked, "A girl, she would be about twenty-two now, she would be called Tan Mliss? Did she come?"

Awkward silence. "No, no," said one old man burned the color of soil by the sun, except for a hat-shadow on his forehead. "Nobody came, I told you."

"Husband!" said his wife, who was squatting down, her arms sticking out from her knees. She waved both of her hands. "There was a girl, remember? I don't know her name, but she came asking for the family that lived here. She asked for her brother."

Map heard the crackling of the field fire. "Did she say where she was living now?"

Oh, the woman waved to indicate far, far away, oh so far that the girl had no interest in coming back and claiming land. "Phnom Penh. She said she was going to Phnom Penh to make money."

"Phnom Penh," said Veasna. "Cool."

There were now two trains a day to Phnom Penh Central from Battambang. So it was back to the beautiful boats, and then on to the train station, which looked bombed and abandoned. The train left at 5:00 A.M. in complete darkness and there was no light to see inside the carriages. You could hear people grunt as they stepped or sat on each other. Cows grazed the grass between the tracks.

Map and Veasna had no money so they rode trains for free. They sat among the spare wheels and track carried by the flat cars ahead of the engine. They would restack the iron to give them some shelter from snipers. If the train went over a mine, they would be the first to know.

Sometimes their extra guns were welcome and their brothers-in-arms let them ride the armoured cars along with the civilians, the chickens, and the piles of vegetables. They were only shot at once, not seriously, though just a few months before Khmers Rouges guerrillas had killed forty people on that same train.

Cambodia was at war and not at war. Every day five or six things happened: a city would be shelled, land mines would explode, or someone would be kidnapped. Prince Sihanouk's rebel force, the ANS, had an agreement with the government's army not to shoot each other. But the Sihanoukists still fought the Vietnamese. On April 13, perhaps to celebrate the start of New Year, the ANS had blown up the Vietnamese gas depot in Samrong.

Phnom Penh town was in worse shape than anyone had told them. Many buildings still had no roofs. The roads were lined with rusty hulks, cars that had been abandoned thirteen years before. There were no streetlights. At night it was pitch black and dangerous. You'd hear people peeing, crying, fighting, shouting abuse, and see nothing. It smelled of rotting leaves, rotting fruit, excrement. The children's clothing hung in strips. Hungry eyes followed them, and even Map and Veasna walked closer together, guns at the ready.

You could buy a Vietnamese whore for fifty cents and fuck yourself stupid and still have money to get drunk. Shanties lined up along suburban roads and the women would stand outside them demanding payment first. In the center of town, they'd stand outside the blackened hulks of apartment houses and you'd have to step over and around families squatting on staircases.

"Make sure their name isn't Mliss," Map said once. He was joking, he meant it to be funny, but Veasna, who was always palm-wine drunk in Phnom Penh, went suddenly solemn.

"Don't look so sad, Brother," Map chuckled. But he was secretly glad that Veasna had been so serious.

"Just watch your money around these thieving Vietnamese tarts," said Veasna.

They took pot shots at their Vietnamese allies. Hun Sen and Vietnamese troops wore almost identical uniforms, except for the insignia on their caps. Map had grown the eyes of an eagle spotting the little red star that meant the soldiers were Vietnamese.

The Vietnamese lived in hotels or crammed together in villas outside the center, but sometimes you'd run across a big shot who thought he was a playboy. Usually they were from the south, not as disciplined or as honest as the northerners. They took bribes, got drunk, boasted and smiled a lot. "More like us!" Veasna would joke.

There were still almost no restaurants, except for those in colleges. The Liberty and the Peace restaurants had just opened on what was now called Achar Mean Boulevard. Only everybody still called it Monivong.

One night a yuon playboy came staggering out of the Peace. They must have thrown him out. Two Vietnamese whores came trotting out after him; the guy was so drunk that he'd stumbled out without his bodyguards.

Veasna was drunk as well. He took one look and fired a bullet just past the guy's ear. Then he shot the asphalt at the man's feet. The man froze, and then sompiahed with respect. Map saw wisdom in his round, watchful face.

"I always greet politely man with gun," the man said in something like Khmer.

Veasna's eyes bulged to hear Khmer from a foreigner's mouth. The shock of it and the aptness of what the man had said struck Veasna as funny. One of the whores slinked her way up to him. "I know good place," she cooed, looking like a housecat gone feral.

The yuon called out, still in Khmer, "You two have one good time. I would like go home."

Veasna thought that was even funnier. "Go home. Hah hah hah, he's right, it is time to go home!"

The girl cooed. "Oh. Don't disappoint me. Big handsome man." She stroked his cheek. He shoved her away.

"It's good you yuon whores are here. Cambodian girls don't suck dicks."

"Cambodian girls are too ugly. No one wants them." She said it sweetly enough not to be shot.

Finally, Map intervened. "Hey Veasna, hey friend, let's go have some fun. I don't like talking to these guys and anyway, these girls…they're too expensive for us." Map turned to the girl and bowed slightly. She had been clever; she had got her client away.

"Go on," whispered Map to the girls. Then explained, "My friend lost all his family."

Which wasn't true.

The yuon intervened. "I am very sorry for your tragedy," he said. The other girl looked calm and smiling but she was pulling on his arm, very hard.

Veasna allowed himself to be led away.

Later he said, "You get the two of us mixed around, friend." He patted Map's neck. "It's okay, we're buddies. But you do keep getting us reversed."

Map had replied, "Nothing is true anymore."

They kept looking for Mliss. They asked in bus stations. They went to the old post office, which had once been red, black, and gold like a temple, but was now a bare and splotchy brown, with the employees sleeping on sacks. Had a girl called Tan Mliss or Koy Mliss come for post?

The employees laughed. What post? There is no post!

People lived in the ruins of what had been the National Bank, washing their crockery in big plastic tubs. A lost girl? Oh, there are so many of those. What does she look like?

Map realized that he had no idea.

The old train station was lined with people sleeping at night. Map and Veasna walked up and down the rows, whispering his sister's name. "Mliss? Tan Mliss?"

Other people were tilling the rows of people in the train station. They peered over the faces, bending as if over rice fields. They too apologized and then asked after other names, names that meant Golden or Lucky or Happy.

New Year came. This was only the second year that celebrations of *Col Ch'nam T'Mei* were authorized. Hand-painted posters promised races: boat races, horse races, and oxcart races. At Boeung Kek Park next to the old French embassy, families sat on the grass. Beautiful girls with long black hair piled high on top of their heads wore new pink sampots and strolled out over the lake on the rickety zigzag walkways.

Veasna and Map went to the Tuol Sleng exhibition. They didn't go for fun, but to look for Mliss. There were rows of photographs of people who had been taken there as prisoners, mostly Khmers Rouges cadres themselves. Many people visited Tuol Sleng, steeling themselves to find the name or photograph of a relative who had disappeared. If they could write, they signed the guestbook, in case relatives came looking for them.

At Tuol Sleng there was a map of Cambodia made out of human skulls, held in place by thighbones. Only the Great Lake and the Rivers were free from bones, painted blue.

The Peoples Republic wanted Cambodians to hate the Khmers Rouges, but they did not have to tell lies to persuade them. Fishermen still tripped up on bones in the mud, or pulled them up in their nets. Children on riverbanks found human skulls used as nests. Farmers ploughing fields found bones, matted cloth, or old rubber sandals.

Map talked and talked all the time they were in Tuol Sleng. He couldn't stop talking. He wanted to drive out the faces. "She was an excellent student, very interested in history. She wanted to be a nurse," said Map. He was making up stories. Everybody's brother or sister was an excellent student, especially if they had disappeared.

They lined up to look at the guest book. It took a long time because most people read the whole book looking for names. It was hot and Veasna was hungover. He did not look big and handsome. He smelled sour, and his unshaven chin did not make him look in the least like Che Guevara. He looked like somebody who was getting too old for shades and slicked-back hair. "*Awh kumlang*, I'm tired," he kept grumbling.

Map tried to make a joke of the hangover. Devil-may-care-lad pays in the morning for the pleasures of the night before. The teasing didn't work. Veasna was troubled and hot and thirsty. Maybe he was getting tired of looking.

Next trip, maybe I'll come on my own, Map thought.

They finally got to the guest book. They signed, and then they scanned the signatures. Family names and nicknames and full formal names and the provinces they had come from and the provinces they had marched to. Some even listed the camps in Thailand where relatives were thought to be.

Down, down, down, past all the names, the names that meant January or Jewel, or Sweet.

121

Map's body knew before his brain did. His breath caught, his heart thumped still. Then he saw the name in tiny neat handwriting—Tan Mliss—and an address.

It was back up Monivong towards the train station, near where you would turn right for the Samarki Hotel.

There was a square portal through a building into a narrow alleyway. Families lived along it, crouching under makeshift awnings, cooking in tiny pans. Smoke had stained the walls black; rain had streaked them. Overhead torn plastic sheeting hung, providing some protection against the rain. Girls lounged in front of staircases.

Map stopped in front of a staircase with a tiled number from the old days. "If she is a prostitute, please still respect her. And please, please don't sleep with her."

Veasna slapped his chest. "Why do you say that to me? I would not do those things. You should trust me by now."

"I don't trust anyone," said Map. "At least not around women."

And for some reason, Veasna took hold of the back of his neck and held it firmly. "Come on, Chubby, let's see what we find."

The light fittings had been torn out all the way up the staircase. Children and grandmothers sat in silence on the steps. They knocked on a doorway and a madeup Vietnamese girl said brightly, "You looking for me?"

Map explained he was looking Tan Mliss. The girl said, "Ah, yes, this way." She trotted up the steps, showing off her legs. "This door here," she said.

They stood and waited for a moment, and then Map knocked.

The door opened only a sliver. A huge brown eye stared out at them and a breathless voice said, "I do not work here, you have made a mistake, try the other doors."

"Mliss? Is your name Tan Mliss?"

Silence. The door hesitated in mid-flight.

"Mliss, this Map, Tan Map. I am your brother. I saw your name in the Tuol Sleng book."

"What was our brother's name?"

"Tan Heng. Mliss, it is me."

The door was opened by the most beautiful girl Map had ever seen.

Map's father had been beefy, bullish with a heavy nose, heavy chin, and thrusting teeth. Their mother had been delicate, shaken inside, with huge staring eyes and fragile cheekbones.

Somehow in his sister, the two had cancelled out.

Mliss was taller than he was, slithery and thin as a reed. A folded headscarf held her hair in place, and she wore a housecoat and earrings. She saw Veasna and skittered backwards, hauling in a breath and saying in a voice that was almost a cry, "Who is that?"

They were frightening her. They were soldiers with guns.

Map quickly pushed his hair in place and under his hat. He saw out of the corner of his eye that Veasna had stood respectfully back.

"Younger Sister, this is my best friend, *samlaing*. He has been with me in all our efforts to find you. This is Comrade Nim Veasna."

Mliss sompiahed and her hand strayed up to her own hair. She invited them in and her eyes avoided theirs. Only once did Map catch her glancing up at his face.

Mliss was a good Khmer girl. She was not like the hearty girls riding mashed together in the back of pickup trucks. Nor did she look like a farm girl nipping about her kitchen. She did not slip-slop cheerfully across the floor in sandals. Even in her own house she walked as if the floor could break, as if any sudden movement would awaken her from a dream.

"I'm sorry," she said. "There is nothing to eat. Would you like some tea?"

Veasna was somehow more at home than Map. "Oh, tea would be perfect. We've just had lunch, so please, Miss Tan Mliss, don't worry about food."

"Tea is no trouble." Her teeth were white and perfect. As slowly as drifting clouds, she turned and put some paper onto the fire ring on her table. She stirred the embers and blew. On the floor next to the table were a bowl, some spoons, and two tin pots.

The room looked like it had once been the service area of a bigger apartment. The walls and floor were covered with rosebud tiles and there was a drain in the middle of the floor. Along the top of the wall some bricks had been left out to make a kind of air. There was no other light. Buckets of water were lined up along one of the walls.

A folded hammock hung in one corner. Three pairs of shoes were stowed under it and some plastic bags next to them contained neatly folded clothes. No sign of a boyfriend; no pictures from newspapers on the wall. There was no radio, no flowers, and no cushions. One clean mat lay squarely on the floor.

Veasna tried to kick-start the conversation. "We serve with the regiment in Siem Reap."

"Oh. I don't know about the war." All her movements were elegant. She seemed confident and smiling, but she kept pulling her hair out of her eyes unnecessarily. "I work in a school. It is a charity run by some East Germans. The big round building near the Samarki? I am very lucky to get a job there; it is the only orphanage in the city. It is not much money, but it is safe and they pay me regularly."

Map turned to Veasna and smiled with relief. "That sounds like a very good job. I am very happy to hear you have such a good job."

Mliss came with the tea and knelt down, laying out the pot and two plastic cups that were printed with flowers to look like china.

"I taught myself some German." She passed a cup and gave Map a wide but somehow blank smile. "My husband paid them a bribe of forty dollars to take me. They keep apologizing."

"You are married?" said Map and could not keep the surprise out of his voice. So where is he? Map thought. Why does she live like this? "I am anxious to meet him."

"I would like to see him too," she said, very calmly. "He paid the bribe and then left."

This was a shameful thing, but her gaze seemed to be steady, even though her smile was a bit glazed. "I think it was his way of making sure I would be all right. We had no children, so perhaps not too many people were hurt."

Veasna was direct. "He must have been a foolish man to leave a beautiful wife like you."

Mliss turned to him, still smiling. "Was he? If you knew me, Comrade, perhaps you would not say that."

"Look," said Veasna sitting forward. "It is New Year. We have all lost so many people. Perhaps we could all go out and walk along the riverfront?"

She dipped her head, slowly, gracefully. It was like watching a movie star. Map involuntarily shook himself. It was not possible such a beautiful creature was his sister. "I do not go out," she replied. "Except for my work."

"This would not be going out. We could just turn at the next street and walk to the river." Veasna hesitated and glanced at Map. "Maybe you would just like to go to see the Central Market? It would be a family occasion at New Year." Veasna was trying to be cheery and punctiliously correct at the same time.

Mliss said, "I don't go out because as you can see, my hair is falling out."

Map paused. He looked. She chuckled. "You cannot see it because I take great care to hide it."

Her hair was pulled back so all her forehead could be seen, and it was not thin. Perhaps it was falling out at the back.

"Also, people throw water at New Year, and that scares me."

"It is supposed to bring luck," said Veasna, gently.

"Not if you are in the back of a pickup going fast. Then it hurts, or it causes an accident."

Map suddenly understood that she was afraid. "Believe me, Mliss. You are beautiful. No one can see your hair, as you say."

Veasna smiled and tried to look lively. "If anyone throws bags of water at me and Map, we will lob them out of the way. Splat!"

"Nevertheless. I do not like going out."

Both of them looked about the empty room. No radio, no newspapers, no games. What on earth did she find to do?

Veasna was still trying to look perky. "Then let your brother and me go out and come back with a meal. A feast, yes no? You don't know how long Map has been trying to find you. He asks everyone, do you know a Tan Mliss?"

"My friend Veasna looked for you as well."

"Map helped me find my mother. So this is a real celebration for both of us. Please. It won't take long. We will come back with the meal, and we can all celebrate New Year together."

Mliss smiled, and the smile could only be described as gracious. It was like talking to a princess. She held up a delicate hand. "Oh! What can I say? Thank you. That would be so kind." She glanced at Map and then fixed on Veasna.

Oh well, thought Map, if I had a choice of looking at Veasna or me, I'd look at Veasna too.

At the door Map stopped, overcome. "It is good to find you, Younger Sister. It is so good to find you." His voice started to shake.

Mliss remained placid, the smile like a distant lighthouse. "Thank you, Older Brother." She dipped in a kind of acknowledgment.

Then she remembered something. "Oh. Please. No snake, no frog, no cricket. I cannot eat those things. And no beer for me. I don't like beer."

"We will get no beer, only soda."

She nodded, and stroked hair back from her face, though it was perfectly in place.

They went to the state canteen in the nearby Central Market. The government had boasted that ninety-two million riels worth of consumer goods had crowded into Phnom Penh as part of the celebrations. The huge old dome of the weird French building rang with voices like the inside of a bell. Veasna gaped and started to laugh at the abundance. There were bicycles, cameras, electric fans, even, on one stall, video recorders. The stalls were piled high with vegetables and meat and drink. One stall had tidy temples of wines and cognac and Thai Coca-Cola.

"I know what your sister needs," said Veasna and impulsively bought a tiny transistor radio with batteries.

The state canteen was offering everyone a five percent discount. Map and Veasna bought hot steaming bags full of rice and pork and fish and vegetables with soup. They would not have bought beer in any case—a bottle of Singha cost four hundred riels.

As they walked back through the market, Veasna said, "Don't worry about your sister. It takes people in different ways. You expect to be overjoyed, and for everybody to be overjoyed. It doesn't always happen as you expect."

"No."

"She's scared," said Veasna. "She's beautiful and scared. Maybe she's scared because she is beautiful. Being beautiful can be scary."

"Veasna, what are you saying?"

"Beauty can make you scared to lose it," said Veasna, holding out his arms, shrugging his eyebrows. Maybe he meant himself.

Map went back to joking. "I don't think she can be my sister. How can someone who looks like that be my sister?"

"Oh, you are handsome fellow."

"I look like a monkey," said Map. "I know that. I don't care."

"And that's what makes you so brave," said Veasna, and for a joke pushed the tip of Map's nose. From anyone else—what an insult!

They bought tinsel. They bought a large plastic star and a candle for New Year.

Veasna insisted on going to the toilets to wash from a cistern of water. He took off his shirt and shaved.

"Ah, you fancy my sister already."

"No, but I do not like looking like a slob with a girl like that. Ah? And Map? Shave, my friend." Veasna held out his razor. "Really. We look like ruffians." He said it with sadness.

In the alleyway, the neighbours' children played a screaming game of *angkunh*, throwing nuts at each other. Inside, Mliss sat cross-legged on the floor as if it were scattered with cushions. With perfect little cries of surprise, she laid out the New Year feast on plates and bowls she had borrowed from her neighbours.

"I told the Vietnamese girls that my long-lost brother had come, and so they loaned me all these plates. They were so happy for me. They know I take care of children, and they say that maybe I will have to take care of theirs. They all think they will die." She shrugged. Then she murmured, "I really only like children."

Veasna asked gently, "Why is that?"

"They see everything fresh. They have no bad past. You make them laugh and everything seems fine."

Mliss ate nearly nothing. There was soup, but she simply sipped some from her brother's spoon. The rice on her plate was pressed once between her fingers. Of the beautiful crisp fish, she took only a sliver.

"Oh, it is so delicious," she said.

"Have some more," Map urged, already worried about her.

She gave her head a little shake. "Eating makes me sick."

"Oh, Younger Sister! This is not good. You should eat."

"Oh, Older Brother. Don't worry. I have survived on my own."

Veasna was inspired. "She eats air and mist. She goes down to the river in the early morning when no one can see her, and she breakfasts on the dew. Sometimes she goes and feeds on the scents of flowers, or the buzzing of honeybees."

Almost imperceptibly, Mliss clapped her hands. "The children would like you," she said.

"Not as much as I do," said Veasna. He meant as much as he liked her.

But Mliss replied, "Oh, I can imagine that you like yourself very much."

Veasna closed his eyes. "That's not what I meant."

He remembered the radio. Map was sure he'd bought it to hear about the races. The broadcast came from a new stadium in a new suburb called Phnom Penh Tmei. In the first horse race, most of the horses took off in the wrong direction and one of them charged the officials. Veasna roared with laughter and said, "That is a Cambodian race, all right!"

The race was won by the only horse to complete the course in the right direction, a mare called *Srey Sramoss*. The name meant Lady in Mourning.

Mliss suddenly said, "You have not asked me about the family."

Map replied, "I didn't like to."

"Heng is dead, but you knew that. Our younger sister is dead. I thought all of us were dead," she said.

Something bristled around Map's heart. "Mom and Dad too?"

Mliss gave a tinkling little laugh. "Of course. Now don't tell me you forgot?" She was smiling.

Map was plunged into nightmare. He felt as if he were falling down into a well. His parents, dead?

"You were staying with Uncle, with the *maquis*. He told you himself. He said you went all quiet and hid in a haystack. He's dead now too, of course." Her voice was light and pleasant, with the slightest rasp to it as if she had been shouting for a long time.

Something stirred inside Map's head. It was a brown background, reeds perhaps, and in front of that, something black, out of focus. A dim memory of Uncle?

Veasna was leaning forward in concern. "Chubby?"

Oh, how stupid. Of course. He'd been told. My uncle told me, he said: both your parents are dead, and then I went and hid in the haystack, and I didn't tell Older Brother when I saw him next and then . . . I forgot all about it.

It was as if all the leaves on the trees had fallen off at once. Their trunks and branches were clear now, bare and skeletal like burned hands.

He'd left the Khmers Rouges because it would be easier to try to find his parents. He'd ridden up and down the country trying to find them. Years he had spent looking. And that little kid had known all along. That little twelve-year-old hiding inside him had never said, Hey, older-self, they're dead.

Veasna was kneeling in front of him. "*Samlaing?* Map?"

His sister was saying, pleasantly, "More tea?"

"How?" Map was blinking; his face was twisted up as if trying to work out a very complicated problem. "How did they die?"

"Maybe you don't remember because you blame yourself. The Lon Nol army knew that you and Heng had joined the maquis. So they came and beat Mom and Dad up. In those days troops didn't usually do that kind of thing. They were very bad at it. Right away, they died, just a few blows." Mliss finished pouring another cup of tea. "I saw the whole thing."

She sat smiling.

"I sat and held them until neighbours came a day or two later. They were very kind and I lived with them. They said I was their daughter and I used their name to hide. How strange. How strange to forget a thing like that." Her round eyes stared at him in mild wonder.

Everything seemed to rush to the front of Map's face: blood, tears, sweat. Everything seemed to swell. He thought of himself at fourteen, a Khmer Rouge soldier guarding the New People, curled up on a floor and staring, because if he closed his eyes he dreamed about his parents and that would make him cry.

Map thought of himself at twenty-five, guarding the Vietnamese labour camp in Kralanh. The Viets had herded six hundred men deep into the hill forests, set them digging trenches and laying mines. More conscripts kept arriving. No food could be delivered, and the forest had been foraged clean. Map had malaria, a new strain that had come out of Preah Vihear. It flattened him, left him prostrate and shivering and helpless. One of the conscripts screamed in his face, "How is this any better than Pol Pot!" They stole Map's hammock; he had to wrestle to keep his gun.

Map had lain on the dirt, his bones quaking with fever. He had prayed then to the spirits of his parents to help him. Which meant he must have known in his heart that they were dead. There was a silence in the world whenever he thought about them.

Veasna let his plate drop down to the floor. "*Col Ch'nam T'Mei,*" he whispered. Happy New Year.

Festivities over.

Veasna and Map spent the night on the floor of the train station. In the morning, they all went to Mliss's school.

With the children, she was a different person.

She picked a little girl up and swung her round and round. The other children clustered around her and she bowed down and kissed them. Immediately she joined their game of volleyball. She shouted encouragement, and laughed when they made mistakes, and got them laughing at their own mistakes as well.

The German headmistress energetically rang a bell, and the older children ran into the classrooms. Mliss gathered the smaller children, sat them outside on the ground, and told them the story of the King and the White Elephant. Then she led them in song. She introduced her brother, and his friend. They were from the wars, far away. She made Map describe Angkor Wat. Map was too ashamed to say he had not bothered to visit, so he made it up, from the photographs he had seen. She took over and told them the famous story of how Jayavarman had driven out the Chams and rebuilt the city.

"So. That is what we are doing. We are finishing the war, and will have to rebuild Cambodia again."

Veasna stepped into the spotlight and started to sing old children's songs to them. Map had not known that Veasna could sing. The children were delighted. Mliss grinned and jumped up and took his hand and started to sing too. And then she asked all the children to join hands and sing.

Map remembered being eleven years old, in school, the bad boy. He fired slingshots at people taking a shit in the woods. He and his brother were in a gang and they had gang wars, firing real arrows at each other. Once he hit an old grandpa by mistake. Map had hidden on the roof in the dusk as the old man searched the village, yelling.

Yet. Map had been good at his letters and at maths. He loved *saprak takraw*, kicking the ball. He had bounced like a ball himself. He suddenly remembered the smell of his mother's fire, how she always sprinkled medicinal plants in it, to drive away illness and mosquitoes. He had a sudden sense of home.

Maybe Veasna did too. Veasna asked the children if they knew

The King's Last Song

about Ros Sereysothea and Sin Sisimuth. Most of them did not. Just a few years before it would have been risky even talking about them. The Vietnamese had banned all old music. But nowadays So Savoeun came all the way from Paris to give a concert in Boeung Kek Park. Veasna began to sing their sad songs from the old days before the wars. A tall handsome man in sunglasses with a nice smile who could sing—the children looked up in fascination.

Is this Sin Sisimuth? No, he's dead.

Sing us another, sing us another!

Lunch came, rice with potatoes, saving Map and Veasna from having to think of more ways to entertain the children.

Mliss loved feeding the children. She pushed food onto their plates, and gave them seconds. She encouraged them, by pretending to nibble the rice herself. She wore a white shirt and sunlight blazed through it and almost through her, as if she were translucent.

She laid the children out on blankets in the shade, and she stroked their heads.

"We have to go," said Map. Impulsively, he hugged her as an older brother might do, and she patted him and stepped back. She sompiahed with self-conscious thoroughness to Veasna.

"I will say good-bye to the children for you," Mliss said. She stood at the school gate and laughed and waved, as if from the shore of another country where there had been no war.

As the train began to pull away, shuddering under him, Map began to heave with sobs. Embarrassed, pained, Veasna looked away, blinking.

They got to Battambang in pitch darkness. They camped out near the bus station. Map started to cry again. Veasna tapped his ribs and got him to shut up. Map fell asleep, his face pushed against Veasna's shoulder. At dawn they slipped down to the docks and found a boat.

They didn't get back until late afternoon. They stopped for a drink in town and got back to camp well after midnight. Their sergeant came out in a sarong and flip-flops to berate them.

Veasna broke into an old song.

Sarika-keo euy
See ai kawng kawng.

Dear sarika birds, what are you eating, very noisily?

It was a happy child's song about a courting couple. Veasna's face rose up into a smile and he started to clap and dance as he sang. What had come over him?

He was beyond the power of the sergeant, who chuckled and growled. "Get out of here," he said, waving them away. "I can't deal with you goons!" He stomped off back to bed.

Veasna's face was swollen with smiles. As they walked back, he drew himself up tall against the stars. "I am in love with your sister," he announced. "I want to marry her. So I will be going to Phnom Penh frequently. I want to check that that is okay with you."

"It is not for me to approve."

"Maybe. But I want to know this is okay with you."

"It is okay with me ..." Map trailed off. Something bothered him. "She seems distant."

"Oh ... she saw her parents killed. Did you see her with the children? She was not distant then. I want a wife, Map, and I want to have children. I am getting too old to be a ruffian."

"Okay, okay, yes. But only if that is what Mliss wants, yes? This is not the old days, and I don't know Mliss well enough to play the head of the family with her."

Veasna nodded. Something was pushing his cheeks up. "We will have to make up new families. Like those Chams in your old house. This war, it will be over soon, Map. Then I will go and be a farmer. What I want to do is buy a farm and have a wife and a house, and children. You could live there with us. You would be the uncle. You could live there with your wife too." He was delighted, and slapped Map on the shoulder.

At that hour the crickets and the geckos and the birds were all silent and still.

"It would be a family," said Map.

"That's it exactly! We lose our families; we make a new one. The brothers share the house and the fields, and everybody works and brings in extra money."

Map started to nod in agreement. "That is a very good thought. That would be a good action."

"Then that is what we do, ah! You and me, Brother."

They shook hands. *Youl prom*, agreed.

The rainy season belonged to guerrillas.

Conventional forces sank into the mud or retreated into garrisons and towns. Map and Veasna sometimes took a boat to Phnom Penh, which was miserable in the rain. Or they bounced in army convoys to Battambang and then took the train.

Their comrades on the trains insisted Map and Veasna ride in the mortar car with its big guns. Even now the railway was so overgrown that sopping wet leaves would trail along the carriages through the open windows.

They smiled and said, "We don't want you outside attracting fire."

Sometimes the ground road washed away under the track. Sometimes a tree had fallen across it. The troops and passengers all ran out into the rain, shovelling mud and shoring up the track. Their stomachs jittered like nervous horses, listening out for the sound of gunfire.

Once back inside Mliss's room, Veasna and Map would listen to the rain on the roof. Outside, they could hear the neighbours' children playing, pouring rainwater from the gutter into jars and then in and out of the big cistern, the *peang tuk*. Mliss would worry about the children getting wet, and call them in. She soaked all her sheets drying the children's bare feet, while telling them old stories.

Their mothers would saunter in, smiling. One of them had a beautiful chess set. They played in teams of two, and they were all very good. The games were long, complex, and clever. Mliss would watch and hide her face when Map or Veasna made a good move. Then it was her turn and when she won, she would bounce up and down and clap her hands like a little girl.

Veasna bought a lamp so they could play long into the night, babysitting for the prostitutes when they had to be with clients. They in turn left little cakes. Lamplight, sleepy children on laps, constant voices, the making of tea, the smell of smoke, the clatter of the rain—all as in the old days.

Veasna and Map now slept in her room. Like any family, they made an art of privacy. A blanket was hung across the room. Veasna and Map were used to the tough life. They slept on the floor. The little room began to fill with things: a vase for flowers, a small, low table, and a statue of a fat cat with a mouse.

Quietly, things were changing. Every year the Vietnamese made a big show of sending troops home. Tanks or trucks packed with young Vietnamese would bounce their way east, their pots and pans jangling, past a state-organized parade. This year, the troops left quietly. Some of the top brass left as well. Cadres from provinces like Takeo or Svay Rieng reported a continual flow of trucks traveling across the Mekong and the border

A bright-toothed young Party worker was buying fruit at the market. Even his spectacles seemed to smile, catching the light. "The Vietnamese are going. They really are going," he said, swinging his bags full of fruit. "Now the question is, can our army fight the Khmers Rouges?" Veasna and Map, in their uniforms, felt a bristling in their cheeks. Could they?

Mliss was more succinct. "If Pol Pot comes back," she said, "I will commit suicide."

In June the curfew went back from nine to ten P.M. Map would take off by himself, to leave the two lovers alone. He went to the Central Market and looked at things he could not buy. He saw boots, blacking, and mosquito nets, things that the army should have supplied to him, but which corruption sold to the black market instead.

He saw very few books, but there was a stall with some hand-copied manuscripts or surviving printed texts. One of these was a history of Angkor. Map's heart yearned for it—a time of Cambodian greatness—and he remembered how ashamed he had been in front of Mliss's children not to know more. He bought the book and went without supper.

Thunder would suddenly explode overhead and rainwater would cascade onto Map's head and shoulders, soaking him in an instant. Old men would slush past on bicycles. At such times Map might buy a girl. Without Veasna to cheer him up, buying a woman felt sad and second rate.

The rooms would have blankets instead of doors. A girl took off her clothes. She was slim and beautiful, beautiful breasts, and perfect firm legs. Somehow he just did not have the heart. He put on his shirt to leave. Had she displeased him? No, no, he said. Everything was fine.

"Oh," she said. "You want love. I can't sell love. Next best thing?" She tried to look cheerful.

He shook his head.

"You should take it. You are not rich and you are not handsome, and you have paid me for it."

Maybe she liked him. Maybe she was just trying to hurt his feelings for not wanting her. She said, with a sideways smile, "It has to be better than going back to wherever you are going and being alone, or the one who is left out."

It was true. He stayed. They even talked a little bit. She was a *Khmer Krom*, an ethnic Cambodian from Vietnam. She had a child, what else was she to do? "I can't wait around to become a virgin again. And no one will want to marry me now."

He came back at nine-thirty. He could still see lamplight through the window, and he could hear his brother and his sister singing songs and laughing. The New Year star was still hanging outside the doorway. He was home.

He opened the door and both Veasna and Mliss cried, "There he is!"

"We've done it," said Veasna, glowing orange in lamplight. "We have decided to marry."

Map saw the fire dance in his sister's eyes. She beamed and looked content, as if finally she had eaten something.

Veasna and Mliss were married that October, when it was dry and safer to travel. This time the train was full of soldiers, including some of their reprobate buddies. The wedding was held in the school. The soldiers lined up in their uniforms, along with some of the teachers and the huge and angular German headmistress.

Somewhere there is a photograph. In it, Mliss wears silken trousers and epaulettes that dangle with beads and a tiny brass Khmer crown on her head. For some reason, she's scowling. Her two teacher bridesmaids look coy or pleased and the German headmistress fixes the camera with a face determined to express amusement and joy, her long arms stretching around almost all of them. Her cold blue eyes chilled Map's blood.

Veasna's mother, Mrs. Hing Boupha, is there with the most fixed and winning smile of all. She had taken to smoking cigarettes and herded all the other guests around using the glowing butt as a cattle prod while effusively correcting Mliss's grammar.

In the photograph Veasna stands much taller than anyone else, holding a basket of plastic flowers with his bride, and he smiles like an old man looking back over a life full of prosperity and grandchildren. His big, smooth, veined hand cradles the flowers. They hide the swelling of Mliss's belly.

People who see the photograph do not recognize Map. They say he looks like a little boy. His big teeth shine out in a huge grin, and his eyes are open with hope. The flash has slightly overexposed the film, burning away his spots. Map is almost young and handsome. He comes up to his brother-in-law's shoulder. He looks beside himself with happiness.

The wedding was happy, but quick, snatched in comparison to how weddings used to be. In the old days there would have been long feasting, music, and chanting by lay preachers. Instead one of the teachers played wedding music on a cassette and the teachers improvised a dance, a ghost of traditional hand gestures and formal patterns.

The soldiers had to get back to Siem Reap; the train would not wait. From Dangrek, from Koh Ker, from all the border provinces there was news of increased fighting.

On October 4, the moderate KPNLF—the "Khmers Bleus"—took over Kandaol. They had intercepted radio calls giving orders to government troops. The Hun Sen Army tanks had refused to go in, saying they had no fuel. The ground troops had retreated, saying that they had run out of ammo. KPNLF videos showed warehouses full of both.

Why did no one understand? Government troops didn't want to kill other Cambodians, particularly not Sihanoukists or republicans. They just didn't want the Khmers Rouges back.

Cambodians wanted the Vietnamese out of their country and China to stop feeding the Khmers Rouges arms. They wanted America to stop supporting China. They wanted the Soviet Union to solve its own problems. They wanted it all to stop. They were exhausted.

By November, Prime Minister Hun Sen would formally request that the Vietnamese reinforce his troops.

Back in Siem Reap, things got tough. The army wanted to show it didn't need the Vietnamese to fight the guerrillas. Map and Veasna were lectured on the war. They were made to play games, running up hills to take fictional resistance strongholds, only the resistance never shot back. Nobody could shoot anything; there was no ammo.

Their sergeant lined them all up and tightened his own belt and announced to the company that there had been many changes. Volunteers were needed for the front. One of the volunteers was Nim Veasna.

Map and Veasna waylaid him afterwards, but the sergeant was ready for them, with a tiger smile and a ready temper. "I know what you are going to say," he said before Map or Veasna could speak, and his hand seemed to fling everything else away from him. "It is no accident you two are separated. You are a bad influence on each other and all the other men. You, Veasna, you're out of my company and at the front. No longer my problem." And he walked on, leaving them standing.

Veasna had been volunteered to help the 196th regiment take back Pailin from the Khmers Rouges. Pailin was a gem-producing town. The 196th regiment had a bad reputation for smuggling gemstones and ducking the fight. People joked that Veasna would see no fighting and come back rich.

For Map, there were other uses. Despite the war, the government was reopening Angkor Wat to tourists. Idiotically, in Map's view, they were restarting the airline. Flights would start landing in December. Map had read his book on Angkor Wat over and over and enthused about it to other soldiers. Someone must have heard him do it, because they made him a tourist guard.

The woods all around the monuments were crawling with Khmers Rouges fighters. Map could imagine the tourists huddled together and surrounded by troops, stepping on snakes or threading their way through fields of land mines. The Khmers Rouges hated foreigners and thought all white people were Soviets and shot at them. The Vietnamese hated the Chinese and despised the Thais, so they would be rude to Asian visitors. Sihanoukists, the ANS, had always been active in Siem Reap, and they would sabotage any effort by the Vietnamese-sponsored state to earn money. Even the KPNLF had revived themselves and made Siem Reap province one of their strongholds. The allied guerrilla factions sabotaged, mined, and took potshots, sometimes at each other.

Map and Veasna said farewell over a bowl of rice at a roadside stall. The army trucks poured out blue smoke. Two friendly guys nodded to them. They were ANS guerrillas, good guys fighting for their king.

Veasna was measured and serious. "The war will be over in two or three years," he said. "We start our farm then. Maybe we could try to get your old family farm back. We could move there."

They didn't see each other for over a year.

Professor Luc Andrade was one of the first Westerners to go back to see the monuments. In one of his albums is a photograph of Map. Map's forearms are as thin as twigs and his face is cratered with acne scars. He stands in front of the Bayon, which looks as ruined as the National Bank, with shrubs and grass growing out of it. Balanced on Map's shoulder is a grenade launcher, aimed, thankfully, away from the monument.

Map began to overhear English and learn it. "Hello well come," he said to Luc, which is how he ended up being photographed. He started to explain the history of the monuments, how the architect of Angkor was allowed to copy only the stables of heaven. Luc remembered.

Map ate plain rice. Map patrolled the monuments and pondered: how did we build these things and then end up where we are? He wondered at the wealth of cameras and sun creams that the tourists bought with them. He heard buzzing and looked up at the tiny, vulnerable aircraft that would be so easy to shoot down. The sound of mortars would come sometimes from Kulen, sometimes from Banteay Srei, sometimes from the town. He saved his money for paper and wrote to his sister and got no replies. He asked everyone for news of the 196th regiment.

That January was, depending on your viewpoint, either the tenth anniversary of the Vietnamese invasion or of the founding of the People's Republic of Kampuchea.

It was decided to celebrate the latter. Map was given leave to go to Phnom Penh for the celebrations.

His bosses must have thought he wouldn't be able to go. Travel through Battambang province was no longer safe—Sihanouk's 27th brigade was slamming Viet positions all along Route 68. And anyway, Map had no money for travel.

He sold his services to a corporal with a line in smuggling second-hand cars across the border to Phnom Penh. The guy had got hold of a Mercedes. Map would get five thousand riels on delivery. Map gave lifts to some of the other guys, which meant they got to go home and he got extra protection. They took off through Kompong Thom province, carrying extra fuel, speeding up through every narrow pass and seesawing up and over ruts and washouts. They could smell the extra fuel leaking in the boot. Nobody smoked.

But it was fun pretending to be playboys driving a Mercedes, swapping jokes and getting out to push when the ruts and dust meant they could not get up a hill. They would jam branches under the tires to give the Mercedes extra grip. Sometimes even that didn't work and they would have to drive off the road, certain that there were landmines somewhere under the leaves. They rode the bouncing seats like broncos, accepting that any moment they could be spinning up into the air in pieces.

You had to laugh.

Map parked the car in front of the Department of Fisheries, walked in with his AK-47 and was actually paid the full amount by a well-fed functionary. He bought presents for Mliss and could even afford to take a cyclo to her flat.

The Royal Palace was freshly cream and gold. All up Monivong Boulevard, the buildings had been repainted. Yellow and red flags lined all the streets, except the ones still barricaded with barbed wire and the wrecks of cars.

Mliss looked pleased enough to see him, and got some dishes from her neighbours. Map called her the Aerial Princess. She smiled and served the food calmly, working around her expanding belly. Map started to wonder how she had survived alone with her beauty. He tried to get her to talk about her first husband.

"Oh. He was okay," she replied. "He has security job now."

"You should write to Veasna," said Map. "He will worry."

"Oh. There is no post. Where would I send it?"

"196th regiment at Battambang. He will get it and be happy. I know he misses you. Things are safer again in Battambang. Hun Sen asked the Vietnamese back." Map passed her a gift of paper and pencils.

"I will write," she said in a mild voice and put the paper down.

Map said to her, "You know, I'm thinking of getting back our old farm. You could be the schoolteacher there. They will need teachers when the war is over."

Mliss's smile was radiant. "The war will never be over."

The smile encouraged Map. "Who knows maybe I will get married too! They'll be babies everywhere for you take care of."

Mliss added, "And orphans."

"Good!" Map was trying to cheer her up, get her to smile again. "We will adopt them. We will have a big farm full of people."

"There will be so many ghosts wandering around homeless that there'll be no room for the rice." She tried to turn it into a joke. She tried her princess smile. It cracked.

Map leaned forward. He took her hand, which was still and cold. "If we went home, we would be close to Mom and Dad's stupa. We would lay out the table for them at Pchum Ben."

She said something very strange. "They will still come back angry."

Peering into her face, Map saw that she had combed her hair so it fell over one side. He watched the curtain of hair move. It seemed to him that he saw the faded ghost of a bruise on her cheek. If Mliss's old husband came back and beat her up, what else did he do?

Map never told Veasna. But.

Who could be sure the child was his?

The baby was due in April.

As February and March passed, Map got increasingly frantic. He had not heard from Mliss; he had not heard from Veasna. The army was clear; it would not give Map leave to attend the birth.

There was a new junior officer called Sinn Rith. Map pleaded with him. "I must go on leave. My sister is giving birth."

Rith shook his head. "You only get leave if your father dies. Your sister should have married."

"She is married. Her husband is my buddy Nim Veasna. He got volunteered to join the 196th. You know where he is? Can you radio him?"

"We cannot radio anybody. You remember what happened at Kandaol? Things are bad everywhere, Map! Look, let your friend take care of this. It's up to him to get to his wife. Not you. We are too stretched, we can spare no one."

Every night, going to sleep in the tent, Map prayed for Mliss and the coming child and for his brother. Prayer was all he had. Hope, he had been taught, meant nothing.

They give Map two jobs, guarding monuments by day, and in the evenings, writing up records. Most of the officers were younger than Map and could not read or write. Map, to their very great surprise, was literate. He was old enough to have lived in a country with schools. He could keep the records and fill in the forms. That gave him access to paper.

Map wrote often to his sister, to reassure her, to ask for news, and to beg her to write to Veasna. Post sometimes got through, but he had no idea which letters. So he said the same things over and over. He had no money for stamps, so he shined all the officers' boots for cigarettes, and then sold or traded the cigarettes. This made the officers think he must be getting married himself. "That Map, he is coming around to life."

Finally, in late March, Mliss wrote to him. A letter from home, the first Map had ever had. He opened it up slowly, and read it.

Mliss did not mention her pregnancy except to say that she herself was well. It was mostly about the children at the school. They had put on a play. She described each of the children and the roles they played. There were, of course, no parents to see it, only the staff, but they all stood up and applauded.

Map folded the letter carefully and put it back in his pocket. Then he worried about it getting worn and creased. He had nowhere to put things. The hammock was kept tightly rolled in his pack. The tents had no shelves; boots hung from poles. Finally he put the letter back in the top pocket of his shirt, and then worried about the ink spreading from his sweat.

Map sat and thought about his loyalties then stood up and visited the corporal who smuggled cars. He went AWOL again. This time he drove a BMW.

On Highway 6, he was stopped by two soldiers like himself. They too would supposedly be paid 1500 riels a month, only they didn't get it. They smiled like skeletons through the car window.

"You're a lucky guy to drive a car. How much you get for that while we stand here like targets for the Khmers Rouges?"

"I'm 118th regiment, I know how it goes."

"So you share with your friends." One of them lifted up his rifle.

"I haven't been paid yet. I don't have the money. I don't get the money till I deliver this car." Map offered them cigarettes. Cigarettes cost fifty riels a box. They stored them behind their ears.

Map kept smiling. From the slightly Vietnamese twang to their voices, Map guessed they were from the southeast, Takeo or even Svey Rieng provinces. They would have families and untended fields. "Hop in with me," he said. "I could get you partway home."

The two soldiers went AWOL as well.

This time the monkeys at the Department for Fisheries played monkey business with him, and did not pay him the full amount.

Outside a civil servant was loading crates of cognac into the car Map had delivered. Both car and crates were going to some army officer. The civil servant looked at Map's uniform in despair. "Is this any way to fight a war?"

"None of that stuff gets to the guys who fight," said Map. "The guys who fight get nothing."

"The likes of us don't either," said the civil servant, his eyes like deep dry wells.

Which, thought Map, is how all this mess happened in the first place.

He walked to Mliss's house. As he feared, Mliss had made no preparations for the birth. She had bought nothing for the baby, not even a blanket. Map knocked on the neighbours' doors and borrowed bowls, baby clothes, and towels.

"We did wonder about her," said one of the prostitutes. "She seems distant from her situation."

Forget the army. Map stayed with her.

The child was born during the New Year.

Mliss looked as delicate as the leg of a tiny bird. The pregnancy looked too big for her and when the contractions started she floated no longer. She held her belly and wailed.

The delivery took nearly a week. The midwife plied her with as many traditional remedies as she could find. Some of them made Mliss throw up. Some of them were stimulants to spark labour and actually made the pain worse.

She couldn't stand the hammock for some reason and tried to give birth on the floor. Map spent hours sitting beside her on the floor. He tried to hold her hand; she fought him, wrestling. He was forced to conclude that she just did not want to have the child. She didn't want to bring it into the world.

On the third day the midwife demanded money for more medicaments. Map gave it to her and it was late afternoon before he finally admitted that the woman was not coming back.

He ran to the orphanage and found Madame. He shamed himself and lost all dignity. He could not smile, he could not accept. He just wept and tried to explain in French to the headmistress.

"Why not tell me?" the woman demanded in her rough Khmer, with her long pink nose and long pinched face. Her name was Suzanne, but Map couldn't hear it properly, let alone pronounce it. Map couldn't understand whether she was angry at being disturbed or contemptuous of him for showing such a miserable face, or enraged at his stupidity. She slammed pots of leftover food onto her gas stove, and spun around her rooms getting money. She gripped his arm and flung him into a cyclopousse and went with him down Monivong.

Her face fell when she saw the room. "*Mliss habite ici?*" Mliss lay on the floor, with the look of death about her.

"*Est-ce qu'elle peut marcher un petit peu?*" the Madame whispered, and for the first time Map understood that she was deeply distressed.

Together they carried Mliss down the five flights of stairs.

"Where are we going? I don't want to leave my house!" Mliss wailed and reached back as if to grab hold of the railings.

The same cyclopousse driver was waiting in front of the alleyway. "I knew you would need help," he said, gently.

"Calmette," said Suzanne. The Russian hospital.

All during the journey, Mliss rocked and sobbed and rocked. She stared about her wildly, and Map realized that she hated leaving her regular route between work and school.

"There are robbers! They drive up alongside cyclopousses and shoot. Oh!"

The cyclo driver apologized. "I'm sorry she is not well. I'm cycling as fast as I can."

Mliss flinched at the white sunlight on the baking buildings. "It's full of bad people here!"

The Calmette was baking hot as well, and the Russian and East

German doctors and nurses seemed to float with fatigue. Their eyes went unfocussed when Suzanne spoke to them and it took some moments for them to reply. They did have a delivery table. One woman was whisked off it, some kind of towelling laid over it, and Mliss was left there. It was a holiday and there were no Cambodian midwives.

It took hours. Mliss would not open up, and there were no drugs to ease the pain or relax the muscles, not unless they had a lot of money. Did they have money? The nurse looked askance and hopeful at the same time.

"Where are the drugs?" Madame demanded. "I'm not paying you until I see them." She disappeared too. It got dark, and Mliss started to tell the child to die. Madame came bustling back, with a clean syringe she had also bought and a tiny bottle of clear fluid. She elbowed the attendants aside. "I was nurse!" she snarled in Khmer. She injected Mliss, and leaned over and stroked her hair, which hung like water weeds to either side of her pinched and feverish face. The drugs took hold and Mliss relaxed. The birth of Veasna's child was suddenly over with, like the easy delivery of a rich entrepreneur's son.

Then they had to make Mliss stand up and walk. The floor had to be swabbed.

"She can come home and stay with me," said the East German.

"*Mliss, elle a peur.*" Map explained in his halting French that Mliss was afraid of any change. "*Elle n'aime pas les rues. Elle fait seulement maison-école, école-maison.*"

Madame paid again for a cyclopousse. Mliss slowly climbed the stairs. The prostitutes crowded into her room, cooed, and helped Mliss into her hammock. They plucked at her stomach to help cure her. The eldest, who acted as a doctor for all of them, warmed some glasses and lined them up on Mliss's back. Purple-brown circular welts rose up under them. Mliss stared straight down at the floor, without her princess smile.

Madame gripped Map's arm. She had rooms. "*Nous avons des chambres pour les assistantes à l'école. Mliss, elle sait ça. Dites à elle que ces chambres ne coûte rien. Dites-ça à elle.*"

Madame went home. The doctor-prostitute wrapped the child in a blanket and gave it to Mliss and it rested on her stomach. Map saw its face, new pink, and scrubbed. It looked like Veasna.

Before he could think, Map said. "Well, there's no doubt it's Veasna's."

Mliss heard him, looked up, and fixed him with an unblinking stare.

Map had to get back to the army. The next morning he said goodbye to his sister. Madame came and Map could sompiah her. Map promised Mliss that Veasna would come when he could. Mliss's princess face was firmly back in place.

Her grin looked huge, but Map noticed for the first time little stringy muscles around her mouth.

"Tell Veasna he has a son called Nim Samnang. Tell him everything is very good, no problems." *Samnang* meant Lucky. She held the child out from her, rather than nestling him.

There was a boat going all the way back to Siem Reap that took passengers. It needed protection. Sitting on the roof of the boat, his gun ready as defence, Map looked at the water, full of fish and reflected sky. Map pondered his newborn nephew. A child in the family. A child in *his* family, the child of the two people he loved most in the world. A double nephew, the son of his sister and of his brother.

He didn't want what had happened to him to happen to Samnang. He wanted him to grow up educated, happy, to pass his exams and work for the government. He didn't want him to be shot at, dragooned, or starved.

Preah-ang Buddha! When would this war ever be over? It has been twenty years! In twenty years, babies have been born, grown up, and become soldiers without ever knowing peace.

Samnang could grow up to be a soldier too, cadging cigarettes and threatening people for money. Let's have forty years of war then, shall we? Shall we? Let's just keep going until there is no more Cambodia, until nobody wants it and nobody wants to live here.

Map lifted up his gun and rattled off a burst of bullets into the air. A cloud of samosan birds rose up from the far shore. The few passengers ducked and screamed. The fishermen thought it was just high spirits and laughed. The silken water, the silver light returned. The Lake was not at war.

In April, the People's Republic of Kampuchea ceased to exist.

It was renamed the State of Cambodia. By unanimous vote the National Assembly removed all mention of socialism, revolution, and Marx-Lenin from the constitution. Cambodians were allowed to own land privately. The private sector would provide what the state could not.

Civil servants were told they must not expect their salaries to be sufficient. They were to get the rest of their living from private enterprise. More of them carried crates of cognac into rich men's cars.

The hot season continued. The government wanted to make one last show of strength before the rains began. April heat had evaporated the tourists like water and army paperwork could wait. Map found himself volunteered to 5th Division in Preah Vihear.

He went back to eating brown rice mixed with paddy and old dried fish. He patrolled listlessly and saw little action. He walked through elephant graveyards of Russian tanks, now just twisted metal. I can survive twenty years of war, he thought, but can I survive twenty-two? He tried to tell himself: the chances are still the same every time I walk onto a battlefield. The odds don't change on horse races the longer there are horse races.

Map saw a boy blown up. Someone, maybe even their own army, had ringed a pond with trip-wired grenades. The little private went to fetch water. One moment he was walking, then, as if Map had blinked, he was on the ground. No boom, but a sound like rain: blood, flesh, dried grass. The boy crawled down the slope to the water.

You drink too much water with wounds like that, you die, everyone knew that. The boy drank and drank. To avoid more grenades, Map followed the path of the boy's crawling down through the long grass to the bank. He sat with the boy and tried to give him a soggy cigarette. "Don't tell my father," the boy pleaded. He meant, don't tell him I killed myself. The spirits of suicides never rested.

Hey, have you heard? the joke went. The Soviet Union has announced its new support. They can't afford an army anymore. They are sending people to train us to run a circus.

Cambodia is already run like a circus!

No, no, you don't understand. In a circus the wild animals do not eat their trainers!

The rainy season finally squalled in. Mud swallowed conventional warfare, miring trucks, tanks, and boots. Map was sent back to Siem Reap. Rivers flowed between the tents. Some of the men wore kramars as if they were going swimming. He saw one of his junior officers, Lieutenant Sinn Rith.

Map told Rith his string of circus jokes. Rith's smile was sideways. He waited until Map had finished and said, "Is your friend still in hospital? I heard he's not that bad."

"What do you mean?"

Rith's face flicked downward. "Didn't you know?"

"Know what? How would I know anything, I just got back!"

Rith backed away. "Go to the hospital in town, Map. That's all I've got to say. Hospital in town."

Map strode after him, grabbed his arm, and spun him around. "Hospital, what do you mean, hospital?"

Rith flung off his hands. "Map, don't go crazy, you're a crazy guy. That's why nobody told you. You shoot off your mouth, you shoot off your gun, so people back off!"

"Told me what?"

"Go to the hospital in Siem Reap and find out. And leave your guns behind!" Rith gave him a half-push away. "Go on!"

It was good luck. Siem Reap was a center of Vietnamese presence and they had built a good hospital for themselves. There were flights, and wounded men from the Siem Reap regiment were sometimes flown there for treatment. Map had no bike, but it was only four kilometres to the hospital so he walked with the rain driving down. He walked as if the rain were evaporating off him from the heat. Somehow he was at the hospital without knowing how he got there.

Veasna was on a trolley with chipped white paint in a tiled room. A doctor was washing his hands over and over, and looked as if he was too exhausted to care who came in and out. Veasna's face was black and red, smeared with blood, and he had huge bandages on his cheeks and forehead. A pumped-up blood-pressure gauge was strapped to his arms. For just a moment, Map thought Veasna was wearing boxing gloves. Then he saw the clumps of bandages were too far up the arms, and that the swaddling of grey blankets below the waist was too flat.

Veasna had lost both hands and both legs.

"Hiya, Younger Brother."

Map sompiahed in silence.

Veasna still had his eyes. He tried to smile. This was to show acceptance of life as it now was. His chest, arms and stomach were covered in blackened dust. Map wanted to brush the dust away. They were tiny wounds, entry points for bits of grass or plastic.

"I will find it difficult to comb my hair."

"I'll comb it for you," said Map.

"You'll have to feed me too. I don't think my arms are long enough to reach anymore." Veasna mimed a snapping mouth.

Map lit a cigarette for him. He sat watching and then realized that he had to take it out again to flick ash.

They sewed flaps of skin over the ends of Veasna's arms and legs. There was not much else to do for him. After a week, they sent him home.

Home. Where would that be?

Map used his belt to strap Veasna to his back, and he bicycled him back to the camp.

He cradled him back into a hammock.

Veasna rocked a bit and shook his head. "Sorry, Map. But I don't think I can get out. I think I would rather sit on a box or something."

Furniture? In a tent? "I will try to find what I can."

Veasna smiled and sompiahed.

"I have to go work. I'll come back with food and something to sleep on, okay?"

Veasna smiled and nodded, fine, fine.

That evening, Map came back dragging a tin ammunition chest and a pillow. It was raining, but Veasna was sitting outside away from the tent and crouching behind a bush. When he saw Map, Veasna whinnied like a horse. A strange smile tugged skywards at one corner of his mouth.

"I messed myself, Map." He dropped down as if ducking a humour bullet. "I couldn't get my shorts down."

Map found himself smiling back.

"I'm really sorry to ask this, but could you find me something else to wear?"

Map stole someone's kramar, and tied it quickly around Veasna. He used a stick to throw the shorts out into the bushes. Veasna walked on all fours into the tent, pulled himself up onto the tin ammunition chest, and rolled onto his back. "Clean and dry," he sighed. "That's better."

At suppertime, Map got Veasna a cup full of rice. They didn't want to give it to him. Rice was their wages. "It is for my buddy, he has lost both his arms and legs! You want to make him crawl in here to get it himself?"

"He's telling the truth," said one of the guys behind him in the queue.

"So why does he need to shout?" the servers said, scowling. "No need to shout, eh? Don't show such disrespect to your colleagues."

Map broke. "I don't have any respect for my colleagues! My colleagues leave their wounded out in the rain to rot!"

Traditionally Cambodians eat rice by pressing it together with their fingers. How was Veasna supposed to eat?

It made Veasna chuckle. "I have no idea how to eat this."

He tried balancing the plate between his forearms, but he could not lean forward far enough to reach it with his mouth.

Map put the plate down on Veasna's tin box, and Veasna, kneeling on the ground, was able to lap at it. The plate kept slipping, and the rice spilled over the edge.

"If we had some wire, maybe we could strap a spoon onto one hand." Map used the word *hand*. "And you could hold the plate still with your other arm."

"That's a good idea. We'll try that."

"Come on, man, let's finish up," said Map. He spooned the rice for Veasna.

Then he combed Veasna's hair. He found his palm oil in his kit, and he slicked the hair down, and combed it into orderly streaks. As a finishing touch, he perched Veasna's sunglasses on his nose.

"Oh, what a stylish person," said Map, managing again to smile.

Veasna gave a civet-like beady little grin. He leaned back on his elbows as if he was on a beach and chuckled.

Map wrote to Mliss. It was a terrible letter to write, but he had to do it. He went back to the canteen so Veasna would not see. Map posted it and then realized that because the post was so unreliable, he would have to write it again.

The army had given Map back his old clerical job. That meant he could stay and take care of Veasna.

Map would check up on Veasna at different times of day, just to bring him food or tell him a little joke. The poor guy was bored out of his mind. Veasna didn't smoke because he couldn't afford to and there were no magazines or books to read. There were government or enemy radio stations, or maybe you could get cheap pop music from Bangkok, but none of the guys had a radio.

All he did was lie on his chest in the tent, out of the rain. When the rain was heavy, Veasna would pull himself out into it, and wash as best he could.

The other soldiers hated it. They thought Veasna made himself into a spectacle and tutted. Why didn't he do what anyone else would do, which was go away? Nobody liked to see his flippers; it was ugly, it was incomplete. It's too bad, said the officers, but it is disturbing, you know? Everybody who sees him is reminded it could happen to them. He should go home to his family or home to…I don't know, there must be places we can send people.

It's that Map. He takes care of him like a mother. Without Map he would have to go away.

Every day, Map would check for letters. None came.

Veasna said, "Mliss, you know, she may not want to stay with me."

How were they going to get him home?

Map would answer, "Mliss doesn't know what has happened yet, probably."

"Or maybe she just doesn't write. Maybe she should go back to her husband."

"He won't want her, she has your baby."

Veasna went quiet. "Maybe it would be better for the baby too." He said quietly, "I could go and live with my mother."

"I'm sorry, buddy, but your mother? It would be like snuggling up to a great big pike that eats small deer. No, no, Mliss has a good job; she gets money, maybe not a lot, but enough. What we need to do is find a way to get you to Phnom Penh."

Veasna nodded, relieved, encouraged. "Of course that is why she can't come here! Clever girl. She has to keep her job to make money."

Map silently pleaded, Mliss, Mliss. Write to him. Reply, please!

Mliss, Mliss, I don't think you are quite right. Mliss, Mliss, I wish you could tell me what happened to you all those years, but I do not want to force you. Mliss, Mliss, I want to be close to you, and be an older brother to you. But you won't let me near; you won't let Veasna near.

Are you even close to the baby?

The sky brightened again. It was October, the dry season, and Map got volunteered back to Preah Vihear.

Map shouted at Rith. "Who is going to take care of my brother! Answer me! Are you going to feed him?"

Rith's smile looked lazy, his eyes half-closed. He did not like being shouted at. "Oh no. That is not my job. That is his family's job."

"Fine. Good. Great. Get him back to Phnom Penh, then!"

"The Khmers Rouges own both roads to Phnom Penh." Rith leaned back in his chair. "Let Veasna take care of himself. Where you are going, you will have to take care of yourself. We can't spare you to take care of Veasna. Everyone else is going to the front, are we going to say, no we have made a special case of Tan Map, because his friend was blown up? Everybody has had a friend blown up!"

So Map had to load up his backpack, and strap on ammo. Gunmetal felt as hot as a pan, the khaki uniform as rough as sun-warmed tent canvas. Map sat next to Veasna, and put his arm around him. Seen from the side, Veasna almost looked like a whole man.

"You take care, Older Brother. Siem Reap is a pretty good place to be."

Veasna saluted. "All alone in a base camp? The NADK are crawling all over Banteay Srei. This place is a target, not an army camp!"

"Hmm. Nothing we can do."

"Nothing we can do." Veasna looked around at him, sunglasses still perched on his nose. "Whatever happens, you have been a true friend, a true brother."

"So have you." Map stood up.

Back in '85 in the K5 camp, when Map lay shivering in the dirt, Veasna had knelt beside him. "I know a way out of this," Veasna had promised Map. He carried canisters of gasoline out into the woods away from the camp, doused the ground, and set it alight. The forest fire billowed hundreds of feet up into the air. The minefields exploded, shooting up gusts of black air as if the earth were spitting out its dead. The fire cooked all the animals in it—snakes, civets, tortoises, monkeys, even one whole wild elephant. The thousand starving workers ate charred corpses for a week.

Veasna's cheeks had glowed cherry red as he watched the fire, but his eyes had glowed even brighter. Life will be wild, he seemed to promise; life will be fun.

His eyes still glowed like that. Veasna grinned and pressed his forearms together.

Map turned and marched away.

He was gone a long time. No action in Preah Vihear so he got sent to help retake Pailin from the Khmers Rouges. The Khmers Rouges won, pushing them back. Then—and this was a very bad sign—Map was sent to help guard Kompong Thom.

The new regiment gave Map time off to go to see his sister, and he was mad. He was going to tell her off. Why haven't you written to your husband? Okay, maybe you didn't get my letters to tell you what is wrong, but you should have written anyway!

Map's anger was clenched like the white knuckles of a fist. His feet pounded up the steps to her room. The prostitutes leaned out after him. He heard Samnang crying.

"Mliss!" Map struck the door just once. It foxed him and flew open. Then he saw that the lock was broken.

Just inside the doorway was the statue of the fat cat with the mouse. It was broken, but had been repaired with Scotch tape. The tape had curled up yellow from the heat.

He looked up and saw chipped plastic plates and torn clothing. The hook for the hammock was bent. Lopsided, as if on a sinking boat, Mliss lay very calmly in it. A scarf covered her head, as if she were a farm girl out in the fields. Her cheeks were swollen and purple.

Her ex-husband.

Map said immediately, "If I see that bastard, I will shoot him and stuff his body down a toilet."

"His boss would come looking for you."

"Has he touched Samnang?"

Mliss was smiling. "I knelt over him. So he couldn't touch him."

Map drew in a breath. It was as if he were heaven's anvil, to keep being pounded. He stood and closed his eyes and he knew, knew in his heart and liver.

Map was certain that all of this was happening to his family because of him. It was his fault, because of the bad things he had done. He had done wicked things and had not earned enough merit to avoid bringing terrible luck down on everyone he loved. He could never earn enough merit. His soul was black with evil deeds. He was a pool of bad luck that drenched everybody he loved.

"Mliss. Sister. I am so sorry for you. Pick up your clothes and whatever you have that is not broken, I will take you to live in the school with Madame."

Did anything matter to her? Without a word, as if tidying up after a meal, she began to put together some clothes, some toys.

"Hold Samnang for me, will you?" she asked.

Map jerked away. "I'm afraid I will hurt him."

She left the baby on the mat. She had squirrelled away plastic bags and string. With dreamlike precision she set in order her few possessions.

I must get away from them all and stay as far away from them as I can. Perhaps if I pray to be killed badly, then the luck will change. Maybe if I am burned in a fire, all of this will stop.

The doctor-prostitute came in and sompiahed Map. "We heard the noise, is she all right?" she asked.

"No," said Map. "We are getting out of here."

"We will miss her. She is a reminder for us of the good old days. We wish her well."

Map nodded thanks.

The prostitute hesitated. "Mliss never was a fallen woman," she promised him.

She was speaking as if Mliss were dead. He turned and looked at Mliss. She moved like a spirit, distracted, hungry, sketching a motion one way and then going the other. He asked the prostitute, "Does she talk about things?"

The doctor-prostitute sighed. "Sometimes. Mostly not. What happened?"

"Her husband, her new husband is alive but...disabled. A land mine."

The prostitute bowed in respect of Veasna. "It will not stop until we are all dead."

Map shouldered up a dozen crammed plastic bags and they walked to the school. Mliss walked looking up at the sky and the tops of the buildings. They came to the school, and its circular yard was full of children, running, swinging, kicking, and screaming. Mliss suddenly looked beautiful and elegant. The children ran up to her to say hello.

"I am coming to live with you all," she said, kneeling down so that she could smile into their faces. Their faces dropped limply, and their eyes stared when they saw the bruises.

Map knocked on the side door and Madame called out anxiously from behind it.

"*C'est la famille de Mliss!*" Map said.

The door opened and Madame's face soured into horror. "*Qu'est-ce-qui se passe!*" she gasped.

Map's French failed him. He said in Khmer, "Her ex-husband beats her up. She has finally left that horrible place. You said once there would be a room for her here. Can you give her a room? *Est-ce que vous avez une chambre?*"

Madame bundled Mliss inside, reached up to take the bags. Map stood outside on the step.

"*Entrez! Entrez!*" Madame implored him.

"I am sorry. But I am bad luck and it would be better if I do not."

He backed away. "Take care of her. She is a good country girl. She was always good at her studies. She used to be happy and play. She is happiest...," he took a deep breath, "when she is with the other children."

Madame didn't understand a word, but she was alarmed for him. "Monsieur Tan? Monsieur!"

He walked away backwards so he could see Mliss as he left. She looked up and smiled sweetly, as if he were walking towards her, not backing off.

"*Bahn bon,*" he murmured. Good luck. And then because this was a big occasion, he wished her luck more formally. "*Soam a-oy ban chok chay.*" The phrase had a note of prayer in it.

"*Lea haoey,*" she said, an ordinary good-bye. She gave him a pretty little wave.

No letters. No phone. Kompong Thom baked in the dry-season heat.

Map wrote a letter to Siem Reap HQ requesting news about Veasna. No answer.

Map jumped on a supply truck going to Siem Reap in a convoy. The sun had baked the roads as hard as asphalt and he was there by evening. He stalked into his old camp.

"Where is Private Nim Veasna?" he demanded. He slammed the desk to shake up the little clerk who had taken over the job of quartermaster. He was a frightened little flower who shook every time he spoke to Map. He stared at Map in surprise and dismay.

Map shouted, "Where is Private Nim Veasna!"

Lieutenant Sinn Rith came into the office. "Who are you talking about?"

"My brother-in-law who was blown up. I left him here."

"Oh, him. I don't know."

"Where is he?"

Rith smiled. "Always the same, eh, Map? You know if you weren't such a coward and threatened the Khmers Rouges as much as you threatened us, maybe you would help us win this war." He pretended to search through papers. Papers, who kept papers on anything? Rith probably couldn't read anyway.

"Ah yes, here we go. Yes, there was no one to take care of him so he...uh...went to rejoin his mother."

Map walked to Battambang along the open road. He was hoping to be shot, but a man who has lost the compassion of Buddha and who is damned will not be lucky enough to be shot. Buddha wants him to see how deep the curse will run.

So Map got to Battambang, and Veasna's mother had been at the palm wine. She had an evil tongue, and smelled of alcohol. Her teeth were black. Map would see her, years later, living in one of the temples as a nun, but for now she was a drunk.

Veasna was not there, and as far as Map could tell from his mother, he never had been. Map did not get angry. He asked her again. Had she seen Veasna since he was hurt?

"Oh," said, his mother, curious. "Was he hurt?"

Map turned and walked out without any further words.

He went back to the camp. By now he should have been shot

several times over. By now he knew he was cursed. He walked into the office and there was the frightened little flower of a quartermaster, even more uncomfortable than before.

"Where is Nim Veasna?"

"I don't know," said the little flower. The little flower was shaking. "People say that he went back to his mother."

"He didn't...," Map bit back on rage, "go back to his mother."

"Oh. Well. Map. You know, when people say someone sleeps with his fathers or has gone back to his mother...especially these days when...when there are so many mothers who have died, that can just mean that they have died...too?" His voice trailed away.

"How?"

"Oh! You know he was badly wounded."

"How?"

"He would not have had a happy life, it was such a terrible thing." The flower really was trembling in the wind.

Map advanced.

He was thinking, I was cursed enough before, it hardly seems that anything I can do can make the curse worse. As if he already knew what he was going to do.

He asked the little flower, "What did you do with him?"

"I? I? I did nothing...except, except, from time to time, I would bring him food, you know. Not many people did that, you know how soldiers hate...to be reminded, and some of the people in this camp are just peasants and very superstitious about bad luck..."

"What did they do to him?"

"I...I..."

There were always rumours. Not enough rice to go around. They don't take care of the wounded anymore. In fact, they think it's a waste to feed them, since they can't fight and transport is so difficult. It was whispered that sometimes they even...

Map's voice was a whisper. "Did they shoot him or just let him starve to death?"

"What? Oh no, nothing..."

Map couldn't be bothered to let the man finish. He swung up his rifle and blew off the top of his head.

The body was flung in an arc against all the unfiled papers nobody could read.

There is no God for me and there is no law in Cambodia, so who is going to track me when there are no roads, and who is going to judge me when everybody in the whole country has killed something to survive?

The dead flower's body still trembled. I've seen this before, I've done it before. You weren't worth a bullet. I should have pulled out all your fingernails first, like we used to do when we wanted to have some fun, and then pulled out your tongue and made you sing a song for Angka. I should have made you dig your own grave naked in the rain and then lie down in it. I should have weighed you down with a heavy stone and found Veasna's shorts and made you eat them and then and only then would I have beaten your head in with a hoe.

You'll try and come and find me. You'll try to kill me back.

But I have to do some things first.

He patted the dead quartermaster's pocket for the keys. He wrapped himself round with belts full of ammo, and a tin of extra fuel. He got into an army truck, revved it up, and roared through the barrier out onto the road. He pushed it bounding up and down over ruts, jarring and weaving around potholes, his headlights full on. Come on and shoot me if you're going to, don't do anything halfway!

He swerved around debris. Piles of cow shit hid mines. Heaps of reeds hid mines, even little bumps hid mines. You people are lazy. I know how you do it; I've done it myself.

He drove back towards Kompong Thom, and down the old track, headlights blazing and beeping his horn. It was dawn, but no straw was burning this time. He pulled the truck up with its engine running and let off a round of ammunition. "Out of the house!" he shouted. "Out, get out now."

He started shooting at the roofs and shouting. The Chams stumbled out of the house. He shot over their heads, but made sure his blank eyes told them: I'll kill you no problem. They begged, they pleaded, they saw he was crazy. He got back in the cab, revved the engine again, and drove the truck head-on into the house. They shouted "No, no, not our house," and he said, "It's my house. Nobody gets it."

He went round the back, got out the gas canister, splashed the truck, splashed the broken bulk of the house, especially sploshed the open cap to the gas tank. He made a trail of gas away from the truck.

Then he took out a cigarette lighter, the one Veasna bought the day he found his mother.

He stood back; fire fluttered forward; there was a whoosh; the truck was alight, and the houses caught and then there was a bone-rattling thump in Map's chest. The back of the truck lifted up and there was a fist of fire going up into the air.

A grand house, we used to call it. It was a peasant's house, full of hope and not much else. Work hard, study, be good, give your money to the poor as if we weren't the poor ourselves, work in the hot sun, drink evil water and get sick. Oh, thank you, Lord Buddha, *Preah-ang Buddha*, for this abundant life!

My parents aren't here, my brother isn't here, Veasna isn't here, nobody's here, not even as ghosts. Mom and Dad, they were dead at the beginning of all of this. There have been so many waves of ghosts since. The spirits of my family will have been washed away on floods of ghosts. Cambodia has floods of murder more regular than the Tonlé Sap.

Well, this is my place! This is the place where my brother Veasna and I should have farmed. Where his many sons and his beautiful daughters should have prospered. This is where my brother Heng should have come if there were any justice. He would have come as a general with his beautiful wife, down from the city, big and fat and army-fed, his children looking down their noses at our cows and hens and supper of catfish.

Somewhere my wife is pouring water over her head, and she is singing sweetly because all she has ever seen is sunrise and sunset and neighbours given dinner because they helped to build a new shed. My plump and happy wife stands at the crossroad at New Year to collect money for the monks. She sends our sons off to school every morning wearing their clean little school shorts.

At New Year she goes from house to house doing traditional dances, her fingers arched, dances that are about fishing and hunting and laundry. My wife dances beautifully and sweetly and she loves her sister-in-law Mliss because they have known each other all their lives and have always been friends. They dance together, and they can go from house to house, and Mliss is not frightened of the sun, she is not frightened to leave the house. Mliss goes up to anyone's house and dances for them happily and in perfect safety. And Mom and Dad died in their hammocks, and their ashes are in urns safe in the stupa, the *cheea dai,* so I know where they are and I can ask the monks to chant for their spirits so they get the food that I leave for them. My sons paint the spirit houses white and they hang tinsel in the New Year and on the porch we lay our table for all our ancestors, and they come in peace and love for these are happy spirits who do no harm.

As they did no harm in life.

But watch out for me, Buddha. Since you can't save me, watch out for what kind of avenging spirit I will become. I will have many heads like the Naga, and staring eyes like a demon. I will be the Monkey King who murders Lord Rama and rapes his wife and joins the demons!

Map walked away. Behind him the fire leapt up joyfully like a troupe of celestial dancers, and the folds of the fire's swirling dresses enveloped the straw, the wood and the lopsided Kompong Thom spire. No Muslims will have it, no yuon will have it, no Angka farmer who butchered people and thinks he got away with it will have it. No one will have it. You won't have it, Buddha. You can't take it.

He could hear the Chams behind him sobbing. He rattled more bullets over their heads. He walked back up the track to the main road, and kept walking.

Map felt he had won. I have nothing left, Buddha, so what are you going to take now?

Mliss committed suicide.

Map knocked on Madame's door, and she saw him, and reeled back, and said, "Oh, Monsieur Tan. Oh, I am sorry." She tried to tell him in Khmer, but she garbled it and it took ten long minutes of confusion and false starts. There was some insecticide and she drank it. It was a bad thing; I won't make you unhappy by telling you. Yes, yes, monsieur, it took her a long time to die and she was in great pain. Yes, monsieur. Die. *Morte? Elle est morte.* Yes, monsieur, yes, yes, that is what I have been saying. She was so unhappy after her husband's injuries, and...monsieur?

Madame was used to little Cambodians who nittered gratefully at her heels like puppy dogs. Madame was not used to great raging Cambodians with round staring demon eyes. Madame was not used to seeing Cambodians when they break open like eggs and everything that has been done to them is done back.

Map was bellowing at her.

"That baby is not an orphan! Samnang is not an orphan! Samnang has a family!"

Map shouted so hard he fell onto his knees. He jabbed a finger at her and roared. "That baby does not get adopted. The baby stays here, I pay. *Il n'est pas pour … pour donner aux autres!*"

"Oh monsieur! Oh! I understand. Do you want the child? Do you want me to get him for you?"

"*Dtay!*" he screamed. It means no, but she forgot that. He waved the child away. Samnang must stay away from him, or the luck will spread like black dye. "*Dtay, dtay, dtay, dtay!*" And he couldn't stand up, so he crawled away as fast as he could, crawled for Veasna, in honor of Veasna who could only crawl, crawled because he was only worthy of crawling. Map would die and not even come back so high as an insect.

Oh, Buddha, what a mind you have, how clever you are, what traps you set. Oh, what else could you take from me? Okay, Buddha, you win! I honor you out of terror; I honor you out of grief. I honor you because you eat my country, licking your fingers like it's sweet fruit. Okay, you win!

On his knees, Map bowed again and again, and touched his forehead to the ground. Now I understand! Now I understand!

You are Angka, God!

Yes, yes, Angka was the palest imitation of you. Perhaps the Khmers Rouges suffer now because they failed. Even Angka made mistakes and let some live, but you, you destroy all. And you tell us to smile, and to accept, well, Okay, look! Look, I'm smiling, see? I get the joke.

It is funny. Ha ha ha ha! I'm laughing, see? Hear me laugh, *Preah?* I bow to you, Lord Buddha, and your superior wisdom and all the people's brains you slammed into the roadway. Oh, I am pissing myself from desire to serve you!

Is that enough? Can the killing stop for just a little while?

Can Samnang live, *Preah-ang* Buddha? Will you let him keep his legs and his hands? Will you stave off making him a deaf-mute, or perhaps even spare him being shot at?

Can he go to school, *Preah?* Please? *Sohm, Preah oeuy, sohm preah oeuy, sohm . . .*

Map was curled up on the pavement, and he was dimly aware that Madame was holding him and rocking him, going ssh, ssh, ssh.

Map became embarrassed. He stood up and wiped his face and sompiahed. Madame was wise enough and scared enough to let him go.

He weaved away unsteadily, to join the police. The police carried guns too.

At least when the army finally came to shoot him, he would be able to shoot back.

The Vietnamese said the war would go on for two more years and indeed the UN showed up in 1993. But the chain of conflict did not finally end until 1998. The Vietnamese lost 53,000 troops in Cambodia, almost the same as the number of Americans who died in Vietnam. There is simply no counting the numbers of Cambodians who died.

APRIL 1151

There were many things about being a slave that Jayavarman could accept.

He could make himself love the mud. Mud could cover his skin and keep out the sun.

He could love nursery rice. It would nourish and give life. He could not love bending over for hours pushing the young and tender plants into flooded fields. He could not love the ache in his back. He could feel pain making him old. It numbed his brain, closing down the world.

At first he had told himself that enslavement would be a valuable lesson in humility and acceptance. He had still been thinking like a prince. He soon learned that aching shoulders could teach him nothing. They shrivelled as they ached, losing strength and skill. He remembered all the foolish tales of heroes grown stronger through labour. He walked now with knees permanently bent.

You called yourself Nia, Slave, out of arrogance. You thought you were being noble climbing down mahogany steps in condescension.

You were a slave all along. It was your destiny. And how you ache for each day to end, so you can rest a body so full of pain that it stops your mindfulness.

You look up at the slow sun, waiting for it to crawl across the sky, so you can crawl into your hammock. Sometimes you cannot even see the sun, your eyes sting so much from sweat.

Jayavarman Nia had learned other things.

He had learned that Buddhists could be evil taskmasters. It made no difference to a slave if his masters spouted empty words of compassion and forbearance. They still looked through you as if you were a beast.

Jaya had taught himself to speak Cham. He had to, to survive. His Cham was crude and halting, and it reduced him to the level of a child. It made him sound ignorant, like a peasant. He remembered laughing at the airs and graces of the Chinese, who had seemed to him to be so ignorant and crude. They were only foreigners, trying to learn and take part.

He had learned that you needed hope and strength to be sociable.

The man labouring next to him said nothing. Jaya did not know his name, knew nothing about him, and cared nothing about him.

The man next to him stood up. This was dangerous. It drew attention. He croaked at Jaya, demanding something in a tribal language. He was some sweaty unwashed wild man, who did not smell any worse than Jaya.

He barked again. He had the eyes of a soldier who had seen too many battles. His voice went high and rough, requesting something. He gestured as if embarrassed towards the knee-deep flooded field.

Then he knelt down into the water and pushed his own head under.

Move, Jaya told himself, and didn't.

Jaya, move. The man is drowning. Jaya looked up at the guards. They shovelled rice into their mouths. One of them glanced up and kept eating.

Jaya felt his way through the water, as thick as a cloak, and he could not find the man under it. Finally he struck an arm, grabbed it and pulled upwards.

The arm was smeared with mud but underneath it, the flesh was feverish in Jaya's grasp. Jaya had a dull thought: he could make me ill too.

The mountain man groaned and gasped and said a word in pidgin. Jayavarman had heard the word used of fish thrown up onto a bank.

The man pointed at himself. Drown me, he was saying. Drown me!

Jaya shook his head. No.

Once again the wild man pushed himself under the creamy green flood, and disappeared. Jaya felt as if the whole weight of the sky was bearing down on him. He had no words. What would he do?

The man wanted to die. But he was ill; maybe it was the fever talking.

Jaya reached down into the mud again, and pulled the man up.

The tribesman had stuffed his mouth full of mud, swallowed it whole. The surface of his open eyes was coated in mud; his nostrils were clogged with it. His bones quaked with an animal effort to breathe.

One of the hot, bored soldiers called from the bank, "Let him go! He wants to die."

Suicide would condemn the man, push him further down so that he would be reborn as a rat or a slug. Jaya tried to gouge out the plug of mud and reed from the man's mouth.

The soldier stood up and waved. "Get back to work. Let him die!"

There was a pop as the plug of mud came free. There was a rasping gasp, and the man swallowed mud, and then coughed.

"Oh shit!" shouted the soldier. He stomped down into the mud, and casually swiped Jaya across the face, knocking him aside. He grabbed hold of the other slave's long queue of hair, hauled him up onto the bank, and left him there.

"Work, idiot! I've got mud all over my jacket!"

Once I had a wife as beautiful a celestial maiden with full and milky breasts and we were as fertile as fruit. I had a beautiful son. I had been restored to my family home, surrounded by fields and the line of coconut palms I had known as a child, the oxen tamely tethered beside the hay. I called to my men, I rode into battle, I was brave and rode my elephant fearlessly. I served my King, my old and failing King. I served the Buddha and so did without noble finery.

How foolish I would have looked to the Gods. My lack of finery meant I was not recognized as a high-born person. The winged blade cut my elephant's throat and down I fell, a prize, a man no longer. I am a slave whom no one knows or regards. Who sees comrades choose death.

Just work, Jaya. Empty your mind. The only way to end suffering is to end happiness as well.

No happiness, not in this life, not now.

Jaya went back to work and prayed for the man. Live, Comrade. Live, and learn. Be reborn as a prince for all your travail. Be a better prince than I was.

The mountain man woke up, was hauled to his feet and was sent back to work. He glared at Jaya as he passed and spat at him.

Work, Jaya, taste your own sweat. The sun will set. Endure.

Time crawled, but night was inevitable, bringing rest and disappointment.

The slaves were herded back into temporary shelters full of insects. Slave women dumped noodles direct onto the slaves' callused hands. The noodles were lukewarm and half-cooked in lumps. No one had the strength to care about anything.

Some new cooks had been shipped in. Their faces were still dusty from the march. One of the women shook lumps of rice into Jaya's hands and widened her eyes at him. No doubt he was in such a terrible state as to inspire pity.

His hands were now as rough-skinned as his feet, and so filthy that it would be rude to point them at people. Let alone use them to shovel food into his mouth.

He dropped onto the ground like a bundle of loose sticks. Be grateful Jaya, be grateful you work the rice fields.

His first torment had been a timber camp up in the hills. The timber camps were cold and damp. He had shivered all night with no fire or blanket.

The stone quarries had been baking hot. The heat slammed back from the rock-face. The sharp broken edges of the stone cut his feet. Boulders fell on men, or crushed their legs to paste.

We build our graceful temples on that.

So, Jaya, the rice fields are best. You have the best work possible for you. You are lucky, but you complain.

The wide-eyed woman approached.

Jaya felt the dullness of his mind. She was so unimportant that the guards did not prevent her walking over to him. What do you want? Jayavarman wondered. If you think this soldier can give you any sex, you are wrong. Work has made this rooster a hen.

What is in your eyes, woman? Pity? Why me? Look at the others; some of them are in an even worse state than I am.

The woman spoke Khmer. She said, in a voice as sad as any song, "Lord. My Lord, is that you?"

Jaya thumbed a fly out of his eye.

The woman reached up and pulled something from her neck.

Jaya had seen it before. An amulet of protection. He stared at it, his lower lip feeling as heavy as a sack full of rice.

"Fishing Cat?" he asked.

Her hands involuntarily flew up to her mouth. "Oh, my Lord, what has befallen you?"

"I was caught," he said.

"Oh, my Prince," her voice slid up and down the scale of notes of pity and sadness and regret.

He was baffled. "What are you doing here?"

"The war washed over my village. We were taken."

"Oh, Cat. We are both slaves."

She knelt in front of him. She dipped low and placed her forehead on the ground.

"Cat, don't. Don't, it will only make trouble."

"You are my Prince." She looked up and she was crying. "You are my kind and noble Prince, who sent me back to my home, my beautiful Prince. Oh! This life is unkind. I pictured you in your home with your family and I thought that you at least would be happy."

"Sssh, Cat. Sssh. That way lies a sore heart."

"I can bear things for myself, but for you ..."

"I am used to it now. Almost."

She looked down at the amulet. "You told me that it could not protect me."

"Do you ... are there ... any noodles left?"

Jaya could not be too proud to ask for more, if she could get him some.

Cat's face worked, with misgiving and sadness. Abruptly she stood and walked back to the temporary, smoky trenches.

The world closed its eyes.

And then bounced back into awareness with the rustling of her skirts, her skirts smelling of charcoal and fish.

"It was for the soldiers," she muttered. Two roasted catfish fell from the folds. She looked away as he pushed both of them into his mouth at once. He chomped crackling bone. There were fish flakes in his moustache.

The other slaves stirred awake and she ran.

❧

No law said that slaves should not love or that slaves should not marry.

In the weary, drugged, hungry evenings the two slaves still found the strength to walk a short way together. They would lie on their backs next to each other, chastely looking up at the sky, not even their hands touching.

Sometimes when the sun had blistered his back, she would lance the pouches of skin with fired needles.

Sometimes, when his legs wept blood from leeches, she would wash them with boiled water.

"Tuh, she looks like a servant girl with her king," the guards chortled.

"Yeah, well, he was one, wasn't he?"

"Naw, that funny little guy? He was a stone carver more like."

"He keeps talking religion. I reckon he dressed up some of their temple dolls." The Cham guard mimed an effeminate priest.

"Aw, let 'em be. They've got to have a life too."

"Yeah. It could be us. It could happen to us. Next war." The soldier grunted as he turned over his helmet for a pillow.

Cloud-flowers. It seemed both of them were buoyed up by something invisible and spinning, something that you could not eat or drink and which would not keep off the sun or the rain.

Cloud-flowers that nevertheless nourished and perfumed, making the sky and the sun and the mud and the rice noodles beautiful, savoury.

In the afternoons as she scrubbed the blackened clay pots she would look to the fields, thinking of him.

By day in the fields, his back was more supple, bearing its load more flexibly. His step bounced even at the end of the day.

As they sagged gratefully down onto the ground together, something else seemed to open up and expand, something that everyone could see.

Love was still possible. Kindly love, alleviating love, love which warmed and elevated. Love which made sweat sweet, feet beautiful, grass into a soft bed. Love gave anyone with the capacity to be happy for others a moment of pleasure. Love gave hope to anyone with a particle of courage left. It gave anyone whose strength was not exhausted a reason to think that life could always offer something.

So no one was surprised, only a few were displeased or jealous, when finally the slave girl Fishing Cat and the man who was ashamed of his name ("Victory" indeed!) announced that they were man and wife. No witnesses, no ceremony. Who cared if slaves died, let alone married?

But the declaration was accepted by all.

And they were left alone to hold each other at night on the cold dewy grass, sharing their warmth.

They shared what food there was. She found herbs during the day, or caught crickets or geckos, and they ate those. It was noted that her respect for him was exaggerated, always something of the servant girl in her reactions to him. About him, there was always something of the relieved and grateful settling of someone used to better things.

Did they screw? There was no privacy, people would have seen them, but it was as if they had promised not to bear children here. Maybe they were both too tired.

Instead, like a cat and a dog by the hearth, they would rest on each other. Cat and Dog became their nicknames.

Until one day two cavalry men on fine horses came to the camp. Between them walked a slave.

"Which one is he?" a Cham noble in a high helmet demanded. The slave scanned the faces and answered. The slave was Khmer, but they both spoke the shared religious language, Sanskrit.

"That's him," the old slave said, pointing at Dog. "That's him. Hello, Lord! Hello!" The old man looked back and forth between the guards, smiling, happy, relieved. "That's the one called Jayavarman."

The Queen consumed herself.

Indradevi Kansru looked at her sister as she collected yet another untouched tray of food.

Even in the shadowed depths of the monastery-temple, heat and starvation had made her skin scaly and coated it in sweat. Queen Jaya's round face rested on a thin neck like a plum about to roll off a plate.

Lamps hanging from the ornate fixtures cast an orange glow. An old woman sat with her legs folded under herself, fanning the Queen.

"Has my sister eaten anything at all?" Indradevi Kansru asked.

The old woman shook her head. She had tiny eyes, wizened and dark.

Kansru turned to her sister. "'Sri? 'Sri, I have some water for you. You should drink at least!"

"I am so nearly there," said Jayarajadevi.

"You are so nearly dead."

"I can so nearly see the great cycle. I can so nearly hear the great deep sound of the void."

Indradevi put down the jug. "Do you want your husband to come home and find that you have died? That there is only your older sister here to greet him and say: she died of a broken heart waiting for you. Consider, Sister, if that would earn merit. Or would it be considered selfish?"

As if pricked by a pin, Jayarajadevi's eyes opened. There were strands of muscle in arcs around her mouth; you could see the skull under her skin; there were pouches of flesh like a squirrel's around her chin.

Jayarajadevi asked, "Explain."

"You focus on your own salvation, when the household needs you to be its head. It is not Dharma to indulge a broken heart and call it the path of asceticism. This is the time for an orderly life in your home with your family."

"I have no family."

Indradevi discovered that she was angry. "Thank you for that. Should I call you Sister, since you have no family? You may well wish that you didn't have a family, but you do! You have a son who never sees his mother!

The Queen swayed. "I did not mean that."

"You say many things that you do not mean. You say them anyway without thought or care for others."

"Sister!"

Indradevi boiled over. "How alone am I and how much more alone will I be if you starve yourself to death, grieving for a husband you do not even know is dead?"

The old servant woman kept fanning.

Jayarajadevi seemed to melt back into herself. "He is dead. What else can he be? He was supposed to die; he was sent off to be killed."

"This is not Dharma! Dharma is patience and forbearance with a cheerful mien. You wish to follow the Dharma, Sister, go out among the women and take up your spindle and busy yourself cheerfully among them. What is your body that you have to take revenge upon it?"

"I seek to understand!" Jayarajadevi's eyes were wide with pain. "How love can be wasted and how vengefulness and hate can so triumph."

"It surpasses understanding," said Indradevi. "Don't try. Accept. Then you will learn. Not this way." Indradevi ran a hand across Queen Jaya's forehead. "You are in error, Sister."

One of the lamps flickered out.

"Oh!" Indradevi snarled in rage. "Why aren't the lamps kept full!"

It's not the lamps that make you angry, Indra. It's not even your sister. It's you, yourself, for letting this happen.

It is not her weakness, but yours that allows this to happen. You are the one who must change.

Indradevi grabbed hold of her sister's arm. "Come on, stand up. You're going outside."

The Queen raised and lowered her hands, like a querulous old woman. "I am in meditation!"

"You are in self-indulgence." Indradevi was the stronger of the two and had no difficulty in pulling the Queen to her feet. It was like hoisting up light, dry sticks.

"Let me be!" The Queen turned to her servant. "Stop her doing this."

"Out!" Indradevi drew a shawl around her sister's shoulders and pushed her. "You do nothing worthwhile. You could barely show up for the funeral of your beloved guru."

The Queen wept petulantly, and her feet made little sobbing steps. "You torment me!"

Indradevi kept pushing. "You are not being ascetic to attain the truth. That is not honest, Sister. This is grief. Unenlightened, all-devouring grief. Accept it as grief. Call it by its right name. Do not call it devotion. It is not."

They came to a flight of steps. Indradevi swept her sister down them as if she were a reed broom.

Sunlight seared an inner courtyard.

On a raised platform there grew a bougainvillaea, a butterfly tree. It was April, the time of butterflies, and the tree was covered in them. Startled, the butterflies rose up from the bougainvillaea in a cobalt, orange, black, and yellow cloud.

Indra pushed her sister into the tree's shade, made her sit, and arranged the shawl over her head.

"The air is beautiful," the Queen whispered. "It smells so clean."

"It's not full of incense." Indra drew a deep calming breath herself.

By all that was holy her sister looked awful—tangled, thin, and worm-eaten. And she had once been so beautiful. Tears ripened in Indradevi's eyes.

Queen Jaya whispered, "We only had a year." She meant herself and Jayavarman.

With a sigh, Indradevi settled next to her and hugged her. Jaya trembled in her arms like a bird fallen from the nest. "It was a beautiful year," said Indradevi.

"Yes, yes it was," replied Jayarajadevi, her voice creaking with a mixture of gratitude and sodden grief. She was as frail and shivering as the butterflies. She looked up at them in the tree. "Sru," the Queen asked, "bring me my little boy."

Indradevi ran.

Her son came, fat and stomping like his father.

The Queen experienced uncertainty. I must look like a ghost to him.

She berated herself. Kansri, this is not good, you have not seen your boy in weeks—a lifetime to a child. While you poke around in the dark, what sort of man is he growing into? How will he be worthy of his father if he is neglected? How can the memory of me be his rock if Yashovarman decides to take him away to the City?

Her sister walked behind him, guiding him by the hand. Indradevi's smile was wide and joyful. She is so pleased that I am seeing him. Oh, Sister, how faithful you are! My Kansru, my delight, my boon companion.

Jayarajadevi said, "Indra, thank you." Then she bowed low. "Hello, my little boy. Hello, my little prince."

Queen Jaya tried to snag his attention with her eyes. He sighed grumpily, and his thrusting, angry male body was difficult to pick up and hold.

She wrestled him up onto her lap. "Mother's-child, mother's-son," she called him. "Suryakumara. Do you know how you got your name?"

Oh, woman, while you were out burning your mind up to heaven, your son was calling. Your boy, all that may be left of your husband, the most precious thing you have.

You neglected him. You even thought of him as a worldly distraction, a bond to the earth. How could you think that a neglectful mother would attain wisdom?

"Your father named you Surya after the Universal King. King Suryavarman loved your father, so that is why you were named after him." Kansri kissed her son's forehead. He leaned away, as if reaching for a toy, but there was no toy to reach for.

"And you were named Kumara, Crown Prince. Which you are, here in Nagara Gotama, City of the Eastern Buddha. Here, you are a very important little man."

She kissed his round, tiny hand.

"There is a new Universal King now. And he does not love your father. Some day, not now, not for a while yet, but some day you will have to go the royal palace to serve the King. That is far from here."

Jayarajadevi remembered her wedding night, out under the stars.

The boy asked, "And Daddy?" The little face was solemn, too solemn, and the eyes too demanding.

Jayarajadevi found she could be strong. "Your father was a warrior, and a king and..." How could she put this to a little boy? "Your father was a holy man. He was entirely trustworthy. His beloved King called for a war, and so your father fought. We have been waiting for him to come back. But I do not think he will be coming back. I know he would come back for you if he could. I saw his face when he held you for the first time, and there was never a father so proud of his son. Your father loved you."

The little boy's face was a blank. He had never seen his father; his father meant nothing to him and perhaps never would.

"Is he dead?" the little boy asked.

"Warriors often die," said Jayaraja, her voice as light as a butterfly.

"Am I King, then?" He looked only slightly baffled.

"Not yet. We do not know for certain that your father is dead. And you will only be a king here. Your name is a loving name, but it is a dangerous one."

Indradevi Kansru came bearing a wide bronze tray piled high with rice and fruit.

"Oh, look," said Jayarajadevi. "Food. Beautiful food."

The little boy held out fat greedy hands, like flowers opening. Like life.

The new King of the Chams was simply dressed.

He wore a jacket, but it was not quilted and embroidered. It was silk, but brown, and he wore no crown or tiara, or anything wound into his hair. It was simply pulled back into a bun.

Jayavarman was allowed to rise up onto his knees.

"I am sorry you have been so badly treated. We did not know that you were Rajanga, or we would not have sent you to the fields." The Cham King made a circular gesture with his hands: turn around, sit cross-legged, and be comfortable.

Jaya found it difficult to shift himself and to assemble words. "I...My commander wanted me dead so he tried to put twelve parasols all around me, to attract attention. I sent them away and dressed like a common soldier."

"A good survival technique," said the King. "Except if you're captured." His intent was fixed and his mouth firm in a half-smile. Sanskrit gave both the Chams and the sons of Kambu their formal titles. The language permitted subtlety of thought, expression, and treachery.

"Was that commander called Yashovarman?"

Jaya's face felt heavy and soft like old fruit. All he could do was nod yes.

"Ah."

Jaya prodded himself: think. Quickly.

The Cham said, "Suryavarman is dead."

It was news Jaya had been expecting. Suryavarman had lived too long and became foolish in his old age. God should not let kings get old.

Then Jaya remembered the old King, as tall and skinny as a mantis with his smart clicking brain and his knife-point eyes. Always making buildings and schemes, and never loving. Marrying a Cham for alliance, never fathering a child, putting his wife's brother on the throne here. Poor man.

Jaya needed time to think.

He asked about the fate of the previous Cham King. "What happened to Harideva?"

"Oh." The new King's voice was mild. "I killed him. I used to be called Harirajadeva."

One of the warring princes, Jayavarman remembered, the head of a faction.

"But now I am called Jaya-Harideva. We both like that word, Jaya, perhaps." Victory. "I've managed to stop the Chams fighting each other and unite them. Champa is not part of your kingdom any longer. It is not even an ally of Kambujadesa."

Jayavarman nodded. "And Yashovarman is now Universal King. And you need to know more about him."

The King smiled. "I'm sorry, I appear to be offering you the chance to become a traitor to your Lord, which nobody of any merit would welcome. You're a Buddhist, I understand?"

Blackmail, threats, inducements?

"Champa's relationship with Buddhism is different to the one your people have; we're closer to it. We were a Buddhist kingdom for a while. So, you might find that we understand your beliefs better than many of your allies."

"If you are about to offer me a chance to depose Yashovarman, you need to know that it is unthinkable that a Buddhist could become Universal King."

The Cham held up an intervening hand. "I am offering you an easier life here. It's ridiculous wasting a man like you hauling rocks or transplanting rice. We'd like to give you a chance to study in one of our monasteries."

Jaya waited.

The Cham shifted suddenly where he sat. He thrust himself forward. "My friend, the Khmers under Suryavarman marched against the Siamese. They marched south to Malaysia. They tried to make us join their wars against the Ammanites and now most disastrously the Dai Viet. They have been catastrophically defeated by the Vietnamese, and Suryavarman is dead. I need to know. Will the Khmers continue to march against all their neighbours under Yashovarman?"

Jaya's mind churned like mud. He felt off balance, saddened, tears bristling in his eyes. All of this was alarming. "I have been trying not to think about my people," he said. "Or my past. When you live as a slave, remembering another life as a prince produces only pain and anguish. A troubled mind."

The Cham went still. Suddenly, in his eyes there was a humanizing light. "You will be more powerful if those memories have no power over you."

The Way.

Yes, Jaya, you could refuse to think, and go back to being an ox in the mud, which is the fate Yasho would wish for you. You could end your days by eating mud to block your own breathing.

There is no safety for you anywhere and little honor; all courses of action are treacherous. But if you are ever to be anything else, you will have to walk away from those fields.

So. You talk.

Jaya remembered Yashovarman the Ox. Bullying, demanding, but also slow and steady. He had seen Yashovarman with the greatest possible deliberation marry Suryavarman's niece. He had even fathered children with deliberation. Jaya remembered Yasho's face, never smiling, always...always...

Always afraid. Yashovarman the Ox was fearful.

Jaya's mouth spoke and what came out of it was surprising. "He is cautious. Cautious and slow and methodical, and the disasters of the last years of Suryavarman's reign will"—here was another surprise—"frighten him. He is personally fearless, but I think he believes people are innately stupid. All his friends are stupid, blunt people. He shines among them—which must be a matter of policy too—and when he talks to you, he listens to you as if he expects you to be stupid. So. He will not trust Khmer troops to fight and to win."

Something in Jayavarman quickened and he looked up. "I think Yashovarman will stay at home. He is no Suryavarman. He will have plenty of trouble at home."

The Cham King dropped his head with relief and then looked up again. "So, we may have a time of peace?"

"You may. I fear Yasho may have to devote more of his energies to controlling his own people." Jaya found he knew something else. "He will turn out to be smarter than anyone expected. That will cost him."

Jaya looked up and felt something frank and honest shared in the space between them. That was dangerous.

"We have not made good use of you, Khmer who is a Buddhist." Suddenly the Cham King looked playful. "Have you ever seen the ocean?"

April 15, 2004, part one

Map does not look pleased.

"I can bicycle," he says.

His captain replies, "With those hands?"

Map looks at them, turns them over. Rectangular patterns of red and yellow have soaked his gauze bandages. "My hands have been cut up most of my life."

The Patrimony Police all stand in ranks; everyone can hear what Map is saying; all their faces are turned towards the ground. William feels ashamed.

The Captain glances at Sangha. "Map. You have a choice. You can stay and guard the temple or you can go out and help question people. But you don't have a motorcycle, we don't have motorcycles, and the army is holding your bicycle hostage. If you want to help find Ta Barang, and I know you do, you will ride that motorcycle."

Map rolls his lips back in and nods, once.

"Mr. Tan Map," says William, bowing with a sompiah. "I am happy to work for you."

"How much are they paying you?"

"Map!" exclaims the Captain and turns to Sangha and Yeo Narith. "Please accept my apologies for this behaviour."

Sangha is chuckling and shaking his head. "We all know Map. He has a big mouth." The other policemen chuckle. "William is getting his contract price, seven dollars a day, when he works."

"I only get twice that for a whole month," says Map, and turns and walks away, out of the ranks.

They all breathe out, shaking their heads.

The police village is on the eastern side of Angkor Wat, at the end of a causeway that crosses the moat. Single policemen, or police-men working away from their families, live in a terrace of wooden rooms, on top of a small rise. The rooms have no doors. Some are entirely open on one side. In one room, a rank of canvases leans against a wall—stylized, repetitive paintings that one policeman tries to sell to the few tourists who enter Angkor this way. A sign in hand-lettered Khmer offers professional haircuts; someone was once a barber. There is a hand pump that they all wash from, soaping all over, wearing their kramars or shorts, and pouring water from a tin pan over their heads.

On the other side of the causeway is the Captain's house, some-what finer, resting on solid pillars, with a painted gable. There is a small café and bar, and behind all of it, a lopsided laterite wall. A gopura leads to tracks through the forest to the temple.

Map doesn't sleep in the policeman's village. Nobody is too sure where he does sleep. This morning he came strolling down the road from the direction of Banteay Srei. The other men were already all lined up. Map gazed at the tree-tops, stopped, and lit a cigarette— to demonstrate that the Patrimony Police did not own him in the mornings.

William scans that road now, anxiously. The pickup trucks are late. He is saddened to think that the boys he recruited might miss the meeting; that no one will know what he has achieved. The Director of APSARA and the Captain stand side by side. They are worried that the attackers will strike at the Wat or other temples, so most of the Police will still guard those. Some, the best behaved, will repre-sent the Patrimony Police at army roadblocks.

Map sits by himself on a tree root, smoking.

A pickup comes along the moat, its reflection flickering around pond weed. It could be any pickup. William focuses. No, no, it's Ea, he can see the army uniform on the arm resting outside the window. William waves.

The APSARA director breaks off his briefing. "Here come our friends from the army now."

Map laughs aloud and springs to his feet.

"Ah! We are going to have karaoke! Music from AK-47s!"

The ranks stir.

Does William hear the click of a safety?

"They're not the army," says William. Sangha turns to him. "They're people from the town. They want to help."

"Until there is any trouble," says Map.

"There will be no trouble," says the Captain, and Map just laughs.

"They don't know who did this, and they need to find somebody fast, and they want it to be me. That makes trouble, doesn't it, guys?"

The other policemen murmur yes.

The Captain's eyes boggle. Sangha shields his eyes, and shakes his head. He works with Map every day; he knows him well; he likes him.

The police like him. Why? Why does everybody like Map? William needs to know.

The pickup turns and jostles along the unpaved causeway, white dust billowing behind.

They wait.

"They're all kids!" says Map.

William says, "There are also many older people in the town who want to help."

Sangha steps closer to him. "Did you do this, William?"

"Yes. I thought they could help your investigation. Sorry."

"When did you do this?"

"Last night, after I drove you to the Phimeanakas."

Sangha raises his eyebrows. A second pickup is now following the first.

The police and APSARA wait until both pickups swing around and stop. The boys stand up, looking a little wide-eyed at all the policemen. They have been taught to avoid policemen.

Map is laughing. He strides forward. "Deputies!" he calls them, laughing at them. "Fall into ranks." The boys look sheepish. "Come on, come on."

"Map," says his Captain. "What are you doing?

William intervenes. "These are all good boys, sir. They all want to help the police find the Book and bring back the words of Jayavarman. They can go and look in many places. They can ask many people, all over Siem Reap, what they have seen. They feel angry that a foreigner has been kidnapped in their town."

All the right things to say. The boys nod. The APSARA director chuckles. "We seem to have more investigators than we thought."

Map says to them, "Kids, this isn't a game." He holds up his hands. "I got this climbing over razor wire to get away from the army. They were going to beat me up. You want to face the army?" Scars, spots, lumps, the punched-in nose, fingernails like.claws—Map is so breathtakingly ugly that the boys stare in silence. They can see; this is history talking.

Captain Prey intervenes. "The army is working with us, Map."

Map ignores him. "Do you want to help?"

The boys all nod.

"Okay, so get down out of those trucks and tell me what you've heard." Grinning at themselves, at their own daring and clumsiness, the boys jump down.

Map's the only one, William realizes, who is accepting their help. He looks everybody other than me in the eye and talks to them without false politeness. But he does the right thing and everybody respects and likes him.

What is going on here that I do not understand?

The boys say that one of their grandmothers saw a foreigner in a punt on the river, that an uncle saw a busload of Thais leave that morning very quickly. One lad tells them, "My grandfather says everybody in Leung Dai knows the old cadres there took it."

When he hears that, Map's eyes shrink back into themselves, shivering. Only William notices.

Later, Map walks off in the direction of the main road and steps into the forest. He comes back out of uniform.

He wears an old T-shirt, a squashed green cloth cap, shorts, and the thick gloves that farmers sometimes use to clear scrub. They hide his bandages. "Okay. Let's get moving."

William sompiahs. "Yes, Sergeant. Where do you want to go?"

"Leung Dai," Map says, as if to the air.

"You mean where the Book was found. We'll have to go through an army roadblock."

"You drive, don't try to think," says Map.

Heading out past Mebon, they come to a row of vehicles waiting in front of army jeeps.

They coast to a halt. An old farmer, his face rumpled and bright red, continues cycling and the troops shout at him. Confused, he blinks, stops and sompiahs as an army officer strides towards him.

Another officer walks up to William's motorcycle. Map calls the soldiers "sir" and takes out his family ID card. Map says he is going to help a friend clear scrub. The officer scans the card, folds it up carefully, passes it back to Map, and lets them go.

"How did you do that?" William asks.

"You're not paid to ask questions, either," says Map.

They make the rest of the drive in complete silence.

Seven dollars a day, William counsels himself, and a chance to help find Luc.

Luc hears Fish Face, Arn, come back.

He calls the boys idiots, but exuberantly. "There is not a tourist in all of Siem Reap!" he shouts. The engine revs and the boat swings around and away. The sound of the water changes from a relaxing gurgling beat to an exhilarating shoosh. After hours of nothing, any change feels good.

Neatly, quickly, the old man thumps down into the hull.

"I have newspapers, barang. We are famous."

The old man tears the tape off Luc's head and holds up the English-language *Phnom Penh Daily*. "What's this say, barang?"

UN DIG TEAM HEAD KIDNAPPED

SHOTS FIRED ON LAKE

Luc tells him.

The old man laughs, pleased. "You see, General, the barang don't care you're here too."

Gleefully, he pulls away the tape from the General's face as well and thrusts the newspaper at him. He pulls out another one and holds it up for both Luc and the General. It says in round, red Khmer script:

KIDNAPPING IN SIEM REAP

THERE MUST BE NO RETURN TO THE DAYS OF WAR

The color photographs show the New Year panic, the dour-faced mass of people caught in flashlights. In the crowded airport, tourists waited, heads slumped onto their hands.

The old man bounces on his knees. "All the tourists have gone. Think of all the money you are losing, General! I drove through

Angkor to get here. There wasn't one tourist. All those APSARA guys in their blue uniforms sitting there like this." The old man mimes head-in-hands desolation and inactivity.

Luc thinks of William. "Many poor people make their living from tourism."

The old man looked pleased, ready for this. "No, they don't. They get, what, two dollars a day? The biggest room in the Grand Hotel costs two thousand dollars a night! The people who sweep the floors walk hours back to their houses to eat a bowl of rice their families grow for them. The rich run their hotels, the tourists have their air-conditioning, and poor people can no longer afford to live in the town."

Luc tries to mollify him. "All of that is true."

"Nobody wants the Khmers Rouges back, but the things that created them are with us again. People with regional accents go to university only to find they are mocked once more. Gun runners, drug dealers, corrupt people of all kinds come to Siem Reap and look down their noses at honest farmers."

"I'm sorry to hear it."

"You hear what I say, General?" The old man gives him a kick. "You can't live on corruption all the time. You can't sell the whole country to the Thais or the Singaporeans without us knowing it!"

"You are a Khmer Rouge?" the General asks. He sounds aged and frail.

The old man barks at him, "What is coming will make you yearn for the Khmers Rouges. The Pol Pot clique were educated men. They had too much education, they were crazy from it, but they had an ideology that you could understand and argue with. The kids now have guns and and are on drugs and have never been to school. You are lucky it's me and not them."

Luc has never heard talk like this before. "What do you think they will do?"

"Shoot up tourists at Angkor Wat. Maybe hold them hostage. Not because they expect any good from it. Just to stop people like this man."

The old man gives the General's knees a slam with the side of his foot. The General squeals and tries to sit up.

"People like Yimsut Vutthy, they look down, *moel ngeay* on the country people. They are always evaluating us as inferior, *an.*"

The old man drops the newspapers in Luc's lap and works his way back on his haunches into the prow of the hull. He settles with a gun in his lap. "So. Read me what they say in English."

Luc reads and wants to cry. They thought they were doing so well. They thought the country was coming back. "You have been very effective," he says quietly.

"You are right there, barang," says the old man.

Gunfire, panic, evacuation, airports. Nothing about the *Kraing Meas.*

Luc asks, "Where is the Golden Book? Have you sold it?"

The old man gives a sideways smile. "You think everything comes down to money."

Luc's voice goes thin. "Do you still have it safe?"

"Why do you care?" the old man asks.

A very good question. Luc goes quiet. "Because I love Cambodia."

The old man looks at him with his fish's face—unmoving and unreadable, perhaps a bit sullen. "Why?"

"Because when I was young I fell in love with a Cambodian, and ever since then I sometimes see the world through his eyes."

His? *Gloop.* You're tired, Luc. They hate *khutoy.*

The fish face does not move. "You are a very lucky barang," the old man says. What does that mean? The old man is looking at him askance. "You speak good Khmer. You were an old colonial." A dangerous statement.

"I grew up here," says Luc.

"So this is your home. You like coming back here. You're sorry the country is so badly run and you think you could run it better."

"I am glad the French no longer hold it."

"Why?"

"I went to France and found I did not like it."

"But you think the country is badly run."

Luc says, "This is not my country, I cannot say."

The old man laughs at him. Luc goes back to reading aloud, shivering with sweat, hunger, fear, and exhaustion.

He has told the truth. Maybe it was good that he had said "he." Otherwise the story could have been one of a rich barang stealing

Cambodian women. Luc is now utterly dependent on whether an ex-Khmer Rouge hammered by thirty years of war will comprehend a common humanity between them.

How much would he mind dying? Luc is surprised at how little he minds. He's over fifty years old and no genius. There are no great works to complete, no children to support, no wife to grieve. He's eaten superb meals, seen the Pyramids, and spent his life outside Europe, the grey place that bored and oppressed him. Perhaps his years in the East have made him crypto-Buddhist. Perhaps he half-believes in samsara, the cycle, the coming back.

If he died now, he would die content. Filthy and sleepless in a fish-stinking boat.

And fearless.

I never knew that. I always thought I was a terrible coward. Was all that fear a pretence? What did I get out of pretending? Nothing. Absolutely nothing. What a waste.

I'm doing what they tell you to do in this situation. I'm talking to them.

Food comes—rice and steaming land crab. The old man waves at them to eat. He stands up and gets out of the hull. The General looks up at Luc mournfully, like a penned animal, round-eyed and wet. He takes the bowl with shivering hands. Luc puts his own bowl down and helps him, breaking open his crab.

"Ugh!" shudders Vut. The main central body of the crab, its brains and intestines, stinks.

The bandages at the back of Vut's knees almost phosphoresce with orange and green stains.

"You should eat the rice at least," says Luc.

Vut groans again. He's sick. Luc eats only the legs, cracking them open and sucking out the meat.

"You said you loved a man," says Vut.

Luc uses the truth to prevaricate. "I love everybody."

The old man comes down soon after. "You eat this part," he says, and shows Luc how, prising apart the central body. It's full of green gunk. Luc's eyes seem to shine a narrow band of torchlight on the old man's bitten fingernails to see what he does. The old man does not touch the guts but expertly tears out white flesh.

Luc can allow no barriers. He shrugs forward and takes the crab.

Its labyrinthine inner chambers scratch his palms like plastic. He eats as the old man showed him.

The old man munches out a question. "What do barang think about the *khmei kraham*, Khmers Rouges?"

Luc finds his mind is dull. "Nothing of interest. They think they were crazy people who killed many Cambodians. Some of them know that the US bombed your country and kicked out your Prince. Some of them know the US and China supported the Khmers Rouges to keep them fighting the Vietnamese. Most of them know very little. It was a long time ago."

The old man shrugs. "What do you think?" For the first time the old man truly smiles at him, and before Luc can answer, he says, "We were crazy people who killed many Cambodians." He grins, watching Luc's reaction.

"We were angry. That made us stupid." The old man shakes his head. "Angry at all the people who used our country for their own wars, angry at all the city people who were corrupt and scornful. All those city people got bribes, money on the side." His face went harsh. "They deserved to die. I'm glad we killed them."

"But my friend died too. He was a farmer from Kompong Thom."

"Ah," the old man's smile now looks regretful. "What we didn't know was that the High Organisation, the *Angka Loeu*, was run by city roostershit as well. Well, I did, because I knew them all, but I was young and thought that all Cambodians must know about rice. Those jerks knew nothing about rice and farming. They made us do stupid things and we all starved. Everybody. So I learned: no matter what educated people say, there is no one that country people can trust but ourselves."

The old man butts Luc's foot with his heel; rude but not meant to hurt. Arn, Luc tells himself, Arn is teasing me. And it seems that, yes, perhaps there is something friendly about the old man.

The old man says, "Sorry about your friend from Kompong Thom. He was a good man?"

"Very."

"Then that's why he's dead, only bad men are left." Grin. Joke. "Like me."

For a moment the old man looks like Map. The same flash of

hatred of the self, of the world. "Cambodia is at the bottom of the well. The only people who come down here are not the people who hurt us. I am sorry it has to be you."

That you imprison? Or that you are going to have to kill?

The old man reaches back round for his gun. He prods the General's kidneys with it. "This one here? We will eat his liver. Maybe we will cut it out of him while he is still alive. Like we used to do."

Luc urges Vut in English, "Talk to him, for God's sake."

Vut replies in Khmer, "You speak better Khmer than I do."

This amuses the old man, who prods the General with the gun again. Vut reacts like a sack of rice. He needs all his energy to stop himself complaining or crying aloud. Pain takes the form of trickling sweat.

Luc says. "He is a broken man. You've won."

"Not till we eat his liver." The old man turns and grins again.

Luc advances. "He was only trying to earn merit by protecting the Book."

The old man sniffs and shrugs as if under a burden. "Ah! This book. What is this book?"

"It is an ancient book. It is the story of Jayavarman's life, written by himself."

They can hear birds in the reeds, calling. They can hear the slop and gurgle of little waves against the overlapping boards of the hull. Like going fishing with an uncle in the warm afternoon.

First, the old man looks solemn. Then he looks angry. "It is our book!" he insists.

"Yes, it is," says Luc.

"Barang," he says, sneering like Elvis Presley. He leans back and looks at Luc with narrowed eyes. "You say you love Cambodia. So do I. I am going to do something very Cambodian with that book. And if you can guess what that is, I will let you live."

It's a game, without significance. The old man could shoot him anyway. Luc finds that he is genuinely smiling. "Okay," Luc says lightly. "Will you let the General live too?"

"Mmmm," replies the old man with no commitment, looking up and down the barrel of his rifle. His smile now looks like Luc's; he likes Luc's acceptance of the basic terms. This is indeed a game, only with bullets.

"How long do I have?"

The old man levels the gun directly at Luc's forehead. "As long as you need. But only one guess."

Well, I could stew for weeks and still get it wrong.

The lapping of the water, the crying of the birds. Time is measured in pulses of thought. Think quickly, and time slows. Speed can make time infinite. So I have as long as I need.

I know he does not want us to have the Book, and I know he regards the Book as his, "he" being the people of Cambodia, but the people for him are country people only; he will not want barangs touching it, translating it to other tongues for other people. He will not want the General and all the people who defeated him and his kind to gain any merit or make any money from the Book. He certainly will not want Thai art dealers to get it. He wants to shoot it over all our heads, but keep it safe and warm and sheltered. He would push it back in time if he could, or push it forward.

What the hell.

Luc says, "I can guess now."

That rouses the General. *"Preah-ang Buddha!"* he whispers.

Keep it simple, Luc.

"I think you are going to take the Book and bury it again."

The fish face freezes. Then the old man bursts out laughing. "Barang!" he roars, this time with approval. He leans back laughing and shaking his head, looking like a happy drunken farmer at a party.

A good Cambodian joke now would be to shoot Luc anyway.

Luc advises him. "Wrap it back up in the same bundles of ten leaves. Don't wrap it in anything modern. Wrap it in the same orange linen."

"Maybe I should burn it so it goes up to heaven!" Eyes twinkling, he scans Luc's face for signs of dismay. The old man then murmurs an emollient sound, as if in some way Luc's correct guess had been a victory for both of them. "What's your name, barang?"

"My personal name is Luc."

"Luc? Luc?" says the old man, his eyes widening. He laughs. Luc suddenly hears his name as a Khmer word. "Luc" means something like "reaching into."

"Are you reaching into a hole to catch a rabbit? Teacher Luc, reaching down and into. That's a good name for you!"

Still chuckling he shuffles forward and tapes shut their mouths. They are going to live a little while longer. To Luc's surprise, he hears the old man's boat start up. It heads off in the opposite direction from which it came.

Luc thinks: he said he knew the Angka Loeu.

That means he knew Pol Pot.

September 1960

The station in Phnom Penh: rain drumming endlessly on the roof.

The Battambang train arrives glossy as if with sweat. Shorts and headscarves are soaked; flip-flops squelch. People's foreheads reflect light through the windows like billiard balls as they hoist up suitcases, cages filled with hens, or bicycles.

The train blows out as if finally able to relax.

Saom Pich feels his way down from the carriage. He is eighteen years old and this is his first time on a train, his first time in the capital. He hopes to pass for a city person. His best clothes—trousers and a good pair of sandals—are smeared with soot and smudged water.

Down to the end of the platform, the brothers said, then turn left and find the row of offices on the other side of the track.

Saom Pich has great difficulty seeing. A train door slams behind him. Some functionary runs past Pich, his white shirt a blur. He fell asleep on the train and now has to run back to his office job.

Pich gets lost. It's nearly dark. Sounds echo high overhead. He looks up and dimly sees a huge vaulted ceiling with round arches. Is that a row of ticket windows to his left? He can hear windows sliding down, clicking shut. The echoes of footfalls are fading away. Already the train station is almost empty.

Pich mops his brow and carefully retraces his steps.

He certainly cannot say, Excuse me, sir, can you tell me where the Second National Congress of the Kampuchean People's Revolutionary Party is being held?

It has been an adventure to take the boat from the country to one big city, and then a train to another. The noise, the mud, the signs, the shouting of people, the sound of so much Chinese, so much French, all of it confounds him. The way some of the women sound as they walk—click, click, click, swish, swish, swish—he can hear that they wear entirely different clothes, lead an entirely different life. They smell of soap, perfume, and alcohol. Pich clings to—what?—his presence. His presence of mind, his sense of self.

I am the real Cambodia. I am who they need to know. They need to listen to people like me.

Pich sees lights to his right. He wanders into the toilets by mistake. They are made of concrete with tiles and taps and smell of soap and sweetness. We use tree-shadow and earth.

Someone comes in and says hello and asks, "What province are you from?"

Lon Nol's secret police?

"Siem Reap," Pich finally admits. He traces the wall towards the door. He can clearly see a pattern of black flecks embedded in the yellow tiles.

"I'm from Kandaol," says the other man. All fourteen provincial representatives are meeting. Could he be referring to that? "Can I help you find something?"

"No, thank you. I am just leaving."

Then the voice says, "Are you Saom Pich?"

Pich pretends not to hear and keeps walking.

"I ... I was asked to look out for Saom Pich."

Pich grunts. The man shuffles ahead of him, probably deliberately dragging his flip-flops. He opens a door and a murmuring of voices cuts short, and there is a flood of light. The man seems to pause at the entrance. Waiting for Pich?

If this is the secret police, they already have my name.

Pich goes in.

Through the fog he can see a sudden and relieved smile. "Comrade," says the smile.

Inside is a hot and tiny room with paint so peeling even Pich can see the patches. In that tiny room twenty other people are crowded, sitting on window sills or along the one desk.

"*Notre camarade de la campagne*," one of them says, swift as a knife.

Pich recognizes the downturned smile of Nuon Chea.

"How goes the struggle in the country?" Nuon Chea asks, the friendliest of them to Pich, and to an extent his mentor.

"We do what we can," says Pich. "Sihanouk has been very successful at eliminating opposition. I am alone. I have no information. I need support."

Nuon Chea smiles. "We are your support, Saom Pich. We are your library, your books." Nuon Chea waves Pich forward.

It has been such a long and tense trip, and to finally be greeted, teased slightly and promised help all at once, is welcome and pleasing. Pich feels himself smile, and the smile seems to ricochet around the tiny, hidden, peeling room. There is a fog of chuckles for him.

In the corner is the huge beaming smile of Saloth Sar.

Pich can recognize Keo Meas and Sao Phim. Thiounn Mumm nods; his brother works with railway cadres, which is how they got this room. The non-party member Ieng Sary smiles through smoke and tobacco stains, more fog.

There are no introductions. Any names used are nicknames. From time to time, people address Saloth Sar as Pot.

"Comrades," says Saloth Sar. "Our situation is perilous. The Sihanouk authorities savagely oppress the mass-struggle movement. Many members have been arrested and killed. Others have wavered and abandoned their duty."

Only last year, the in-country leader of the party defected.

"Of our old established leaders only one is left."

That is not quite true, there are other old guard cadres in the room, but Tou Samouth is still head of the party. There is a murmuring and dipping of heads towards someone sitting next to Saloth Sar. Pich squints, trying to get some idea of who Tou Samouth is as a person.

And why he is so silent and weak? Pich knows what this congress is about—replacing the old guard with all these educated young men from France.

Including the mysterious, sweet-voiced Saloth Sar.

Who spends the next five minutes praising the international revolutionary effort and the brotherhood of the Laotian, Cambodian, and Vietnamese peoples.

He's good at this, thinks Pich. You know there is a contradiction to follow and you sit smiling and waiting for it. I'd follow him. I've seen through him, but I would follow him. I think he's probably at his best sweet-talking students and sounding like everybody's idea of an enlightened man.

Sar summarizes. That same month, the Vietnamese workers party had resolved to liberate South Vietnam.

"And of course we support them in this. And of course they look to us to work primarily towards this aim."

The liberation of someone else's country. I see where this is going.

"That is why our comrades asked us to hold this meeting in circumstances of great danger. We are being asked to support a monarch because of his supposed anti-imperialist stance."

While he is murdering us.

Saloth Sar continued. "And because he supports the Vietnamese in their just war against American imperialism."

This, Pich realizes, is an anti-Vietnamese cadre.

Which could be useful. Some country people hate the yuon. All those ancient stories of the Vietnamese using Cambodian heads to make a table for their teapot.

But being anti-Sihanouk as well? Is that wise?

"The people love Sihanouk," interjects Pich. After all, I am a blunt country fellow.

"Indeed, they do." All Pich can see is the forgiving smile. "An example of false consciousness."

"He was more clever than we were at claiming credit for getting rid of the French. The people love Cambodia, and so love him. If I understand you correctly, Comrade Pot, the idea is to use nationalism to build a movement of class struggle."

Saloth Sar has to chuckle, and Pich thinks he sees the man's eyes widen. "You do not need books, Comrade."

Pich knows then that this man makes assumptions. He thinks a blind country person does not read. It is only things out of arm's reach that I can't see. I can read. I read anything I can, all the time. Which is why I am a dedicated and useful cadre.

And why I know that mingling nationalism and socialism has produced deadly effects elsewhere.

The representative of Siem Reap province leans back and lets the debate trail on.

They are soft, fat, friendly, Paris-educated, and aggressive, thrusting everyone else out of their way. A Communist should have no other virtues save one: they fight for communism. What happens if they have no virtues and spend most of their time fighting for position?

Rain starts to drum again on the roof. Pich begins to wish he'd used the toilet when he had the chance.

"To work, comrades," says Saloth Sar.

He coughs, then smiles with a self-deprecation that may not be entirely feigned. "We are small in number. Our friends and colleagues from the days of Issark are dispersed or in Hanoi. We must assist our Vietnamese comrades in any way we can. Our situation is utterly perilous and so we masquerade as teachers or functionaries. What are we to do? Go home and give up?"

Pich corrects him. "Some of us are rice farmers."

Saloth Sar's eyes seem almost fond. "Some of us are rice farmers," he says in a warm, gentle voice.

Pich's turn to relent. "And no, we do not go home and give up."

"No, Comrade," says Saloth Sar in a low, warm voice that suggests he is near tears. "No. We do not give up." He coughs. "So what is left to us?"

Pich is surprised to hear this from Sar. That is indeed the question, the only question worth asking.

Nuon Chea speaks. "We begin again. I propose that we here form a new movement that is more responsive to our unique situation."

Saom Pich inwardly groans. How many names do we have to give ourselves? We will now spend two days writing a constitution and electing new members to give the new brotherhood power.

And that is what they do for the next hour. They discuss a new name. Saloth Sar says, "I propose the foundation of the Workers Party of Kampuchea. Workers because we are socialists. Workers because we are teachers, functionaries, clerks, and rice farmers. Party because we are a united movement however small, comrades together.

Saloth Sar glances about him with sadness and love at the tiny room, the tiny party. "And Kampuchea because we are also a nationalist, self-reliant movement of the Khmer people."

Pich asks, "What are we going to do?"

Nuon Chea chuckles, very heartily considering it is the middle of someone else's talk.

Sar answers. "Be dedicated to socialism and to anti-imperialism and"—getting to what is different—"to the real people of Kampuchea."

Pich says, "Me."

Sar says with his slow warm voice. "Yes, Comrade."

"Who else?"

Nuon Chea chuckles.

"Those who demonstrate by their actions that they recognize the Khmer people."

"By doing what?" Pich is bored, fervent, and unfooled.

Sar is doing a good job of not being annoyed. "That is for the party to decide. There must first be a party."

Pich says, "So okay, we all risked prison by coming here, that is a party. What I want to hear, Comrade, is what we are going to do to help my brothers."

Pich's poor eyes cannot see who speaks next. "I think we might say...in advance of discussion...that we will privilege them."

Pich is hungry. "How?"

The same voice. Pich peers. He finally sees a face that looks like a skull with the lightest covering of skin. He looks a bit like the skinny little librarian back home. "By giving them jobs. By making sure that all jobs are open to them. Perhaps...if only foreigners have a skill, by making sure that the foreign specialists work for them?"

Pich says, "Through socialist revolution."

The skinny librarian nods. "If the people think as you do, we have already won."

Pich corrects him. "Socialism deals with class, not nationality."

Sar is backed into a corner. "Perhaps..." He shrugs. He looks about him. "This would need debating. But. They are colonists. Perhaps we send them home."

They? Pich checks to make sure he has understood. "The Chinese. The Vietnamese. The Chams. The ethnic minorities?"

Sar sounds more firm. "It needs debate."

Pich makes a sound like wind between his teeth. Why does this feel as if it has gone utterly off the rails? Why does it feel like the train has crashed into the station?

"The Chinese kill pigs because we feel our religion forbids killing and so we eat pork. Many Vietnamese lead blameless lives fishing on boats."

Sar nods. "We are not talking about those."

Pich realizes something. You have never even seen them. You have never been anywhere near them. You have not had to share the same bed with them. You have not had their sweat flicked into your mouth as you work together. You have not looked at their laughing beautiful daughters with delight.

Pich considers. "So. We are talking about our oppressors in the cities."

A murmuring of assent. But, thinks Pich, the oppressors in the cities are your own families.

Pich asks again, "What actions are you suggesting?"

Sar shakes his head. "We need your ideas, it is the discussion."

"The yuon, the jeun, the Chams—they do not have homes to go back to. They have fished the lake from the time of their grandfathers. They came here as envoys from China in the time of Jayavarman. They are Chams, who have been in Indochina as long as we have, and became Muslim when they intermarried with Malays. What we have to do is welcome them instead."

Sar's turn to say, "How?"

And for this, Pich is ready, he has imagined this, dreamed this, for a long, long time. "We take them into our homes. We take them out of Phnom Penh, away from their cars and their bars and their *lycées* and their ballet. We take them away from their banks and their stalls and their sweatshops. We take them to our villages and say: work with us, live like us. If we do that, they will become us. We will all be home. We will all become Khmer."

Nuon's downward mouth dips even lower. This may or may not be a smile. How would you know if this man is pleased? "Re-education."

"No. A change of situation, leading to a change of heart. A stripping away of class. Not nationality. I don't need the Chams to be Khmer, I need them to be brothers. That's different."

"A stripping away of class, not nation," offers Ieng Sary. He approves.

There is a kind of warm chuckling as if they are all toasting a colleague with warm white spirit.

Geoff Ryman

"This is just the kind of debate we need to be having," says Sar. "Action, Comrades! Shall we vote? Shall we be a party? Shall we be called the Workers Revolutionary Party of Kampuchea? Hands up for yes."

All hands go up together.

Things get rapidly less interesting. They discuss governance. They discuss procedure. They talk about it all the next day. They get very excited about lines of reporting, independence of cells, and formulation of policy.

We may be small, but we do have power over our own administration.

The agenda of the meeting is fulfilled. They elect officers to carry out their administrative schemes of governance.

Ieng Sary is elected Number Four. Saloth Sar is elected Number Three despite his speech. Even Nuon Chea is only elected Number Two. Tou Samouth is made Secretary-General.

Someone is elected Number One, but this proceeds through a series of facial expressions that are a blur to Pich. There are shared smiles, raised eyebrows, and satisfied closings of eyes. Who was Number One? Something? A principle? They all seem to derive pleasure from it, and laugh out load when Pich asks, "So who is Number One?"

At a secret meeting in the train station of Phnom Penh in 1960, Saom Pich was elected a showpiece Brother Number One, and did not even know it.

The man with a librarian's face got him a pair of glasses.

The glasses were the greatest thing the party ever did for him. He used those glasses to read the rumples around Saloth Sar's smile.

Two years later Secretary-General Tou Samouth vanished. That tended to happen to Saloth Sar's closest friends and allies. He later declared that he and Samouth loved each other.

He destroyed the reputation of Nuon Chea, forcing him to resign. Saloth Sar then controlled the party.

With his mentor gone, Pich adopted a policy of silent and effective administration. He cultivated the librarian Ta Mok and did nothing to attract the friendship of Saloth Sar.

In 1963 Pol Pot and Ieng Sary fled for the maquis, and almost unnoticed the wars began.

April 1152

Jaya had not known that the sky could look like the inside of oyster shells.

He had not known that in a country by the sea, the beaches would be polished hard by the water like wood. The sand here reflected the sky like mother of pearl. Sky, sea, and sand would merge.

The wind would change, blowing one way in the morning and another way in the evening. In high winds, the sea would dance, as if churned by white horses.

On dry days, blowing sand would sting his ankles like biting insects.

On some mornings, mist clung to the shore, muting both light and sound. Sometimes rain would come and go and come again, all in the space of a day, trailing rainbows. Some evenings, mountains of clouds floated overhead, with sunsets of their own.

The fish tasted different. The air tasted different, salty. Was it cooler? Were people happier here, more relaxed, laughing as they pushed the hulls of their flat-bottomed boats shushing over sand?

Jayavarman, also called Buddhist-Khmer, would get up each morning from a bed of straw, and stretch and look out over the lines of palm trees. The sound of the wind blowing through them would mingle with the sound of surf.

The hills rising up suddenly behind him were always green. The sky was always pregnant with rain; there was no dry season. The vivid lime of the fields and orchards hurt the eyes. There were no wild forests here, full of beasts. The land by the sea was crossed and crossed again with waterways, roads, pathways, temples, fields, and villages.

The buildings were different too. The Chams built their temples out of brick, not stone. Their Buddhist shrines were made of wood.

"Let the buildings die too," said the monks. "Everything rises and then fades."

Each morning, turning away from the pearly sunrise, Jaya would look at his family and feel the flower of love open up in his breast.

On a bed of straw, as warm as the landscape, was his wife. Her face was delicate: a tiny jaw, wide cheekbones, a ridged nose. Enfolded in her arms, their first child slept. Cat always kept his body covered. Their son had twisted, undeveloped limbs and sparse hair. Their beautiful, angry little cripple rocked his head trying to move, tossing his legs that would never walk.

He was the child of overwork and hunger. They had decided not to have children born into slavery; they had tried to withhold themselves but in the end the need for love was too strong for them.

Jayavarman looked at their house, at the bare wooden floors, the straw bed, their few garments hanging from rafters, and their measures of rice in reed urns mixed with rat droppings. He heard the morning song of sea gulls, surf, and hissing sand.

A kiss on the hollow cheeks of his wife, on her fine-boned temple, and on the fragile mouth. A loving, yearning groan from her. The sweet milky smell of the baby.

Then to work.

Love made his step light. Love of the trees, the broad beaches with their hushed surf, the pathway, his family, the birds, the sky, and the silhouette of the temple. Jayavarman's step was cat-like, prowling on perfectly placed legs, alert, and somehow predatory.

His job was to sweep.

Sweep and ensure the water vats were not only full but pure, no crust of leaves or insects.

The crust was removed by scooping it out and pouring the water that came with it over himself, over his feet, drenching and washing his clothes as he wore them.

He put straw on the brazier, breathing life into the fire. Then he set water to boil for the tea and the rice noodles and he swept the temple floors. After that, he sprinkled water over the swept ground, and by then the water was boiled.

He served tea and noodles to his master, and massaged the old man's knotted shoulders and freckled flesh.

"You have not yet clothed the images," the Master said, slurping noodles. The Master was a tiny, embittered man, and Jaya had long ago given up expecting wisdom from him. All the Master had was scholarship. Jaya smiled as he massaged the old man, bowed from too much reading.

Jaya no longer thought of himself as ignorant. Firstly, because he was quietly learning everything this scholar had to teach him, and secondly because he knew now that wisdom came from doing. This poor, frightened, wheedling little soul had done nothing all his life. Jaya beamed on him, as detached as the sun.

"I will clothe the images as soon as you are happy that I have finished here."

"I do not wish to have to take responsibility for everything," said the Master. Jaya smiled. The man took responsibility for nothing. "I should not have to remind you. Have you looked at the water?"

"Yes, Master."

He's afraid of me, poor soul. He knows who I am, even though I have tried to disguise it, and he is terrified. He knows I remember everything he tells me. He knows from the questions I ask that I am his equal in mind. He knows from my smile that he has absolutely no power over me.

He knows that his King comes to see me once a year, and treats me, within limits, as a person of rank.

At times, I even think that Hari chose this man as my master deliberately, to teach me both knowledge and disrespect for it.

"Master, repeat to me another *jataka*."

"Tooh! You have been told enough jatakas for a servant."

"Nevertheless, Master, they are an inexhaustible fount of wisdom."

And the old man, who had to do something with his time, told him another tale of the Buddha in one of his previous lives.

"And what," Jaya asked him, "are the duties of a king?"

To be abundant in generosity, to show by example, to attain wisdom and compassion. To care for his people as if they were his own children, to know their anguish and their pain. To care and, having cared, act.

It was an idea of kingship that touched Jaya deeply.

He remembered Suryavarman, crazed by the desire to expand the boundaries of his kingdom. A wizened stick of man, as if he were a roasted chicken sucked dry by his own ambition. The old, dry bones had a marrow of love that no one had tasted.

Jaya thought of the Cham King, all wise policy, his good kind heart always at war with the need for a king to be a warrior. A sword resting on his lap even when at peace, even when welcoming allies.

He thought of Yashovarman, inflating himself to an enormous physical size to hide his bestilled heart. Yasho was like a ship on a lake without a breath of wind to fill its sails. He would be a king secretly consumed by fear and inactivity.

Gradually, the thought had come, as he massaged the bookish, withering shoulders: I know how to be a king better than any of them.

A king would be almost invisible, not out of fear, but in order to be powerful over a broad range of action. A king would need to be able to walk his kingdom in peace without pomp, so he could talk to people without causing fear. A king would gain power by listening, knowing what was actually happening in the temple fields, or in the village lofts. Having bathed his people in the glow of his attention, he could gently tell them stories, small quiet stories that would guide them onto the Dharma, the Path.

Such a king would have no need of war to aggrandize his glory. Indeed, war would be the distracting, draining enemy of his task. War would destroy the wealth he had built up; it would take him and his mind away from the people he was getting to know. Such a king would gain his power from the love of his people. His people would love him and defend him. Inspired by him, they would work towards merit in this life and progress in the next.

Who among the people had loved distant, insect-like Suryavarman, when their sons had been killed in war? Who would love the swollen Yashovarman, occupied with rites and rituals and buying the favour of the Gods?

A good king would content himself with a land no bigger than a day's walk.

Such a king would live in happiness in a small palace, open to all, a place as tranquil and beautiful and holy as any temple, where visible virtue and kindness took the place of invisible gods and expensive images of them.

Such a king would live in such a place as his family home, off in the low hills, by a small undistinguished river that yet provided fish and irrigation. Such a kingdom would be far away from the exhortations and rituals of the City. It would be safe in its humility: no threat to the Universal King.

One day at dusk, having been beaten with a fly whisk for charring his master's grilled fish, Jayavarman squatted on the ground under his one-room house. He tickled the ears of the guard dog and looked at the plump and contented hens picking at the ground. His tiny world.

His tiny wife was blue in the dusk, as if carved of turquoise. He smiled up at her with love. "Are you with child, Wife?"

"No, no, why do you ask?"

"Because we are going to walk home."

Cat's eyes boggled, and then she went still. "Is that wise?"

Jaya smiled and shrugged. "Of course not, no. But I have learned all I can here. And life is suddenly flowering within me."

"How far is home?"

He had no idea. "Many weeks' walk? We have to go south, where there is a pass through the hills."

"How will we eat?"

"I will carry rice. We will fish and catch crickets. We will eat."

"And," Cat swallowed, "go home to your wife."

"I have more than one wife. Many men do." He pulled Cat to him, and kissed her.

She looked sad, but ready. "A king cannot have a slave for a wife. People will say you broke the natural order. They will say"—she indicated their son and his shrivelled limbs—"that our son is what comes of intermarrying."

"You are a slave no longer, Cat."

She put a finger on his lips to silence him. "Then I have a choice. I can stay here, among these people, and let you go. I might be able to bear it. Or I could go with you and be"—she sighed—"whatever you think best for me to be. Once you return you will be a king."

"You will be a lady of the house…"

Her eyes were steady. "It would be better for you to give me the most likely answer."

He sighed helplessly. "A kind of a wife. A wife in my heart."

Geoff Ryman

She blew out. "Consort. Favourite concubine."

"That's how it will be seen, that is why we should marry..."

"And what will you say when people ask who my grandfather was? Shush. A consort. A king's consort. Let's see how it works." She moved towards the door of their hut. Surf was hissing up onto the beach. "I will miss this little house."

The King put his arm around her. "It has not been a bad life." They both had been perfectly contented with their daily round, the oyster-colored sky, and the smell of Cat's own milk.

They slipped away from the hut, bearing their loving burdens of baby and rice, and it was as easy as making love. They walked into night and a different history.

Night was their cloak.

They walked at night, fished and ate at night. Day was their time of rest. They hid in reeds or scrub, shading their eyes, listening to wind billow through leaves. They tensed when they heard the crackle of peasant footsteps on paths.

Jaya and Cat left the coastal plain and climbed up into the hills. Skirting the main trails, they dodged through airy mountain forests streaked with tall, white-trunked trees.

Finally they came to the Wat where travelers decamped. There they joined a caravan of traders, who would give protection from the hill tribes.

Hidden among so many people, they climbed up into clouds. Cat shivered, never having experienced air so cool. Shawls over their heads disguised who they were. Rain was another veil to cover their faces. The mountains closed in on either side, and the mist cloaked them from the view of the military towers.

At Buon Me Thout the caravan came to the Srepok River that gushed through the passes, westward all the way down to the great Mekong. The trail sloped downwards.

All along the narrow Srepok valley, the Cham army camped. Crouched amid other travelers, Jayavarman saw the night fires of the army along the hilltop trails. From below he heard the raucous laughter of soldiers and the shouting of their wrestling matches. Walking past their encampments, he smelled the heads left on stakes to terrify tribesmen and fugitives.

202

So Jaya and Cat took to the night again. They swam down the river, tied together with ropes made of their own clothing, Jaya holding the baby over his head. As quiet as moonlight, they rode the river's currents, dreading rapids and crocodiles. Fish brushed past them and took tiny bites of their legs.

The river widened, becoming swift and rippling. They waded through shallows or marched on the banks, struggling through thorny scrub. By day they slept as best they could, hidden in thickets.

Once they were seen by tribesmen. They were fishing from rocks at sunset, heard a cry, and looked up to see men with tattoos on their faces. The tribesmen might have been friendly, but Jaya and Cat ran nevertheless, swift and hardened of foot.

They joined another caravan. It followed the Srepok westward down out of the hills onto a dusty plain. They arrived with a great wave of folk at the confluence with the Mekong. There was a town with houses on stilts. An old man greeted them in Khmer.

All along the banks were landings and skiffs for ferrying people across, but Jaya had no money for the fare. The old man turned out to work on the ferry. He let them cling to the stern of the boat as it was rowed across. They hung on to the ferry, trailing in the water and shivering inside, for the Mekong was full of devouring asura-fish and crocodiles.

They stood up on the opposite bank and were home. Now Jaya and Cat could walk openly on the road, south and west from the northern confluence.

Dawn here was silver. The sky was silver with white dust, the soil bleached, the trees sparse and spreading far ahead on the flat, dry ground. Their feet were grey like ash.

Sunset was copper, even more stained by dust. The low light made everything glow.

They came upon category houses by a river. "I think this is it," said Jayavarman. He shuddered with something like a chuckle. "I don't quite remember."

Then over the tops of trees, they saw glowing and golden the modest temple towers of the Eastern Buddha. They walked dazed, hollow-eyed, not sure they entirely believed they were there, wondering what kind of welcome they would have.

Here, it was an evening like any other. The market was empty except for some children playing in a puddle. They came to the wall that surrounded the central complex. It was decorated with the usual sandstone carvings of celestial maidens and kalas, but Cat saw now how much more graceful they were than the rounded heaviness of Cham statues. She was grateful.

The gatehouse was guarded. The soldier demanded, "Who are you, peasant?"

Jaya replied in a low, calm voice. "Bring the lady of the house and she will know me." His eyelids sagged.

Cat held the child and found she had wound him up in her thin scarf, to hide his bent and twisted legs.

"You have served here before?" the guard asked. He eyed Fishing Cat. If your little slave husband bores you, woman, you would find a real man under this armour; perhaps you like a fighting man better, no? He rocked on his heels, grinning.

Fishing Cat made her lip curl in disgust. A fat oaf like you? She bounced her son as if he were firm and healthy.

The guard had no other use for her. "No one cares for the likes of you. Come back tomorrow. Or don't come back at all. We have a full supply of nia and pual and kamlaa."

Jaya answered, "We are none of those."

"Whatever you are, get out of here."

Jaya smiled. "Why do you despise category people?"

"You have no courage, you work in fields."

Jaya's eyes gleamed like the sunset. "What would you eat, without category people?"

"Yah. It is your role to make food so that I can fight."

Jaya still smiled. "I wonder what a king makes of soldiers? I think some kings think soldiers only exist to die for them, to make them great."

The soldier wanted to show he was up to thinking. "I was more virtuous than you and so I was born of a higher rank."

Ah, thought Cat, if a soldier can say that then the people here are all educated. Jaya's head jerked back with amusement. "Then I would make sure you are as virtuous in this life as you were in the last."

"I could strike you down," said the guard.

Jaya's voice was as gentle as wind in the reeds. "No, you couldn't."

The guard discovered that he did not really want a fight. The wind whispered with a hollow sound as if blowing through a clean-pecked skull.

There was a sound of tiny bells tinkling with the rhythm of walking. Sandals flapped on the paved courtyard. A woman's voice was raised as she approached. "Who is this man, Liver? Do we know him?" She was perhaps a little put out by having to cross the courtyard herself. "I saw him from the upper floor."

The woman stood in the gateway, and turned towards them. Her face went still. Cat's heart was as bated as her breath—was this his wife?

"Hello, Sister," said Jayavarman.

The woman was lean and handsome, with a diadem on her brow and a tiara above that. A shawl of gold embroidery warmed her shoulders. Fishing Cat could not help but duck and lower her head in respect.

"Jaya?" the woman whispered in a wan, heart-stricken voice. "Jaya?" A rising note of hope. "O Jaya!" A squeal of joy, as if a heart was an egg to be broken open.

"Jaya, Jaya, Jaya!" This great lady hopped up and down like an excited child. She bounced overjoyed into his arms, and he hugged her and picked her up and swung her around. "Kansru," he said and his voice broke apart into sobs. "Oh, 'Sru, I'm home."

The woman covered her face, and tears streaked it. She put her hands delicately on his chest. Then she turned and wailed into the house. "Sri! Sister! Jaya! Jaya, he's hoooooome!" The word home was a lost eagle wail. "The King has come home to us! 'Sri!"

Then she gave a quick, questioning look at Cat. A woman with a child?

The sound of sandals running and a wailing voice. "Husband! Hus-band!"

The three of them fell against each other and wept. Fishing Cat waited outside the circle, listening to the wind.

The last of the light faded, and Jayavarman reached out an arm for Cat and pulled them all together.

The King called a banquet for all the household.

He went to the kitchens himself and called for rice and noodle dishes and fish and vegetables to be cooked and laid out in all the household bronze dishes as if honored guests had traveled from afar.

Then he invited the kitchen girls, the temple workers, and his soldiers. He invited the fat guard at the door. When he had learned who he had insulted, the man had flung himself flat on the ground. The King said to him, "You were mistaken, and we are all mistaken sometimes." He put a hand on the guard's shoulder. "But do not combine foolishness then, with foolishness now. Get up and show respect, as a man would to his uncle."

The household was a duststorm of joy. Curtains were taken down and washed and rehung properly, fresh and golden. The category people, knowing that they were to fill their bellies, cleaned all the halls with a will, pursuing dust and spiders and rooting them out of corners. The halls were so full of the sound of flapping sandals and bare feet running that it was as if they had been invaded by flocks of birds.

The King was as tireless as the sturdy working women. He followed them in their work, asked after their husbands and children. If someone was sick, he made sure that the apothecaries came with medicines.

On the night of the banquet, the hall glowed with burnished bronze, and the Little King stood up in their midst.

He wore silk, but with no flowered embroidery, brown silk as if he were a monk.

"My household, my children, and the children of my household. I am home. I have traveled far and faced dangers to be back among you. First I was guarded as a prisoner and then regarded as an equal by the Cham King. I escaped, and I am home. Home with my beautiful wife, Victory Queen Holy, whose first name I took."

There was another woman with him, as simply dressed as he was. Brown silk, fine stuff but simple. Some kind of consort, best not to question a king too closely.

"All of us together will create a new Path," said their Little King. "Our quiet, prosperous, happy fields will be like a corral that is kept safe for cattle. No one will notice at first. People notice war, not tranquillity. But as part of that corral, I will restock and rededicate the hospital here, for all to use, every category of person."

Sompiahs and a polite warbling of approval.

"This house will be open to all who need succour and comfort. If a hungry person comes, we will feed him. Rest houses will be built next to my own house for the weary. Then we will build a school. My great-hearted wife Jayarajadevi has shown the way to me. We will build schoolrooms for all the children of the Eastern Buddha so that all can earn merit through wisdom. All of these things will be consecrated in the name of Lokesvara, the creator, and Gotama, the Buddha, and to the memory of my parents."

The King's beautiful face, already fattening, permitted something to tremble in its cheeks and eyes: human sadness and mourning.

The servants remembered his watchful mother and kindly father. He combines the best of them both.

"This will be a happy house," he promised them. He held up his arms. "Now, eat!"

And the category people looked at the wide ears and the wide eyes of his senior wife, bat-faced but beautiful. What, what was she feeling?

Queen Jayarajadevi Kansri had not remembered how her husband bustled.

He stomped, cheerfully, lovingly, and relentlessly. In an instant, he had started to run everything. When she had run everything before.

Whatever good she had done, such as the religious school for the women, was praised and then appropriated. Schools, hospitals, rest houses were founded or restocked. It was as if everything devoted and quiet and private in her heart had been flung open and out into the street.

The First Queen ate, maintaining her visage, working on her heart.

"Sru had reminded her that goodness had to be made into public acts. That was what men were for. That was why she had loved him, wasn't it? Because he was responsible, he took the virtues and made them manifest.

Why didn't she? There was a little catch in her virtue and it was tripping her up.

Then there was his little slip of a concubine. Oh, he was a man, men took second wives; they had creatures like these on the side. But she sat here at table as if high-born, and then went down to work in the kitchens. How was she supposed to react to that?

The idea made Jayarajadevi weary. The truth you have to face, she told herself, is not in scriptures or in meditation. It is lodged in your heart.

What kind of man would you love? A man who would have left the slave-wife who had sheltered him? Left a baby because it was born incomplete? Would you love a man who vented himself into palace girls and ignored them?

No, the man you would love would be a man who treated his category concubines with kindness and concern. Look at her, Queen Jaya, this is a woman of true intent. This is not a schemer; this is not a woman who saw advantage and pressed it. Ev3en now every gesture is the gesture of a servant girl to her lord. Regard and learn, throw out useless things like fear and mean-mindedness.

Look, she keeps her eyes downcast. Look at her face; it is a refined face that is as delicate as a bird's foot.

You have your strong sister Indradevi Kansru whose selflessness abides beside you, even at the cost of having a household of her own.

Can this not be a second sister? Out of place, friendless, without anything except the love of the King? A beautiful sister who will know more than you do of hardship and loss? Can you, Queen who prided yourself on your virtue, fail to show her kindness and love? For if you do, you will show yourself to be little and false.

When your husband has given you the opportunity to be grand, as big as the sky.

This is your opportunity, woman, to work with him on the project that you yourself started.

To build a different kind of king. A different kind of kingdom.

And therefore a different kind of court.

Oh yes, we could build another hell like Yashodharapura, the City. All the King's wives scheming to get their relatives positions in the hierarchy and their rivals' children disgraced or even murdered—poisonous hypocrisy, slicing wit, killing smiles, and the silent pounding of fists of frustration against stone.

There is a seed in your heart, woman, of that kingdom. And there is a seed in your heart also of something new, a fine, tall, fruit-bearing tree.

That's the seed I choose to nurture.

The King's wife looked about her at the banquet and saw a low bronze table set out with baskets of food. She rose to her feet and walked to the table, a magnificent piece cast in the shape of flowers and birds.

The Queen leaned over the table and as if picking flowers selected the fattest most finely battered prawns, the greenest onions, and the most fragrant pickles. She arranged them in a dish.

Queen Jaya carried the dish to Fishing Cat. "Here, good woman. To recompense you."

Something in Jayarajadevi clenched with strain, but she held firm. Look at her face, she told herself, look into her eyes. Who is this? This is a kind and faithful woman.

The servant eyes were horrified. "Oh, Lady, no!"

Do you believe in category advantage, Queen? Will you do this to show her up, to make her look small? That is what they would do in the City. You could take this same action and turn it into a weapon, and even be praised for it.

Or you could stay true to your new Way. The Way your husband is holding this banquet to establish. You can do this to elevate both her and yourself.

"You fed my husband when there was no else to do it. You were his friend from childhood and you remembered that friendship always. It is a pleasure to return the kindness."

The King beamed. His hands urged Cat to take, eat. His eyes turned up to Queen Jayarajadevi and beamed approval, joy. And love? Of a kind?

You will have to share him, Queen Jaya.

The servant girl bowed deeply, as was her place, and Queen Jaya returned to her cushions.

Her sister Kansru took her hand as she sat down and with the subtlest flick of her eyes and hands said: *a good action, Sister.*

The King's wife thought: you have served me bowls of fruit or rice, 'Sru. You have played with my child as if he were your own.

Not for the first time, Queen Jaya wondered: what are your feelings, 'Sru? Have you learned to let someone else have the love you wanted for your own? If so, as always, I have much to learn from you.

Oh, come lamps and burn with joy! Come honey and sweeten us, come music, come let us have light and joy and peace and kindness. Let us have love, which has to unfold and change or wither. Let everything be as abundant, as generous, and as temporary as a fall of flowers from the trees.

"Where are the musicians?" Indradevi said, as if reading her sister's thoughts. "Come, play, play for happiness and the restoration of our Lord, and the Way."

The two sisters' eyes met and both were glassy in the lamplight.

You grow used to everything with time.

You grow used to wearing clean clothes and eating well. That comes quickly. You get so used to the other girls giving you food and bowing that you cease to notice after a while, and then you realize you have forgotten them all together.

You grow used to your husband, your love, your King going off most nights to sleep in his wife's bed. You grow used to the fluttering of gratitude, of love and of, yes, desire, when your beautiful husband returns to you for a night, and you rest in his soft smooth arms.

And oh, how the waves of love pass through you then, how desire sighs through you like a gust of wind, how you drape and curl around him, how you open up to let him inside you. How well you sleep.

You get used to him going in the morning.

You cease to be flustered when his grand wife talks to you kindly. You cease to be bewildered by the generosity and the good behaviour, and the balancing act that goes on behind her eyes. You grow used to wanting to respond in kind with similar acts, only to find it is never appropriate. Nothing you have can be given to a queen. You accept that she has everything over you. She and your husband spend hours discussing the Gods, as if they shared rice with them. Together they analyse the teachings of the Buddha as if they could penetrate his mind or his previous lives just by thinking, by talking.

You grow used to the ache in your heart because you can never give him that. Your mind, like your fingers, is blunted with work. You will go thick-waisted and stolid from all the sitting and all the feeding, for you cannot stop your peasant hands and mouth flying to food, stuffing it in just in case you do not eat tomorrow.

You accept that though you yearn to be friends with the servant girls, it can never really be. The ones who are friendly are simply being smart, currying favour. The ones who are friendliest are the very ones you trust the least, the ones who have the brightest, hardest eyes.

So your choice is stark. You can melt into the shadows and start to die. Or you can pray, pull in strength, and say: I am a good and chaste woman who deserves respect.

You go to the Queen and say, "Queen Victory, I have a suggestion."

Jayarajadevi puts down her palm-leaf book and looks smoothly pleased. "Yes, Cat."

"You and the Princess Indradevi work so hard at the school, at the hospital, with the medicines. It seems to me that I should help in some way."

The Queen smiles approval. This strange, wise, virtuous, woman who is made of smoke says, "Yes, Cat." Again.

"I could take responsibility for the kitchens and the household."

A pause.

"That is rather a large task."

"It is a task which the Queen will understand is very familiar to me."

She drinks you in. She always leans back and takes you in, like you are a perfume. She does it to remind herself of who you are, why she likes you, how she can bear you.

"I must ask my sister the Princess Indradevi Kansru. I cannot simply make a decision that involves her. It is good that you wish to do this."

Education and grace and training and a fine mind and a good heart. And one whole eldest son, to your incomplete one. She has the ability, just by sitting there and shining, to make you lower your eyes with shame.

Lady, I would ask you to teach me how to read, if I could bear to have you do something else for me, to climb down so far. I would ask you about the Gods, but you would never finish explaining, and I would never finish misunderstanding.

You work so hard and so sincerely to make me part of the family. You do this for our husband's sake, for the sake of the Way, for the sake of virtue and your own salvation. You just cannot quite do it for your sake or for mine.

"I...I could mention the idea to Princess Indradevi for you."

And yes, that is a challenge, a hesitant foot forward.

"Oh, the Princess and I are sisters, it will be better and easier if I do it."

As simple as that. She's bested you by speaking from the heart.

So it is the way of acceptance. She will always be Queen. You never will.

It is not even clear that you want to be, Cat.

This dreamlike life will go on, cut off from all things that make any sense. You will learn, Cat, but slowly.

Your task, Cat, will be to make a place of simplicity the King can return to, a place removed from palaces or temples or power or prayer.

You are dismissed by your pleased and grateful Queen, and you think.

You want a New Way, Lady? You shall have one.

Fishing Cat moved into a hut.

She cast aside her fine robes. She dug a trench for a fire and made a clay oven to roast and bake, and she strung hammocks. The only concession to her status was a hanging golden curtain that could be lowered, for privacy, when the King visited her.

"Fishing Cat, what is this I hear about a hut?" asked the Queen.

"Oh. I am happier there," said Cat.

The Queen looked stricken. "Have we been unkind in any way or made you unwelcome?"

Cat felt bigger, happier, and the Queen looked more frail. "No, no, not at all. But I am not comfortable in a palace, with all its finery. I am happy with my palm-frond roof, and fine handsome shed."

"But I feel terrible, as if we had said or done something!"

Quite sincerely, Cat took the Queen's delicate hand in her own. "No, not at all. You have been an inspired vision of the virtues. But I'm sure the Queen can see. The girls come to talk to me. We sit and do our chores and joke. They come and rind the fruit, and so do I. Really. I am happy."

And so, my Queen, is the King when he comes to stay here.

He remembers the oyster sky, and the green grass. For he has another home, in another land. And I have something that you cannot have and over which you have no power.

Part of your husband will always be a slave now. He is that with me.

So let him have his other life, Queen, a life in a shed, with a fattening category woman and the deformed child of a slave, in the open air with the smell of cooking charcoal instead of incense.

You are graceful and wise and beautiful; and you will not only reflect his greatness, you will help build it.

So, go back to the palace, Lady. I will always be grateful and respectful, though I cannot in all honesty say that I love you.

You try to look reassured, and you cannot think why you have such misgivings. You have already understood that if I am happier here, it makes no difference what people make of it. How virtuous you look—or perhaps don't look—is of no significance even for you.

Walk away, Lady, so graceful, thin, and reed-like. Of course we are not equals.

We are different.

And this, this, will be my home. I am content.

So people spoke.

They spoke in the royal household. They began to speak in the villages that owed rice and fealty to the City of the Eastern Buddha.

The King of the Eastern Buddha rested part of the week with his slave woman in a slave hut. He allowed himself to be called by his old palace name, the name of Nia, Slave.

If anyone asked, foolishly presuming the King could be teased or made to look weak, he responded, "Slaves own kings."

And he would explain how God was present in all things, even the smallest. How kings were a tiny pinpoint of creation, so tiny compared to the mass of the trees, the grass, and the slaves who tilled the ground. You traced power high enough, and it circled back and came to earth.

It circled back, to a charcoal stove, a worn hammock. Power settled like a bird back onto a crippled son playing in the dust. Power pressed between its fingers unseasoned rice in a reed bowl.

The King called Slave delivered his thoughts to a circle of young acolytes, while his concubine worked over an earthen stove, humming peasant songs.

The beautiful Queen did the noblest works.

Her talented sister composed poetry in Sanskrit so fine that Brahmins came from India to study her technique.

The King sometimes shouldered a leather bag and walked out to the fields of his tiny kingdom. He staggered down into the moats and reservoirs to help the serfs drag out the choking plants, and dredge black soil up onto the banks. He skittered down into the rice fields, bending over to help his people replant the nursery rice. In the lumber yards, he would laugh aloud and spring forward to help the sinewy, black, sweaty men who sawed timber.

On these sudden, joyous, bounding voyages into the life of his people, his companion was the slave woman, who helped catch fish and crickets.

As intended, the only possible response from the people was love.

The soldiers noted that the King's first task was to build a wall all around his city. That one knows the value of defence as well as prayer, the soldiers said, and tapped the sides of their noses.

With the walls, and the great new gates, there was carving to be done. Craftsmen, yearning for both work and a gentler atmosphere, crowded into the City of the Eastern Buddha.

A stonemason, burning with love, sat and looked at the King's meditating face as he rested.

Alive with the flame of heaven, the stonemason suddenly thought: I can remake that face in stone.

He went to work with a chisel, and then with a wire brush and then with sand in the palm of his hand. He stroked the stone to life. The living stone showed a plump, kind, beautiful, strong, and peaceful spirit. The white stone face seemed to glow with a holy light.

There had been no other image made like it in all of Kambujadesa. It was not the face of a king who was a god. It was the face of a beautiful man, smiling with content, yet stressed with compassion.

Something new. This was a kingdom of new flowers, all about to bloom.

"If only words could do that," said the King, over the stonemason's shoulder.

April 15, 2004, part two

On the road to Leung Dai, Map hangs onto the motorcycle, slow and heavy with fury.

It's you, isn't it, Saom Pich? You've done this.

You'll have some shiny intellectual reason for it, but it won't do the rest of us any good and it will lose us the treasure. The army have already clumped all over your house and found nothing. Well, I don't want you to think you've fooled us. I want you to know that you're under suspicion, that your life will be hell, that we'll never let you get away with this. I'll burn your farm for you.

Map is tired.

He has now gone for two nights without sleep. But it's more than just physical fatigue. The whole effort of being Tan Map—of boasting, of being merry, of ignoring the throbbing ache in his fingers, of being fearless, of not letting a word of bullshit come out of his mouth—just suddenly today it's all got too much.

And now I have Ly William to drive me.

Pich will know who I am, his whole family will. Maybe they'll recognize William and ask him: what are you doing with this murderer?

This is the guy who killed your parents.

Well, I'm just too tired to care today. William's the one who wanted to drive me. He can just find out. I shot his mother and father. And maybe then he won't be so happy about his seven dollars a day. Or so peaceful.

"Who are we going to see?" William asks, turning around on the bike.

"Your worst nightmare," says Map.

The bike bounces down an incline into a village with hedges tight up against the road. They pass a fenced, boarded-up building. In 1979, that was the Angka regional hospital. They made pills of paste and traditional herbs, only the little girls they called nurses didn't know one herb from another.

They come to the corner where the road dead-ends with only a dike beyond it. They pull into a yard surrounded by kapok trees. A corral pens in an ox, away from the fruit. The house is solid, made of matching wood with a roof of wooden tiles. The stilts are square like beams, not round, and they sit on top of smoothly formed concrete posts to keep away the termites. From within comes the sound of a TV.

"*Sok subbay!*" calls Map. Two small boys in blue shorts, with paper animal masks—a monkey and a tiger—come out giggling, squealing and twisting each other's arms, overexcited by some afternoon TV show. This would be a second crop of kids, from some new young wife.

Map feels something like despair. Even this murdering old pirate has settled down; all of Cambodia has gone home, it seems. Except for Map.

He asks the boys if their father is home. He isn't, but their mother and their great-aunty are. The boys point to the fields behind the house. Map walks around the house; the boys clamber boisterously back to their TV. Next to the house is a tall haystack. A large palm leaf with its stalk is folded down over it, to help keep it in place.

Map remembers haystacks like this, smelling of sun and dust. He thinks he smells a warm and human smell. He lifts up a lid of hay, and there is a child's nest, with a round colored ball inside it.

Oh, big brother, you and I would sleep like this, giggling long into the night, making wicked plans.

Gently, as if hiding it from foes, Map scatters the hay back down over it.

Next to the haystack is a well, with a wooden lid and a bucket on a rope and a neat smooth concrete wall around it. No UN markings. Old Ta Pich made this himself then. Dug it, poured the concrete. An accident did not cripple him. The well walls did not fall in on him, nor did the rope break as he climbed out. So where is karma?

"Made it himself. Nice job." Map talks before remembering that he has a policy of saying nothing to William.

"Sergeant," says William in a low, anxious voice but with merry, encouraging eyes. "You think maybe the farmer took the Book?"

Map only shrugs and walks on. He can't be bothered to answer. *I thought you were smart this morning, but you've gone back to being soft and stupid. We're trying to get Luc back, and for that we need brains.*

Ahead of them there's an earthen oven with a grill over it. Women in faded sampots are weaving palm fronds. Map remembers the hours he spent as a soldier over ovens, melting plastic sheets to make oil for lamps. The sheets were blue, and as they melted, they smelled of fire and rotten fish. The smell would combine with the hollow in his belly to make him feel sick.

A different world, now.

"This is a nice farm," says William. He looks nervous; he's only just realizing how nasty this could get. *If Saom Pich is here, he may start shooting.*

It will feel good to shoot him, even if he hasn't taken the Kraing Meas.

Why isn't the house filled with spirits every night, demanding food and justice? How can Saom Pich sleep? How does he go unpunished? Or am I punishing myself? I sleep out on the ground. I have no home, no family. This old man led all the murders around here; he was the number three man; he did all that but he is the one with the handsome house and the healthy sons.

As Map draws closer he adds still one more blessing: the beautiful young wife.

She is folded as neatly as a pocket handkerchief next to the stove, a young woman with a new baby and a sweet, calm expression. A Khmer beauty.

She escaped it; she escaped the whole thing, the wars, and the jeum-room camps on the border, all of it. What is a leathery old murderer doing with a wife like that? A home like this? Hens, fruit, a tethered ox, children warm in hay?

As they get closer, Map smells pondwater, stale and slimy. Wet palm leaves are piled high next to bamboo rods. Away from the house because of the smell, the women are making old-fashioned

Geoff Ryman

roofing—soaked strips of palm leaves doubled over bamboo poles. Not for this house—oh no, this house has tiles. They're to sell to poor people, to make Pich even richer.

Map remembers as a child looking up from his hammock in the rainy season and seeing the overlapping rows of palm-frond ceiling. He loved the neat way each rod did two jobs, supporting one layer of leaves like a curtain rail while propping up the higher layer from underneath.

Next to the palm panels, lengths of thick, hollow bamboo are roasting on the fire. They will be full of sticky rice and red beans. He remembers breaking open bamboo to eat as dessert at New Year.

Home.

Next to the wife, an old, black-toothed crone pokes the embers under the fire and feeds in scrub. She looks up with eyes as mean and narrow as Map's own. You old stick. We are just the beaten husks, you and I. All the juice and sugar has been pounded out of us.

"*Yiey,* Grandmother," Map says to the old lady, then to the wife, "*Loak sray.*" They blink at his old shorts and farmer's gloves. The young wife recalls her manners, gives Map an unclouded smile and, as he is an older man, sompiahs.

"Your husband must have much merit. He has such a beautiful farm."

The wife goes back to folding the leaves around the rods. "Thank you. We like it. It is pleasant enough."

"You have a TV."

"But no electricity. Maybe that is best. I like natural light." She smiles again. The presence of William reassures her. William, who looks so harmless, so friendly, so polite. William bows and smiles and strains forward like a friendly dog.

Motoboy, I know you. You can't wait to start chatting her up, to find out who she knows and how you can help each other.

"A good life," Map nods. "Everything on this farm is well done. The house, the fields, the well—they are all solid."

The little, beautiful girl still doesn't get it. She looks pleased. "My husband does things well."

The old woman knows what Map's about. She stands up and keeps a fistful of scrub between them. "He had it bad during the war."

"No, he didn't," replies Map. "He was district representative. An

218

old-fashioned maquis. They did things well, the old ones, the old-time Communists. They'd been to school and the Party gave them books, taught them all kinds of things. They were educated. In a way."

The old woman grunts. "The army have already been here. They turned the whole house over. There are no guns, nothing. You can go home."

The wife's face falls, and her eyes close. Map is sorry to see her beauty hidden away. He's sorry to make her unhappy and also glad to trouble her. She has had it too easy; she knows nothing.

Map lets the wife have it. "We were both communists. I worked for him for a while, before and after the yuon came. Were you with him in the jeum-room in Thailand?"

Of course she wasn't. You don't stay sweet and kind in a refugee camp.

The wife gives her head a mournful little shake. "That was before my time," she murmurs, her voice a pleading whisper that means: I am innocent, keep me out of this.

How he must love you, Map thinks. You are the comfort of his old days, young and beautiful, giving him baby sons. And you look happy, so maybe he is good to you. Tigers are tender with their cubs.

Suddenly Map finds that he does not have the heart to involve her.

Great-aunty stands her ground like an old stake charred to a spear point, ready to defend. Map knows her type. You bounced back and forth across the border, didn't you, old woman, fleeing whenever the yuon shelled the forward camps, scuttling back into Thailand. The NADK kept going on the backs of women like you. The Americans gave you food, while we marched up and down Highway 6 stepping over people who slept in the road because that was the safest place.

Map turns to her. "You've had a lot of people here. Since the Book was found in the fields." He waves over the hedge of trees towards the dike and the rice fields.

The old woman grunts, watchful.

"Have you seen any people around the village? Anything odd? Any old-timers come to the house?"

"Gaaaah!" the old woman mouths in disgust.

"Where is your nephew, Loak Saom Pich? He isn't here, I'd like to talk to him."

The great-aunty bends down and busies herself turning over the roasting bamboo. The wife lowers her head even more.

"When do you expect him back?"

The wife speaks, eyes still downcast. So, she doesn't want to be spared. Map watches her carefully, for any tremor, any wiping of the mouth. The young wife says, "My husband has gone to town to get some things."

"So he will be back this afternoon?"

"I...I expect so. I do not know. I...think he said he would be back tonight."

"Tomorrow," says the old woman.

"Oh. So it is that kind of shopping. To the bars and the girls?"

The wife stabs him with her eyes. "No. He is not that kind of man."

"He spends all day in town, I know. Possibly in prayer. I will come tomorrow then."

Then the wife gives it all away: she wipes her mouth, wiping away the lie. She can't stop herself. "No! I mean, he has another farm, so he works there all day."

"And another wife, perhaps?" Map gives a smile that he knows is his least charming.

"Where are your manners, Maly?" croaks the old lady with a false, sideways simper of politeness. "Go get Loak Sergeant Tan Map some of our sugar, to show respect."

The great-aunty smiles like a dog baring its fangs. Round-faced and miserable, the young wife stands up. She rebalances her baby on her hip, and walks back to the house, swaying as naturally as a palm tree in the breeze.

The great-aunty says. "I know who you are."

"You know my name. That's not the same thing."

"You and your older brother were holy terrors. My nephew worried about people like you. What you did even to Base People; it was disgusting. He came this close to shooting you, more's the pity that he didn't. He knew you would end up a turncoat."

"At least I fought against Angka. Does he have the *Kraing Meas*?"

The old lady is more than ready. Her half-smile is grimly amused. She says nothing.

"People from around here say that old Khmers Rouges took the Book. They say everybody here knows that. If he has the Book, we'll get him. You can tell him that."

The old woman snorts in disgust. "I don't know what you're talking about."

"But you knew what I meant when I asked about all the people."

"Oh, that. They found something in the field." She waves her hand as if all of that nonsense was nothing to do with her.

"Maybe I should stay and wait for him to come back. Maybe he'll have the Book with him."

"And if he had this book with him, what of it? Maybe he's been looking for it too."

Peasant cunning. Always so blunt, so smart, so dumb all at once. Map has to smile. William looks uncomfortable, scowling and confused.

The wife saunters back with a parcel of wrapped leaves. Palm leaf has been made into ribbons to bind it shut. "Home sugar," she says with a twist in her voice that could mean: you need sugar, in your life, in your soul.

"Thank you," says Map, pauses, and then smiles.

Away from the house, Map makes William stop the bike.

By jabbing him in the ribs. Then he gets off the bike and without saying anything takes out a mobile phone.

"It's the same as mine," says William, as if he does not notice how rude Map is being. "Luc Andrade gave it to you."

He's said something Map cannot ignore. "Yes," says Map.

William sighs. "He made many good actions."

Captain Prey is now at APSARA HQ in a meeting. Map says to him, "Saom Pich is the leader, Saom Pich is behind all of it."

Prey asks, "Why do you think that?"

"Because he invented art theft. Ta Mok needed money and it was Pich who had the brilliant idea of cutting up the temples to get it. Having said for years it was the one thing we must not touch. I was there, remember? He's not at his farm, he's not coming back to his farm and that's because he's on a boat holding a gun to Luc Andrade's head."

Prey sighs. "Okay, Map, I'll pass that onto the army."

Map chuckles. "It would be more effective to throw it down a well."

"No, Map. They are restructuring the investigation, a new man is coming in to run it, and he might be more interested. If they decide to set up a roadblock around Leung Dai, I'll call you back, and you should get out of there."

"Can't do that. Someone has to watch the house."

"Map, you're a suspect."

"If Pich's old aunty creaks out of here on her bicycle I'm going to follow her. Something else you can tell the army. They should write down the identities of everybody who goes through roadblocks. They'll need to know everybody's travel patterns, who goes where, when."

Prey sighs. "I'll pass that on too. But as soon as the army think you're at Leung Dai, they'll go there to arrest you."

Maps folds shut his telephone and says without looking at William, "You better remember all of that, motoboy, because I'm not going to say any of it again."

They wait in silence, listening to the dust expand in the heat, the swishing of a cow's tail somewhere in the reeds, birds, a woman talking somewhere in a house.

William sits on his bike and wipes his forehead.

"Loak Sergeant. The old woman said the army has already been to the house. Maybe it is not news to Saom Pich that he is a suspect. So maybe nobody will go from the house today to warn him."

"Getting hot, huh?" says Map.

"We could go to the Lake..."

Map has to chuckle. "Nice and cool on the Lake."

"There were the shots on the Lake. Now that you know it's Saom Pich, you can ask people if they've seen him. You know, an old man with glasses."

Map stands, arms folded.

"You are not in uniform. Maybe people will tell you things they wouldn't tell the Army."

Map shifts, looking at his feet.

"Maybe you speak Vietnamese? I speak some Vietnamese. I bet the army don't, so we could ask all those people on the river or in the floating village."

Map turns to him. "I told you. You're paid to drive, not to think."

They sit and listen to the wind in the trees for an hour. The heat buzzes around them.

Finally the phone vibrates. Map opens it up and Prey says, "Map, do you have any evidence other than a gut feeling? Have you found out how Pich could know the Book was being moved?"

Map feels William's eyes on him. "No."

Prey sighs. "They say the roadblocks they have are enough. They did like your idea about names, though. They will tell their men to write down names of everyone who goes through the roadblocks."

Map says. "You have a pencil? Tell them this. Make sure they pass this on to all the roadblocks. Saom Pich may be using the name Chuor Preuk. It's what he was called for a while in the 1980s. Other family names of his wife and uncle are Kem and Ung. His cousins are called Soeun. Okay?"

Prey checks the spellings then says, "I'm telling you again, get out of there. Sinn Rith has been prowling about the place like a caged animal and suddenly he isn't here. He may know where you are, and if he shows up, he may arrest William too."

Map laughs. "That's a good reason to stay."

Map catches William looking. Could he hear all that? Map says good-bye to the Captain and then turns to William. "You should go home. I'll wait here."

"It's okay. I can stay."

"You should go. You'll still get paid."

William says, "I work for you. I will wait."

"There's not going to be any lunch. I'll be here all day and all night if I need to, with no food and probably no water."

"I've gone without food before," William says.

He isn't leaving.

Sunlight creeps slowly across the track. It and the birds are the only things that are moving in the heat.

William clears his throat. "Loak Tan Map? You should get someone to watch here for you, so that you can look elsewhere."

Map chortles. "What, pay them seven dollars a day?"

"I have a girlfriend who lives here …"

"I get it, you'd like to visit your girlfriend. Okay, go ahead. I'll stay here and work."

William cuts him off. "Her family were ANS. They have no love in their hearts for Saom Pich. They had a land dispute with him; he took over one of their fields. They can see his house."

A Sihanoukist family in Leung Dai?

"They're smart people; the father was a soldier just like you; he fought in all the wars."

Map does not need to see another old soldier with a beautifully tended farm and family. This farm has a palm- and rice-wine distillery and a cloud of hens circling under the house. There are many children, all of them born after the mid-80s as life became possible again.

After the war, everyone else went home.

The girl, Sra, tries to look offhand with William. Maybe he's not been paying enough attention to her. Of course she's beautiful and of course William behaves like a civilized, educated man around her. Sra looks at Map like he's dirt, a peasant, but William explains. This man works for APSARA, he is in disguise, he needs your help.

He clears a space to let Map talk. The father is serious and seasoned. Map has never even met him before, but he likes him, the kind of responsible man you trust in war. Let William talk to children; this is men's business.

"Saom Pich. You think he took it?" the father asks.

"He's an art thief. I think he shot up the town. It's how he works."

"What do you need us to do?"

First off, Map told them, nothing obvious. We don't want you to get into trouble with these people. All you need do, all of you, is watch who comes and goes. Write down the time and what they look like and anything unusual about the bike. You know, if the bike is carrying firewood, or if it's old and rusty. Do you have a phone?

The family don't have a well and the daughters have to carry all their water on their shoulders. They don't have electricity and there is no road to their house; but they are modern Cambodians and of course they have a mobile phone, just like they have a TV attached to car batteries.

"Okay. If Saom Pich himself comes home, you give me a call right away. Okay?"

As they leave, the father asks, "Is it true that the Book was written by Jayavarman?" Map says yes, and the farmer shakes his head. "The idiots."

Back in the field, William says, "Many people want to help you, Loak Tan Map."

Map can't stop himself having the obvious thought: It's you they want to help, William.

Okay, this is a nice, smart boy. It changes nothing. I owe him a blood debt, and I should not be sitting here pretending to be his boss or pretending to be his friend.

"Do you wish to go to the Lake now, Sergeant?" William's voice is so light and breezy, you'd almost think Map had suggested it himself.

The damnable thing is that the kid's right. Map says curtly, "Okay."

William takes a footpath back, his rear tires slipping sideways in the dust. They hear motorcycles roaring up the main road and turning off to Leung Dai: Sinn Rith.

Closer to the Great Lake, the land flattens out and even at the end of the dry season the fields are streaked with water that looks like shards of mirror.

At the crossroads in front of the gateway to a hillside road, army vehicles again block the traffic. Map sompiahs, and produces the ID card, and again they are waved through.

Okay, reasons William, ID cards are not always accurate. He lived with another family for a while and his personal name could be different. So no Tan, no Map. He's kept it like that because he is a criminal. He looks like a criminal sometimes.

The road becomes an elevated dike. Palm-leaf shacks cluster along its edge, lining the road, the houses of people who did not find farms after the wars. These houses have no stilts nor floor, only an open entrance. Men squat in doorways, washing themselves. They sit in hammocks, staring.

Ahead, the dike is washed out and there is no bridge across the breach. Truck tires have milled the mud into patterns like woven reed. Only a single plank of wood crosses over the morass. A boy stands in a punt offering to take the bike around it on the river. He smiles with embarrassment when Map asks the price.

With the boy, Map is gentle, smiling and chiding. "How much?" he repeats, miming astonishment. The boy's white teeth glow like lamps against his weather-beaten face. He says the price again in a shy voice that trails away, like the direction of his gaze.

Map says, "Oh, that is a very good price." He turns to William, suddenly merry. "I am the *bong thom* here, yes?" He takes off his flip-flops and gives them to William to hold. Then coughing once as if summoning the courage to ask a girl to dance, he hauls William's motorcycle up onto his shoulders. He holds it in place with the heels of his hands. The torn fingers, even in gloves, arch away like claws.

William yelps in surprise and jumps back. "No, Mr. Tan Map, don't do that! You will hurt yourself!"

And my bike!

Map carries the motorcycle on his shoulders, wobbling barefoot across the single plank of the walkway. Even the punt boy laughs, leaning backwards then twisting around on his heel in surprise.

"Thank you!" calls Map from the other side. "That was a very good price for a punt." A crowd of men laugh. Map goes up to them to cadge some cigarettes. "Only one, for lifting a bike!" The men give him more, and he lights up. He asks questions. Have any of them seen an unfamiliar boat? Maybe yuon or Thai? Any small boats that go in and out at strange hours? Seen an old guy with half-moon spectacles?

The men shake their heads, no. Just fishing boats from around here. Yes, they heard the shots, but they'd seen and heard nothing after that. The army has been all around here asking questions.

Map gets back onto the bike. He only says two things to William. First, "Don't call me Map where people can hear." Second, "Take us to the boats." Then he stays silent.

The river widens and deepens and is lined with shops and big tourist ferries to Phnom Penh. The first shop they walk into faces the river, not the road. The dock is cushioned with old car tires. Bottled water and gas canisters line up under plastic covers. Inside the shop, on the countertop, there are pickles in glass jars and hot coffee in thermos flasks. Glass cases hold AA batteries, shampoo, fruit juice, oil, and medicaments of all kinds. The toilet perches out from a gangway, directly over the river.

The owner is a bustling middle-aged woman who is sweeping the floor. Map shows her his police badge and asks questions. Any new boats show up to buy supplies? Anybody new in charge of a boat who doesn't look like they know what they're doing? Anybody slam into the dock, or anything like that? An old guy with glasses?

The woman is polite, her face closed. Map looks poor, solemn and dangerous. People are afraid of you, William thinks, you look like a ruffian. They want you to go.

Teacher Luc could be wounded, could be shot, he could be dying. He could be lying alone in a boat wondering if he has any friends.

And you don't know how to talk to people.

William says to the woman, "Isn't it beautiful here now, with the lotus fields so near?"

The woman nods. "It's the one good thing about living here. That and catching fish from the ponds. I wouldn't eat fish from the river, it's too dirty."

"I always wanted to live by a lotus pond. If I were rich, I would own one," says William. "I would go out every dawn and every evening just to see the flowers."

He talks about his uncle's four rice fields and how he had to pay neighbours to work on them.

As William thought she might, the woman suggests that her husband could help. "He does little enough around here!"

William says, "Sure," and gives her his village name and tells the story about how they got their farm back after the war. They traded farms with someone who wanted to move back to Battambang.

Map says, pointing to William, "This guy here, he just talks to everybody all day long."

"That's a good way to be," says the woman, finally smiling at Map.

"Yes, he went around and got half the town to help us find the people who stole the *Kraing Meas* and took the barang hostage."

"Oh, yes!" says the woman, pleased. "I heard about that, what a great thing to do! Look, have some coffee and we can sit outside." She pauses, and wiggles. "Don't worry, this is polite, I won't charge!" They sit on plastic chairs on the dock, and the woman brings her thermos and tiny plastic cups.

"People say that there are farmers who take boats out at strange times. They leave at night and come back at night, or they go out at lunchtime and come back only an hour later. I haven't seen them myself."

Map uncoils. "Do people say from where?"

She waves vaguely upstream. "People say that they're farmers."

They talk a little longer about the lack of rain, and the level of the lake. Map asks where the boat has docked. Oh, different places. They finish their coffees, and to William's surprise, Map pays for them. They say good-bye sociably and leave.

They go from boat to boat, asking the same questions. If people react badly to Map, William takes over, being young, respectful, and easygoing. They talk to people in boats made out of just one log, with a tube of palm-frond panels to shade it. The owners fry noodles on tiny grills balanced between bricks.

William and Map talk to people in larger boats with flat-roofed canopies and rolled-up blue plastic curtains to protect against sunlight or scrub in narrow canals. Boys in their best black clothes sleep on board. Have they seen anything?

One floating house has a sunburst gable and a blue roof. A woman leans out from the porch, looking into a floating box of fish. She wears black and a conical straw hat. She is Vietnamese.

William says hello in Vietnamese and tries to explain. The woman has not even heard of the kidnapping. The army did try to talk to her about something, but they went away again. No, she has heard nothing strange.

William looks pleased, and tells Map, "The army have not been asking Vietnamese people."

Map says nothing.

There are bars with big red Angkor signs. There are stalls on wheels and large floating houses with TV aerials. Everywhere, the army have been first.

One small boat has a long metal drive shaft trailing behind it. The young girl inside it wears a squashed pork-pie hat and neat shorts. She's Vietnamese. William translates some of her answers.

"No, she has seen nothing, but she says that a new boat comes and goes from the floating village."

Map's eyebrows raise. He nods and looks at the sun, now lower in the sky. "Ask if she knows someone who can take us around the lake cheaply."

William can't stop himself jumping ahead of Map. "She's already offered. It's a great idea. My friend Chea works in a blacksmith shop near here, we can leave my bike with him."

Map eyes him. "You know everybody. Ask her the price."

Done.

They zigzag back and forth across the river. The engine putters under a loosely covered poop deck. The girl sits on the red fuel canister and steers with a tiny polished aluminium wheel.

The girl knows all the Vietnamese people. Women duck out of their barges carrying babies, and catch the twine she throws to them. She explains, looking to William as if he were the boss. Most of them have not heard of the Book or the kidnapping, but are shocked that the Cambodians would be so stupid as to hurt tourists. "That explains why they have all gone away!" they laugh.

By now, it's past three o'clock. The day will start to die soon.

Grandfather Luc, thinks William, we are doing what we can for you.

The tiny boat braves the wide waters of the lake, approaching the floating Vietnamese village.

A scaffolding of thin, stripped branches holds a boat up out of the water. The Vietnamese owner stands chest-deep in the lake, hammering wedges between the hull and the scaffold. Vietnamese music, more treble and wavering than Cambodian songs, drifts across the water.

The girl calls out. William makes out the Vietnamese for hello, Sir, something about boats, and violence. Has he seen any strange boats?

"Yes," the boat repairman answers. "You." He grins, showing horsy yellow teeth. William and the girl laugh.

They talk to people in barges full of vegetables or hanging laundry over their decks. They wave and chuckle at merry naked children. The mothers have seen nothing.

Their boat chugs up to a floating timber merchant. Firewood and piled planks swell out over the sides of the barge, supported by uprights. There's even a tree growing out of the deck, a medium-size silk-cotton. The timber merchant swings in his hammock, wearing pyjamas and smoking a pipe. The girl asks again, you see any strange boats around here?

The timber merchant sits quietly thinking then says in broken Khmer, "One boat. Small. Small boat. Come go, far south, in out, no fish."

"Sir. Please," says William in Vietnamese. "Very good man. Very kind man. Hurt by violence. Please. Where?"

The Vietnamese girl explains that a very good man has been kidnapped. Did he see an old Cambodian man wearing glasses?

Yes.

"He's seen him," whispers William. The timber merchant becomes voluble. He and the girl talk for a long time. The girl translates. "He says that Cambodian men in a very small blue-and-white boat came and stayed a whole afternoon. He says there was thumping from inside the hull, over and over. An old man with glasses came and then the boat left. That was yesterday. They haven't been back."

"Did the boat have any kind of canopy?" asks Map.

No, no canopy at all. The girl doesn't know the name in Khmer for the particular kind of boat it is. But medium size. Very low in the water.

Where did it head when it left? South, out into the reaches of the Great Lake.

No, the boat did not come back, at least not to the Vietnamese village.

Then Map says curtly to the girl who has been so helpful. "Back, back!"

William looks at the girl and he can't stop smiling. The girl looks happy for him and laughs. William thanks her again and again in Khmer and Vietnamese. They pull up alongside her house. It's a poor house, a flat-roofed box with rickety walkways. One of the rooms has no floors, just planks of wood over the water.

William would take her for a meal, buy her a hat, and pay her extra for all her help and trouble. Map jams the four riels into her hand, and thanks her but briefly. When William bows and says thank you again, Map says, "Come on, motoboy, we've got to get moving."

William feels humiliated in front of the girl and ashamed of Map's behaviour. He holds out his hands and shrugs. The girl shrugs back and thanks him. Maybe four riels are a lot of money for her. William feels something hot in his chest constrict. He reaches into his own pocket and passes the girl a dollar.

William balances his way back onto land and by now he recognizes what he is feeling. He's angry.

He breathes in deeply and finds that his breath has stuck. This has got to be cleared up or he will lose his temper and that could lose him his job.

As they walk back to his bike, William says, "Grandfather Luc gave you work running his Web site."

Map grunts.

"It takes a wise man to see talent in others. He is a good man. That is why I want to help you. I have no other motive."

"I know," says Map.

"Then why are you so rude to me?"

Map tuts, smiles and shakes his head. "You haven't seen me be rude."

"I have seen you be friendly to other people."

"Look, motoboy, I don't have to be friends with you. You are a very lucky guy, everybody in town knows you. Just be content with that. There is only one person in Siem Reap who doesn't want to have anything to do with you."

William is bewildered. "You said that you didn't like me because I am peaceful. What is the alternative? War? You want war?" William's voice starts to rise.

Map suddenly jabs a finger hard into William's chest. His eyes are staring, and encircled, like the bottoms of two glasses full of beer. "You call me Loak and you don't joke with me." He jabs him again, hard. "Do you understand that, motoboy?"

William is startled, and then unexpectedly afraid, as if Map's breath is a wind that blows right through him and stills his heart. If Map got angry, he would hurt him. That was clear: Map could be crazy and dangerous.

It's good that you're devoted to Grandfather Frenchman and that you care so much about the patrimony. It's good you have the courage to say things that other people won't say.

But what is the value in that, if you would rather your people were being bombed?

Map goes back to Leung Dai, to watch all night.

William gets home long after the family has had its evening meal.

His aunty has plainly been fretting. She sees him, and without saying anything, trots out to where his cousin cooks liquorice over a fire trench. She comes back with a fish she has reheated. "You are hungry, I can tell just by looking," she says, and strokes his hair. "Did you eat anything?"

William is too exhausted to lie. "No." He's almost too tired to eat his fish.

Even his uncle looks sombre. Uncle is as slim and willowy as a teenager, and usually views the world from behind a hazy, beneficent smile. His eyes look forlornly at William. He pours him a glass of water. "What happened today?"

"We went to Leung Dai, we went to the Lake. Do we know Tan Map?"

His uncle and aunt shoot a look at each other. Aunty takes over. "We did once. Not well. How long will you be working for him?"

"I don't know. Until APSARA runs out of money or until they decide to stop investigating." With a start, William reaches into his pocket and pulls out his daily fee. Perhaps they look worried because it's less than usual. "I had to pay a Vietnamese girl to ferry us around. I'll ask Sangha to pay me back." His aunty nods a hectic little thanks and darts away to put the money in the house.

William asks his uncle. "Did...did we do something bad to Tan Map?"

"Us?" his uncle sounds at first surprised. Then to William's alarm, his kindly uncle's eyes fill with water. "No. Nothing," he whispers.

Then Uncle stands up and, without saying anything, walks away. This is something he never does. William is left alone under the strip lighting.

William thinks. They never talk about the war; they never say anything about it. They think that if I am kept ignorant, the war cannot touch me. I think the war cannot touch me too, but I breathe it in every day. William sees dust and smoke and something dark within it.

April 1160

Jayavarman passed into the City and fear brushed him like feathers.

Once again an elephant jostled him up the main road into Yashodharapura. He remembered being a captive child all those years ago.

Once again he passed the great, foreboding temples. He saw the stalls, tasted the tang of smoke, and heard the babble of merchants. All of it dragged down his heart, and made him feel small and threatened.

Jayavarman told his memories: hush, child. Be still, little one. Little frightened prisoner, you are here no longer. You are now a strong warrior, tall and arrayed with arms and elephants and sons to defend you. Your kingdom is famous for its peace and prosperity. The King has called you because he needs you and your cheerful, robust armies. He cannot, dare not, hold you against your will.

You ride, son of Dharan Indravarman, on the back of an elephant, and even the elephant wears embroidered cloth. A servant crouches on the elephant's back to hold aloft a parasol, and another marches behind bearing your pendants and signs of office. Your troops march in front and behind.

Your Crown Prince, Suryakumara, rides beside you, and he is fierce and strong, and does not look on the City with fear. Little Cap-Pi-Hau, your son is already twice the age you were when you first arrived, friendless and one of many other captives. Your son comes in state alongside his father with a cadre of soldiers.

But, oh! the faces in the streets.

I don't see any of the old faces. Time has wiped all the old faces away, like the breath that mists a mirror.

Different people, replacement people. They still gawk at the higher categories. Their cheeks are sunken; their mouths are full of broken teeth, and the muscles around their mouths swell out. The flesh around their eyes is dark as if they have not slept; and they stare, baffled.

They remind me of wild dogs that no one wants. These are not men who share the air, rice, and water of a home. They have come to the City for advantage and find thievery and prostitution and the kind of poverty that eats the soul from the stomach up. They smell of sour fruit rinds and baked mud. A cat that lives wild has no fleas, but a cat that stews all day with other cats amid the rinds is full of fleas and worms.

Something is brewing in those replacement faces. It has been brewing for some time, for it is worse in these new faces than it was in the old. It is bafflement curdling into rage.

The caravan turned and even Jayavarman had to gape in amazement. There, finished finally, the Vishnuloka—Vishnu's World—thrust its way towards heaven like five mailed fists. Clad in bronze, its five towers were topped with high masts bearing flags. From their lotus-flower petals hung long banners, black and red but mostly gold. The sacred mountain of Suryavarman the Great was as big and yellow as the rising sun.

"That's it, Son, that is where your uncle-king rests, joined now with his god. His name now is Paramavishnuloka."

Their elephants turned, following the moat and passing the main causeway leading to the western entrance.

Jaya said, "It is Mount Meru come to earth here. You cross the causeway and go up two levels. On that high level there are four great pools, each representing the four holy rivers. From those towers you can see all the city precincts."

His son's face was blank, unmoved as children often are by things that are too big for them to see, too bare of any association to make them feel joy, nostalgia, or regret. Suryakumara had his mother's thin face, but more demanding. "Why is the middle tower blue?"

"Because it is the color of Vishnu whom Suryavarman worshipped. Oh, Surya, I remember seeing this when I was younger than you are now. It was the day of its consecration, and I remember thinking, what will it look like when it is finished? I never thought I would see it. This day seemed very far off then, all the banks were mud, the towers were still unfinished."

"Are those bells?"

From within the walls there came a kind of tingling, ringing sound, too swift and rhythmic for bells.

"Chisels. Those are chisels. They are still working on the bas-reliefs."

Surya sniffed. "So it is unfinished."

The amazing capacity of youth to be unimpressed by the old. How strange to live in a world where King Suryavarman is no more and his great temple is just something old that disappoints.

Jaya wanted to protect it. "Oh, a building of this size always needs additions and repairs."

Suryakumara promised, "We shall build a bigger temple, but it will be to the Buddha."

"The Buddha is so great that he does not need big temples." Jayavarman's voice was gentle with a father's love.

He remembered Suryavarman the King. His eyes. How they gleamed. Always thinking. An unattractive man in many ways, at least when he was old and narrow like a knife. He always pawed my shoulder and jammed me under his armpit. But he also made an exception of me. Loved me. Poor man.

Childless, loveless. But how clever he must have been.

"Suryavarman was not born a king," said Jayavarman to his son. "There was a time of terrible confusion, many kings competing. And Suryavarman won by war but also by stealth. And he did sometimes bring peace, and he did sometimes bring a kind of justice."

"He did not follow the Dharma," said Suryavarman's namesake.

"No. No, he did not. But he knew your mother and I should marry. And he kept all the promises he made to me."

"Including leaving you imprisoned by the Chams." Nothing Jaya could say seemed to erase the hatred his son had of the Chams and of the Universal Kings. It was as if he preserved his love for his father by blaming them for keeping them apart all those years. Surya leaned backwards and rubbed the top of his head against his father's chest, demanding. Demanding what? Love? You have my love, my son.

Jayavarman put his hand on his Crown Prince's shoulder.

"Even if you did name me after Suryavarman," murmured the boy. "I will be a Buddhist king."

"Some of the Chams are Buddhists," said his father gently.

The boy sighed. "Everything except the Buddha is in confusion."

That was true. Jaya chuckled. "You are as wise as your mother," he murmured.

To their left they passed the high mountain with its thousand stone steps, the Yashodharaparvata, its own high temple out of sight.

Skirting the mountain, their procession straggled on, not much regarded as it served no holy function. They passed into the City, which lacked walls and gates. The temple of Mount Meru was on their left, looking small in comparison to the Vishnuloka, but still clad like a warrior in bronze.

Then they took another turn and headed northeast, to Yashovarman's new palace.

How things change.

The wooden-toothed nanny will be dead. The Brahmin who banished Fishing Cat now sleeps with his fathers. Half of the Oxen are dead and the beautiful maidens they fought over are now matrons. You won your queen, the beautiful Jayarajadevi whom Yasho had wanted for a second, perhaps more loving wife. You won, and absolutely no one now cares or even knows.

It has all passed into dust.

Yashovarman's new palace still smelled of wood stain and the carvings were in the delectable new style of the Vishnuloka bas-reliefs, detailed and less full of old stories and demons. I like that, Jaya thought. Interesting, Yashovarman, how similar our tastes are. Though if we show great ladies on the palanquins, why not the working women who feed them?

Kamlaa-category people gathered up the leads of their elephants. Conch shells sounded, gongs were beaten. Suryakumara flicked his jacket shut with a twist and a snap, and glared at everything about him.

It is not fair. Little Surya soaks in my own anger and distrust of this place. He does not regard the City as his own. He could feel pride in his people, in their greatness, but because of me, my old fear, he does not.

Jaya murmured, "Behave well, Prince."

"I promise," said his son.

They ascended the wooden steps, and there were spotless new floors, the polish still tacky underfoot.

Surya breathed out. "These floors are rough. Watch out for splinters, Father."

Little commandant, thought, Jaya, smiling fondly.

Jayavarman maintained the smile as a mask, to indicate cheerfulness, contentment, and power. Puals led them into a great airy room, curtains pulled back, open to the gardens and the grazing cattle.

The room buzzed with the sound of kings and generals, greeting, bowing, and moving between groups to build alliances. The recently defeated general of the northwest looked uneasy. Well he might. Any one of these little kings, rushing to his aid, could or would replace him. Other kings had brought their sons to train them, great strapping lads on the cusp of manhood. They scowled like Surya did, looking angry and disdainful.

Anything to avoid looking afraid. And so, they looked afraid.

The kings and generals looked relaxed and jolly. The vengeful Little King of Poduli, the mountain, bounced on his heels, jiggling, beaming. "Hah! A small rebellion like this! It is good for the young men to have something to fight; it has been too long a time of peace!"

A general grinned at him. "Oh, but my dear friend, this old religion was once based around your hill."

"I know! I know!" chuckled the King of Poduli, looking delighted. "But I have no trouble with it. The people know they must be disciplined. I tell you it is always that western region that has trouble. It is a lack of discipline, but also it's too dry! The place is wretched!"

His own hill was at the meeting of the three great rivers.

Jaya said to his son, "Watch when the conches sound for the King, they will all scramble for the place just opposite the dais. They think sitting there somehow mirrors the position of the Universal King."

"Hmm," grunted Surya. "That is very much like the little children in the courtyard."

Gold-embroidered cushions were scattered about the dais. Servant girls slipped into the room and placed carafes of water and reed bowls of nuts and fruit near the cushions.

Someone whom Jaya did not know, but who bore signs of high office, sailed quickly into the room. He wore a quilted jacket, embroidered with flowers and very fine wrapping round his legs. His hair was pulled back and wound with an image of Siva.

Who? For just a moment, the plucking at Jaya's heart made him fear that the man was King Yashovarman himself. He looked something like Yasho: the bulk, the huge jaw. But his eyes snapped like the mouths of baby crocodiles. Yasho would have had to become quick and clever like Suryavarman to have eyes like those.

Neatly, quickly, the personage folded himself down, like a wolf.

In the position directly opposite the throne.

"Hmm. Greedy boy." said the Little King of Poduli.

"Who is that?" Jaya asked.

Poduli's eyes sparkled with mischief. He evidently enjoyed the fact that Jayavarman was not informed, and would enjoy both alleviating and contributing to that ignorance. "Oh, *that*. That is the *Kanmyan*, the Servant," he said. Poduli turned and addressed his equals. "Which means the King will soon be trailing after him." The chuckles that followed showed no trace of respect.

Yet, when the conch sounded, they scrambled. Those who tried to maintain some kind of dignity found themselves with no obvious place to sit. Jaya had been prepared. He simply swept himself and his son two steps back, out of everyone's way and into a place on the side.

In the jockeying for position, someone, an army officer, forced his way in behind them. He then had the nerve to tap Jaya lightly, gesturing for him to sit out of his line of view. Someone else, a Vishnuite, promptly sat next to Jaya, establishing where the circle of seating ran.

Jayavarman smiled. "No need to crowd in behind me, please sit next to me."

Jayavarman was no doubt eccentric, but was also undoubtedly a successful king. Put in his place, the army officer ducked, smiled, and crouched to his feet and sat to the left of Suryakumara.

Is it any wonder, Jayavarman thought, that I loathe this place?

Then scribes rattled forward into the room and the Universal King himself came billowing in, in robes of black silk.

Shock. The shock came almost before Jaya recognized Yashovarman. It stilled his breath and hushed his heart. Then protocol demanded that he bow and lower his eyes. When Jaya looked up again, Yashovarman had arranged himself on cushions. Jaya saw then why he had been shocked. Yashovarman looked like a scholar. His bulk had reduced; he was thin; he had ribs. He had a scholar's patient, almost kindly face.

Have I lost the chance of a friendship, Yasho, by staying away?

Yasho spoke quietly, in a direct and businesslike way. "We will begin. Welcome to you all." He is not a bad king at all, Jaya thought. After all, Suryavarman did choose him. My Lord chose well.

It was a relief to know that the Universal King was someone to whom you could be loyal. It was a pleasure to see at once that this Yashovarman had become someone Jaya would enjoy talking to.

"We have a small problem to cope with. I'm sure we will deal with it. I'm sure no one here thinks that Bharata-Rahu has the favour of the Gods. There is no way in which his destiny will be to triumph. Unless there is anyone here who favours the old religion?"

Yasho's eyes were amused, but watchful. They rested briefly on Jayavarman. "Jaya, my old friend, you do not follow this religion, do you?" It was a statement, a joke, a threat, and a kind of recognition. The room chuckled.

Jaya found he could laugh unforced. "No indeed, my Lord."

Yasho nodded downwards once, smiling. "It's a very great evil. Our people did well to drive it out when the true religion came. You, Poduli, you know all about it."

The fat, comfortable, clever Little King was more discomfited than Jaya. "I . . . I know very little, Lord."

Yashovarman educated him. "They once used Poduli's mountain to worship the Earth. Their way of worshipping the Earth was to kill some poor hapless soul, so that the God could be made manifest in the body of the dead man, and speak to his followers. Of course the voice always said what the devil worshippers wished it to say. This is the kind of filthy business Bharata-Rahu engages in."

"Perhaps Bharata-Rahu would care to be the vessel for his god," suggested one of the generals.

Yasho pretended to be amused. "I shall suggest it to him in person."

More laughter. Yashovarman appeared to be genuinely outraged on religious grounds.

So this Bharata-Rahu dressed as a demon to scare the witless and uneducated peasants. Jaya remembered the sour faces on the road and thought: but who leaves the peasants in ignorance, King?

This Bharata-Rahu wears his hair long in a mane, and keeps his nails as talons, like a village exorcist who drives out demons.

He drives out the demons that category people blame for disease, because we leave the ill to die uncared for. Women die twisting in childbirth in their huts. I would rather the categories blame demons for their dead wives than us, *Chakravartin*, Universal King.

Yashovarman looked calm and confident. "So the business at hand is simple. We need have very little discussion. I require troops from each of you, and we must march before the rains come. We need to finish the business off in the name of the Gods. Then, we can have lunch."

More chuckles. Uneasy this time; this was all too simple.

"My servant will explain what is required."

The Servant stood up from his position opposite the King. He stomped forward on legs so thick that his thighs met. He glowered. "We will need 5,000 men from each of you. Except of course Kavindrarimathana who managed to lose all his army to these peasants. We will form an army of 100,000 men, with attendant cavalry and batteries of elephants. This is April; your rice will be harvested. The corvée must begin at once. We need each of you to go home, and return immediately at the head of your own troops. Then we march."

Who was this strutting, prodding little man?

Yasho of course has unpleasant demands to make, but this man does not make them gently. Nor, must it be said, with much of an air of deference to his Universal King, or any other king in the room for that matter.

This is not a man used by the King to do his prodding. This is a man who prods Yashovarman.

The Servant cast his eyes about the room, with his thick jaw thrust out. Is he challenging us to disagree?

Jaya spoke calmly. "There should be some discussion of strategy. Before asking for numbers which may not be needed. Or which may not be enough."

"Numbers. We get enough troops to win, that is all. The King has had all his discussions, but to keep your knowledge timely, since you are from the country, Bharata-Rahu has roused all the peasants in the Northwest. They burn temples and seize the riches and the rice. They dedicate them to their old god. They drive out the holy men and tear down the dedications. Counting them is difficult. They are many, poorly armed, and so the full might of the righteous must fall on them hard."

Jaya asked, "Who will plant the rice in the northwest region if we fall on them hard?"

"People from other regions."

Ah. The air around Jayavarman seemed to tickle his face and ears. Jaya said mildly, "Such people may be needed in regions of their own."

Jaya said this in such a bobbling tone of voice that the others laughed. But they had seen his point. First their troops and then their labour was to be taken from them.

Yasho, Yasho, you have allowed yourself to fall victim to one of the Oxen. An Ox who is both blunter and more energetic and possibly, under the wall-smashing bluster, more clever than you are.

The Servant bristled. "You seek to deny the King his righteous request."

"I seek to have an informed conversation that will remove this scourge without destroying the other regions."

"The regions are always a potential source of rebellion."

The kings and generals groaned. What?

Jaya laughed. His felt his whole face beam. "My nameless friend, I don't know why you think calling us rebels is a good way to get us to quell a rebellion. When we have hardly had a chance to say anything. Even the King himself has hardly been given a chance to speak by you."

Assenting chuckles. Jaya pressed on. "Can I suggest a morning of polite discussion to determine how we can best serve the King?" Jaya paused just long enough. "And to give the King himself time to speak."

The Servant was outraged. "This talk of time is just to delay. You do not want to give the troops, and so you hope to wheedle and duck and escape." The relentless prodder spun on his heel. "You see, my Lord, it is as I said. They will delay and cavil and question and try to deny you. They will want your help soon enough if the rebellion spreads to their own lands."

Yasho held up a waving, placating hand, to soothe and make his servant more gentle. "They have not yet refused. Let them speak."

The Servant's eyes shot spears at Jayavarman.

It was the King who told them the true extent of the devastation. He sounded aggrieved, wearied, and pained.

As well you might, Yasho.

For it has come. The hungry face has started to devour.

The people no longer care that you pray for them, or drink purified water on their behalf. They see no benefit to the squads of devotionaries who do no other work than to feed and dress statues, while real people go unfed and unclothed.

That is the real source of rebellion, Yasho. As I think your wise and weary face would admit, if I pushed you.

But we face a religion that kills people so that a dead god might talk. That does not advance the Dharma. Nor would Buddhist institutions be spared. The hungry face was untamed as a tiger's.

"I will certainly bring my troops to your aid, Universal King," said Jaya, deliberately addressing Yashovarman and not his servant.

So the Servant thrust himself forward. "The King himself has committed all three of his sons to the task. He asks less of you than he does of himself."

The air tickled Jayavarman again.

The Servant turned on Jaya. "You! There is your son, are you sending him?"

Jaya answered in a patient tone of voice. "As you can see my son is not yet of an age to fight. And he is the oldest. So no, none of my sons will fight. Will yours?"

The Servant was ready. "I have none, but if I did, of course."

No sons? Neither did Suryavarman.

Jaya beamed. "Oh, so I see! You want us to lose our troops, and then the workers for our lands, and you also want as many of our sons to die as possible."

The other generals chuckled. They may not have much time for little Jayavarman the Buddhist, but they had plenty of time for seeing the King's obnoxious servant dressed down.

Jaya blurted out what started as a laugh and became a growl. "And as many of the King's sons as possible as well, I see! I knew a man who worked as you do, Servant, and he became Suryavarman."

The laughter of the generals was loud and ugly, raucous in its determination to get back at the Servant.

"Following a period of revolt and confusion!" shouted the King of Poduli.

Someone else added, "Over the backs of other men who had better claim."

The air seemed to thrill. This was open revolt against the power of the Servant.

"Watch out for your servants, King!"

Like a caricature in a dance, the Servant folded his arms in disgust, looked away, and tapped his foot. Was he being serious? He cast a look at Jaya and then tossed his head in another direction. He looked like an angry little girl. Jaya had to laugh at him. The Servant was naked, shameless, unreasonable, blunt, demanding.

And dangerous.

Jaya looked at the King, and saw that Yashovarman was looking askance back at him. Their eyes met. Jaya thought: If you prefer this little strutting monster to us, perhaps because you know of no other way of placating him, then you will be fooled. You will be like my Cham Buddhist master, all book wisdom and asceticism. Not much point if your servant strips you of your sons, and then of your Kingship.

But that look, that question in your eyes, King, is weak. For it is full of regret; it shows you know I tell the truth.

If I were you, I would make this little monster head of your troops and dress him in brilliant lime green, put him on a lime-green elephant, and surround him with troops that carry only parasols.

And if he came back, I'd send him on a campaign to the lands of the Pagan.

And if that failed, I would sail the little man in a ship with sawn timbers.

Who knows, if I think he is dangerous enough, I may dispatch him for you in the heat of battle.

Jayavarman stood up. He bowed to the King. "I accept the King's request for troops. I will not send rice workers to the region. The loyalty of the rice workers in these lands must be won back by showing them that the true religion treats them with kindness. I will not send my sons. I will march in brown cloth, so I will not be a target. I also suggest you find yourself a general who has fought a campaign before. I remember our rout by the Chams only too well. It will be unfortunate indeed if this time we suffered defeat at the hands of peasants."

The King remained gracious. "Stay some time here, Jaya. I would like to talk to you." Yasho's voice was mellifluous. Perhaps he even meant it. Perhaps he yearned to discuss wisdom-literature and the savants.

Feather brush of fear.

Or perhaps to detain me.

"My Lord is gracious, direct, and kind. But your servant tells the truth for all his bad manners. It will be a journey of three days to return home. It will be longer than a week to call my men and arm them and stow provisions. There will be no rice in the fields to forage. If I am to be here again in time to march before the rains, then I must be on my way."

And I did bring my son here, and I must get my son safely away.

Yasho's face was full of affection. "We could talk about the old times and undo the damage they did."

Jaya paused, and breathed in strength and courtesy. "The old times damaged many people, Universal King, Chakravartin, though we both appear to have done well." The room, supporting Jaya now, chuckled. "But, Chakravartin, we did not damage each other."

Yasho smiled. "It was a near thing, Jaya. But I know that you do not like the City and yearn to be away." The great King waved the Little King on his way.

Jaya stood and bowed, and then dipped in respect to the rest of the circle. Their faces now gave him colluding smiles, for he had said what they had all wanted to say. He did it again. He said, quickly, sharply, "Keep two sons behind, Lord."

The murmur of the generals showed they agreed. Yashovarman smiled tolerantly and let the loyal, honest little eccentric go his way. Jaya safely ushered his son Surya ahead of him.

Yasho sent all three of his sons to the battle, and all three of them were killed.

LEAF 60

*How bold was Yashovarman's heir, the glorious Samtac Sri Indrakumara!
How my young Lord was quick in the attack, keen in the forethought.
He sniffed the terrain of the battleground as does a tiger. I remember his
young knife face, eyes gleaming like sunlight on the Great Lake. He was a
guardian door, bolted shut against all faults, stalwart, ready for the fight
or for the retreat, strong beyond the norm, and wise beyond his years. The
Samtac was Rama reborn again to embody all the kingly virtues and to
harrow evil. Like Rama, he collected and attracted many friends to fight
for him. Call me Hanuman the Monkey, for I joined him in battle bringing many troops. I was strong and I was loyal, and by my eternal soul,
how war made the maidens in my blood dance.*

LEAF 61

*I remember the faces of the two noble brothers the Sanjak Arjuna and
the Sanjak Dharadevapura, sons of Yashovarman. Their faces were fresh
as though Vishnu had given birth again from his own flowering stomach. The Sanjak Arjuna sang as beautifully as the sarika bird and danced
with grace, wreathing his warrior hands into the ritual shapes. He played
chess with the skill of demon. He would gently question the Samtac, test-
ing the path for his brother as a scout surveys the terrain. The Sanjak
Dharadevapura was fleet of foot on the field, and so devoted in his pursuit
of virtue that the unworthy could count his ribs. How I wished then that
my own son Suryakumara had joined them on the field of battle. How I
wished Suryakumara had friends like these, a noble company of productive fighting youths. Our handsome sons, how happy we are to send them
to their deaths, when the blood maidens dance.*

LEAF 62

I looked across the western plain in the rain-shadow of the mountains of Siam. I saw a fierce and foolish gathering of category people, armed with wooden swords, forest axes, and ragged shields of torn cattle hide. Yama (Death) swelled in the sky overhead, but we mistook him for the sun. At midday, we saw Bharata-Rahu, the ignoble man. He came like a festival magician with long spears on his fingers like claws. He came wearing an absurd mask, calling on his god, holding a dagger as if it could speak and making nonsensical, moaning noises. His people led forward a stumbling man who smiled. He was simple, or drunk, or made to drink potions. We saw Bharata-Rahu plunge the dagger into this man's heart. The bare-chested victim smiled down at the dagger inside him as if it were a delightful wonder, a child's puzzle. And he began to speak in a calm, sad voice, like one in a fever.

LEAF 63

I remember the face of the dying man. It was the face of a man who saw through the world, the face of a lover full of regret at parting. His high voice carried like the wind, saying to the category people: You have nothing. What is there in this life to keep you? If in dying you take two of them with you, then we will win. I will go in advance and be there to guide you into the palace of the earth. For the poor are beloved by the earth, all categories of people are beloved by me. He sank to his knees shivering as if on a cold morning. He fell asleep smiling. He had been made a spectacle to bolster a false priest, but I knew in my ancient soul that I had heard God speaking through him. Pray for him, sons of Kambu, transfer merit to him, for the Gods will know his name even if you do not.

LEAF 64

The dancing maidens are now still in my old heart. I want to pull that knife from the nia's chest, and help him to his feet. I would talk to him as one man speaks to another about the good crop of rice, the kind sunrise that is the flowering of Surya, the nurturing of livestock and the love of a wife and family. I would make that man my friend and together we would weave peace. Poor smiling man, I give you part of the merit earned by the great temple I built on the plain of that battle. May my donations to that temple earn merit for you. Now, in my old age, instead of commanding words in the stone, I cut them onto palm leaves. The merit of this book is transferred to all Khmers who die in battle, the sons of both kings and peasants, and particularly those who die in wars against each other.

LEAF 65

In the soft grey dawn we came running, feet hissing through the grass. We fell on the warriors of Bharata-Rahu, no music, no gongs, no songs, no parasols of office. I drove my sharpened sword deep into the bodies of slaves. Their muscles were so taut that the blade was gripped tight as wet wood closes on an axe. They flung off the blankets of sleep, and sprang to their feet, more ready to die than we were. With eyes as disarrayed as a nest of wasps, they came at us. Never give your enemy nothing to hope for. They embraced our swords. They hugged us as unseemly as public lovers, and killed us as they died. They latched onto our necks with lacerated arms and bit out our throats. It was as if Yama had suddenly stood up over the horizon, turning what had been sheltering darkness into his burning day.

LEAF 66

Our swords rose and fell like the rain. We waded through a swamp of blood, sinking in ooze, having to be mindful that the fallen men would still strike. They clawed and bit and kicked and would not be still so we cut them into pieces. The sun was hot when the rainfall of swords ceased to drum on the plain. We won, but oh what we also lost. I saw the Samtac fallen on his back, two peasants on him. They looked like boys wrestling. The peasants were dead, opened up like fruit fallen from the trees. The King's son blinked; he had clasped a hand over his throat. I knelt and said, "My Lord." He looked at me in great sadness and regret, for his throat had been cut. He tried to speak but his only words were a welling of blood. Yama the devouring sun was full upon us.

LEAF 67

Bravely the Samtac faced his own death. How calmly he lay there, accepting that in this life he would never have his throne, his Kingship, his wife, or his children. He would have this swamp of blood, these flies, and these category people for companions. The Crown Prince could not speak. He could only choose the moment to move his hand. I called to our soldiers, saying, "Despair! The King's son is fallen." They called back: Which one? For Sri Arjuna has fallen and Sri Dharadevapura has fallen. The Crown Prince Sri Indrakumara wept and he looked at me. His eyes said: the Servant did this. His eyes looked up at the sky and the clouds. Then he lifted his hand from his wound. There was a purifying fountain as if from the springs of Mount Meru, a fountain of cleansing royal blood. I held his hand as it washed over me.

LEAF 68

The Kumara's hand struggled and then fell still. I sat still listening to far-away birds in the trees, the birds of morning. Then I shouted for a chariot. Bellowing at the men in anger, I raged at them to move. I ordered all three of Yashovarman's sons to be taken home. I lifted up the vehicle for the royal soul into a chariot, and, holding him to me, I lashed the horses' backs. We thundered over the broken land and the neglected road, and I spoke to the King's son. I spoke of my anger at the Servant. I raged at myself who was older and who was pledged to protect him, and who had failed him. I raged and the body did not answer, but kept its sad silence. I thought of all those who had died, and what was to follow. The floodplain of my soul was inundated with sadness.

LEAF 69

I canoe through that inundation of sadness now at the end of my days. I have canoed through all my other battles on that same lake of tears. For we are angels, we are demons, we can be anything we care to be, but when the blood dances, the blood spurts. And then tears follow. How I had admired my young friends, warmed at the thought of their virtues. How well my friend Yashovarman had filled the throne. How well he had peopled the world with noble sons. I learned then that many things are beyond prayer, beyond hope, and that this is why the Path lies in acceptance. I came to Yashovarman as the sun set, dust coating the blood of his son. Neither of us could speak, and we fell together weeping. How I longed for my home then! How I vowed never to fight a war again!

But Yama rises each day with the sun.

APRIL 16, 2004

Sinn Rith comes to arrest Map while it's still dark.

Lying in his hammock, Captain Prey hears the roar of motorcycles. At first he thinks it's an airplane flying into the airport, but the sound is too prolonged and lacks the high-pitched whine of a jet.

Prey swings out of his hammock and looks outside. On the other side of the south moat, along the main road, there is a blaze of headlights. His wife, puffy-faced and worried, has got up as well.

He murmurs, "Mother, take the kids for a walk around the temple." He goes to the cistern and pours water over his face and hands.

Then he strolls out into the village.

He sticks his head into each of the terraced rooms. "Get up, the army are coming," he tells them. "Put on your uniform." He pauses for a moment. "Take your guns."

"Huh?" One them looks up, slack-jawed, his mouth a pit of fish and beer.

"Just so they see we've got them." Captain Prey pats the man's arm. "Quick, hurry, we must look ready."

The man screws up his face. "Chubby's really done it this time."

Across the moat on the Siem Reap road, batteries of lights play between the tree trunks. Prey thinks quickly. This can't be the main investigation; it must be the Siem Reap regiment. Captain Prey hears his men calling to each other. He sees them hopping one-footed out of their rooms, pushing on shoes.

Prey smiles with fondness and sadness. They're good boys. Most of them were soldiers once.

The motorcycles turn the corner of the moat and mill the dust of the roadway. It diffuses the glare of their headlights. They move onto the causeway to the Police Village, rocking over the ruts in the track. Captain Prey stands waiting, counting only ten headlights in all.

One by one, Prey's men join him, sauntering up to stand beside their captain. Every hair is in place. They're doing this for Map, thinks Prey.

There could be a fight.

The army motorcycles fan out and come to a halt on the plain between the houses and the tiny restaurant.

One by one the bikes fall silent. And there, sure enough, looking aggrieved, is Sinn Rith. Captain Prey calls out, "Hello, Lieutenant-Colonel!"

"Hello," says Rith, with no real politeness. "We want that man of yours."

"Which one?" Prey indicates he has so many men, and that the army are invited to inspect them. They stand feet apart in ranks. They look ready, if not exactly military.

"You know which one, don't get clever," says Rith. Oh, yes, he's angry, like a little boy. A little boy with guns.

"Sergeant Map is not here. He is working on the investigation. With some productive results."

"Do you mind if we look for him?"

"You can go into the temple and the park. Any Cambodian is welcome to visit the temples free of charge."

Rith is not about to be humoured. "You should have turned Map over to us the moment he showed up. You haven't disciplined him; you protect him. Now we've come for him."

Prey stands his ground, arms folded. He's shorter than Rith, older, with a bit of a potbelly, but he is on higher ground. "Does General Nhiek Kosal know you're doing this?"

Rith's blank stare is enough to tell Prey that they are all in trouble.

No one has felt it necessary to tell him another regiment now runs the investigation. He looks like he knows he's been sidelined, but no more than that, so he's here for a quick win, some kudos, and revenge.

Prey says as gently as he can, "I think it would be wise for you to check first with General Nhiek Kosal."

"That's army business. I'll tell him after we've made the arrest."

Prey's face snaps shut, like as turtle's mouth. "Map had nothing to do with the theft. He thinks you'll arrest him and try to get information he doesn't have. You may hurt him. You'll certainly take him away from the investigation when we need him."

Rith shakes his head. "We'll just see if he's here."

"He's not."

"Good. We will prove that." Rith waves his men forward towards the village.

Prey puts a hand out in front of Rith and stops him. "My men don't like this. Don't go into their homes. You'll turn things over. Both sides will want to be big men and have a fight."

Rith's face is as immobile as stone, but he inclines his head back towards his men. "Don't mess up their homes. These are poor people, they don't have much."

Captain Prey holds up a hand up to make sure his men stay put. "They will just go through our houses. Let them see we don't have Map."

The houses are open, and bare. There's hardly anything to riffle through. Being on a rise, the houses are low off the ground. The soldiers crouch to look under floorboards, frightening out hens.

Prey glances anxiously at his men. They paw the ground with their feet.

Rith's men come back, shaking their heads.

"I told you," says Prey to Rith.

The Lieutenant-Colonel does not answer him. He waves his senior officers over and huddles with them, murmuring.

A sergeant starts issuing commands. "We're going to look through the woods inside the temple area. Sam, you take your men by the north track; Nunny, you take the south. Chea and I will look through the temple itself."

A thudding of dust, crackling of twigs—seven of the soldiers move out through the gopura into the grounds of Angkor Wat.

Ignoring Prey, Rith and two of his officers walk towards the policeman's café and sit down at the table. One of them has a bandaged nose.

Rith says, "We will wait for this fat fellow to show up."

Prey sits next to Rith. How to break the news about Nhiek Kosal to him gently? "Lieutenant-Colonel," he says, "let me offer you some tea. This will be a day of surprises. For both of us."

The old man comes back and gives Luc the Golden Book.

Inside a battered old suitcase decorated with a New Zealand sticker are packets wrapped in newsprint. Luc peels back the paper and sees the torn, black-and-brown cloth, and he yelps.

"*Kraing Meas?*" he asks.

The old man doesn't answer. He reaches back onto the deck and tosses Luc a child's school notebook. "Get to work," he says.

Luc, dazed, turns the notebook over in his hands. It has a picture of a white rabbit on the cover.

The old man jams a pencil into Luc's hands. "Turn it into modern Khmer."

Luc's eyes boggle. All is confusion.

The old man starts to look grumpy. "Start writing!"

Luc swallows. Hands shaking, he gently pulls back more of the old newspaper. Inside the first packet are five whole, uncleaned brown rectangles of gold. He gently lifts one of them up. Inside the incised grooves are flakes of baked ink, just enough to make reading easier.

He looks back down and counts 155 wrapped parcels, plus the ten torn circles in plastic envelopes. It's all there. "Do you want me to translate all of it?" Luc asks.

"Depends on the time," says the old man.

The time before you have to shoot me?

The old man settles into his favourite position in the prow. "Kru Luc! Teacher Reaches-Into! Reach fast. It's long, you'd better start." The boys hand the old man his AK-47, and they unwind the tape from around the General's face.

"Hey, *Ko'hh*," the old man says to the General, clicking off the safety catch. Ko'hh means Unable to Speak. "Watch and learn, ah? We will have what Jayavarman tells us. But you will not. Neither will the Barang. We will have it, the people, not some museum, not some army, not some rich Thai banker."

Luc says. "It would be better in pen. Pen will photocopy better. More people can read it."

"Pen?" says the old man. "You think I'm a rich man?" The old man's face darkens. "Just write fast. Hey! Hey, Ko'hh, tell me why don't we know the language of Angkor? Why don't you people who run things educate the people? Why do you keep us down?"

Vut finally says something. "There are many Cambodians who study history. We do what we can. We are trying to feed our families too. We work like you do, day in day out, just trying to have a clean place for our sons, a safe and happy place for our daughters."

"Yeah, but you are higher up, you could do more."

"I started out a maquis like you. I fought to bring Sihanouk back."

Good, Vut, good. Talk to him.

The old man almost spits. "Then you sided with the yuon."

The General sounds softly pained. "The yuon beat the Americans. Pol Pot was being paid by the Americans. You tell me who a good Cambodian would fight with?"

The old man laughs again. "There was no good Cambodian!"

"Kong Sileah? He was a good man."

The old man nods. "Hmmm. Yeah. But he was killed."

The General says, "By you."

Maybe I should not be listening to this, Luc thinks. He starts to work on the Book.

The packets are entirely out of order and some of them have spilled open. The first packet was damaged, which makes it easier to spot, and Luc knows what it says at the beginning. He finds it, slumped somewhat sideways on top of other leaves.

My name in death will be Parama Saugatapada.

The General says, "Son Sann was another good man. You and the KPNLF had a lot in common. Both of you were against Sihanouk. Both of you were against the Vietnamese."

"Son Sann? That elegant intellectual? He wanted to hand us over to the Americans!"

"Who supported the Khmers Rouges after 1979."

The old man laughs.

My real name will never be written. For much of my life, I bore a King's title: Jayavarman.

The old man says to Vut, "Anyway, we did beat America. We got them out in '75."

"So why did you take their money?"

"It was China's money. China is a good Communist Asian country. The US just wanted to stay friends with China."

I am Jayavarman the something of a new . . . Dharma . . . way? morality? that overwhelms? pushes under? the . . . old and surmounts? overcomes? it. The old gods . . . had to listen to the big/ great soul . . . Buddha . . . for enlightenment.

I can do this, Luc thinks. It would be wonderful to do this. It would give the Book first to Cambodians. Something like this . . .

Well . . .

Doing something like this could make your whole life worthwhile. As quick and as tense as a breath, Luc begins to write.

The General says, "We were just doing what other countries wanted us to do."

"We agree on that," says the old man with a suddenly sombre air.

The second leaf is under the first, but not the third. The old man says, "So read me what it says."

Luc feels something like a wind move through him—all his Cambodian past. "You will have to help me," he says. "Tell me what Cambodian people would really say in modern Khmer."

Then Luc turns to the General to deliberately include him. "And you help me too."

"Kru Luc," says the old man with an unreadable face. He says it in the most complex way, as a tribute and a warning. *Teacher Reacher, do not reach too far.*

Luc hears another female voice, his nurse old Kunthea. He always loved talking to Kunthea. He sees her in the kitchen making lunch forty years ago. Her voice warns him. *Khla krap kóm tha khla sampéah.*

If the tiger lies down quietly before you, don't say it respects you.

Wincing with pain, the General rolls over so that he can see the Book.

Luc involves the old man. "So how can I say this in Khmer? *I am*

Jayavarman, the . . . porter? of a new way?"

"Bringer," says the old man. He begins to help.

William sees army officers in the police village, and he has Tan Map on the back of his motorcycle.

Map chuckles. "Just keep going. This will be fun."

Fun? The army motorcycles gleam like huge black insects, and the pickup trucks are there, full of boys who crouch in the back, looking miserable.

Map laughs again. "Maybe we'll both spend the day in jail, moto-boy!"

Map looks terrible. He seems to have spent the night prodding his spots. They've gone a livid swollen purple. There are claw marks across his forehead the color of deep bruises. He looks like a gun has gone off in his face, and his speech is woozy with fatigue. And no, he did not eat anything at all last night.

Does this man want to die?

William can see three army officers around a table at the gateway café. They sit up, take their feet off the stools, and touch their comforting holsters.

William looks back at the number of army motorcycles and thinks: where are the rest of the men?

At least Map had stopped on the way back from Leung Dai. He walked into the forest and came out armed and in his uniform. The army won't know he goes through their roadblocks looking like a farmer. With the gloves off it's evident that his hands are infected now, yellow and purple.

"You want to go on, Loak Sergeant?"

"Sure. What, you think you can drive faster than army motorcycles?"

William works the motorcycle around the ruts in the track. It takes him five minutes to cross the causeway.

He parks his bike next to the pickup. "Hiya, guys," he says to the boys.

"The army's here," one of them replies. "They don't look friendly."

Map hops off the motorbike and strides forward. "Good morning, Lieutenant-Colonel! Good morning, officers." He's laughing.

William is allergic to conflict. It makes his stomach cramp. He looks at all the guns.

Map flings his hat onto the table in front of Rith and swings onto a stool. "It's good to know that officers have time to relax. It means the rest of us can get on with our work." He turns to Captain Prey as if reporting to him. "Saom Pich did not come home last night. No messengers came to the house. So he's out there somewhere with the Book." He turns and grins at Sinn Rith. "Or have you managed to arrest him?"

"No," says Rith. "We've managed to arrest you."

"Not yet," Map laughs and waves a finger in Rith's face.

William thinks: this isn't an act. He really isn't at all afraid of them. Which means he really doesn't care what happens to him.

"Oh, something else our investigation has found out. We have a sighting of Saom Pich getting on a boat and heading south onto the lake. Someone was thumping inside the hull. I think your General may be hurt."

Sinn Rith is glowering. Map laughs at him. "You mean nobody told you? That is because General Nhiek Kosal runs things and your team doesn't."

"Map...," warns Captain Prey.

"Your own colleagues don't trust you. Maybe they think you stole the Book too."

Map's face is doing the most extraordinary things. The squeezed spots have swollen into huge hard lumps, and grinning traps them between muscles. They rock back and forth all by themselves under his skin.

Map leans forward. Parts of his face seems to be hammering to be let out. "I remember you, Sinn Rith. I saw you in that café in Phnom Penh where all the Tamils went. Tamil food, Tamil talk. You were a captain then, and I asked myself, why does the Captain sit there? Then I remembered. The Tamils come there to buy guns for their civil war..."

Sinn Rith looks deadly, like a snake. "You keep talking, Map, you'll be in trouble..."

"Your poor privates, they didn't have any guns. They saw their guns and their ammo for sale in the market. You're the one who sold it, for lots of money." Map is chuckling. "You know, you're a very smart guy. How much money did you make selling army guns to terrorists?"

Captain Prey cut in. "Map, let up. Sorry, Lieutenant-Colonel, Map does this to show how easy it is to make charges."

Rith shouts over Prey, "He is the one who will be sorry!"

Map drawls on, enjoying himself. "Some corrupt army people need a new way to make money, and there is this Book made of gold. They don't care who wrote it! And there's an old General over their heads, blocking promotion, so it's a good way to get rid of him as well."

Sinn Rith draws his gun.

Someone shouts, *Mother-fuck!*

William jumps back, pulling some of the boys with him towards the pickup.

From the laterite wall of the ancient temple comes a cascade of clicking sounds. Safety catches.

"Putto!" says one of the army captains.

All along the walls, police guns are pointed at them.

Captain Prey stands up. "Idiots!" he shouts. "I didn't say to do that!" He turns to Rith. "I didn't order that!"

Map sits still in his chair, with his back towards the guns. He starts to giggle. He shakes his head, enjoying himself.

Captain Prey is furious. "What do you want, both of you? You want to start shooting? We have a truckload of kids here. Have you never heard of crossfire? Haven't there been enough children shot in Cambodia? What good would it do either of you to have a gunfight at Angkor Wat? You, Rith, what would that do for your career?"

Rith looks at his boots. "Your men pulled guns."

"You pulled yours first and they reacted. Look, there is a new general who runs the investigation. You don't run it, Rith. Not you, not your colonel. You just want to get at Map and get a quick result to show up the new guy. And you!" Prey points to Map. "You have the brains of a shrimp."

Map chuckles. "That's true. But I didn't take the Book." He flicks a hand at Rith. "I think these guys did."

Captain Prey is beside himself. "Enough!"

Rith's eyes go darker; his cheeks are white with rage. He cranes his neck back and around to look at the wall. There are at least fifteen policemen ranged along it, sheltering behind the crenellations. William looks at the big, beautiful bikes and thinks, Rith has more men, where are his men?

Prey shouts at the police, "Put your guns down. Down! Now! Come out here where I can see you."

Shuffling sounds come from behind the wall.

"Come out!"

One of the policeman jumps down from the top of the wall, just to show how strong he is. The others step around and over fallen blocks. They still carry guns. The army is still outnumbered.

"So, the Patrimony Police protect murderers," says Rith.

Prey sighs. "They wouldn't do that if they didn't trust Map. If they didn't know that he works all night and then sometimes all day to protect the monuments. My men think Map is a good man." He glowers at Map. "Underneath it all."

Rith is cornered. His face closes up and he sits back down at the table. He's humiliated, William thinks. He won't be able to leave without doing something.

Prey looks over to the boys beside the pickup. He waves them forward. He wants to use them as a distraction. "Boys. Come here and tell us what you've found out."

William thinks: get the boys out of there! They hang back, hugging themselves as if cold.

Map salutes them. "Patrimony Deputies. Don't be scared of Sinn Rith, he's a nice guy. It's only me he hates; isn't that right, Rith?"

Then from out of the eastern gopura, other soldiers emerge, and William knows. They're going to have to hurt someone.

William spins on his heel and begins to walk towards their machines. At first he only wants to get the army away from the boys. "Nice motorcycles!" he exclaims.

There are three officers at the table, and three soldiers have just come through the gate. That means there are four others somewhere.

One of the captains at the table calls to William, "You stay away from those."

William sompiahs but keeps walking. "They are so beautiful!" William turns and glares at Ea. Ea understands and begins to walk towards the bikes as well.

"Man," Ea says, "how is it that you guys get these great machines?"

The two officers at the table follow Ea. "They're too good for you."

The last four soldiers come out of the gate. They see William and head straight for the motorcycles. The first three have headed him off and now put a proprietary hand on their bikes.

William greets them. "*Chumreapsooah*. Just looking."

Ea talks as well. "You guys happy? I just got out of the army but they never gave us bikes like these!"

The two officers from the table come up behind them. William's stomach cramps with fear. He leans over and peers at the splendour of the chrome. "How many horsepower?"

By now, only Sinn Rith sits at the table.

"Don't touch army equipment, farm boy." Two of the soldiers get on their bikes to protect them. The four new arrivals do the same.

William looks up at Ea. "What a great job. I always wanted to be in the army."

"The army only takes men."

William laughs as if that were very funny. "I'll remember that answer!"

Then he squats down next to the machine. "Oh, and I used to think a Honda Dream was the best bike. Look at the suspension." He reaches out to touch it.

The soldier swings up onto his bike and kicks Williams hand away. "Ouch!" says William, looking pained, and shakes his hand.

At the table, Sinn Rith explodes. "What is all of this!" he shouts. He jumps up and strides angrily towards his men. He moves very quickly.

William hears him mutter, "Can't even protect our bikes from children." William pretends to be very afraid and scuttles away. "Sorry, sir, sorry, I meant no harm!"

By now most of Rith's men are sitting on their bikes. The most obvious thing for him to do is mount his cycle as well.

"Come on," growls Sinn Rith. "Let's go work with professionals."

The last two officers finally climb onto their motos, and together, all of Rith's men start up and rev their engines. William can feel the soil throb through the soles of his track shoes.

He glances up and sees that Captain Prey is already on the phone.

Ea looks at William and chuckles. "Man. I thought we were in trouble for a second."

"We were."

In order of their status, the army men roll out along the causeway, up and over the humps in the uneven ground. William turns and walks back.

Map has stood up and is organizing all the boys into a group. Captain Prey raises a hand as he talks on the phone. "Map, hold on."

Map keeps talking to the boys. "How many of your families have boats? There is a particular boat on the lake that we need to find."

Prey hangs up and jumps to his feet. "That was the General. He wants you to go to APSARA HQ."

Map shrugs. "I'm going to the Lake."

"Saom Pich went through a roadblock near Battambang last night."

Map's face falls. "Battambang?"

"He used one of the names you gave us. He said he was going to his cousin's house."

"Well, go there! That's where the Book is."

Prey is holding up a hand. "They did, but Pich was already gone and there was no Book."

"So he went to Battambang by boat, saw them writing down his name, and went another way back to his boat as soon as he could. He and the Book are on the lake somewhere."

"And you're going to come back to APSARA HQ where we can keep you away from Sinn Rith and you can get some food and sleep. Have you seen your hands? And Map. You must be polite to these people. The General's on our side. None of that stupidity we just saw. If you work well with these guys . . . I'll try to get you a pay raise."

Map's gaze fixes on his boots. "We're going to get the bastard," he says.

Map looks up at William and finally smiles.

This time they let William into APSARA HQ.

There is a big meeting inside the villa. William is left to wander. Behind the main building, there are long, grey warehouses. Outside them on grass or pavement are Angkor artifacts, some of them larger and more phantasmagorical than anything left out in the monuments.

There is a huge temple guardian who looks like Jayavarman except for his fine headdress and thick legs. Under the shelter of a walkway are multi-armed Hindu gods two or three times taller than a man. William is stunned to see it all. How is it that all this richness was here and I never knew it?

Behind one of the workshops, identical temple lions and the heads of gods line up. One of the busts is neatly sawn in half, and William sees that it is made out of hollow concrete. Are APSARA replacing the real artifacts with fake ones?

Dik Sangha comes out and shakes Williams hand and says how pleased they are with him and Map. He sends William out for pizza. Map wants pizza. They both chuckle.

By the time William gets back, Map is sitting outside under a tree. He sees William and raises his hand high. It is wrapped in a clean bandage and someone has put bandaids on the gouges on his forehead. William gives Map his pizza and walks on into the villa, to deliver the lunch. There is one huge room with open French windows, a vast oval table, and heavy chairs. William glances at all kinds of uniforms, brown, blue, and green. He sompiahs and passes them the pizza boxes, but he is not wanted and soldiers rapidly step forward to bar his way, and walk him backwards and out.

Map has already finished his entire pizza, and is sitting on a bench, sharing a beer with an older man. When he sees William, Map rocks himself to his feet. "There's something you should see. I told them that you are a Cambodian and trustworthy, and who else are these things for? I also gave a beer to the guardian!" Map rocks forwards.

The old man limps with them to one of the warehouses and opens it up. It smells of mildew and is full of statues and large, polished stones with inscriptions. "This is the kind of writing the Book is in, here," says Map. "The top is in Sanskrit, the bottom is in Old Khmer, but they say different things. The Khmer is a list of real things. We are more practical."

William peers. He can make out some of the Khmer words and thinks: It really was us; we really did do this. Map taps one large tablet. "This one was from the Pre Rup temple. Luc told me what this part here means: 'Oh you who are wise, may you come more and more to consider all meritorious acts as your own.'"

That seems to mean something to Map. He stares at it for some time. "Useful if you have no merit," he says, and smiles. He's very tired; the smile is faraway and distant.

He flicks his fingers forward and walks to end of the warehouse. They come to a statue of what William thinks at first is the Buddha, wrapped in orange cloth and protected by a shell made of Naga heads.

"That's Jayavarman," says Map. "After his reign there was a Hindu revolt. They threw this statue down a well. The French found it and repaired it and put it in a Wat, until they realized what it was. People think it's still there, in the Wat by the Bayon. But this is the real one."

He sits cross-legged on the concrete floor. "Eat your pizza."

William sits down next to him, and thanks Map for the opportunity to see these things. He tries to find out what Map knows, and Map starts to laugh at him. "Too much to tell you in a single afternoon."

Map starts to talk. Perhaps it's exhaustion, perhaps it's the beer. He tells William that his last woman got so mad at him, she took a hammer to his mobile phone. Another decided to brave the forest and sleep beside him there, but she was like a tourist, frightened of the bugs and the snakes. "Anyway, they only want me because all the men my age are dead." He looks wistful, and sips a beer. "So many gone."

He tells William some war stories about a boy who drank too much water after stepping on a tripwire; another about a comrade who was so tired he fell asleep on top of the ammunition dump. It went off. In the morning, all they saw was a huge, flat, blackened ring, and right in the middle of it, looking like he was still asleep, this guy dead. "He was smiling."

Map's face looks as infinitely sad as the face of Jayavarman is infinitely serene. William summons courage to ask him about the scratches on his face. "The ghosts do that when I sleep," Map says. "They're mad at me." He sips another beer.

He asks William his real Cambodian name. William tells him the story; Map starts to look tense. For once William unbends, in part because he wants Map to relax, to be tranquil again. "I did have a Cambodian name my mother called me. But it was a silly, grand name. You couldn't call anyone that name in the Pol Pot era."

"What was it?"

William doesn't usually tell people. He doesn't want people to call him by his Cambodian name when his mother can't.

"She called me Veasna."

Map's face looks even more tranquil than before. "I knew another Veasna once. I'm bad luck for people with that name. When this is all over, and we find the Book, you should stay away from me, young Veasna."

But he isn't angry. He is looking at William as William always imagined his father would but does not, even in dreams. His father's spirit cannot find him, perhaps because he calls himself William.

"You be happy, young Veasna. Marry, have children, make money, and stay away from me."

Map starts to drift in and out of sleep.

"Jayavarman came to me last night," he murmurs. "He told me that we're going to get the Book back. But not in the way we think. He also said that he was sorry, but he needs Teacher Luc."

At the foot of the statue of Jayavarman, on the concrete floor, Map finally falls asleep.

Outside the warehouse, inside the APSARA compound, workmen are staging a rooster fight. The birds jump up and gouge each other with their huge red feet. William goes outside to laugh and to joke.

Map has won William's loyalty for real.

At sunset, William drives Map back to his forest to sleep, and then he drives on, to Army HQ.

William sits in Operations in a plastic chair by a table. He says to a private, "Tell Lieutenant Sinn Rith that I know the truth about Tan Map."

He waits for an hour, and finally is shown into the Colonel's office. As almost always, the Colonel is not there—that's why he has a lieutenant.

Sinn Rith does not even look up from the desk. The room smells like the house of the man who rents cars to tourists: ozone and plastic from the TV, wood and polish from the floor and furniture. The

TV's on and draws William's eyes like a magnet. Karaoke, with the sound turned off.

"So, tell me what you know," says Rith, still without looking up.

William hunches where he stands as if the polished wooden floor were ice and his feet bare.

"Mr. Tan Map is a good man. He really does not know where the Book is, or your general."

"You waste my time with that? Get out."

"I am just a motoboy. I drive him around, that's all. I have no reason to say anything else. He really does try to find it! He works very hard, I don't know what he did before that was wrong…"

William knows who Sinn Rith is. His family were fishermen; he probably even has some yuon in him. His family might have been a target of the Khmers Rouges; he had been genuinely loyal to the Vietnamese. If he has done well and is a big man now, it does not change that he started out a peasant like William. He swaggers because he has won things for himself. William still knows how to talk to him.

Rith glares at him. "You are messing with me. Don't mess me with me; I can cause you trouble, motoboy."

"I'm messing with you to find out what he did. If he is a bad man, maybe I need to change my opinion."

"He was Angka."

"I know. But he changed sides."

"He killed someone. He killed one of my men, and then ran off to the police and they protected his hide." Rith's eyes glare at William with righteousness.

"If he is a murderer, that is a terrible thing."

"You should have seen it."

"But you still need to get the Book back, and the General, and there's no point fighting a war now. Do you doubt Map is smart? Do you doubt he is tough? Do you really think he took the Book? Perhaps working together you could find it and your general."

Rith's face is murderous. "What's it to you?"

"I don't like to see Cambodians fight."

Rith can't stop his face tightening into a smile. "You shouldn't live in Cambodia then."

"Aren't you sick of it? Map will never be sick of it; it's all he knows.

But you, you are younger. You are smarter; you have this office; you have this TV; you have the army to give you training. Do you know what those police are, who they are? Peasants like me who get eaten by mosquitoes and who catch frogs for supper. It is up to you to bridge the gap."

"Why is it up to me?"

William gestures at all the electronics and the polished desk. "Because you are a more important man than he is."

"You can't flatter me," says Rith, but his hand rests on his forehead. "Okay, okay, I will think about what you say. Will you now get out of my Colonel's office?"

"How else are we to finally stop the war?" William asks. "We're still fighting it."

"Okay, okay."

"Map says the war is still going on, and he's right. He's crazy, but he's right."

"He's drunk more like. Crazy for sure." Rith draws in a breath. "Look. I will say this once. What am I to do when I see the *police* protecting a murderer? You're right. This is Cambodia. Police, law, puh, it means nothing if you are connected. It's how things are. But I don't have to like it, and I don't have to treat a murderer like he is my older brother!"

But, thinks William, you shouldn't try to arrest him for something he didn't do. He expresses gratitude and respect and then leaves.

William walks as softly as possible down the army arcade. Map, Map, his feet seem to whisper, I hope I have done the right thing for you. Who did you kill?

Was it the other Veasna?

The hatch is left open to let in cool air and the last of the natural light.

Luc translates, scribbling. The old man looks relaxed, sitting with a newspaper and a rifle across his lap.

I'm not even Scheherazade, thinks Luc. Scheherazade just had to keep talking. I have to keep translating. What happens when I run out of text?

Luc looks up. "What's the modern Khmer word for the front of a boat?"

The old man arches an eyebrow. "*Khaengh muk kaphal.*"

Luc shakes his head. Sanskrit and Old Khmer often shared words. "Doesn't sound like that's it."

"What's it for?" the old man asked.

"He is describing a battle on the Lake. The battle that saved Angkor."

The old man sits up "Really? Where?" He crouches forward and takes the notebook from Luc. "Could be *khaengh kruy kaphal* if it's the back of the boat."

"It could be anything."

"Yup, *eu-uy*," says the old man.

"I'll just leave it with a question mark." Luc reaches for the notebook and writes the Sanskrit word next to his translation. To help those who follow.

The notebook is full of notations. After the first ten leaves, each packet seems out of order. Luc has to assume that no one will be able to refer to the *Kraing Meas* itself, so the notes say things like: second packet translated, leaf two ...

The old man pauses, appraising him. "Give it to me to read when you are finished. I want to read it."

The old man goes back to his newspaper. Luc writes Khmer quickly and simply, the pencil scratching continually, like a loom heard on a transistor radio. The old man says, "You write like my old schoolmaster. You write"—his tone goes from affectionate to bitter—"like all those intellectuals."

"The Angka Loeu?"

"Yeah. Angka Loeu. They wrote like you, like they were running to catch a train. Like the words were leaving the station without them."

Luc agrees. "That's how it feels."

The old man half-smiles but his eyes are stony. "Your whole lives are a train that is leaving without you."

You, thought Luc, are a very considerable man.

Keep talking.

"The sunset is the train that I'm trying to keep up with now," Luc says. "I want to keep working."

Silence. Luc is coming to the end of the notebook. "I need paper."

The old man holds out his hand for the notebook. "I want to read." He starts to read about the battle. His eyes widen. His hand drops, still holding the notebook. "This is about being Khmer."

Luc shifts forward on his haunches. "What does it mean to be Khmer?"

The old man replies, "We are a people who are perpetually in struggle. We are always about to disappear. But we don't."

"That does sound like the Book."

The old man sniffs. "Some of this is wrong. You say things and I can see the barang peeping out." He turns around and shouts for one of the boys. "Sam! Samrin!" Ah, thinks, Luc, at last, the boy's name.

Head through hatch. "Yes, Grandfather?"

The old man passes Samrin money. "Go to the bookshop in the old market and then the one in the Central Market. Buy four more pencils and ten notebooks from different shops, don't buy them all at once. Go on! Take the skiff. And don't talk to anyone. Just be quiet and polite. I want people to forget you were ever in the shop. Go! Go now!"

The old man turns back to Luc. "I'll correct it." He reaches out for the pencil.

Luc inclines his head and passes it to him. "Can I see what you change? It will help me learn."

He shuffles forward and lies next to the old man, leaning over his shoulder. No gun, no knife. Luc could almost—only almost—turn and run.

Except he wants the translation to be correct.

The old man laughs. "Look at this here. *Maych baan jee-a?* That's a colloquial question. From a king?"

Luc smiles, groans with embarrassment, and nods. "*Hait ay bann!*"

The old man smiles back. "I will have to be your Kru," he says.

As he reads, his eyes mist over. "He loved his wife," he says, the notebook pages crinkling as he turned them. "Hmm. He wanted a new beginning too."

He looks askance at Luc as if to say: get my meaning?

"Like Angka?"

The old man whispers. "Yes. Only he did good things. The Angka were jerks, that was the trouble."

They read the notebook together. The old man shifts to make room for Luc. "What's this Madhyadri?"

"The Bayon. That's what it was called then."

"Ah, yes, it's all there carved on the walls, just like he says. Yes!" The old man looks pleased. "Boys in fruit trees, turtle hunting, a woman giving birth, it's there on the walls. And here in his book."

"Why did Angka destroy so much?"

The old man keeps reading; his answer was ready. "They killed all their best people. They gave control to boys and peasants, running things for the first time ever." The old man looks up. "We thought we could change people by forcing them to have the right experiences. You don't change them, you just break them."

"You thought you would move them to the country and they would learn to live like country people."

"Yes." The old man reads on. After a while he says, "There is no one else I can talk to like this."

The old man makes marks in the notebook in the clear hand-writing of a schoolmaster. He finds plainer, more direct local expressions for objects and emotions. He makes it into a book for country people.

It gets late. They close the hatch and light a lamp. Even the walls start to sweat.

"Gah! This makes no sense. How do you fall from a boat into a water *lotus* of fangs and drowning? Lotus is a good word about holy, peaceful things."

"Ah, now that I'm sure of. The word for lotus flower in both Old Khmer and Sanskrit is *padma*, the same word." The notebook shows the original Sanskrit next to the translation.

"You're sure?"

"The people of Angkor had hundreds of words for lotus, words for every part of the plant, and lots of different words for different colored flowers, but yes, I'm sure."

The old man peers over his spectacles. "Hmm. You're sure it can't mean different bad things too?"

Something tickles inside Luc's head. One of the great hells was called *mahapadma* in Old Khmer. Padma was also the name of a hell?

"Hmm. Perhaps. Change it to hell instead of lotus and I'll check it later."

Later? As in going to a reference library? When would that be? The pause between them goes on slightly too long.

They hear a noise. "Ssh!" says the old man. Luc's heart catches in fear. Fear? Almost as if he doesn't want to be rescued.

A boat grinds its way towards them and shushes to a halt. The old man stiffens and then relaxes. He rolls forward onto his knees and blows out the lamp. The boy opens the hatch and swings inside the hull. He drags the hatch back over him and only then clicks on a flashlight, holding out pencils and notebooks.

The old man commands, "Okay, you write in this new book here, I'll keep correcting." The hatch slams shut and the lamp flares back into life.

Luc carefully unwraps another packet. This one seems to be about Jayavarman being a slave. In Champa. This will change our view of him, Luc thinks. He picks up the leaf and realizes: the last time this was touched was a thousand years ago.

The old man reads as the wick in the lamp glows white and the air in the hull heats up again. From time to time he wipes the sweat out of the hollows of his eyes. The General wakes up. He groans, rolls away and covers his eyes. The old man keeps reading, calmly and methodically, sitting bespectacled and cross-legged. His sweat drips once onto the notebook and after that, he holds the book up.

Arn, Luc makes himself think. Arn's name means Reader or Reading and he often comes to my house so we can read together. We can hear laughter from outside, club music, birds and traffic, all from a Phnom Penh in which nothing is dangerous or unhappy.

The old man finishes the first notebook. He folds his spectacles, and goes still and quiet, trying not to show emotion. After a time he sighs and says, "He wrote it for us, for his people in the future."

Luc thinks: I've got to him.

The old man asks, "How much have we got done?"

Everything aches: Luc's eyes, back, knees and hands. "Six packets, thirty leaves out of 155."

"You want to keep working?" the old man asks.

"Yes, okay."

"I'm staying here from now on," says the old man, as if in passing.

APRIL 1165

In the late afternoons, after napping, the women of the palace gathered for instruction.

Queen Jayarajadevi had once so enjoyed this part of her day. Recently, it had become a trial.

The servant women waited under a white awning that kept out the sun. They greeted Jaya with a sound like many bells. *Rajadharma*, they called her, Queen of the Holy Path.

Jayarajadevi Kansri took pleasure in her women, looking so healthy and fulfilled. One could tell at a glance that this was a well-governed land of happy people.

For how much longer? There had been terrible news in a letter from the King. He had written from faraway Champa, where he was building an alliance.

Yashovarman had fallen. The Servant now ruled.

Something rustled, coughed, and shifted its way across the floor.

Queen Jaya's heart sank. Here he came, late again, today of all days, when there was so much to discuss. The King's second-born son, Rajapativarman.

"Apologies, Aunty." Rajapati had a full male voice, deep and mellifluous. From the voice alone, one expected a handsome prince of legend.

Prince Rajapati walked on all fours, a long sausage body with tiny hands and legs that were the same size. He had to wag his spine from side to side, a movement that his brown silk clothing, with its glimmers and rustles, only emphasized. He did not have the round family face, but was hawk-like and handsome.

Queen Jayarajadevi forced herself to confront her faults. She hated looking at him. She hated that ignorant people said that he had been sent to punish the King for a fault. The fault of marrying a slave? Not so if you counted Fishing Cat's two comely daughters. It had been a lesson for Queen Jaya to love her husband's consort. She had hoped to capstone that with love for all the King's children.

She could not love Rajapativarman.

He was a king's son even if his honorific did not include the title Crown Prince. So Queen Jaya waited in respectful silence as he hauled himself across the floor. Think, Kansri, how much more taxing it is for him.

But it would be less taxing for everyone else if he came on time. And he would get less attention.

The Prince said, "It took me longer than I thought to walk from the second hospital." His smile was fluttering and shy like a coy girl's. And like so many coy girls, his shyness masked a fixed determination.

His very presence at a school for women seemed to say: I am not fit for men's work, so I might as well learn along with the women. That was well and fine, but the women wanted to discuss all subjects, even those men should not hear. He could have tutors if he wanted them. It was hard not to see something aggressive about his behaviour.

As if he had heard her thought, Rajapati said, "Sorry to be such a bore. But I come here so that I will be less alone."

She had to say something. "And you are welcome, Prince."

"And perhaps I'd be more welcome if I didn't keep everyone waiting." He finally arranged his pillows and settled, as attentive as a bad conscience.

Jayarajadevi began. "Today we have had news. Our Lord's Lord, the Universal King Yashovarman, has not only been killed in battle..."

The ladies dutifully groaned.

"...but his Servant has given himself the honorific of Tribuvanadityavarman and declared himself without right to be the Universal King."

The women tutted and covered their mouths with their clean right hands.

"Tribuvanadityavarman. It's not even a royal honorific."

Rajapati blurted out a laugh. "I can't even say it!"

"Protégé of the Three Suns. What's that a reference to?"

Rajapati's voice went darker. "Being a servant, he has to be original."

Queen Jayarajadevi wanted to work her way to truth with her women. "I wish to clarify for myself why this seizing of the throne lacks virtue."

Rajapati sniffed in a kind of reversed laughter, and looked at her, blinking and grinning, as if the question were absurd.

Queen Jaya continued. "I think of the behaviour of Rama, who was an avatar of Vishnu. When Rama discovered that the throne, which should have been his, had been given to Bharata, he took himself into exile voluntarily. This is how someone who follows the Path treats issues of succession. He steps aside. The King of the Eastern Buddha, Lord Jayavarman, similarly has never even considered making himself a Universal King. How can a servant lay claim to any virtue when he makes himself a king?"

Jayarajadevi felt something pluck the air: a mistake.

Rajapati smiled. "Like my mother made herself a consort of the King?"

Queen Jaya's eyes boggled. "No! Nothing like you, beloved mother, who is an exemplar of all the virtues!"

He was smiling, the little rat!

Queen Jayarajadevi wrestled with anger. "Virtue elevates as naturally as plants grow towards the sun. Virtue never seizes like the tiger. Virtue awaits invitation."

Rajapati leaned his head back. "Tribuvanadityavarman was invited, I'm sure. By his men in the court. Perhaps they felt he had all the virtues."

Fine. To be challenged was to be forced to think. "Your mother did not send a king to his death in order to achieve elevation."

Rajapati smiled. "She achieved it through love."

"Yes!"

"Love is a worldly distraction from the Path; so is murder. Maybe ambition needs no excuse."

The First Queen drew a breath. "Your father would never send someone to his death to be rid of him for policy, or to advance himself."

Did Rajapati's smile mean he thought his father would do such a thing? "I am reminded again of the virtuous Lord Rama," he said. "I'm thinking of his behaviour towards his wife Sita. In some *versions*—and there are so many versions, I wonder which one, if any, is true—the virtuous Rama burns his wife to death."

Separation from Sita had made Rama doubt his wife. In the end, Sita was rejected, humiliated, unjustly cast aside by her Lord. Every woman knew the potential truth of that.

Oh, wretched boy, you always touch the most painful parts. And you always have this slight wrench in your love for your father. Who, as it will be apparent to everyone here, I have just likened to Rama.

Jayarajadevi stood back from her anger and took root in the genuine puzzle of his question. "Rama was a god come to earth, perhaps to learn the difficulties of being human. Men are cursed with a need to be master, even over their wives. If they feel their wives reflect badly on them or suspect their wives, they behave badly. On the other hand," she sighed, "there are men such as your father, who is always open about his faults and tries to live up to the things he stands for."

"Such as having three wives and at least one consort."

Some of the women gasped, for the King had two wives and a sister-in-law.

He was referring to Queen Jaya's unmarried sister.

"Two wives," corrected Queen Jayarajadevi. "The illustrious Rajendradevi and myself."

"I made a mistake," he said, so lightly you could almost hear the air whisper: *It's an easy mistake to make.*

It's a difficult age, thought Jayarajadevi. Most boys become rebellious at fourteen, but they can be sent to army camp or off to the mountains.

He switched tactics. "So is it war, Aunty? If I can call you Aunty, exactly."

"I fear so," she whispered.

"Father will be happy, then. I suppose that's why he took his able son Surya with him to Champa."

Silence. "Your father hates war."

"He feels bad about it after it is over. I don't *think* it's because he's sad there is no more war. I think it's because he sees the results, you know, guts in trees. But his eyes and his smile gleam when he knows one is coming. I suppose he forgets all about the blood and the killing."

"Your father has to deal with whatever is real."

That smile. He's about to come out with that horrible laugh. How could a woman as lovely as his mother have such a son? Sometimes I think his heart is as shrivelled and twisted as his legs.

"I cannot," he said, "deal with what is real. So really, what I have to say is of no value."

"If you say so, Prince, it will be true."

"Ah! How terrible for you, if what I had to say went unattended."

Patience, Kansri. He deliberately annoys because he feels mean inside, and who can blame him, poor boy? "I find it terrible if anyone is not listened to."

"And you make such efforts to listen to me, and I am grateful. I can see you working so hard at it."

Oooooh! He really is trying to make me angry. Enough!

"People are not perfect, Prince. Even if their limbs are. Perhaps you expect too much from people who are whole. Forgive us for being frail. I am afraid the sad truth is that even kings and queens have much to learn."

It may have been the point he wanted to make. "I will remember that lesson," he said, in his beautiful voice. Something deep inside the voice made the teak floors quiver.

Late afternoon, golden light, silken footsteps, rustling of cloth— Fishing Cat entered the upper storey with a bronze bowl.

Queen Jaya had not asked for anything, and it was generally known that she was not comfortable when the King's consort served her. "Cat," said Queen Jaya. "This is kind of you, but I ate earlier today."

"It's no trouble, Lady." Fishing Cat lifted the bronze lid and vapour rose smelling of cardamom and rice and fish.

Cat and Princess Indradevi were in a conspiracy to make Queen Jaya eat, to help her resist what they called the Bird Temptation.

The Temptation was to starve away all the flesh and take to the heavens in spirit. Intellectually Jaya knew that it was wrong; starvation did not, finally, improve the spirit. But her heart felt like a caged bird; she wanted to open up her ribcage and let the bird fly free.

"Oh, that all looks so delicious. I will take something, thank you."

Cat stayed, arms folded. Watching to make sure that I swallow something? Am I so far gone?

Queen Jaya reached forward and pressed together rice and fish. Cat moved behind her and began to unwind her hair.

Really, this sisterly attention. Jayarajadevi almost understood why people felt that mixing categories broke the natural order. It produced awkward situations like this.

Fishing Cat said, "I'm worried. I fear my son has been troubling you again."

Should she prevaricate, deny? "Yes, Cat, he has."

"He is too combative. I don't think he realizes yet he has the power to wound."

Oh yes he does, thought Jaya. But then it would be difficult for any mother to believe wrong of her son.

Cat sighed. "He is a warrior, trapped inside that body. We have to get him away from here."

Queen Jaya blinked in surprise. "How? Why?"

"He's turning in on himself and outward on everyone else." Cat's hands, soothing the Queen's hair, were calm, but her voice caught. "We need to get him to his father. We need to get him into a war."

Queen Jaya turned.

Who is this woman? She is stolid and blunt and yet she always manages to astound me. I certainly would never have prescribed war for any of my children, and yet what a relief, and how selfish of me to feel relief.

I do want her son gone.

Queen Jaya turned to look at her. "It's not for me to say, Cat. You're his mother. But I have to say, I think you're right."

The look on Cat's face shocked her. It was smiling, knowing and kindly all at once. It meant Fishing Cat knew. She knew that her son needled the Queen, that he was more than an annoyance. He had become a trial. The look meant that Cat saw through her. Queen Jaya had a slight inclination to stand up and leave. She resisted it.

Cat said, smiling, "You are allowed to sigh with relief."

Making light of it, Queen Jaya, blew out an exaggerated showy sigh of relief. "Whew!"

The slave-consort's chuckle was simply a rhythmic hissing of breath. "My son assumes everybody thinks he is a monster, and, without realizing it, tries to live up to it. I tell him he's rude and will lose friends, but he is not wise. So. We must make him wise."

"But send him into battle. How? What will he do in a battle?"

"I don't know," said Cat. "If we make him think it's his idea, he'll tell us what he can do."

"Cat, this is a plot."

"Tooh! It has been a plot since his birth. A mother knows; I knew when I held him. The way he writhed. He was a little devil then." Cat's eyes gleamed with a smile.

But I must not play along with this, Queen Jaya thought. This must be her doing. Jaya said nothing else.

Cat said, "Tonight at supper, we will gather all the children, and talk about the situation. We might suggest that his brothers go back with the messengers to join the King. All except him. That would do it."

Her eyes were suddenly sad.

Aunty Indradevi mentioned it over supper.

The boys' excitement danced like the light from the tiny oil lamps. Even bookish Virakumara became agitated. "Oh! Yes! I will note all the great actions and write an inscription!" he said.

Little Rajendravarman said, "I will go and Suryakumara will teach me to throw a spear!"

Vira bounced up and down. "We can all travel together, we can all protect each other!"

Queen Jaya was becoming frightened for the boys. "How can you forget strategy! Remember the Lord Yashovarman, who sent all his sons to the same battle! That is why we have this war now, all his heirs were killed."

Rajapati had stretched himself out on the middle of the table. "Perhaps you should send his useless son instead."

Queen Jaya was beginning to get annoyed again. "None of the King's sons are useless!"

"Except the one who cannot walk. Or resist breaking things."

He looked at the Queen askance. He was forever looking at Queen Jayarajadevi askance, as if there was something about her he could not believe.

"If you keep degrading yourself, Prince, sooner or later people will start to agree with you!" Jayarajadevi felt her eyes flash.

"Heaven forfend, no, that's an outcome I had never imagined!" His voice was mocking. Ooooh! It made Jayarajadevi angry. He knew what he was doing to himself, so why was he smiling?

Rajapati said, "I'll tell you what I could do in a battle." He was coiled now, like a cobra. "You know the bronze standards, the tall ones? With an image of the Monkey, borne aloft for luck? I could stick myself up on top of one of those. I could be carried for luck, like Hanuman, God of Strength."

His mother is right. He is a sword swung inside a house that will either cut his family or cut himself.

"What good would that do?" said his half-brother Vira.

"Well, at first I thought that my deformities would terrify the enemy. But then I thought: I could be a bronze image with eyes. If you held me up high enough, I could survey the battle. I am not unintelligent; I can understand the basics of warfare even if I can take no more part in it than a floor rag."

Silence. Vira looked down at the table, in some kind of embarrassment or shame. Rajapati could say things that reduced everyone to silence.

"Then that is what shall happen," said the Queen. She tried to keep her voice soft and kind. "You will get your wish."

Cat spoke. "And none of your brothers will go. Only you. And understand, Son, that this is a punishment. For being rude."

"Only about myself." Rajapati sounded surprised. His smile slowly faded.

Rajapati left at dawn with a detail of soldiers.

He was put in the care of one of the soldiers, who had been blinded in a battle. Rajapati detested the man. He was always smiling; what on earth did he have to smile about? The soldier's name meant Root Vegetable. He was a soldier nia, who followed the troops and cooked them noodles—a peasant, stupid, always cheery and smelling of sweat.

But today there was a breeze, the sun shone pink and gold on the clouds, and the clouds scurried in the sky like pennants in a battle. Rajapati felt himself soar, being carried on the back of a man who was as incomplete as he was.

"Sing us a song, good Root. I will warn you of potholes."

"Okay, Little Master, okay." Root kept thinking Rajapati must be a child, to be so small and wriggly. "You boom along well too. You have a voice like a drum, sir. Despite your age!"

And Root sang a children's song about the tricky white rabbit. That's me, I'm a rabbit, thought Rajapati. I must survive on my wits.

Rajapati tapped Root on his left shoulder and Root edged to the left. "No need to guide me, sir, I can hear from the men ahead of me where to go."

Which of us is worse off? Rajapati wondered. I would give anything to have your strong legs. But blind? If I had been blind since birth, then I would be used to it. But if I knew that someone had taken a knife to my face to cut my sight from me deliberately, I would never forgive.

I would never forgive the world. I would never smile except if I had hurt someone. So how does this blunt peasant keep his good cheer?

"How long have you been blind, Root?"

"I don't know. Hard to say." Root turned his head back over his shoulder, dipping respectfully, with a slightly abstracted smile.

"What...four years, five years?"

Root answered. "More, more than that. At first I would not walk, I was too scared, I thought I would fall over. I was very angry. But your father came and talked to me, and I was not so angry afterwards."

"Dharma," said Rajapati, exhausted by his father's virtue, and his father's distance.

Root nodded up and down enthusiastically. "Yes, yes, the Dharma is good, it takes away my anger." Up and down and smiling.

Peasant, thought Rajapati. Bumpkin. I would not be so easy to talk out of anger.

But you are happier for it.

I suppose peasants are happier, I suppose they just live, I suppose they have no little beast gnawing at their hearts. They also have no

279

ideas. If someone of a higher category tells them something, they believe it. They are grateful for it. They smile and bow. They are only just one up from the beasts of the fields. If a blind elephant could talk, what would it say that was any different from what this bumpkin says?

Someone took my eyes away, but I got used to it, and now, hey! I'm happy.

Root said, "Sounds can make a world too, you know. You hear a world as well as see it."

Rajapati tapped his right shoulder. One side of the dike had fallen in. You didn't hear that, thought Rajapati.

"And anyway, if I fall over I just pick myself up!"

"And if you roll into thorns?"

"Then I pick the thorns out."

"And what if your wife is cheating on you and you don't know it?"

Root roared with laughter. "She did! She left me!"

"Ho, ho that sounds like a good joke."

Root made a sound of sympathy for his wife. "Aw. I don't blame her. She needed a husband who could provide. It was not that she didn't love me. In the dark, I tell you, a blind man is as good as one with sight." Root made a boastful gesture with his fist and then grabbed his own genitals. "Ah! Ha-ha! I ask the girls, was I good, and they all say, oh, Root, you are so energetic! Ha-ha. I tell them it is because I have to be good or I may not get another chance. Ha-ha!"

Rajapati felt a stirring down below. "You buy women? How can you afford them?"

The three soldiers in front had been listening. One of them, a real brute called Scarface, turned back and grinned. The Bharata-Rahu had tried to blind him as they had Root; there was a healed gash across his nose and forehead. Scarface said, "Sometimes we buy one for him."

Root chuckled. "I have very good friends. Sometimes your father does. So I am one grateful boy."

Scarface grinned. "The young prince is interested, eh?"

Anger writhed inside Rajapati like a serpent. "My hips are so twisted I can't get my dick inside a woman. My bones get in the way."

Blessed silence. It was as if his words had scorched the air, blackened the earth. The troops looked down at their feet and marched on in silence.

Once they left the province of the Eastern Buddha, they had to march at night. The darkness was no disadvantage to Root. He took part in the whispering debates. He could hear forests or rivers ahead; he knew marshy ground from dry by the sound of wind or the smell of the earth. The others saw the fires of their own patrolling Khmer troops.

They were avoiding Khmers, for Jayavarman was a traitor to the Usurper.

They crossed the great river at night, in a canoe. Rajapati lay on his side on the floor of the boat like an awkwardly shaped piece of driftwood, and the others took turns paddling.

Rajapati was pleased with the discovery that he was not afraid. Not of the night, or the river, or the crocodiles, or the Khmer troops. He was edgy and alert, but not anxious. He knew that Virakumara would have been jumping at every noise, his hands crawling about the boat in fear. Is it only that I have nothing to lose? That I really don't care as much about leaving this life? For if I'm born into another life, then it is at least likely I will have straight arms and straight legs.

Or is it just that I am a soldier at heart?

"If we're caught, let me do the talking," he told his troops.

He felt a kind of jolt go through the messengers. "I am a good liar," he added. "All I have is my tongue. I wield my tongue like a sword. I hope one day to behead someone with words."

Rajapati had meant it as a joke. The silence again, the shocked air, as if the world had gone breathless from the extremity of his words.

Root spoke. "What will you say, young Prince?"

"I will say that you are taking me to the temple hospitals at Champa in the hope of a cure. They will ask me why can't I go to a healing temple at home, and I will answer: because I am an affront to my father, who feels that many people say he must have done something bad to have me for a son. And so I am really being sent away from my homeland in exile, to keep me out of sight. I will lie so well, that I may even be fooled myself and be so moved that I start to cry."

Root said, as he drove the paddle into the water, "That will make it look like your father is a small man."

"That is why it will be believed. The easiest lie is one that invites people to scorn someone else. I will say that, and you will all agree. You might even grumble about having to be exiled with me. Agreed?"

It took some moments. What they were really adjusting to was the fact that Rajapati had become their leader.

Finally they all murmured, "Agreed."

It is well you agreed. After all, I am a prince, and I intend to be obeyed.

They entered the lands of Champa, and from there the danger lay in being killed as Khmer spies. An escort of Champa warriors was supposed to guide them into the hills, but they were not waiting at the appointed place. The little detail of troops would have to travel unaccompanied across Champa lands.

"Can you read, Young Master?" Root asked, fingering a fan of palm leaves.

"Of course I can, you oaf. What else would have I been able to learn? Javelin throwing, perhaps?"

Rajapati had finally wiped away Root's cheerful smile. The nia said, "Don't be angry with me, Prince, I am just a simple man."

One should never treat a mount cruelly. Firm but fair was the way to train an animal. Or a dolt.

"Give it here, then, Root, and don't go taking everything personally, as if you were the center of the world and every shaft was aimed at you."

Rajapati felt bad. He snatched the palm-leaf letter from Root's hand. He had to twist his arm upside down to do so, and he dropped the letter.

He sighed. "That was my fault, Root. As you will learn, it is difficult for me to hold things. Can you kneel down and pick it up? It's in those reeds by your right foot."

Root knelt down, leaning Rajapati far forward and to the right. Rajapati nearly toppled. Both of his hands bent inward at the wrist, and they flailed trying to get a grip on Root's thinning hair.

Finally Root felt the letter, and righted himself. He held it up and Rajapati read it. It was a letter of passage from the Cham Lords, commending these Khmer troops as allies.

"Give me the letter," commanded Rajapati. "It was very foolish for you to carry it. What if Usurper troops had found it? No one would think I am anything but a cripple. They won't expect me to carry letters of state."

"Sir," said Root gently. "You needn't cut yourself all the time."

"How do you mean?"

"All this talk about your legs and hands. It hurts you."

Rajapati suddenly seethed. "I am just stating what is true. Acceptance is Dharma, isn't it?"

"Anger is not," said Root.

They marched by day through Champa lands, the wide, wet, green fields. And then suddenly upwards into the high hills.

Life was at its worst whenever Rajapati had to do his business. Root would lower him to the ground and offer, "Do you need any help, Prince?"

"No, I do not!"

"There are snakes, my Lord."

"And what could you usefully do about snakes? Sing them a song? You can't even see them. I can wipe my own bum, thank you."

Rajapati would shrug his way into bushes. He couldn't quite reach his wrappings. He had to double up from the middle of his back and pick at the knot. He could only do them up again by tossing a neatly rolled package of linen up and under himself. The whole process took many minutes, as sun blazed, insects buzzed and creaked, and the messenger warriors slumped in the shade.

The Prince would then came crawling out from the bushes. "I hope that gave you all a chance of a good rest," he might say. "I have my uses after all."

"Sir. It would go more quickly if I helped. I don't mind, sir."

"No. I suppose you don't, you're used to mucking out animals."

"Sir, don't say that," Root's eyelids had scarred closed, and his gaze was always slightly misdirected. Talking somewhat to the skies, he added. "Who better than me, sir? Many people are modest like you, sir. I have the advantage of not being able to see."

"You can still smell," said Rajapati. "I can assure you my shit smells not one bit better because I am a prince."

"Oh, sir. I'm not the man to tell you that your royal shit smells like cardamom and honey. But it can't smell any worse than mine."

"I'm not a baby to be nursed."

Root sighed. "Consider, sir, the military problem."

"Military problem?"

"Sir, we lose time while you go off. It holds everything up. And, speaking frankly, sir, you don't become a footsoldier without having to see other men taking a shit."

Root was right; of course he was right. If you're not frightened of war or dying, Rajapati, what frightens you about this level of personal service?

You are frightened that it makes you seem helpless. You are frightened that he might mock you, or say your dick is small. Good Lord, 'Pati, look at the man. He's a dolt, but he's good-hearted.

He would never do anything to hurt you.

If only because he loves your father.

"All right, Root, next time you can help me."

Root nodded, and reached back and gripped Rajapati's knee, which was as bumpy and fragile as a cat's skull. "That is good, sir. I am glad you let me help you."

Was it possible this dolt felt sympathy for him? Was sorry for him?

Rajapati hated people feeling sorry for him, but he found that this time, he didn't have the heart to kick back or take revenge for it.

He patted Root's neck, as if he were a good bullock. Root began to sing another white rabbit song. Rajapati suddenly understood; the song was meant to amuse Root, not him. He was not singing it because he thought Rajapati was a child.

'Pati, 'Pati, sometimes you make yourself into a fool. You get angry and mean for no reason.

Remember the morning you left, Rajapati, and all of the world felt like a flag that was unfurling? It could be like that all the time. It's the same world, the same sky.

So Rajapati joined in the singing. The white rabbit was fooling the small brown bear. He did it through stealth and cleverness, not power. Everyone knew and loved the white rabbit.

Rajapati never sang. Cripples always ended up making music, sawing away at instruments off in a corner where they couldn't quite be seen. Music was what cripples did.

But it felt good to sing, anyway.

And Root sang with him, rollicking his head from side to side. Root was laughing. He's happy, thought Rajapati. He's happy for me.

The army of Champa was gathered in the high hills.

The encampment was vast and hidden in the woods that clung to the sides of the hills. Rajapati's detail were expected, greeted and then led ducking under branches, past shelters made of bowers. No fires, not tents or banners—nothing to give away the presence of the Cham army. Even the path was not worn. Evidently the troops took a different route each time so there were no paths to be seen.

"Root, it's enormous," said Rajapati. "It is huge, there must be 100,000 men here hidden away. But there's no smoke from fires, almost nothing to give it away. And you wouldn't think to spy out this many men clinging to hillsides. The plan must be to swoop down from the hills, cross the river, and do a forced march before the Servant can gather his forces in one place."

"Your father is a wise man."

"Can you hear where the soldiers are walking? Keep ducking low, we're going through leaves, you will scrape me off!"

"What do the Chams look like, sir?"

"Like us, only they wear too many clothes. Their helmets look like lotus flowers upside down. They concentrate all their wealth on their heads."

Root smiled blindly over his shoulder. "A wise place to concentrate it if it stops a sword."

"Root, a gathering like this, it must mean that there will be a battle soon!"

Root's back twitched like the haunch of deer. "Don't wish for that, sir."

"Oh, Root, I'm so bored at home. And I don't care if I die."

Rajapati unsheathed his soul and swung it over his head. I shall see a battle; I shall be part of it!

Root stumbled on the loose rocks, the slippery layers of fallen leaves. "Keep heading north," murmured Rajapati.

You had to admire the genius of it. Dappled with shadow, the camp of the Chams spread out on either side of them, silent, disciplined, and still. The eyes of the Chams followed them with suspicion. These are hard faces, Rajapati thought, these are murderous faces.

We both write in Sanskrit. We use the same titles and even the same names. We are cousin peoples. It is like looking in a mirror that tells unwelcome truths. The reflection is not unfailingly beautiful. We are suspicious of them, they are suspicious of us, the alliance is temporary, uncertain; and our swords can be turned on each other.

Danger tickled Rajapati's belly and made him smile. By God, this is the real thing!

His father sat under a tree, as round as a ripe pear. You may not *look* dangerous, Father, even with your back wisely turned towards the downward slope. His father looked up, and his eyes smiled at each of them in turn—Root, Scarface...and Rajapati, Son, how good to see you.

Rajapati explained, "I was becoming a nuisance, so my mother sent me to you to get me out of the way."

The King floated to his feet, gracefully. His whole body said: nothing can deflect or distract me.

"I'm sure you were," said his father smiling. "Your mother is a wise woman."

"You can just bury me in a ditch, if I am too much trouble."

The King smiled. "You? You are no trouble, Rajapati. A prince must be able to judge his impact precisely."

Jayavarman turned to his men. The messengers all dipped in respect. As he always did, the King bowed back to them. This indicated that respect was due to all beings on the cycle of samsara. Oh, we're all potential Bodhisattvas aren't we, Father?

The letters were produced. Jaya read them himself, flipping the dry palm leaves over with a snap. He chuckled at something. "My wives are telling me many things indirectly," he said, glancing up at his men with smiling eyes.

You think more of your men than you do of me, Father.

Jayavarman finished and looked up. "Root," he said warmly, and "Root," again with a happy chuckle. "My wise friend, how are you?"

"I am well, sir. Rajapati and I have become friends, sir. I am his elephant, and he is my guide."

Jaya turned and looked at his son with an equally friendly eye. "And what have you learned, Son?"

"To be a leader," Rajapati said.

Jaya bowed once. "That is a lot to learn in such a short while."

Root intervened. "Sir, he is a wise one. He knew what we should say to the Servant's troops if they caught us."

Scarface nodded. "He is brave."

Jaya's smile was imperturbable. "It seems to me you have also learned how to win friends, Rajapati."

They ate packed cold rice and dried fish. Rajapati hated dried fish, because his hands had to hold the leathery flesh and tear it with his teeth. Impatient people would be tempted to help him, feed him like a baby, or cut it up for him like he was a child.

The soldiers and Jaya sat joking after their food, exchanging news from home. Jaya asked delicately of his first Queen's health. Was she looking thin? They moved on to the situation here, how things had nearly come to the point.

General Namasivaya strolled casually up the hill to join them. A Buddhist like his King, Namasivaya squatted on the ground next to the soldiers. How they followed the Path, these kings and generals.

Namasivaya explained that they were to march soon, now that their strength had gathered. It would be a forced march, down out of the hills; and the Chams had a plan to build a temporary bridge across the great river. Elephants and war machines could cross and swiftly overtake their troops. They would march as far as Poduli if they could get there before meeting the Usurper's army.

Rajapati found he was yearning to tell his father his plan, the plan for him to be a useful lookout. He kept trying to catch his father's eye. He wanted his father to talk to him as easily as he chatted with the soldiers.

Root said, "Rajapati has a good plan, my Lord, for how he can help."

Jaya turned the full focus of his attention onto his son. "Excellent. What is it, Prince?"

His father's gaze was like a blast of sunlight full on a delicate flower. Rajapati found his idea shrivelled in this hot, revealing light. Suddenly, it sounded small and stupid. "I . . . I sit on one of the standards. I look out high up, and I see what is coming."

Jaya nodded. "How would you stay on?"

Rajapati felt a flicker of annoyance. "I have strong hands, I would hold on."

"The march would last all day and all night. You would be rocked and buffeted."

Rajapati found himself turning to Root. "Root . . . Root would buckle me on to the image."

Geoff Ryman

"Root won't be able to march and carry you, Son. How would you tell us what you had seen?"

"I...I would just say."

"Over the sound of battle? You would have to shout. That might make you a target for arrows. The enemy might hear you. If you were right, it might discourage them, but if you were wrong, it might mean we made mistakes."

Root spoke. "My Lord. If I walked with the bearers, he would just need to whisper. I have sharp ears. I would hear him."

Jaya turned, his eyes full of affection. "You are a valuable man to risk in battle, Root."

"I am a useless blind man, but you find a place for me. Your son, sir, has the heart of a prince! He is so smart, sir. He would not mistake the deployments; he would be like a bird in the air who could tell you what he saw. And he is brave, sir."

Jayavarman's eyes were wells of sadness. "I don't doubt he is any of those things." He looked round at Rajapati. "If the standard is dropped, Rajapati, you would be left tied to it on the battlefield. I would not send in anyone to find you. I would not ask anyone to risk his life, and, frankly, I would not risk my own. Do you understand that?"

"I am a soldier," said Rajapati.

"Yes, you are," said Jayavarman.

The conch shells sounded over and over.

The Chams, squatting at the ready, stood up, sniffed, and folded away their dice. They seemed to Rajapati to be unbelievably calm. He felt nervous, shaken. The musicians began to beat the drums to get them marching and he was still not aloft.

It was noon on the Mekong plain and beds of reeds as tall as a man shivered and waved with the hidden passage of the Usurper's troops. The gongs began to moan out their great long notes repeatedly, meaning: *The enemy is here.*

The standard lay on the ground. Rajapati lay on top of it. "Root! Root!" he called.

"Here, sir, here," said Root, carrying long loin wrappings, light and soft. Fumbling, he tied the young prince to the top of the standard, lashing him to a holy image of the Monkey God.

Standard-bearers scuttled past them. "You! Boy! Standard-bearer!" Rajapati called to them to carry him. They ran on, or stopped to take another one of the standards, their backs turned firmly towards the Prince. "Standard!" the Prince called. They pretended not to hear.

"Cowards! None of them want the responsibly of carrying me."

"It's all right, sir. I knew this was how it would be." Root felt the ground for the pole. "So did your father."

With a wrench of his strong shoulders, Root hoisted and held the young prince twenty-five feet above the ground. The brass standard rocked and swayed like a heavy pendulum. Rajapati could see the mass of Khmers crawling towards them through the reeds in three great deployments, with cavalry ranged in front, like the prows of great ships.

Their own troops marched in two great separate blocks, hoping to slam the Khmers from two different sides.

Root called up, "Can you see anything, Prince?"

Rajapati turned what he saw into a battle plan in his head. "The Khmers are laid out in the Formation of the Gods." This meant battalions ranged in three wings as Siva, Vishnu, and Brahma.

"The forces, particularly the elephants, are concentrated in the Vishnu." The other two wings would be lighter, faster, and able to close in like pincers. It had been less clear than it might have been; there was a mass of infantry also in the Vishnu center.

Booming, bashing, wailing, the Cham troops advanced.

Root began to jog to catch up, fighting to keep the standard balanced. "Can you see the Cham generals, Sir? Can you see your brother or Namasivaya?"

"Yes, but they are far from us..." Rajapati broke off. Soundlessly from this distance, the Vishnu wing launched itself forward, cavalry and foot soldiers only, sweeping towards them.

"Root, the Vishnu wing is driving between our two forces!"

Root bellowed, "Messenger! Messenger!"

"They will separate our two blocks!"

"Messenger!" Ducking between legs, a slip of a boy appeared, lightning-footed.

"Are you there, boy?" Root bellowed. "Tell the generals that the enemy are in the Formation of the Gods, Vishnu wing driving between our two blocks."

"How can *you* see that?" said the boy in scorn.

"Look up. The King's Eye is borne aloft. Now run, or the advantage of knowing that will be lost."

Like an arrow shot to skid along the ground, the boy turned and was gone, darting through the wall of men ahead of them.

"Keep going, Root, catch up."

"You see anything else, sir?"

It was the reeds. Chams were not used to fighting in them. The wedge of Khmer troops whisked through the high grasses unseen between the two blocks.

"They've already separated us and we haven't even seen them!"

Suddenly, as if seized with a paroxysm, one of the Cham formations shuddered to their left and charged.

"The Chams have realized. They are charging!"

Root called up. "That will be your doing, sir."

Like a dam breaking, the Siva wing suddenly poured round in a great arc, mowing down reeds.

"The arm of Siva is swinging round to the left."

A Khmer horseman trotted towards them, led by the messenger boy. The horseman was a high category warrior in scintillating colors on the back of a white mare. He reined in the horse and shouted up, "What now?"

Rajapati shouted, "Siva wing circling to the left. It's coming round behind our southern block!"

The cavalryman said, "Namasivaya wants you to join him. The boy will guide you." Then the horseman clicked his tongue, flicked the reins; his horse spun around and spurted off towards the lumbering elephant on which Namasivaya rode.

The boy seized hold of Root's arm, to lead him. Root shouted up, "Hold on, sir."

Root began to run, the messenger boy holding his hand. The standard lurched. The elbow of the bronze Monkey God rammed Rajapati's fragile ribcage. The whole world spun crazily, as if the countryside were drunk. Wincing at the battering of his ribs, and the chafing around his wrists, Rajapati still tried to see. Ahead was a jolting, blurring mass of lances, reeds, heads, and cavalrymen.

Everything bounced and jostled. Rajapati suddenly felt the wrapping around his wrist give. Root stumbled, and with a jerk, the cords suddenly loosened more. Rajapati felt himself drop down slightly.

The boy still guided them, pulling Root's arm. "Make way, make way for the King's Eye," the messenger called. Rajapati turned and tried to wrench his hands round to tighten the cords. His tiny forearm bent double in the middle, and his huge hands, long and slightly limp, wriggled, trying to reach.

Rajapati looked up. The Chams had bitten into the Vishnu wing, but Siva had closed on their southern wing, and now the Brahma wing had moved, sweeping down on their northern flank.

"Brahma wing moving on our north!" he yelled. "Brahma wing moving!" The messenger boy took off, leaving them. Rajapati tried to see his family in the mêlée. His father always made it his business to be relatively invisible on the battlefield. But Surya! Despite arguments with his father, Surya was under parasols in a howdah, posed like a god.

Oh! to be astride an elephant, bow in hand, to call encouragement to troops, to swing around and let fly arrow after arrow, like Brahma on his hamsa.

Instead of being tied wriggling to a stake. What a stupid idea, what an absurd, undignified, silly way to die.

To die.

The cords were coming untied. He couldn't blame Root; he'd had to tie them quickly. The whole idea was flawed, his father had seen that, but he didn't stop him.

It's one thing to kill yourself with your stupid notions, Rajapati, another thing to kill Root. You hang on and do some good, for a change.

Rajapati stopped trying to tie the cords. He gripped the Monkey's arms and held.

Root stumbled, still trying to find his way. The standard pitched forward, nearly flinging Rajapati from it. Another cavalryman reared up on another white horse. "What do you see?"

Rajapati shouted, his voice breaking, "Surya's been caught between Vishnu and Siva. Same on the north with Brahma. Both our blocks are fighting on two fronts! No movement. They're bashing each other to pieces!"

Root repeated it. The horseman charged off towards Namasivaya. A huge Khmer footsoldier helped Root to steady the pole. Rajapati's hand slipped from the Monkey's shoulder. It was as if the smooth bronze were greased. His long, limp fingers found the Monkey's mouth and the serrations of the image's teeth. Okay, teeth, pierce me if you will, but just hold me!

It was only then that he realized he had been turned round the wrong way, away from the battle.

He tried to twist around to see, but his hunched back stopped him like the limits of a hinge. "Turn me around!"

Root and the solider quarter-turned him. "More! Right around!"

He was turned and saw disaster.

The Vishnu formation had split in two, opening up a corridor. The Vishnu elephants began to advance down it

"Vishnu elephants going deep in. Right down the middle."

Root repeated it, calling blindly, but there was no messenger. The big infantryman signalled to him and sprinted away to carry the news, leaving the pole to swing wildly. Root struggled to right it, but it slammed into the forest of other standards. Rajapati clattered against them. A prong of metal struck and numbed his hand. Another forced itself between Rajapati's hip and the legs of the Monkey God.

With a flip and a twist, it levered him free.

Rajapati fell, shouting. He thumped onto a warrior's head and rolled down onto the man's shoulder. The Khmer blindly cast him off as a distraction.

Mud slammed up into him, reeds sliced his skin like tiny knives. As if it were threshing time, many feet in unison pounded the ground.

Helplessly Rajapati thrashed on the ground. His hand cracked under a heavy foot. "Root! Root!" he shouted. "Idiot! Don't step on me! Root!"

An ignorant Cham face peered down at him in horror. It did not know what it saw, something half-human speaking on the ground, some kind of battle sprite, some *garuda* or demon or emissary of death.

The Cham made a vomiting sound and kicked him.

"Stop, stop, you idiot!"

He doesn't speak Khmer, 'Pati.

Rajapati flailed himself forward and out of the way. His right hand was now as useless as a flipper. His bent, wishbone legs slipped, tying to find a purchase on the wet ground; his aching knotted little belly heaved and inched him forward like a caterpillar. "Root, Root!"

Suddenly the tide of feet swung around. There was a cry, a wail of alarm. What now? The feet broke into a run.

Running away.

Hands fumbled in the mud next to him, feeling the ground.

"Root! Root! Here!"

Root crawled forward, patting the ground. Running men fell over Root's back, piled high over him. They all fell on top of Rajapati, hands extending, knees ramming their full weight onto him. They stumbled their way to their feet, stepping on him. Root lunged forward, diving for him, finding him. Like a mother, Root seized Rajapati, and pulled him to his breast, fought to his feet, and ran blindly.

Feet thundered; drums beat; long horns sounded retreat. Billows of sound swirled around them booming, clanging. Root lifted up his head.

Rajapati guided him. "Ahead. Dead ahead. Run!"

Root spun instead, in waves of noise.

A wall of the Usurper's troops bore down behind them.

Root ducked like a bull and charged. An elephant trumpeted. There was a sound like rain, a sound like a tailor cutting silk.

Arrows.

Root hunched over the Prince, his back fanned over him like a parasol.

He stumbled, fell.

Root heaved himself up and thrust Rajapati further down under him, into the mud. Root's hand reached out, found a leather shield and hoisted himself up and pushed the shield under himself.

Over Rajapati.

With a sound like an orchestra beginning to play, a blade sliced into the earth next to Rajapati's cheek.

Through Root.

There was a drumming overhead. Clubs pounded on a ribcage, on a back, over a heart.

The singing blade slipped upwards. Voices roared, feet pounded, milling the mud. Over him, Root shook and shivered.

Root? Root?

Rajapati writhed out from under the shield. Chest hair was in his face, and blood. He wanted to see Root's face while it still had life.

The weight of the body was too great for him to shift. Rajapati was pinned. He arched up, his back locked again, and all he could see was Root's neck. He could smell Root, all over him. If he ever smelled that smell again, he would cry.

"Root? Root? I know what you did, Root. You saved me. Root. That was stupid. Why did you do that for someone who wants to die?"

Because you don't want to die, Root seemed to answer.

Because you have worth, little prince.

It was me who didn't mind dying.

Root, Root, I will never forget you. Root, Root, you were my true friend. Root, you are worthy of princes and kings and diamonds; you are worthy to have temples built for you; you are worthy of inscriptions in Sanskrit and bas-reliefs that name you and show how you fell.

Oh, Root, where will I ever find a friend like you again?

The sound of the battle passed over them. Root's blood ceased to pump over the Prince. Rajapati tried to pull himself free and couldn't.

All was silent except for the wind. Rajapati started to sing. He sang the song of the white rabbit, who was tricky.

Life was tricky, it was a game, you had to accept that too. You march off into eternity and that in itself has no meaning.

Oh, Root, Root, I hope we meet again in another life, and I hope I know you, I hope I will recognize a friend. For your merit I hope you are born a prince, and for mine I hope I am born crippled again, and blind, and that I will have a chance to save you and serve you as you served me.

The white rabbit tricks you. The white rabbit fools. Rajapati realized that he had been howling the song aloud.

Let them hear me, I don't care if they find me.

"Brother? Brother!" said a voice. Suddenly Root was hauled off him.

There, surprised, full of alarm, pity, and joy, was the face of his brother Suryakumara.

"Rajapati!" said his brother, and hugged him up and lifted him away.

The rout had been complete. King Jayavarman had survived and both of his sons, but the Chams felt there must have been spies in their camp. Perhaps there had been. In any case, the Chams did not ask for Jayavarman's help again. Nor did they attempt to remove the Usurper again for another twelve years.

APRIL 16, 2004 NIGHT

Rith drives home.

He pushes the accelerator pedal flat onto the floor as if it were Map's face. His black Toyota roars ahead, sounding like he feels.

Let's say for one minute, he thinks, that Map had nothing to do with the theft or the kidnapping. Say for a minute that Tan Map actually cared about temples and carvings, or even about a book.

Was that any reason to stop treating him as an ugly, sneering criminal? To forgive murder?

And that motoboy of his, may his liver fall out. Sitting, legs folded on top of a chair like a peasant, who was he to preach to an army officer about not fighting other Cambodians? What does he know about it? I lived through the Pol Pot era. I lived through everything that followed.

We had to take the Khmers Rouges back, we needed somebody to do the work, so we let them all come back in. The result: we live with murderers. In Samrong, there's a guy who turned his whole family in to the Khmers Rouges. Both his parents were killed because of him, but he still swings in his hammock. It's one thing to have to accept breathing the same air as those turds. It's something else to be preached at by a boy who only knows how to bargain tourists out of a meal.

A small animal darts across the road, a flash of red on its belly.

Rith swerves to miss it, tires squealing in the heat. Rith's heart pounds as if he's woken from a dream. It was a cat, a beautiful *chmaa*. He glances back over his shoulder to see if he's missed it.

That motoboy has got him so angry he's driving like a madman.

Okay, Sinn Rith, you're nearly home, so calm down.

Rith lives in a side street near the old colonial town. From the outside, his house looks like a wall of streaked corrugated iron.

Rith beeps his horn, waits, and beeps again with impatience. That old slattern of a servant Jorani pulls the gate open, bowing, trying to look pleased, and covering her broken teeth with her hand. Rith glowers at her and thinks: not good enough, Jorani.

The driveway is a narrow passage forced between two houses. Rith has to push down his side-mirrors to be able to edge though it. That *yesh* Jorani stands in front of the gate. Rith glares at her and beeps at her to step aside, and she looks pleased. She gestures for him to drive on. So he drives on. She soon gets the point: the side of the car grinds her against the corrugated iron. She giggles and finally gets out of his way.

Rith swings the car round into the courtyard and then reverses into the garage. Rith's son slips into the house through the back door. Where's he going? Rith whips protective sheets over the car, to keep off drips.

Rith leaves his shoes on the doorstep and steps up into his house. Grey concrete floors, whitewashed walls, bars across all the wide and open windows. He hears the front door slam. Rith shouts his wife's name, storms through the smells of rice vapour and spices, and rams his nose and eyes between the bars of the front window. A narrow alley full of potted plants runs along the front of the house to the gate. Rith is in time to see his skinny teenage son spin round its edge and pull it shut after him.

Rith shouts his name after him. "Sok! Sokhem!"

His wife shuffles up behind him in fluffy slippers.

"Don't worry," he says at once, "I'm not mad at you. Why did our oldest son go slinking off?"

"He said he was seeing friends."

"Well, if he misses his supper that will be too bad, don't cook him another."

Rith's daughter lounges on the floor, hypnotized by the TV. A Thai woman in a shampoo ad stands in front of skyscrapers, tossing her beautiful glossy black hair.

"*Chavy*," Rith calls her, Little Angel, and he kneels down and kisses her head. She grins with pleasure, and they fold up together in a hug. Her eyes stray back to the TV—a Thai serial about teenage vampires.

Though it's modern and made of concrete, the house is bare. There is a photo of his wife on the wall, but clothes hang from the top window bars or from hammock hooks in the walls. The hammocks in turn lie folded in the corner. There are no chairs and the thin plastic mats fail to cushion the floor.

Rith hauls off his hot, heavy shoes, feeling sore at heart.

He pads out to the waterbutt in the courtyard and wrenches himself out of his clothes to wash.

All his money is tied up in his General's hotels. What will happen to that investment now, with all the tourists gone?

"Get on with the food," he says to his wife, through the window bars. He riles up his sweaty hair and starts to pour water over his head.

I provided for my family better when I had a few more things to sell. Yes, okay I sold government guns, but only when things were at their worst. It was that or my family starved. Hasn't my wife suffered? She is as nervous as a butterfly. How many kids has she lost to illness? How much worry did she have all that time I was fighting?

Who is Tan Map to accuse people? What was he doing in Phnom Penh, then? How did he know about the Tamil café, if he wasn't selling guns himself? Who is he to humiliate me in front of my own troops?

In front of everyone. They put someone else in charge of the investigation and didn't even tell me. So I show up to do my job and arrest a suspect, only to find they know more about the investigation than I do! How is the army to hold up its head with all this internal rivalry and division? It turns us into a laughingstock.

Rith scoops more water over himself, cooling, cleansing.

That Map, he's just a killer who thinks he's got away with it. I can't stand it when he grins; he's grinning because he has escaped. They all escaped, all of those Khmers Rouges, from ever being called to account. He is utterly without shame, without remorse. He's like an animal.

The water freshens his skin. Rith feels the dust and heat sluice away. He sags into comfort, a numb, slow comfort that is so much like despair.

It looks so bad. We are the army and we said the Book was safe with us; nobody else should be allowed to take care of it. Then it was not only stolen from us but the thieves took our General and a foreigner and shot up the town and chased all the tourists away. I can't blame Tan Map for all that. I can't blame him for getting all that information on Saom Pich.

But I can still hate him.

In the end it is the murder that is the root of this evil. All these years I have sat and tried to forget, knowing it was Map who shot my man. Okay, that quartermaster was a coward. Okay, gunfire made him shake. Everything made him shake. Okay, it was fifteen years ago. But that man was in my care and I owed him protection and he didn't get it. Map killed him and got away with it.

I never can stand losing.

Rith pulls on shorts and slumps down shirtless onto the doorstep to be cool.

"Husband," says his wife. She lowers a plate of rice laced with pork and greens. It's even scented with coconut water—a very good Cambodian meal.

Rith wants to kick the plate across the courtyard. At the very least he wants to say he is not hungry and push the plate away. His insides seethe. He belches and holds his tummy.

"You will feel less angry when you eat," says his wife. Then, in a softer voice, "You always do."

Shrugging as if she's made a grudging compliment, Rith leans forward and eats in a rage, pressing rice and pork with his fingers into a fragrant parcel and jamming it into his mouth.

She's a good wife. I shouldn't be bad-tempered with her. Regret passes through Rith like a sigh. The good food turns round and round in his mouth like everything bad he has ever had to swallow.

No, it's no good; he can't stand it. He can't stand the thought that Map is not to blame for the loss of the Book. He must have taken the thing. He's turning on Saom Pich to save his own hide. Saom Pich was his old boss, they're in this together, that's where all his information comes from.

We've found nothing, for all our motorcycles and roadblocks. Map has even sent children out to find the Book. It's like he's saying look, even children are better than the army.

His wife says, "Your eldest son was thinking he could join the search."

"Join that rabble? No!"

His wife looks down towards the floor. "But, Children's-father, if it does some good? More and more people join in the hunt."

That's it. "So now even you join with the enemy!"

Now Rith can slam down the plate. Now he can take revenge. He feels justified in being angry with his wife. She blinks back at him in fear and surprise. Join the enemy? He stands up and begins to shake his way back into his uniform.

"Where are you going," says his wife. It is not even a question, her voice is kept so carefully flat and neutral.

Rith buckles up his belt and buckles on his gun.

"You should eat," says his wife. "You should not go out with a gun."

"I know what I should do, Wife. I know what I should have done." Rith nods and feels wild and actually has no idea what he's going to do. He simply has to move.

"Give my dinner to that boy and tell him to expect trouble if he joins the rabble! Jorani! Jorani! Get the gate open!"

You couldn't go hunting men in a Toyota sedan. Rith stops first at HQ and gets out his army motorcycle.

Rith drops himself down on the kick-start like an avalanche and the bike roars under him. He shoots out of the gates and up the dusty track to the main highway.

He feels like a stone flung from a slingshot. The air cools him, as if a woman with forest breath was blowing on him, teasing.

He feels launched through all of his life so far: the early days with his brothers laying out reed fencing for the fish farm. Late at night they kebabed a small part of the catch, smelling smoke, looking up at the stars.

Now, when people speak of corruption, his belly tightens. They are talking about people like him. He takes money for promotions; he takes money whenever he can. For Chavy, for Sokhem.

Of course it's not ideal. What is? But it's how people of position do things. Who could live on an army salary?

And still his son does not respect him. How could he? The house has no furniture, and after all these years he still swims after

General Yimsut Vutthy for scraps.

This was peace? The peace they yearned for all those years? Why does peace feel like one long, unending headache?

Rith sweeps past the crossroads where APSARA checks passes to the monuments. His bike spits out a spark and a puff of smoke. The boys stand up open-mouthed. I'm army, you stupid schoolkids. What a useless job you have, what a useless life!

A useless life for the whole country, sitting on top of these temples as if they were eggs that could hatch a future. All they hatch is a fortune for Thai airlines and Thai businessmen and people in the government. We live off these stones like wasps on fruit. Maybe the best thing for us would be if someone did steal them, then we would have to find something else to do.

Rith slows alongside the Angkor Wat moat. They had not found even a trace of a camp in the main temple area, so Map must sleep somewhere outside it, within walking distance. Rith knows where the villages are within the forest, and the footpaths that go to them. He knows which sections of forest would be deep and tangled enough to hide Map's camp.

He sees a couple of likely looking partings in the low scrub. Nothing too well worn, but enough for a man to duck through twice a day. He works his way on his bike into the forest. He imagines the bike shooting him forward to take Map by surprise. The motorcycle trampolines up and over tree roots, and skirts damp patches.

Then his machine slips on a polished tree root. Suddenly the bike slides sideways out from under him and onto his knee, slamming it painfully onto something knobbed and hard. With a choke and a chortle, the bike falls silent.

In a rage, Rith kicks the bike off and staggers to his feet. His knee crumples under his weight.

The pain punctures his anger. It settles like a flat tire.

Calm down, Rith, he tells himself. Calm down, you have to be clear-headed. He stands the bike back up and sees with regret that roots have scratched it. He licks his fingers, rubs some of the scratches away and takes a deep breath.

Then he realizes he's smelling a fire. He knows this kind of fire, it's made from green twigs torn from trees. It smokes and keeps away insects. Rith pats his gun, still firmly in its holster. He hobbles on, springing lightly off the hurt leg and swinging it forward like a suitcase, into the dark.

What a soldier you are, Map, what a hard man. No one can find you in the woods you are such a fighter!

The smoke is laced with incense, sweet and heavy, like in a temple.

Red light glimmers between the leaves and Rith eases his way forward.

Map is kneeling, his back to Rith. He lights a row of five candles. Beyond these, two coconuts have been cut to stand upright by themselves. Stuck into the white flesh of each are three incense sticks tied together with red thread. In an old condensed milk tin, three more incense sticks burn.

Rith smiles in scorn. Such an advanced man, so modern.

Tan Map thinks he's a *kru doh ompoeu*, an exorcist.

Tiny fish from the baray smoke on sticks over the green fire.

"Feeling happy, Rith?" asks Map without looking round. "Have you come to shoot me?"

Rith suddenly finds with a lurch, that he has not. That's not why he's come. His jaw flaps. He looks at his raised gun. He discovers that the gun is there to protect him against Map or his friends in the police. He slips it back into its holster.

So why *is* he here?

Map turns around. "In that case, could you help me? Put that star-fruit branch in the water. I must not touch it."

Rith's anger has a strange wrench to it. "Ah yes, the *lok kru* must never even walk under a star-fruit tree." Nevertheless he lifts up the branch and crouches forward. "Trying to drive out the spirits of your victims, Map?"

"Yes," Map says.

Rith moves the star-fruit branch over the bowl. He can't believe it. He's actually taking part in an exorcism. He's helping Map.

"You do this every night?"

"Yeah." Map sniffs, and turns back to his cooking fire. "So why are you here?"

The answer is to hand. "I want to know why you murdered my man."

"Which one?" says Map, stretching round. His teeth in firelight glow yellow-green. "I've shot so many."

"I'm not here to joke! We found my man with no head and everybody said they'd seen you. Was it because he tried to stop you thieving?"

"I don't remember shooting him. But I must have done," says Map.

"Were you drunk?"

Map's eyes are bleary. "Who shot Veasna? You tell me that, and you'll tell me the person I should have shot instead." His eyes were Khmer Rouge eyes: like a stone dropped into a dark well at moonlight.

"Veasna? Who was Veasna?"

"The best man in the regiment. He got volunteered to go out to Pailin and stepped on a mine. Remember? You remember. He had no hands. He had no legs. Come on, you don't notice much but you must remember that." Map's voice goes raw. "Veasna married my sister, he's the father of my nephew, he was my brother!"

It produces something like vertigo to see that Tan Map is just as angry as Rith. It's like hearing your own voice echo back to you from the bottom of a well.

Who are you to feel pain? Rith thinks. Who are you to be angry?

Map quietens down. "He never complained! He used to drag himself to the toilet and all the army had to do was feed him, just one bowl of rice a day, but even that was too much, so someone, somewhere, just decided it was easier to kill him!" Map turns back to the fire.

"I do remember," says Rith and slumps down onto the leaves. This is confusing. He feels something like motion sickness.

"So your poor quartermaster was just the first guy I met when I found out. Maybe if he'd just said, those fuckers shot your brother, I could have taken it. He tried to pretend it hadn't happened." Map shrugged. "Veasna was the nearest thing to a brother I had. So I just lost my head, and your man lost his. Pow!" Map looks round at Rith. "I went back to my old farm and Chams were living in it and I cleared them out and burned the place down so no one else would have it. Then I went to Phnom Penh and found out my sister had killed herself."

Rith says very quietly. "So did your friend."

Map's neck snaps around. "*Thaa mee!*" Excuse me?

"Your brother killed himself too."

"Ah," says Map. "Ah."

He leans the twig with its tiny fish back over the fire. He goes immobile. His eyes gleam brighter and Rith can see the man is trying not cry. His mouth crumples.

Who would have thought this wild man had any feelings at all? This is embarrassing. Rith wants to hide.

Map says, "That's why he keeps coming back."

"What, you mean his ghost?" Rith tries to chuckle. It's not that he doesn't believe in ghosts, it's just that ghosts are so unmodern.

Map's eyes look haunted. "He can't rest. I leave him food out there..." Map jerks his head towards the forest all around them. "He comes out of the trees like he's mad at people, and walks around their houses like he's looking for blood. He holds up his stumps at me!" Map pokes the fire. "It's why I can't live with people."

"Those are dreams," says Rith. "I have dreams too. The dreams are true, but only part of the truth. I think they can do less than mist."

"They're not dreams. I make rituals." Map waves at the circle of coconut shells. "He glares at women. He wants them and can't have them. I try to tell him about his son. But I think he hates his son for being alive."

"It was the war," says Rith.

"They all keep coming at me! There are not enough stupas for them all. I give them food, they sniff it, but are not satisfied. All those men, all those women, all those children, they all come and ask me: Why are we dead? Why were we killed by our own people?"

Rith thinks: I thought you had no shame or remorse. You are made of shame and remorse. It's why you scratch your forehead, it's why you have those spots; it's why you do those crazy things.

You are a poor, ugly, tough little fellow, and we both came through it.

Map looks up. He presses one nostril shut and blows out snot. He's trying to look like a tough guy. "I'm sorry about your man. He was just in the way. I was crazy then."

"Don't worry, that quartermaster is among the happy dead. He has gone on. I hope he was reborn as someone more brave."

It's strange, thinking now, but Rith had never really liked that little squirt of a quartermaster. He had not been a friend. He was just someone in the ranks whom Rith should have protected. In fact, Rith and his friends had mocked him, played tricks on him, made him miserable. Funny how you forget things. We stole his account books; we moved things around on the shelves just to watch him scratch his head. Naw, that quartermaster had not been a friend. Rith was just angry that he was shot on his watch.

"How..." Map dips suddenly as if under a heavy load. "How did Veasna kill himself?" Map almost chuckles. "He had no hands! What did he do, roll under a truck?"

Rith has to think. There was something... "He...went to a cistern, and just kept drinking. He drank one whole water butt, and crawled to the next, and drank that one too. Too much water will kill you."

Map holds up a kebab stick. "You want some fish that a ghost has sniffed?"

"That's a fish? It's so small I thought it was a cricket." Rith hunkers down onto the leaves. "Yeah, why not? I just kicked my dinner back in my wife's face."

Map grins. "So, were you going to shoot me?"

"I think I just wanted this to end, you know? Thinking about how you killed my man."

"Has it ended?"

Rith thinks. "He wasn't my man. You thought we'd killed yours. I don't know. I'm sick of thinking about it." A different kind of feeling writhes inside Rith. "I'm sick of all of it."

"Have some fish," says Map again.

They pass the stick back and forth between them, exchanging bites of crunchy-boned fish, crisp and tasting of smoke.

Rith admits, "You've done good work on the investigation."

"So have you. The roadblocks have got everybody pinned down."

Now it's Rith's turn to fight down emotion. "We've got to find out who told Saom Pich when the Book was being moved and how."

"Yup," says Map, laconic and strong again.

Rith says, "Somebody must have told the thieves 'It's leaving now, by air.' We've asked everyone on the UN team and none of them knew. Luc Andrade hadn't even told his own people. He hadn't told APSARA! So we thought he must have told you." Sinn Rith raises and drops his hands. "We hoped he had."

Map squats down beside him. "Did you ask the Phimeanakas staff?"

"What, those nice little girls in shoulder pads?"

"No," says Map, and rolls to his feet.

Rith and Map drive up to the Phimeanakas gates at midnight in an army van.

Once again, Mrs. Bou's guard Prak shouts back from behind the closed gates. "I told you, Tan Map, that Mrs. Bou says you are to stay out of this house."

Rith answers him in a low, clear voice. "Tell Mrs. Bou that this is the army and if you don't open these gates we will take a tank to the front of her hotel."

Map glances about the street. The usual gang of motoboys has gone home. Good. In the old days, you always had the watchers watched. Underpaid motoboys would be easy to use as spies.

Barefoot, in loose green trousers and a fluttering white shirt, the security guard toddles forward, his hands held in prayer in front of a fixed, sweaty grin.

"Yes, Lieutenant-Colonel. Yes, sir," Prak says. The keys rattle in his hand, and he has no strength to slide open the gate.

Prostitutes wait outside the bar next door, alert, necks craning. Map thinks, motoboys string for prostitutes. Old Ta Pich will have many ways to keep an eye on things.

Map and Rith catch other's eye. He's thinking the same thing. They fling the gates back, and hustle Prak into the shadows of the courtyard. They draw their pistols, click off the safety catches and point them at the guard's head.

"Keep your voice down," says Rith. "What have you done with my general? Where is he?"

Prak first looks scared, and then confused. Wrong way round if you are actually innocent. Then he wipes his sweaty mouth. "Your general, I don't have your..."

Rith nods to Map. They grab Prak's arms and wrench them round.

Prak jumps inside his own skin. "What are you doing?"

"Shut up!" hisses Rith. They drag him forward and Map crams him into the front seat of the van, then rams him down onto the floor so he can't be seen from the street. Rith starts the van, and repeatedly slams the knob of the gearstick into Prak's face to get him out of the way. They pull out, leaving the courtyard gate open. Map kneels on Prak's back.

They start play-acting. They threaten Prak, they threaten his children. They tell him they know he told Saom Pich. They pretend to be crazy guys who want to hurt him just for the fun of it. They pull over outside of town and Map says, "Oh, let's just shoot him!"

It takes longer than they had thought it would for Prak to dissolve, to lose all dignity. He starts to tell them, then contradicts himself, then denies it, but finally, his whole skin weeping with fear, he tells them.

They are not that much further ahead. Prak told Pich when the Book was being moved, but he knows nothing else. He doesn't know where Luc or the Book are now.

Rith starts up the van again, heading for Army HQ. They may have pushed Prak too far. He lies docile on the floor of the cab, staring ahead, Map's knee still pushing him down.

Part of Map has enjoyed himself. He really yearned to hurt Prak.

"I'm wrecked inside," Map says forlornly, even though Prak can hear him. He remembers he once got angry with a girlfriend and started to hit her. He couldn't stop. He has crossed over some kind of line and he can't go back.

"I know," says Rith. "All the more reason to get people like Saom Pich."

But how?

Then Map remembers to ask Prak, "How did you pass messages?"

Luc and the old man work late into the night.

Vutthy groans and rocks, looking up and around at the light, wild-eyed. His skin glistens.

"Fever," says the old man, still reading. He chews the inside of his cheek.

Luc feels as though they are walking along the edge of a cliff. "Get him to a doctor?"

That hard, amused half-smile. "So he can say where we are?"

"You could drive him to a hospital, leave him there and just drive away."

Geoff Ryman

The old man chuckles and shakes his head. "You don't know when you are lucky, Kru Luc."

"Drop him and just keep driving, drive away. Don't come back here. Leave me tied up. Take the Book. Just disappear."

The old man looks directly into his eyes. "I would have to leave my family, my children. I did that once before. Once was enough. Anyway, there are roadblocks."

Between them was the bare fact: the old man was going to have to shoot them both.

Never accept, warned a cat's-paw voice, *that you are going to die.*

"Then take me with you," says Luc.

The old man is flabbergasted, his jaw drops. "What?" His wide, angry eyes seem to say: Don't you know where you are? Don't you know what this is? I don't want to be trapped with you.

Luc says, "You don't have to kill me."

The old man splutters in surprise.

Luc continues. "I don't have to turn you in. I could pretend that I have no idea who you are. Just some Cambodian guy."

The old man rocks again. He shakes his head. Almost teasing, he tosses the notebook at Luc's head. "Why wouldn't you tell them who I am?"

Luc scoops up the notebook quickly before it slides into water. "Because I don't believe you are a bad man."

"You don't know me. I am not soft-hearted."

"That is true. But you are not destructive. You are not wasteful."

"Words," says the old man. "You are made of words."

"So are you."

The old man shakes his gun. "I am a man who acts."

Luc pushes. "You also ask yourself questions. You remember your past. You plan the future. All of that is done through words."

"And bullets."

"Yes," says Luc, but thinks: I'm not scared. I'm really not. And you know that I'm really not. "And it's also done through letting people go, and signing treaties, and getting back to work."

The old man sighs over his half-moon spectacles, a wise old soldier in a yoke.

Luc keeps on. "You could send one of the boys to the hospital to buy antibiotics."

"No we couldn't. The people in the store would know something was wrong. My people can't buy drugs. They don't buy drugs." The old man looks resigned.

Vutthy crows aloud. Sweat pours from him. His eyes are as wild as a horse's trapped in a forest fire.

"Where is the merit in letting an old man die?"

The old man peers at him. "Don't presume that I believe in merit."

Enough, said the cat's-paw voice.

The Book. I must also save the Book. Luc passes the full notebook back to the old man and goes back to work on another.

William sleeps securely in the moonlight, cool night breezes delicious on his back.

Something is chirruping, making some kind of noise he can't identify. He doesn't want to move.

My phone! I left it on, it will wake up Aunty, I shouldn't have left it on. He catapults himself forward onto his knees and starts slapping his clothes, his bag. Where did I leave it, where did I leave it, I'll wake up everybody in the house. His hand hits something solid in his trousers, he fumbles inside the pocket, pulls out the phone and hunches over it. "Hello, hello?"

The phone that Luc Andrade gave to him.

"Motoboy," a voice growls. "I'm coming to get you!"

William recognizes Sinn Rith's voice. Then there is a cackle of laughter, and wuffling sound as the phone is passed, and another voice shouts. "Pay no attention to that animal, William. This is Map. We've done it! We've cracked the case! Listen, the security guard at the hotel helped Luc a lot, he knew when it was being transported and Pich scared him into helping. He's told us everything. So we have all the army roadblocks alerted."

"What, what?"

"We've solved it. William, we might get Ta Barang back yet."

"Why did Rith ..."

"That was just a joke! Rith and I are friends. So look, William, I need you to come now and meet me. The whores saw us take Prak and they tipped off one of the motoboys who drove out to Pich's place at night with no lights. We arrested him ..."

"One of my boys? Which one?"

"…but another messenger has left the farm and we're sure he's on his way to warn Pich. So come now!"

William is already shaking his way into his clothes and starting to chuckle with excitement. "Yeah. Okay. But which motoboy was it?"

"The one called Mons. We arrested all the whores as well. It's a party! I'll see you outside the bus station, not the guesthouse. We still think it's being watched. The bus station, understand?"

As William drives, his mind begins to clear and his heart inflates with joy.

They just might do it, they just might get the Book back, get Luc Andrade back. William starts to smile.

He coasts into the bus station with his lights off. The bus station is more like a dusty broken concrete triangle than a building. Map is waiting behind a closed-up food stall.

"Are you happy?"

"Very happy, and you?"

Map whispers. "The messenger just went past the last roadblock into town. The guys there say he's heading down Sivutha Street towards us." Map has to laugh. "He's got three hens strapped to the back. They got his name, everything! So whatever happens that's one more arrested."

They push the bike farther out of sight, around the corner to the riverfront. They wait under a shop awning in darkness. They hear a motorcycle coming. It buzzes out of Sivutha and turns right. William wheels the bike out silently and starts it so gently it purrs. They follow the sound out towards the south.

They drive back out of town over the dike. The first day's drive seems a week ago. They are shooting along a road in the dark. Ahead of them, they see the break in the dike. William brakes, and eases the bike down the slope.

He rides across the single plank of wood in the dark with no lights. History repeats like moonlight.

"Young Veasna," says Map, and lays a hand on William's shoulder.

They get to the docks. Ahead of them, still some distance away, overhead lights blaze down, an old man hoists hens off a bike and then disappears into darkness. They hear words across the distance, and a sudden revving of an engine.

People. Connection. "The Vietnamese girl," says William. He revs the bike and turns it back around, and slips and slides the bike down a grassy slope to the moored house, the little skiff. William calls in Vietnamese: excuse me, sorry, excuse me, sorry, we need help.

A frightened older woman answers, bunching all her clothing in front of her neck and tummy. William tries to reassure her. Hello. Sorry. We hired boat. Need boat now! Need boat now.

William sees the girl. He pleads, he nearly weeps. Please, please, please, we need to save the man.

The girl nods her head and says something soothing to her mother. She dresses with a series of quick flicks, and flip-flops out. She motions William to follow. They slip down into the boat. A rail-thin older man staggers out and croaks in dismay. The daughter smoothly says something about motorcycles.

"My father watch your bike," the girl says.

The old woman gets in as well, still in a loose old dress, to chaperone them. The boat heaves itself slowly out from the house. It gradually gathers speed. Map scrambles his way into the prow. William makes excuses and follows him.

Map turns and points. William cannot see or hear the other boat. He looks back. The girl is tucking her hair under her hat and easing the boat to the right at the same time.

For a while at least, both boats have to follow the river channel out onto the lake. For a while at least there is hope.

Moonlight reflects off the sweat on Map's face. His jaw is clenched. "I thought that if I got the Book and Teacher Luc back that would be enough merit to keep me out of hell."

"There are many ways to earn merit," says William, quoting a monk, knowing that kind of stuff got no listening from Map. The answer was in the air.

There's not merit enough in a thousand good deeds for a Khmer Rouge.

The little boat slips out into the lake, but there's only a sliver of moon and few stars. Even the lake is plunged in shadow. From time to time the girl kills the engine and they listen. The other boat is running without lights, but they can hear it.

The sound stretches over an entire quarter of the horizon. "Over there," Map says. He points south and west, towards the Battambang side of the lake.

The air overhead starts to cough. Suddenly, light blazes down from overhead. An army helicopter. Map waves. The light goes, the helicopter sails on.

It passes, still chopping air.

They cannot hear the boat anymore.

They rest, bobbing on the open water, waiting for silence.

"Maybe the helicopter will find them, maybe the army or the Lake Police will get them."

"We cannot give up," says William.

They push south anyway. The lake is at its most shallow here. Soon they are scraping the bottom and scrub brushes their faces.

"I used to come this way by night all the time," says Map.

"With the other Veasna?"

Map just nods. The boat grinds to a halt on the river bottom.

William hates water. Water is dirty and infects. It hides roots and stones and snakes; it washes away shit of all kinds, and washes it back. But just as the sound of the helicopter fades, they think they hear a boat in the channel ahead of them.

Map jumps over the side, in his best Patrimony Police uniform. William can't swim, but what else can he do? He clumsily drops down from the boat. The water is only just over his knees.

"Well done, Younger Brother," says Map.

Together they pull the boat. The channel narrows. Map starts talking.

"You know Luc, he was trying to figure out why Angkor died." Map looks as if he is talking to the fingernail-cutting of a moon.

"He thinks it's because all the canals silted up. No more boats, no more trade, so everybody moved to Phnom Penh where three rivers meet and never silt up. But it was something else. I know what killed Angkor. Do you want to hear it?" He definitely says this to the moon.

"Yes," says William anyway.

"Jayavarman killed it," says Map, and his voice wheedles like a string instrument. "Ta Prohm, just one of his temples, had 80,000 people working for it, to grow its rice, to tend and sweep and to feed the civil servants. Buddhism doesn't have temples like that. With Buddhism, you build a temple for a time only. You take away Hinduism, you take away any reason to maintain those temples."

Suddenly the riverbed underneath them falls away. William and Map slip down into deeper water, a channel. Map flips himself onboard and reaches back for William. William sputters and coughs and has no idea how to pull himself back into the boat. Map chuckles as he pulls him back in. "Younger Brother, we'll have to get you into the Police and train you to get you strong."

William is laughing at himself, his shirt and trousers streaming water. The old woman laughs too, having decided that these are decent Cambodians.

"My clothes are heavy!" says William. He feels bad for laughing, for having forgotten Luc.

"We never know what our actions will achieve. That's why it takes so long to be reborn sometimes." Map is looking back up at the moon. "Big actions take a long time to work out."

They listen. It's so late at night that the channel is silent, no insects or frogs. They can hear nothing.

"Maybe he's got to the other boat," offers William.

"Let's hope," says Map. He stops the young girl starting the engine again and motions for silence. He whispers, "If we go by engine now, they'll hear us coming. Into the water again, Younger Brother."

"I can't swim."

"Hold onto the prow and kick."

Silently, in moonlight, they pull the boat with them. Gradually William gets used to it, half floating, half swimming.

Map says suddenly, "That is why Jayavarman has not been reborn."

It takes William a moment to remember their previous conversation. "The consequences of his actions are not all yet clear."

"That's why he needs the Book to appear. He can't be reborn without it."

They go on for half an hour; then stop, rest, and listen. They start again and pull for longer. William starts to shiver in the cold water. Map pushes him back into the boat. He pulls it by himself for a while longer and finally says, "Let's go back."

The sky goes silver; the lake looks like a mosquito net in moonlight. The breath of heat is in the air.

Map sighs. "Maybe the helicopter spotted them and followed them. The Lake Police will stop and search every boat for weeks. Maybe they'll find them."

But we won't.

"Good work, Younger Brother." The girl starts the engine looking sad.

Suddenly everything is grey, just before dawn. They see purple heron, cormorants, jacuna, and even kingfishers darting among the plants. Overhead, fish-eagles turn in the wind. History repeats.

It's daylight by the time they get back. Map pays the Vietnamese girl, evidently well, because she gives him a delighted smile and sompiahs. William's legs drag him up the bank, and his head feels heavy and slow. "Thank you, Older Brother, for asking me to come. It was an opportunity for me to help Luc Andrade."

Map waves it away. "Thank you for talking to Sinn Rith. You went and sold me to the army!" He pretends to punch William in the arm.

Something in William gathers. He feels sorrow, sorrow for Map. He thinks of him alone, with no family, getting older, having no one to care for him. He mulls this over as the old Vietnamese man wheels out his motorcycle. Map has gone farther up the dike to stare out at the lake and the sunrise. He looks smiling and gentle. Sopheaktea, that's his real name.

Sunlight, the sounds and smells of water, river birds. Life is good. William wheels the bike up silently behind Map.

"I've been thinking," says William. "Why don't you come and live with my family?"

Map's eyes roll and his eyelids flutter.

"You could still work for the Police, but you'd have a place to sleep. There would be people around, good meals. My uncle and aunty are old, and you could work in the rice fields."

Map hangs his head. "Not enough to work off a blood debt."

William is not sure he heard right. "They would be grateful for the help. They would welcome you!"

Map is exhausted again. He pushes the heels of his hands into his eyes sockets and breathes in. "That will never happen."

"I could ask."

"It's a good action, young Veasna. But it's not possible."

"Why not?" William feels confused, and wonders if he has not strayed into ill-advised territory.

"Ask your family," says Map quietly, and indicates with a flick of the finger that they should drive back. "Thank you, young Veasna. You are trying to do a good thing. Throughout you have done good things." He looks worn, enduring, grateful. William just feels confused.

"My name is William," says William, feeling distraught.

"Not to me," says Map. His smile is impossible to read. If anything, it looks scared. Map gives William's shoulder a weary shake. "We both need to get home."

They drive on in silence.

William is aware of a kind of shivering behind him and assumes that Map is crying or shaking with rage or doing something extreme. He avoids looking behind him; he does not want to embarrass Map or be involved in another emotional scene. If he says let's have breakfast, William promises himself, I will say I am too tired.

You win, Map, okay? You win. We finish this job and I have nothing more to do with you.

They roar back into Siem Reap. The Phimeanakas is cordoned off, its forecourt empty of cars, the windows dark, scores of army men standing in groups.

Stupid thing to do, without asking my family. I can't just invite people to stay, it's not my house!

Out through the town, and the modern building where tourists buy their Angkor passes is empty. With nothing to do, the boys in uniform sit on the steps of the booths and chat to the girls.

The odd quivering motion starts up again. They are now on the long road through the forest to Angkor Wat. Map jerks suddenly and the bike swerves. Finally, William stops to ask him what is wrong.

Map has been squeezing his spots and they have finally burst. They were not full of inflammation but scar tissue, and the scar tissue clings to his face like prawns, and out of the gaping holes blood trails, coated in dust. The wounds look like bulletholes. One is just under his eye but the blood is welling up from inside the eyelid. Map weeps blood. William stares.

Map swings one leg around and leans on the back seat. William can't drive on now. Map looks strangely calm. "I've been a coward."

William wants to wipe Map's face. "You? You're not scared of anything."

"I've been everything now." Map means everything bad. His mouth purses together, he swallows and says, "Ly William. I killed your parents."

The very air seems to curdle.

"I was in a cadre that opened fire on them and some other people. We told people they could move to the Lake if they wanted. It was a trick to see who was Vietnamese. Your parents went. I saw your aunty snatch you out of your mother's arms."

Nothing in William functions. He's not thinking, he's not moving.

Map glances away. "I could make excuses. I did warn your aunty not to let any of her family go. The people we killed didn't think that five of us would do anything to forty of them. We made them sing Angka songs as they marched." Map sings, in a little boy's voice, a brief snatch of an Angka song. It sounds almost nostalgic.

Then he snaps open his holster and takes out his gun and holds it handle first out towards William. "Remember to return it. It's police property."

William, startled, recoils. *Get that horrible thing away from me!*

Map's voice is low. "I've got nothing to do anyway." He looks down at the ground and still holds out the pistol.

"Come on, William. It's a blood debt."

William just shakes his head, no, no, no. He would need to explode with rage, and he just doesn't feel that.

Map barely indicates a shrug. He sighs and snaps the gun back. He rocks himself to his feet.

"Peaceful man," Map says, but not in mockery or with rancour. It's more like an acknowledgement.

"*Bahn bon*," he murmurs. Good luck. And then more formally, "*Soam a-oy ban chok chay.*"

William says nothing.

Map turns and begins to walk towards the police village. This time William lets him go. The thought of having Map on the back of his motorcycle repulses him. As he watches, Map's hands go back up to his face and tremble as they push.

William just sits.

He feels abandoned, but he doesn't know by whom or by what. He feels lost and alone and strangely terrified. Out here on the deserted tourist road there is no one to see him. He starts to weep.

"I'm a coward," he says. By now he thinks that any real man would have taken the gun and shot Map. "I'm sorry, Mom and Dad. I'm a coward."

He tries to think of anything that links him to them, any memory. He thinks of all the things his aunt has said about them. His father wanted to start a car-repair business; his mother was a good cadre in the maquis in the early days; she was good at dancing...

"I've been trying!" he tells them. "I've been trying, and trying..."

But it doesn't do any good. He learns languages; he brings in money; he tries to go to university; he smiles and smiles and smiles, and the thing, whatever it is, the darkness, the nightmare, is still there inside him, the thing that never goes away.

The thing is what he sees staring back at him out of Tan Map's eyes.

The war. I'm part of it. Of course I'm part of it, I see it in my dreams; it's in the air I breathe.

Connection doesn't work. It doesn't take it away. Which means that love doesn't work, or reason, or knowledge, not working hard, nor seven dollars a day, not little notes about all his friends who never write back or any of the things William uses day in, day out, to make life bearable.

"Stupid, stupid, stupid," he sobs and slams his own knee.

I tried to make a friend of him. I chased after him like some kind of puppy dog. How many other people know? What would I look like to them? He killed my parents. He's the reason I live in someone else's house.

University. Clean little shoes, Internet, and smiling, smiling, little sompiah, oh, sir, you are a nice man, kiss, kiss, kiss, you want bike? You want me to stay a nice poor smiling little Cambodian? Stay here until I'm a fifty-year-old motoboy, a starving old man on a rusty bike outside a fallen-down hotel, and I'm still saying, Hi! Bonjour! Guttentag! Sawakdee!

William can't stay still. He hauls himself back around onto the bike.

He thinks for a moment he'll roar after Map and ask him for the gun. Then he knows he won't. He knows he'll turn the bike around and slink back home and have a long kindly chat with his aunt.

Peaceful man.

Live with this.

APRIL 1177

The King seemed to have forgotten that his wife had just given him a son.

Second Queen Rajendradevi sat posed in a hammock, cushions behind her back. She was lightly wrapped in gold-embroidered cloth, her hair was scented and piled up on her head, its tendrils holding in place an image of the Buddha. The aftermath of giving birth had left her looking plumper and younger.

The entire household was arrayed around her for the presentation. Even the King's Brahmin waited to bless the new prince.

The Prince Rajapativarman had arrayed himself on a bowl of fruit and was eating a banana.

"Poor man has so many children already, he's bound to forget one or two of them." He swallowed. "Like all his women, really." He batted his eyelashes.

Fishing Cat was at the end of her patience with him. "Shut up, 'Pati."

Being a slave was useful at times. You could be blunt, and the people who were grateful for it could admonish you in public and reward you in private.

"We all understand Rajapati, Cat," said Queen Jayarajadevi.

"I was just trying to lighten the mood," said Rajapati.

"You were trying to be noticed."

The lamps guttered in the breeze. Cat went to lower the curtains against the cool night air.

The Brahmin shifted uneasily from foot to foot. He was at his most uncomfortable at formal occasions when he had to speak. He believed most of the people in the room had allowed their devotion to Buddha to drive out due observance of the Gods. He studiously avoided even looking at Rajapativarman.

"Sisters?" said the Second Queen, looking at the other wives. "Perhaps this is not a good time. We can ask the King to come later."

Cat turned and caught Jayarajadevi's eye, and then glanced at the Queen's sister Indradevi.

There really was something wrong.

This was a son, and the King needed sons. Suryavarman had turned out to be savagely ambitious. He had already suggested that it was time for the King to step down in his favour. Virakumara would make a great scholar and an invisible king, Rajendravarman loved sport, looked good, but liked girls and gambling too much. The birth of a new healthy son was the answer to the King's prayers. And he had been looking so restive and unsettled lately.

You go or I? Fishing Cat's eyes asked the First Queen.

Jayarajadevi said lightly, "Let me go and talk to the King." She touched the Second Queen gently on the shoulder. "You do know how much he wants to see his new son, don't you?"

The Second Queen gave a brave little nod. Fishing Cat admired her. She'd been chosen for beauty and was no match for Jayarajadevi and her formidable sister. She had gone through being regal, resentful, then withdrawn but had come out a sweet and reliable presence.

The First Queen gave Rajendradevi a delighted smile, and slipped out of the room.

The Prince Rajapati lolled on top of a pineapple. "I know," he said, sitting up. "Why don't we swap me for the baby?" He hooted. "What a terrible shock." He mimed his father picking up his newborn and finding him instead. "Oh no! Not another one."

Fishing Cat snapped forward. "That's enough. You want to act like a baby, we'll treat you like one." She snatched her twenty-five-year-old son off the bowl of fruit and dumped him into a wicker cradle. It was too high off the ground for him to climb out.

Immediately she felt awful.

He's always at his worst when it's something to do with children, she thought. He hates them; he's afraid of what they'll say. *Nanny, why doesn't that man have legs?* He can't stand to see the King around his other sons. He starts acting like a clown.

She looked around the circle of the family, bowing apologies to each of them.

Lastly, she bowed to the Brahmin. He looked pityingly at her and shook his head. This, he seemed to say, is what comes of such disordering of categories. This is what comes of radical Buddhism.

They all kept waiting with nothing to say.

Virakumara stood still with beautiful patience, his kindly face placid and withdrawn. His fat wife looked bored. Some of the younger children asked to leave. "Yes, you can go," said Rajendradevi and looked at Indradevi with begging eyes.

"I know!" said Indradevi. "Let's all go out and look at the butterfly tree in torchlight."

Indradevi gathered up the children and led them away.

"When do we eat?" one of the little girls demanded before climbing down the steps.

Rajapati struck again. "My friend Brahmin, I have a question for you about the scriptures."

The Brahmin turned and looked at him with a kind of practised patience. "What interest would you have in the scriptures?"

"It amuses me how unlike reality they are, but how much devotion you show to them."

I have to get him out of here, thought Fishing Cat.

At that moment she heard the King's unmistakable hammering footfall on the wooden stairs.

The Second Queen had a moment to sit up straight and pick up her sleeping son before the King thrust aside aside a curtain and swept into the room. Jayavarman scowled as if outraged, his mouth bunched up. Beads of sweat lined up across his forehead like helmets on a distant battlefield.

Queen Jaya followed with her hand over her mouth. Everyone's eyes caught each other's. Surya? wondered Cat. Has Surya been killed in the war? What in the name of all that is holy has happened?

The King apologized in a deep, angry voice that Fishing Cat had never heard before. "I'm very sorry, everyone. Some news has come. Please begin."

The Brahmin was discomfited. What was an appropriate blessing for a prince in a Buddhist household? A prayer that he makes due observance of the Gods? The counsellor fell back on a Jatataka tale of Vishnu coming to test the young Buddha and finding him generous and truthful.

The King rocked back and forth on his heels throughout.

The Brahmin ended with, "May this young prince similarly embody virtue before the Gods."

The Second Queen held up the babe, and Jayavarman's face softened. He went to the hammock and kissed her forehead, and the family chuckled fondly.

He looked at the babe's face. "My son," he said, warmly. "Oh, but he's a handsome fellow." He picked the babe up and cradled him and bounced him. "And he's born big too. Fine and healthy and fat."

The baby gurgled as if he could talk and everyone responded with appropriate and somewhat edgy affection. The King looked around him, pleased. Sweat still armoured his brow.

He wiped it with a swift sweep of his hand. He looked into the baby's face. "What will we call you, little fellow? Eh? We can't call you by a great big religious title yet." His face clouded. "You won't have to fight a war yet, either."

Rajendradevi asked, "What's happened, my Lord?"

"Ugh!" he grunted and shook his head and passed the child back to her. He clamped a hand on his forehead.

"The City Yashodharapura has fallen. Not only has it fallen, but all its propitiations of the Gods achieved nothing. The palaces have been burnt and looted."

Vira's wife, Cat, Rajendradevi, and some of the servants cried aloud.

The King rolled on. "The Usurper has been killed and Jaya-Indravarman, the Cham King, has made himself Universal King, over all Kambujadesa. Over us."

Virakumara looked perplexed. "What on earth are we going to do?"

The King said, as he folded himself down onto the floor. "We will have a family conference. Most of us are here. The Crown Prince is not."

Rajapati said, "Admittedly, we can't do anything without him."

King Jaya found him in his crib and glared at him. "I want to make sure he behaves. I wouldn't put it past him to be part of this."

"Like we were once?" said Rajapati.

The King smiled, crookedly. "Pati, I can always rely on you to silence any discussion. Do you have a view or do you just want to create confusion?"

Rajapati whispered, "I have no view."

Virakumara did. "If...if they are more inclined to Buddhism, and you were an ally of theirs, is this not a good time to put yourself forward for preferment?"

Jaya blasted back at him. "And be a traitor? They burned the City! It is one thing to be the harrow of the Usurper, it is quite another to destroy the kingdom...all those beautiful buildings, the carvings, the cloth...the wealth...just...broken, squandered, ruined. They're barbarians!"

"And we're not," said Rajapati very carefully to make sure it sounded like a statement, not sarcasm. "As when we burnt Vijaya."

"No wit, 'Pati. Intelligence please, but no wit. From someone! Anyone!"

Princess Indradevi, summoned by her sister, entered the room.

"Queen Indradevi!" said Jaya, which was a mistake as she was not a queen. "At last, somebody will talk sense!"

Princess Indradevi was rocked by this. The King was not generally so dominant or so aggressive. "My Lord wishes to do something," she said, recovering.

"Our strategy was this: to perfect the art of ruling over a Buddhist state, a state in which compassion was the main principle of rule. The well-being of the people was to be the primary sign of a successful ruler, not the addition of territory, or the aggrandizement of the person. In that we have succeeded. And it means nothing!" The King hid his face in his hands.

Then he snatched his hands away.

"The Chams gave no sign they were doing this because they blamed their defeat of a dozen years ago on us. We went home, and recovered from being traitors to the Usurper. We were grateful for being unnoticed. We pulled shut all the curtains. We meditated. We perfected our graces. In the small circle of our tiny kingdom, we made sure we earned merit for ourselves while the rest of the country sank under an illegitimate ruler. And now, we wake up."

The King lifted up his hands and brought them down slapping onto his knees. "We wake up to find that there is no Kambujadesa anymore! We find that allowing the Usurper to continue in his misrule was an irresponsible, heedless act! It was irresponsible to allow ourselves to pay no notice to the Chams or their intentions, to assume that they had forgotten and forgiven all those years of war. Now we wake up to discover we are their vassals. I was enslaved by the Chams once. I was determined never to be their slave again!"

The King was shouting. He slammed his fist down on his own knee.

Queen Jaya ventured. "How ... how did they do this?"

"By ... following ... my ... advice!" The King had the face of a tiger. "I told them the first time, I said, if you try to march across land, you will give the Khmers time to organize. I told them to wait until April, when there is no rice to forage and no food for an army. Come up the rivers by boat and sweep across the Great Lake. From there, go by canal. You will find all of Yashodharapura unwalled, undefended, open to attack because its Kings seriously believe that drinking water washed over a stone penis keeps the City safe from harm!"

Cat had never heard the King talk this way. She looked at the Brahmin. He was still and grey.

The King was shouting and bouncing up and down on his haunches. "So they thought I was untrustworthy but they still took my advice!"

His hands pressed down on the top of this head. "And now I find I don't like playing the Little King any longer. I find that I have learned a hard lesson, that it is not enough to make a ... what did you call it, Indradevi? A little island of safety. Well, come the monsoon and the little island is flooded just like everywhere else!"

This was Jayavarman the warrior. This was Jayavarman the Great, who wanted to be King.

And had realized that only too late.

The First Queen said in a quiet voice, "So what do we do?"

Jayavarman shrugged like a great ox under a yoke it cannot bear. "We ... do ... nothing. Not for a while. The Khmers regard us as traitors. The Chams have no need of us. Both would prefer us dead or gone. The only thing we can do is stay unnoticed for a while and build. Build new loyalties, build new armies, new weapons, new means. We must smile and lie and prevaricate and hide until we can strike. Then I will set out to do what I should have done from the first, which is to make myself"—he slammed his own chest with the point of his finger—"the Universal King! And make all of Kambujadesa a Buddhist state. A state that does not rely on empty ceremonies AND THAT BUILDS A WALL AROUND THE CITY!"

He calmed himself and all of his round body was pumping like a heart. He said, more quietly, "It is, after all, only a city like any other."

He glanced up at the Brahmin, whose eyes were cast down.

"I will send the messengers back to the City with word to Jaya-Indravarman ambiguous enough to be read as congratulations without making myself a legendary figure of hatred. I will lie. I will tell him that we are content as always to be part of the greater state. For I am just an eccentric odd little king with a religion for a harmless hobby." The King looked up at his son Rajapativarman. "You see, I can wound myself with words too, "Pati."

Rajapati was almost smiling. It was a bitter smile, not amused, and not particularly cruel. "That is because you are a cripple, Father."

"We all are. That's why we hate to look at cripples so much."

Both could scorch the air with words.

Rajapati's smile did not move. He said, in a very quiet voice, "I suggest that you start building those loyalties, Father."

Both he and his father blew out air in unison.

Cat looked up and saw the Brahmin was no longer there.

Invited Brahmins should leave with all due ceremony. A slave, however, could slip out of rooms unnoticed to carry out her tasks. Cat signalled for a torch, gathered up her skirts, and ran. She and not the Brahmin could take the shorter hidden way through the royal apartments to the main western gate.

She ordered all the torches lit around the gopura and then climbed the staircase onto the walls to wait. As she suspected, the Brahmin came trotting out of the gate, hunched under a shoulder bag.

By the time she had slipped back into Rajendradevi's chambers almost everyone had gone. The King was holding his newborn son, and looking at his face.

"You will be a big, big man, my son. You will have to be a warrior."
The baby—huge, pink, and calm—looked back at the King with a
complete lack of excitement. Rajapati, trapped in the crib, looked on
forlornly.

"I know," the King said rubbing his nose against the baby's. "We'll
call you *Tlos*."

Chubby.

The Brahmin was found on the road to the City, stabbed to
death.

LEAF 59

Kambujadesa is country where rivers flow backwards. You think the clear fresh water has washed the land, sweeping away the old dead leaves. Then look! The season of rains and flooding comes, and the rivers change course. Here the dead leaves come again, carried back by the floods. Look through the floorboards of your house and you can see the old dirt, flowing backwards, drowning your hens. Your children weep. The mud rises up your ladder, step by step. It swirls into your house, soiling it. Kambujadesa is a country where the past washes back. We are like the fish who swim choking on the past, not knowing why our mouths are full of mud, or when the fisherman will haul in his nets or strike us with spears. My life has been a tale first of war and then remembrance.

THE SEASON OF RAIN AND FLOODING

An officer's shirt with a bullethole through it arrives at the offices of Phnom Penh Soir with this note.

> This is your general's shirt. You will not be getting him back nor the Golden Book. There is no point negotiating. You have nothing we want. We would not believe any promises you make and we expect nothing from you. All we want to do is hurt the tourist trade as much as possible. We don't benefit from it. Hurting it is the best way to hurt you. Why do we want to hurt you? In a city where a hotel room can cost as much as two thousand dollars a night and people die for the price of antibiotics, where pirates make fortunes and look down on hardworking people, it should not take you long to think of a reason.

The letter does not mention Professor Luc Andrade. The French is perfect. Reading the note, Sinn Rith thinks: is it possible that Ta Barang helped them do this?

Rith is not the only one.

Since the shooting, Luc has begun to shake inside all the time.

At first he thought it was shock. A boat arrived in the middle of the night, and an another older man got off it, and said that someone at the Phimeanakas had been arrested. He himself had been followed;

the police now knew Saom Pich had taken the Book. Luc finally learned the old man's name. Police had visited his wife.

The General lay on the floor of the hull. He was yellow and howling, streaming sweat and demanding water. In that instant the old man turned with his rifle and shot him in the heart. The General was lying next to Luc, and Luc felt him jump. Everything went dark; the boys started the engine and the boat pulled away. Luc was left shut in the hull with the body and blood.

Finally the hatch opened, letting in grey early light. The old man told Luc to help move the body. Sprays of blood covered Luc's arms; his back was wet with it. Calmly, the old man began to push rocks down the General's still-warm throat. He held up the General's shirt and shot that too. The sound made Luc collapse inside—for an instant he thought that he'd been shot as well.

Then the old man said in a quiet voice. "I need you to write something for us in French." He passed Luc the notebook, open to a fresh page with a letter already written on it in Khmer. Feeling eerily as though he had shown up late for an ordinary office job, Luc translated it into French.

The letter and the shirt were given to the boys to post. They climbed into their uncle's boat. "Tell the police you've been working at our charcoal smelter. The illegal one. Let them force you to admit it. They'll believe you then. Your uncle came to fetch you. He sold the hens at a dockside market."

The three hens were left with Luc and Pich, and the other boat headed back north towards Siem Reap.

Pich started their engine and headed west. Somewhere on the lake, with no other boats in sight, he rolled the General's body over the side.

They chugged their way into the marshy channels at the mouth of a small stream, reeds and scrub scraping the sides. They stopped somewhere and Pich jumped out and dragged the boat under overhanging branches.

He sat cross-legged on the deck and waved Luc out of the hull. "What packet are you translating now?" he asked.

They remain hidden without moving for weeks.

No further messengers come. The heat and insects buzz. Pich will not allow a fire, so they eat the chickens raw. Luc is still shaking as if from the sound of the gun.

At first he cannot keep cool. Then he cannot keep warm. It's the shock, he tells himself; I'm worn down. It's the food.

They eat raw fish like mangoes, peeling the flesh away from its skin with their teeth. Sometimes the flesh twitches or Luc gets a mouthful of gut. Saom Pich says nothing that is not brief and practical. He uses fish bones for toothpicks. His whole intent seems to be to keep Luc working on the translation. He says nothing about his family or his old life. To Luc's utter horror, Pich takes off his glasses and his wedding ring and throws both over the side.

Luc is covered in bites. The insects torment him. At night he can hear them whine in the air all around him. They crawl on his skin and nip him before he can slap them away. The worst are the flies; they seem to tear off whole steaks from his arms and legs, leaving smears of blood. He scratches himself raw. His head aches and he wants to throw up.

The task of translating is getting too much for him. He finds he can work for only about two hours each day, in the early morning when it's light but cool. He jumps overboard first thing every day to wash and escape the insects. He plunges right down under the water. He drifts off to sleep and jumps awake, realising that part of his mind has been counselling him to breathe in deeply.

The Book, Luc. They will never get the Book if you do not work.

Sometimes, Saom Pich is almost sympathetic. He pats Luc's arm in a comradely kind of way, and lets him dry in the sun before passing him the notebooks.

All the leaves are out of order; the cut circles don't seem to fit anywhere; and Luc's handwriting gets smaller and smaller to conserve space. He has to write notes more frequently.

This leaf might fit with the battle scenes.
We're missing Leaf 59 just before Bharata-Rahu. Is this it? Transition to history of the battles?

At times, as birds sing, as shade creeps, as water gurgles, Luc feels something almost like peace.

Then his joints begin to ache. His head seems to squash down on top of his body; his eyes cross so that he's unable to see; and he rocks back and forth, soaked with sweat.

Pich takes Luc's old shirt and uses it to mop and cool his brow. He starts to use a word long since fallen out of favour. It took the place of loak during the time of the Communists. He starts to call Luc comrade.

Comrade? thinks Luc. When you're going to have to shoot me?

"Read them to me," Pich asks sometimes in the mornings or whenever he thinks Luc is well enough. Pich blinks. He can read without his spectacles, but it's uncomfortable. So Luc reads and Pich hangs his head or looks skywards. Sometimes he laughs or shakes his head in sadness.

Sometimes, when the wind blows, the heads of the trees and the tallest reeds bow, and huge and blue, over the horizon, the peaks of the distant mountains show, gently pushing back clouds.

Showers come, short bursts only. Pich leaps forward and shoves the notebooks into the plastic sacks.

Sometimes, the rain is welcome, cooling. Luc turns up his head and lets it wash down over him, over the decks. It always seems to find more grit to send tumbling along the gaps between the planks, as if the rain bore dust with it. Luc looks down over his body. Every muscle in his body shows, lean, in strands. I always wanted to look like a Cambodian, thinks Luc, and now I do.

One day, as rain pounds down, misting everything over, they hear the throbbing of a boat's engine.

They both pause, listening.

The boat is approaching them.

The notebooks are already in a plastic sack. Pich ties them more tightly. He loads both the real book and the sack full of notes into a tourist's old rucksack. He picks up the gun, but his hand shakes. He lowers it.

"Ah," he says. "They know it's me anyway. There's no point shooting you."

His eyes stare at Luc and seem to ask: what will you do?

Pich climbs into the water. Luc watches him. There goes the Book, he realizes. It's only half translated. He's even taking the notebooks with him. He'll bury the Book, and the translation will remain incomplete. What happens if it gets lost or damaged?

Luc sees the boat coming between reeds, through hissing rain, and suddenly the only feeling it inspires is fear. They will take him away, the Book will be gone, and they'll want to know why he is alive. Maybe they'll even accuse him of the theft. Complicity in the murder of the General.

I'm not young; I'm sick; I don't want to go through any of that. Luc is scared to be alone. He looks out at the reeds and thinks he can see Arn, with the great book held safely above the water. They'll be too close soon. They'll open fire soon.

Luc slips over the side of the boat and into the water. The water is lime green and smells of rotten reed. Yet after sunlight, it smells fresh. Water is Cambodia's blood. The Great Lake is Cambodia's pulsing heart. Luc takes a deep breath, and as if he were swimming in the Olympic-sized pool at the lycée, he shoots forward underwater into the reeds. He finds mud and scrub; a branch tears his leg; he shakes badly. He comes up for air. Sweat and water drip off him. He cannot see the boat, only ripples washing towards him. He ducks down again, using the reeds to pull himself deeper.

A voice like a robot squawks. "Saom Pich! Come out!"

Luc waits in silence.

"Anybody on this boat, come out. Slowly and showing your hands, which must not hold any weapons."

Luc waits. The men shout again. Then their engine starts up, and Luc takes a breath and lowers himself under the water. He lies back, forcing his head down into the mud.

The engine sounds different under water, a bit like a pepper mill grinding. It chokes suddenly into silence, and very clearly, as if next to Luc's ear, there is a thunk as hull collides with hull.

Gingerly, Luc raises his head by degrees. He doesn't want to stir the reeds or make a splash. He breathes lightly, shallowly, without a sound. The rain has lifted and now, through the reeds, dull sunlight is reflected on grey water. He hears heavy feet on their tiny deck.

He thinks of the fishing, and the lamplight at nights, and the cleaning of the decks and hull, and going over the side every morning and every evening to wash, and he feels as if he is losing a home.

Then there is a shout. "It stinks down there. It smells like somebody's died."

"Is there nothing?"

"No, it looks abandoned. Maybe it's a wreck."

"Keep looking."

They stay for hours. Radios squawk. More boats arrive. Luc gets a cramp and grimaces and, as silently as possible, tries to force his toes to curl downwards. Slowly he circles his feet, round and round underwater.

He feels alone and afraid; even his mother's voice has deserted him.

What if Pich has already gone, taking the Book and the translation with him? Then the Book will disappear and it will never be read. What is the point of hiding here then? What am I being loyal to? The Book? Saom Pich?

You said, you promised, you said the Book would be number two from now on, you'd let it go whatever happened to it.

But I know what it would mean to them. Luc remembers his imaginings of Cambodian schoolchildren hearing Jayavarman's words; of families reading at night, their pride glowing like the lamps

I can't let the Book die.

I don't want to be left here alone.

He shivers in the water and his teeth start to click together with fever.

"We'll take the boat back with us. Hitch it up."

Pich has run off and left me alone and they will go off as well, and I'll be alone out here and there won't even be a deck to climb up onto. Luc's eyes sting. He is going to cry. He has no strength left. He has been stretched as far as he can go, and any moment now, he will just blubber out: help me, help!

And pretend he has been held as an unwilling hostage all along.

Then he hears a fluting frog call, something like a whistle.

Pich. He's still there in the reeds. He's telling me that.

Was it Pich? What if it's just a frog?

I must be an idiot to be doing this; I need my head examined. Here are the Lake Police; they are on your side; they'll take you home, and everybody will be happy. You'll be safe; they WILL remember who you are; they WON'T have forgotten you. Sangha and Map and Yeo Narith and…and…he tries to remember other people. It is truly alarming that he has forgotten them. He gets distracted wondering how he could have forgotten, forgotten … the other Frenchman who works for … for … EfeeEFFee. What's the name of the school? He can't think. E F …

The motors start up. With a sloosh and a slosh, the boats withdraw.

Well, that's that then.

Luc feels relief. He didn't have to make a decision. He can just stay with Pich. He can translated the Book.

Five minutes. The frog keeps fluting.

It's getting dark, it's getting cold. The little boy inside Luc comes all the way out, and he starts to sob. He starts to sob uncontrollably, and shiver, and he dry-retches with grief and confusion, as if he's five years old and just woken up from an anaesthetic in a strange place, a strange life he doesn't know.

And suddenly, Pich has his arms around him.

"Well done, Comrade. Brave Grandfather, well done. There, there, we'll get up on land, we'll get you warm."

Pich pulls Luc's hair out of his eyes. "You stayed, Grandfather Luc. That means something. I don't know what." Pich looks amused, and shakes his head, a tough, wry old smile.

"Come on, my friend, we are now guerrillas together."

True to his word, Pich pulls him up onto the bank. "Can you walk?" He helps Luc to his feet, and helps him hobble through scrub onto dry and dusty land. "It'll be hell when it rains," he says. "Until then. Well. This is the life I'm used to. We are maquis, Comrade, resistance fighters. We fish, we sleep, we have water. And"—Pich holds up and shakes the notebooks and the heavy clanking bag— "we have the Book." His face softens. "You can still work."

He pauses. The wind is coming in off the lake, the reeds rustle, the lakeside is full of sounds so it's safe to make a noise. "It's me they'll shoot."

Luc whimpers like a baby. He settles into the still warm ground and its bed of leaves. There's a shelf of cloud in the sky and the last of the golden light streams out under it. Luc realizes that he is warm and dry. Habit takes over. Out comes the pencil; Luc goes to the Book and suddenly he is in command and the world makes sense.

They live wild for weeks, Luc slipping in and out of fever.

Some days he feels quite well. They have plenty to eat and drink. Pich looks at home. Luc lives in a kind of suspended state of reverie.

War, thinks Luc, at its base, life is a war, and without going through war, you don't know life.

That thought keeps repeating over and over. Each time Luc is impressed by its clarity, its multiple implications, the blank truthfulness of it. The thought has the power to make him content with hunger and with sleeping on a bed of dried reed. Rousseau, was it? He can't quite remember.

By evening he is often insupportably bored. Boredom tosses his head back and forth and yet he is so tired and sleepy that his eyelids droop down with the sun.

He begins to shake all the time, day and night, a light, subliminal quivering. Once, in the Jura in France, Luc had seen a frozen river, and underneath a clear piece of ice he could see the river rippling. Him, now.

Sometimes in his best hour, when golden light matches the Golden Book, striking it sideways so the incisions are so clear he can almost hear Jayavarman speaking, somehow then it is an acceptable fact that this translation will be his last act.

It is very far from being a bad or pointless act, even though his concentration wavers, and sweat sometimes drips onto the notebooks, or muddy pawprints smear them. When the pencils grow blunt, he gnaws the wood and sucks the graphite to make them sharp again. He paces himself, translating for only a couple of hours a day.

When the heat of the day buzzes around him, he lies prostrate in the mud and feels chill goosebumps on the back of his arms though he is drenched with sweat.

Then one day, he begins to quake. This is much more than a shiver. He rattles like a tall hotel in an earthquake. His arms dance all by themselves. He watches them dance. In confusion, he thinks he is at the Monterey Pop Festival in 1967. He'd gone there after all, and was a hippy; he's in the field rocking out, his arms going wild.

Does he make up the following story?

Pich goes away for a long time, days, and Luc thinks he's dying. He can feel the insects on his arms and he's sure that they've come to consume his body and drag him down into the mud for storage.

Then suddenly Pich is next to him saying, "Okay my friend, I've brought you medicine. I told them my brother was dying and I begged at the hospital and they didn't recognize me because my face is no longer everywhere. Here. Here."

Pich cradles Luc's head. "These are supposed to be taken with food," he says and pushes a pill into Luc's mouth.

Luc tries to be a good boy and swallow, but the pill sticks in his throat. He coughs. He's suddenly scared he will cough out his medicine and lose it, but Pich comes with water in his cupped hands. "Drink this."

Luc slurps and coughs. He can feel the pill stick in his throat like a leech. More water comes. The pill goes down.

Luc wakes up feeling better in the morning, but he is not sure he isn't making that up either.

They begin to have conversations again.

"The Americans were so stupid," says Pich. "We never would have won without their help. Before they got rid of Sihanouk, we were losing. There were only four thousand of us. Then the Americans start bombing in '69. Three thousand bombing raids in one year, illegal. Then they get rid of Sihanouk because he was neutral. Vietnam and Cambodian Communists were nearly fighting a war with each other over Sihanouk. An American-backed coup against him was the only thing that could possibly unite us. By December 1970 there are four Vietnamese divisions fighting alongside Pol Pot. All of Cambodia joined us. The Americans are so stupid that they pick Lon Nol to rule. Lon Nol, head of the secret police, who was nuts. He's so crazy, he wages a war against peasants. All peasants. All you have to do to be shot by the police is be a peasant. Lon Nol kills thousands. You don't have a single Cambodian on the Lon Nol government's side outside of Phnom Penh!"

He goes on shouting like this for some time, and Luc and Pich rock each other from side to side howling with laughter at the Americans.

"Then in '73 they started bombing us again after the peace agreement! Two hundred days and nights of raids, half a million tons of bombs, and they called it a Peace Accord and wondered why everybody in Cambodia wanted the Americans out!"

By now Luc's sides are aching with hilarity.

Pich wags a finger. "Mind you, mind you, no one could be as stupid as the Cambodians!"

They collapse helplessly against each other, propping each other up.

"Pol Pot, he's got the Vietnamese fighting with him! Four divisions show up to make him king. But Pol Pot is crazy, out of his mind, so in 1971 the CPK Congress names Vietnam..." Pich has to stop and draw in a long breath. "And these are the actual words, 'the long-term acute enemy'! Saloth Sar kills about a thousand trained, sensible, politically aware, intelligent Cambodian Communists because, only because, *they've lived in North Vietnam*. And he passes...oh!...passes the party over to twelve-year-olds. And he wins! And he wins! But only because the Americans were SO STUPID. He takes over the country. He's so incompetent; he kills a million people without even knowing he's done it! How do you kill one million people by mistake and not know?" Pich is shouting. "And now nobody, nobody in all of Southeast Asia, wants Communism ever again. They don't want socialism ever again! They don't want liberalism ever again. It all smells of death to them. So who was dumb and who was smart and who won? The Americans!"

They howl again.

"Sony billboards in Ho Chi Minh City!" Luc remembers the last time he was there.

"Vietnamese client rulers!" Pich's laughter sounds more like a wail. "Rigid class system, stupid royal family bickering over who is king! We're right back at the beginning of the twentieth century! All that war! All those bombs! For absolutely nothing!" He's howling now with hilarity, and tears are streaming down his face.

Luc's laughter has shuddered to halt. He marvels at this new extremity that their situation has brought them to.

Pich snores in his sleep.

He sometimes farts. He blames Luc and giggles.

He talks about his sons, his little boys, and the games they play, and the toys he's made for them, and what they want to be when they grow up. He says calmly, "I will never see them again, and they will not be able to be educated because of what I've done. But they will be there. Long after I'm gone, they will be living and thinking and doing things. That's enough."

Rainy season is mild that year.

Some days it doesn't rain at all. Some afternoons it pelts down so hard that raindrops bounce back up from the ground.

They use the rain as a curtain to hide behind. They slog farther inland to escape the advancing shoreline of the swollen lake. Pich hunches over the rucksack to stop the notebooks getting soaked.

Luc remembers movies. He tells Pich the plots of movies as they walk, and that his favourite movie is *Singin' in the Rain*. He sings him the song. He would dance, but his legs feel too scrawny and taut and he fears he will fall over. To please Luc, Pich says, "Oh, that is a very good song. Teach me the song." By the end they both are singing it, but Luc has translated it into Khmer.

> *Chanting in a monsoon*
> *Chanting in a monsoon*
> *My spirits are rising*
> *Remembering happiness*
> *With a smile on my face*
> *And happy smiling verses*
> *I'm chanting, chanting in a monsoon.*

To respond in kind, Pich tells him the entire story of *Tum Teav*. Luc already knows it, he has read it many times, but Pich saw the film version in which the King is a good guy (Sihanouk was in power then). So Pich recites it fondly, as a relic of a different age. The rain keeps falling. Pich holds Luc in his arms to warm him and stop him shaking.

The morning air is close and heavy, and Luc can't breathe.

"I cannot go back for medicine again," says Pich and shakes his head.

"Am I making this up too?" asks Luc.

The only thing that makes him feel better is the Book. Luc lovingly strokes the notebook pages, his stomach turning over and over. "My hands won't write," he says.

Pich takes the pencil. "Then you tell me what it says."

Luc lies bouncing on the ground as if he's riding in a jeep; his teeth knocking together. He gasps for breath; but he keeps working.

The leaves slip and slide and won't stay in place, and they get the packets confused, and the cut circles get separated from their supposed home leaves, and Luc weeps and weeps. "We've lost it, we've done it all wrong! It's not in order, it won't make any sense!"

His voice trails away to a whine, his face screws up until eyes and mouth disappear and all that's left are strings of muscle.

"Let's match," says Pich. The storm clears. Calmly, methodically, Pich goes through all 155 gold leaves. "No, no, shush, be calm, don't let the sickness master you. No, shush. All you have to do is tell me what this circle says, okay? I'll lay them all out in order. Okay?"

It helps. Luc calms down. He snuffles and wipes his nose, and his head aches so badly he has to squint, and his joints feel as large as oranges. All the leaves are laid out on the ground in order. Crumpled gold leaves are smoothed flat. All ten damaged circles are fitted back into what they think are the correct leaves. Slowly, moving through a fog of confusion, Luc finds their translations in the notebooks and corrects the leaf numbers.

"I'm sorry, I'm sorry," says Luc. "I've been silly. I'm sorry." He's still crying.

"No. You've done very well," says Pich. He sits cross-legged as if in meditation, and both hands are held out as if to say: behold!

"We've finished. That's all. That's why we're confused. They've all been translated. The Book is complete."

"It's over?" Luc suddenly feels very vague, as if the world itself has ended.

"Yes, yes, you rest, okay?"

Luc lowers himself to the ground, and he feels like a little boy again. He says "Read them to me."

"My eyes are not good," says Pich.

But Luc wants so much to hear them all in order. Pich goes back and forth through the notebooks. Sometimes he swaps leaf numbers in the notebook. "I think this April leaf belongs earlier."

He tires and asks, "How long is this thing?"

Luc says, "In Sanskrit it's exactly 22,500 words and then another 750 in the last five leaves. But those were added later. That's important. Each leaf is exactly 150 words." Luc grips Pich's arm so hard that he winces and coaxes Luc's hand away.

"Yes, Comrade, I understand."

Luc drifts in and out of fever. Pich sits cross-legged in moonlight as he reads, and Luc becomes convinced that it's Jayavarman who is talking.

"Are you going to take over the government now?" Luc asks.

Jayavarman rocks slightly.

He clears his throat and continues reading from where he left off, as if the answer was there.

> *I made a foreigner my crown prince and Brahmins my advisors in order to show that external forms mean nothing, and that there are no good or bad men. For it is a miracle of God that all men have right on their side. God is with all of them. All of them speak for justice. No one speaks for evil. The evil only comes when they think their small part of justice is all the justice there is.*

Luc asks Jayavarman. "Why are you crying?"

"I'm not crying, it's just sweat on my face."

"Then why are you whispering? Why does your voice sound strange?"

"I'm thinking of the waste," says Jayavarman. "I'm thinking of all the things that are too big to be put into words. I'm an old man at the end of my life, and life just keeps getting bigger. I'm wondering how big it would get if we didn't die, Comrade. If we didn't die." Jayavarman shakes the top of Luc's hand.

Luc's mother comes and sits down with a slump, dropping into her chair. "Oh, such a day I've had. You too. You look flattened! It won't be long now, and you can rest."

His cousin, who came to Cambodia several times and with whom Luc was secretly in love, drops in bringing a gift of favourite comics. Tintin. And a new one, *The Adventures of Jayavarman*. The cousin talks about all the things he plans to do when he grows up. He died at fifteen in a skiing accident.

Luc says aloud in Khmer, "Isn't it lovely the way Mother and my cousin are sitting here so quietly with us?"

"Your dead are with you?" Pich asks.

There is light all around, blazing on the water.

And Arn comes and sits with him.

Arn is a fifty-eight-year-old man in a white shirt. He takes Luc's hand. "We were so beautiful," he says.

"You're alive," whispers Luc and goes to sleep, holding Arn's hand.

In the morning, he wakes up sane.

"This is not going to get any better, is it?" Luc says.

Pich shakes his head. "I'm taking you in," he says.

Pich loads Luc up on his back, the gold book on his shoulder and the paper book on Luc's. He starts to walk, carrying Luc, at a slow, even, military pace. There seem to be miles of scrub. They batter their way through it. It is still broad daylight when they come in sight of a roadway.

"You go this way. I go that," says Pich, indicating different directions with his head.

Long pause. Both of them waver as if a cord tied between them is unbalancing them.

Pich asks, "Can you make it to the road?"

Luc nods yes.

Pich is smiling lightly, the tough guy amused by life. He shifts his bag and it clanks slightly.

Luc looks at the bag containing the *Kraing Meas* and his throat aches with longing. "Bury it," he says, and realizes just how big a commitment he is making by saying this. He starts again. "Bury it more than two metres deep, and metal detectors won't be able to find it."

Pich closes his eyes and bows very slightly in acknowledgment. "There's nothing you want to check or look at again?"

"My eyes won't focus and I'm hallucinating. I'm the last person who should be changing anything in those notebooks."

Pich nods. "They won't believe you," he warns. "They will think you know where the Book is."

"I know," said Luc. "But someone will publish the Book. The words will be out there."

"They might arrest you for the theft."

Luc shrugs and wavers. He feels like the shimmering air that rises up over tarmac on hot days. "There is nothing else to do, now."

"Nothing else to do."

Luc wants to shake hands, but Cambodians don't shake hands; it's a meaningless gesture they only use with Westerners. He wants to hug Pich, but Cambodians don't do that except within particular relationships.

Their eyes latch. Beautiful faces, thinks Luc, they have such beautiful faces.

Saom Pich sniffs, nods again, and turns and walks off towards his fate.

Arn, thinks Luc. This is Arn and me saying good-bye, which we never did properly, and off he goes. He's survived gunfire, hunger, disease, and age. There they all go, everyone for whom the last thirty years mean anything, off into the reeds. The Great Lake dries, the forests are cut down, the wildlife dies out, and the kids buy mobile phones and Game Boys.

He let me live. He helped me. He took me to the road. What a miracle.

I'd better move before I disappear.

A tall, torn, bloodied barang staggers half dead from dehydration, dengue, and malaria onto Highway 6.

A pickup truck stops for him, and he climbs into the back. He's plainly half-starved, and the sun has peeled off his skin in patches.

A woman with a kramar wrapped around her face gives him water. A farmer with a big plastic bag of bananas pulls some off the stem for him to eat. They are all surprised when the barang starts to sing old Sin Sisimuth songs, his face streaming with tears. He gets all the words perfect. He begins to sing another song with Khmer words, about chanting in a monsoon.

He looks up at the old woman. He has the eyes of a dead man, flat and dry. He pulls a notebook out of a plastic bag, grasping it so hard that it crumples and he says, "*Kraing Meas.*"

The old woman was once a schoolteacher and has weathered all the storms. "This is that book," she says. "The one that was stolen."

Slowly as if underwater, the foreigner takes a chewed pencil and writes in Khmer.

For Cambodian

Then he writes

Loak Tan Map
Police Village
Angkor Wat

He looks into the old woman's eyes and something of his spirit passes into her. A good man who has accepted death has a task for her, a task of particular merit. She takes the plastic sack and sompiahs.

It starts to rain. The people try to shelter him with their scarves and their bags of produce but water flows over him; the truck lurches and slams him. Looking utterly spent, he dies.

The rain passes, and the old woman looks at the notebook.

"These are happy words," says the old woman. "That means he died happy, bringing good luck."

She starts to read them aloud. As they bounce and rattle around new construction, dipping off the roadway onto temporary tracks, she keeps reading. The farmers sit in silence.

The truck stops in front of a hospital. The old woman shows the name and address the Frenchman had written, and everyone in the truck agrees. She slips away with the bag under her shirt.

It is not yet evening when she comes walking towards Angkor, out of the rain.

Map sees her from a distance. He sits drinking beer at the café by the east-facing gate. In most temples, it would have been the main entrance, coming from the direction of sunrise, the direction of life.

With Teacher Luc so long disappeared, Map has no daytime work, except drinking beer. His smile is crooked. Why is this crazy lady walking up here in the rain?

She walks straight up to him, and says, "Are you called Tan Map?"

Map nods. What of it? The woman doesn't seem to like his looks much, but most people don't. "A Frenchman on a truck died, but he gave me these for you." She passes him the rain-soaked rucksack.

Map fires questions at her. "Where, when? Where on the road? Did he say where he'd been? Did he say how he had escaped, or how he got there?"

The old woman shakes her head. "He sang old songs. He was very sick. I think you'd better look in the bag."

Map pulls out ten ordinary school notebooks. He recognizes Luc's handwriting, then the Khmer and then the words, reading the first two or three leaves. By the time he jumps awake, heart pounding, the woman has gone, taking her name and address with her.

Map takes off on his bicycle after the woman, cycling through the rain. He needs a full statement from her. He might need her to come to court and verify the story.

It's as though she has melted into the downpour. He doesn't know that she is not walking back towards Siem Reap, but walking westward, towards the setting sun through Angkor Wat. The last of the sunlight catches the clouds, burning them bronze.

He cycles almost all the way to Siem Reap and then stops. Leaning one foot on a muddy bank, drenched, he takes stock for a moment, wiping the rain and sweat out of his eyes.

What now?

The notebooks.

He cycles back as the sky clears and night falls. The moonlight is reflected on the glossy tarmac. It keeps pace with him. Map begins to hear a squeaking sound. The moon is bicycling beside him.

"What now, Jayavarman?" Map asks. By now, out of respect, he can only look at the reflection on the road as the King keeps pace with him.

For Cambodian, says the King.

Luc didn't want it to go to other people. He wanted it to go to a Cambodian person. That's what he said first.

He wants us to have it; he doesn't want it to be a book like a western book, one of those guides in English, French, and German but not in Khmer.

A different way, says the King.

I have an elementary education. I don't know the history. I have no books. Who am I to do this, Jayavarman?

A Cambodian. The moon smiles at Map with forbearance.

One particular Cambodian. A Cambodian who lived through many wars and lost many friends and who still smiles.

Like I did.

Map cycles on. The moon starts to falter and fall behind.

The moonlight says, This will get you into a lot of trouble, Map.

"I like trouble," Map replies.

You like trouble, Jayavarman Chantrea repeats. Like me.

Map sets up a gas lamp under the café awning and reads everything, the translation, the notes, the sections of copied Sanskrit, and he realizes how much work there is to do. He will need to set it out in order and get some help with the Sanskrit words. Then he will need to get it to other Cambodians, to publish.

A sarika bird starts to sing.

"Okay, Luc," Map says to a spirit he is sure is not in hell, a spirit he is sure stands by him. "We begin."

April 1181

Jayavarman returned to the land of the Chams, as if on a pilgrimage, as if they had never made him a slave.

The Cham conqueror looked on this with favour. Jaya's visit seemed to imply that the two kingdoms were one, and also got the Little King out of the way.

Jayavarman spent six months in the city of Vijaya, smiling calmly, as round and sweet as a melon. Like a melon, he attracted flies.

The sons of Jaya-Harideva, his old protector, needed to talk to him. The new Cham King had killed their father. The sons sent Jayavarman gifts of maidens, supposedly from some other, minor prince. At night, next to the King, the girls whispered messages along with allurements. Jayavarman made sure he resisted both. He praised the beauty of the girls, kept an arm's distance from them, and said nothing that could get him killed if they were spies. He went to the temples and was as devout a Buddhist as always.

Jayavarman had other, more original ways to pass messages.

"Hmph!" he said aloud to one of his enemies. "I don't like the way people keep trying to pass me messages. I tell you, the only way I would trust anyone is if they came and spoke to me out in the open." The way he said it sounded like a rebuke to the dispossessed Chams.

Then, professing himself pleased to be part of a new empire and expressing gratitude to his hosts, he made preparations to leave.

Oh, he added, he was looking forward to seeing the lords of Vijaya when they visited the Universal King in Yashodharapura. He would recommend to the Chakravartin how well the shadow government ruled in the lesser city.

Thus he chafed wounds while pretending to bandage them.

A month after his return, Fishing Cat came running to Jaya. "Lord," she said, her eyes sharp as knives. "It has happened as you said it would. Three Chams at the gates, and they talk like aristocrats."

Jaya streamed forth, all affection and generosity. "Food!" he called, "Food for our cousins!"

The sons of Jaya-Harideva looked as if they had risen from the grave. Their families were hostages; their elder brother was dead; and their eyes burned with the desire for revenge.

Rice and fish arrived, wafting cardamom and lemon grass. The Cham princes feasted and went faint from the impact of food on an empty stomach.

They spoke of their military might, the numbers of their men and elephants. Jaya pretended to be impressed. He did not have to pretend to look pleased. The value of Cham allies would be mostly symbolic. If the Cham King needed murdering, then Chams had better do it.

Cat watched Jayavarman for any slips of comportment. Years of enslavement had built a huge and ugly temple of resentment in the King's heart. He had had to dismantle this bitterness stone by heavy stone and even now the task might not be complete.

Cat also knew what the devout Queen Jayarajadevi did not. Jayavarman had changed. This was now a man who was determined to be Universal King.

While Queen Jaya invented the ideology of the new land to come, Cat had found a way to hide their army. She made them into monks. In deep discussions with Queen Jaya—who was pleased to see that her adopted sister had grown so interested in debate—Cat convinced the First Queen that in their new state all men should be monks for a while. In that way, all men would have religious instruction.

"Let's begin with the troops," she said. "Queen Jaya, you must teach them."

Cat had learned to love her adopted sister, whose heart was bottomless and whose learning surpassed that of anyone else in Kambujadesa. Cat felt her own heart soar when Queen Jaya spoke of goodness, wisdom, and compassion. Cat was sure that the many angry rebels would benefit in their hearts from her teaching.

Cat also knew that they would fight better the more they had to fight for. A new and more human Way would serve.

So she sat, humble Cat, still accepting that she was lowly, stitching monkish robes and listening to the teaching of the First Queen.

Jayarajadevi still had the figure of a slip of a girl, and she had a girl's open face, wide-eyed, vivid, full of hope and happiness and delight. Her too-wide mouth would open up in a smile that was full of love for the world. This beautiful, beautiful creature spoke from her beautiful heart.

Cat feared for her. Oh, Queen, you are not of this world.

"Consider the King's Consort," said the Queen at one lesson. Jayaraja's eyes shone out at Fishing Cat with joy, with love. "There you see before you the proof of my husband's great heart and great sincerity. In his own house, at the core of his domestic life, where you might expect to see hypocrisy arise, you see the King follows the Way. If he follows the Way in his own personal life, rest assured, he will follow it wherever the Path might take him."

Queen Jaya looked up at the skies beyond the dark ceiling, as if she expected to see her husband embodied there in the clouds. Her eyes shone like candles; the oil lamps made her skin golden. "You will be fighting for a new age, a new beginning for all the land."

Fishing Cat looked down in something like shame.

The peasant warriors gaped, open-mouthed.

Cat had to smile: they think they are seeing a celestial maiden come to earth. Okay, Sister, they believe you. Okay, that was a smart thing in its own way.

Maybe it is best you do not know all the truth, that your philosophy has become a weapon of war. Cat continued to cloak trained killers in the robes of saints.

In the fields, in the temples, in the houses of district administrators, people began to sing songs about a white rabbit.

The white rabbit disguised himself as a white royal elephant, said one song. No one thought that he was a sharp-witted Khmer bunny.

The white rabbit pretended to be good friends with some hunting cats in the next forest. The white rabbit learned to sing songs that lulled the hunting cats to sleep, but which told the other animals of the forest what was true.

In one of the songs, the tiger pounced on the burrow of the white rabbit and found him in his hammock looking fat and well fed.

The tiger demanded, "Why are you so fat and well fed?"

"Because I eat so much lovely grass," said the white rabbit and pushed some at him.

"No, thank you," said the tiger in disdain. "I demand a richer diet than grass. I eat rabbits."

The tiger looked up but the fat, slow white rabbit was already gone.

Rabbits reproduce. The land was full of burrows. Peasants would sing the songs and smile and say, "There are more white rabbits in the fields."

The peasants hid young warriors in their huts and said they were their older sons. The warriors would say to them, "Categories. Tooh, categories, who cares about the categories, that is the old religion." The warriors were dressed as mendicants or traders or rice farmers. "When the white rabbit raises his parasol over us, everyone will be shaded."

"They burned our city," the soldiers said to the slaves, "but they can never burn our hearts."

This white rabbit preaches compassion. This white rabbit cares for his people.

This white rabbit will fight for us, as no one ever has before.

The songs also carried messages to all the other little kings. Hide the many rabbits safe in burrows. With so many rabbits, how can the tiger eat them all?

The other little kings thought, this man Jayavarman, he is honest, a bit awkwardly so. Unambitious. He's got the favour of the Chams, and he's bumptious enough and naive enough to put himself forward, but he'll never be Universal King. Let him clear the space. For me.

The little kings did what the songs bid them do.

The Cham King invited Jayavarman all the way to Yashodharapura to ask him, "What is this white rabbit?"

Jayavarman had a mouthful of noodle, and he made a show of suppressing a laugh so he could swallow. "Ah, you must be learning the peasant's language, King."

"I hear much of talk of him."

"He is a way for the lowly people to express resentment. They tell stories of how the white rabbit tricks predators. You are very wise to pay attention to it, for I am sure that the lower categories have long resented their kings. They are an easily led people, full of complaint and free from all action." Jaya chuckled. "What are they to do, strike your soldiers with hoes?" He seemed to find the thought amusing.

"I built them a hospital," said the Cham King. Well, he had repaired one. Just beyond the western reservoir.

"And you removed the hated Usurper. But, peasants! Politics, statecraft, even religion is beyond them. Everything is at the level of superstition. Or folk songs!"

It is a ticklish thing to be summoned to counsel and feign friendliness with a tyrant who suspects you. He looks for slips, for shivers, for unintended words.

But you are one spider trying to catch another. I can walk on your web, King, and spin one of my own.

We are much alike. You were wise to take a title-name that sounds like everyone else's. You hope the people will get confused about who is who. Oh, Jaya-Indravarman, Cham King of the Khmers, perhaps you do not believe in nationality.

Jaya-Indravarman was an old man. Lines radiated out from his eyes like rays of light. His eyes were yellow and blotched with red and his teeth worn and brown, and he was beginning to suspect it was sheer foolishness to remain in Yashodharapura.

It was Jaya's job to keep him there, for the City still had no walls.

"Why do we need these stone temples?" the conqueror asked, eyes fixed on Jayavarman.

"Tooh! They are to worship the Gods who are so far beyond us that it is pointless. But our ignorant people are terrified of any king whom they believe has the Gods with him. The trouble is that if you leave, they will think it is because the Gods have rejected you. It will be interpreted as you abandoning the throne, and all these petty princes will come crawling out of the soil just when you thought you had rid the world of them."

"Ah!" said the King, letting his hands rise and fall, as if helpless.

You feel helpless, King, because you do not know who to trust, including me. Which means you will distrust the best advice I could give you if I were truly on your side.

Jayavarman said, "You might, of course, take some time to return to the city of Vijaya. That might be wise, very wise. One never knows what is happening at home."

"Why, what did you see when you were there?"

"Nothing. Would you believe it, your people seemed to distrust me because I am Khmer? I kept telling them, I fought with the Chams before against tyranny, and I gave signs of my devotion to you. But I was watched all the time. They kept trying to express how proud they were of the conquest...I thought they were grinding my face in it. I felt rather humiliated." Jaya feigned a pout. *A fat, foolish little eccentric. That is my reputation, no? And a man must guard his reputation.*

"I must speak to them and remind them that you fought on our side," said the King of the Chams in a perfectly even voice.

If I had not the clear intent. If I had not the knowledge that I am nothing compared to what it is that I would do. If I had not the certainty that the intent is the intent of the people, so that even if I die, my sons or their sons, or some other prince would press on. If it were not for the truth that I must keep from blazing out of my eyes, then I would be unsure, unsteady, and open to you.

For I sit in your pavilion, watched by your armed guards, forced to sit on boards while you sit on gold cushions, eating food that could so easily be poisoned, with no possibility of leaving here alive except through what I say and how I say it.

But I am now fearless; I have been made fearless. And so I will elude you.

Jaya-Indravarman sighed and said lightly, "Somebody told me that the white rabbit was you."

Jaya chuckled. "Well, I am fat enough. Me? Ho ho..." Jaya stopped and knew he had to pretend to be terrified. "My Lord, what are you saying?" As if involuntarily, he looked up at the guards. "My Lord, my Lord, no, you cannot believe this thing? Who has said this! Who?" Then he wailed, "Why have you brought me here?"

Very satisfying for a king.

Jayavarman, a little king, began to crawl. "My Lord, I have been loyal. My Lord, I fought for you! I build temples in your honor. You cannot believe this of me!"

This was a leader of men? It was the question this false Jaya had to ask. No wonder the Little King's help in the first invasion had led to disaster. This was the thought he had to have.

The Cham conqueror smiled. "Now, now, Little King, I did not say I believed them."

Jayavarman shook and trembled and sat back and looked at the food as if it now made him ill. He gasped and wiped sweat from his face.

The false Jaya chuckled and shook his arm affectionately.

Jaya found he could weep. He wept from determination. "My Lord, you mustn't make such jokes with your servant! Do you have any idea how t-t-terrifying your displeasure is? Oh!" He put his hand over his heart.

"My dear Little King, be more of a man."

"Oh, oh."

"Here, have some water."

Jaya drank and said. "Your Lordship should be more careful who you trust, whoever told you this is simply currying favour by making up stories, and trying to separate you from your allies."

"Hmmm," said Jaya-Indravarman. Unconvinced, neutral, considering. Undecided, concerned, bemused. But certainly not at all afraid of this easily unsettled, religious Little King.

The best that could be hoped for, under the circumstances.

Jaya still pouted. "I can see I had better stay here. I'd better just keep an eye on you." He found he was imitating his waspish, crippled son. "Yes, if you fall prey to stories such as these. You may send me home, but I won't go. I shall stay here and direct your temples for you, and keep you out of trouble."

The Cham King looked as if he had just eaten rabbit. "Will you, now?"

"Well, I must do something to defend my interests. There are plenty of Khmers who resent the favour you show to me. And they won't tell the truth!"

The false Jaya was leaning back. He was amused by this petulant little man, playing at politics.

"I shall decide where you go," warned the Universal King.

And he sent Jayavarman home.

In his eastern kingdom, the King walked with his sons into the fields, where spies could be spotted from a distance. Jayavarman said to Surya and Vira, "It has to be done now. The Cham King knows something is afoot and grows too watchful. I very nearly did not get back."

Virakumara cautioned, "So we attack after May, when the rains swell the river and the Great Lake."

"No," said the King. "Now."

Suryakumara scowled. "But I thought the strategy was to attack from the Lake."

"It is. They attacked from the Lake, but in December. They will be less watchful when the Lake is at its lowest."

"But there is no rice left in the fields, there will be nothing for the soldiers to forage."

"Exactly. Again, the Chams may relax. The people will give our warriors their rice to march on."

Jayavarman gathered his own warrior-monks, in the depths of his temple.

"The white rabbit has many sons. He sends them out to all the hidden burrows. The new song is: all the family is invited to go fishing. Afterwards, we will have a banquet. The main dish will be the tiger."

He sang it to them in a voice that was just good enough to be entertaining.

The soldier-monks chuckled. One of them said, "That will be a good song to sing."

"You leave tonight. You are prepared. Those of you who go to this side of the Great Lake, wait three days before moving. Those of you that have to travel far do not wait to begin. Arrive, sing the song, and get the troops moving immediately. Those of you near Malyang in the west, you launch onto the Great Lake from the west. Those of you here in the east, from the eastern shore, and those of you on the rivers, from the south and up. We will gather in the middle of the lake and sail on together. Tell your boatmen, tell the other soldiers. The aim is not to fight the enemy on the lake or to destroy their boats. The aim is to shoot past them, up the canals, and deep into Yashodharapura to kill the Cham King. My own brave warrior son, Suryakumara, will lead the land forces in the south, to prevent further Cham forces arriving from their own lands."

And also to feed my hungry son's appetite for war, and to keep him far from the Great City.

"The Cham King will know something is afoot. He will guess that many of his supposedly loyal Khmers will desert him to join us. He has already surrounded himself with many Chams. Do we have the Cham princes? Good. They will be in my boat, to share the glory."

And to keep them in view.

"We will not lose. The very stones of our countryside will rise up! The peasants will drive their cattle into the war; the fishermen will hurl their nets over the heads of the enemy. We will take back our city, and rebuild it again, with new towers, and above all else, with walls to protect and shelter it, so that it can never be taken in this way again! For we are the Khmer people, with a language and a way of being of our own. We are not every nation; we are not Universal. But we are us, ourselves. There will be two results of this war: a happy people as you see here in this small kingdom. And peace! No more war!"

The soldier-monks howled and shouted and pledged loyalty and looked overjoyed, overjoyed to be marching at last. They jumped up and punched each other's shoulders, clambering up each other's broad and bellicose backs.

My soldiers, my people. You are so beautiful in life, young and strong, so happy to be fighting at last. I myself will sing songs over your funeral pyres. You will be like flowers that never wilt, no man or woman will see you in age. You will be beautiful in glory, young and strong and brave.

For we are glorious. Right now, we are the flower of creation.

And we will win.

"There they are," said the King.

As if the Great Lake had grown teeth, the horizon was serrated with the prows of many boats approaching.

"That's the West and Malyang and maybe even Louvu or Ahodya." Jayavarman spun around to face south, to see if Poduli had answered the call. To the south, the lakewas rippled, like silk upon a table. No boats yet from the three rivers.

The Little King stood in a small roofed pavilion, crammed into the middle of his long boat. He was safely nested within a formation of twenty boats from the eastern shores of the lake.

"Either the timing is wrong, or Poduli's fleet is not coming. If they are late, perhaps they can act as reinforcements when we need them most."

The Cham prince Vidyanandana tapped King Jaya's arm. "Here comes the tyrant's fleet."

The northern horizon had grown teeth as well.

"Battle by midday," judged the King. He looked down and the creamy green water churned. What looked like a rough-backed log drifted past. Crocodiles. The Great Lake swarmed with them. In battle, as blood ran down the sides of the barques, the crocodiles would stream towards them. Even if the Great Lake was shallow enough to walk in places, to fall into a sea of blood would be to know that jaws would slam into you, knock you from your feet, and gouge out your chest or stomach.

To fall overboard would be to die; to be on a boat that sank would be to die.

Jaya smiled. "Our crocodile jaws close," he said. "See how our two fleets of east and west close on the tyrant's navy. Without doubt, this will be a day to remember."

"Let us hope it is a day that is remembered for its justice," said Vidyanandana. He was not only the subtlest and bravest of Jaya-Harideva's sons, but Jaya found he could talk to him as a friend. He had not felt that for another man's son since the days of Yashovarman's noble princes.

He who would rule must always make friends among the young.

"Justice will not be forgotten and it will be done," promised Jayavarman.

A crocodile thumped the side of the barque. The men jumped, groaned, and then chuckled to themselves.

In the high, flawless light of heaven, even at a distance, the details of both fleets could be seen. Turning behind him, King Jayavarman saw fifty barques catching up with him. Those bearing troops had eleven rowers. Their prows rose up as images of the beaked garuda or makara monsters. Some were plain and unadorned. The rowers sat protected by wickerwork panels. Between their rows were crammed the kneeling soldiers. You could just see the tops of their heads and long lances, as if the boats carried a crop of rice-straw and nuts.

The King's own boat was the largest. The trunk had been made from a single huge silk-cotton tree. Its prow tapered to a carving of a makara monster but with real elephant tusks for fending off boarders. The makara's open mouth disgorged a carving of the seven-headed serpent Naga who guarded the Buddha.

At the back of the boat, a poop deck carried a royal throne, borne up by a wooden garuda. From there the King could survey the battle behind them.

From his central pavilion, the King could loose his arrows and take some shade.

Twenty-one paddlers lined each side of the royal barque. Paddlers faced forward and needed less direction than rowers. Paddles made the long, slow boat more manoeuvrable but still slower than the fighting vessels, whose rowers could put their backs into it.

The soldiers of the white rabbit crouched down between the paddlers.

How different these infantry were to the troops of Suryavarman. This was a rebel force, stripped bare. They wore a motley of quilted jackets or no jackets at all. There were no breastplates, and few bows or arrows. Their weapons were made of hardwood, long shafts that could be hurled as spears or thrust forward as lances. Both ends had been polished into blades that could whack like swords.

The men trusted to skill and God. Most wore only modest twists of cloth around their hips. Bands of rope criss-crossed their chests, lashing javelins to their backs. Around their necks were bronze or wooden amulets for protection. All of them had pulled back their oiled hair into tightly woven buns at the tops of their heads—too tight and slippery to grab hold of.

In my childhood, Jayavarman thought, the soldiers wore totemic topknots of beasts and birds. Even their ears are stripped now, all earrings removed.

In the prow, soldiers nursed ropes with grappling hooks.

The King's heart thrilled, like a bird taking wing.

All about the placid lake, fishing boats were turning, pulling up nets, fleeing the closing of the great naval jaws.

The art of naval attack was to avoid fighting, and shoot through the enemy's lines of defence. They would try to grapple your boat and pour over it in a solid wave of men. You fought them off, hand to hand.

Well, thought Jayavarman. We have done whatever we could. Now fate decides, not us.

We either win or we don't. We will have done what we can.

He apologized to the Buddha.

I am sorry Cittamika, Saugatauma. I could have spent my life improving my wisdom, tending my little kingdom. I have had the conversation with Mara, the world, and I did not choose the Way. I decided to become a king.

So I do not pray on the grounds of my greater virtue or even the greater justice of me being a king over any other man.

I do not pray on the grounds of injustice against the people of Kambujadesa. What difference does it make who inhabits the land or rules others? We would rule the Chams if we could, as we rule in Siam. What difference does it make if there is a Kambujadesa or not? All peoples die eventually. Whether they are great or not, all cities end in ruins.

It will make no difference if I make my kingdom. It will be unmade in the end. It will still be based on categories of people and I will still have to give patronage to the Brahmin and the powerful families. It will not make people wiser. It is nothing to you if your religion is spread among the people.

I suppose I can ask on the grounds that the people seem to want it.

I am attached, Lord Buddha. I am attached to my people. I am attached to my old kings Suryavarman and Yashovarman. They were human and faulty, but as good as they could be.

I was not as good as I could be. I let the Servant rule. I let the Chams win. I made myself a little man.

Now I make myself a big one. That is who I always was, like a silk-cotton tree who tried to be a flower. Do not blame the tree for towering. It shades the flowers.

So. I do not pray to win.

I pray for the right thing to happen.

I pray for the strength to be whatever I really am.

I pray to stop praying and simply to be.

I am here, at the edge of my limits.

And therefore utterly in your hands.

The King turned and saw his limits ranged all around the horizon behind them, boats streaming from the south, the east and the west, and now even from Poduli.

All of them called forth by a song about a white rabbit. Called forth by some mystery that even Jayavarman, at the center of it, did not understand.

To be at your limits with brothers around you, and to know that this would be a day like no other. That was something.

To know that things would finally be decided after years of talk, years of lies and pandering, and biding, biding, biding your time— that was a very great relief.

So Lord Buddha, cast me up or down, give me my full and just return for being my full self.

You do your job, I do mine!

Part of his job was to know the names of all the men close to him. The King looked down the ranks of the rowers, reviewing their names and the names of their wives and children. Then he reviewed the single file of soldiers crammed in the aisle between them. They knelt in the sun, Yama, death.

He began to hear far off and muffled the beating drums of the enemy.

The beating kept pace with his heart, faster, faster.

Vidyanandana said, "I think the Chams will be on us before the two other fleets catch up."

"We push on," said Jaya. "We have twenty boats with us from the east. If they get into the canal system, that will be enough."

Jaya cocked an eye back at the poop deck and said, "Tillerman? Keep going."

A conch shell sounded, the agreed signal to keep advancing. From the decks of the other eastern boats captains smiled and waved.

Jaya spoke to the men. "Remember, our job is to get the troops on land. The aim is to avoid fighting on the water. The battle will not be decided on the lake." Arrows always seem to accelerate towards their targets. Like arrows, the Cham navy advanced. Very suddenly Jayavarman could make out the round, high-cheeked faces of the Chams and their glittering lotus-bud helmets.

"Have I ever told you, Vid," Jayavarman said, with a voice as airy as clouds, "that I cannot swim?"

Vid caught the spirit. "That must make this more interesting for you, then."

Jayavarman shook his bow and his fistful of precious arrows. "It is good that I have been so hard at work at my archery. I don't intend that the Chams give me swimming lessons."

A crocodile thumped the side of the boat again. This time the men laughed.

Two of the King's smaller boats swung up on either side of his barque, like horses protecting an elephant.

And very suddenly the Cham fleet was on them.

The conches blew from boat to boat. Drive on, drive on, drive through! Jayavarman bellowed, "Get past them, push past them!"

A particularly large Cham vessel, hewn from a single giant tree, nosed its prow towards him at rowing speed.

"Spin right!" shouted the tillerman. In unison, the paddlers on the right reversed the direction of their stroke, pushing against the water. The whole boat turned as if on an axis for less than a quarter arc. Then all the paddlers stroked forward in unison and the boat leapt forward.

The Cham boat shot past their poop, water shushing out from it, as the enemy oarsmen cried out and their boat tried to change direction. The Cham navigator shouted and pointed at the central pavilion. Jayavarman had been recognized.

"Down," cried the tillerman.

The paddlers ducked and the soldiers lifted up their tall wooden shields. A volley of Cham arrows sped with a sound like birds, then bit with a sound like talons. They tore into the deck or thunked against shields.

A Cham boat slammed along the left-hand side of one of the King's side-boats. Grappling ropes uncoiled in the air. One missed; two others bit into the sides of the ship. Rowers spearpointed the tips of their oars at the eyes of boarders, and crouched forward to throw off the hooks. The Khmer soldiers then pushed off from the side of the Cham barque with their long lances. The side-boat shot free.

The King laughed aloud. His little arrowhead of three boats was already through. Ahead lay the undefended waterways of Yashodharapura. He nipped between his crouching soldiers along the boat to climb onto the rear deck. He peered behind, into the morning sun, shielding his eyes.

Come now, remember, he told his other boats. Do not engage. Treat the Cham ships like shadows and slip past them.

Jaya saw one of his seventeen other boats disengage and push forward. Then he saw, unmistakably, the spider-web grappling lines fly across from the Cham ships.

The boat that had nearly rammed him seemed to lose heart. It slowed as if foundering and then turned south.

Lose heart nothing, they're joining the battle. Where we don't need one.

"Slow down, stop," the King said to the tillerman, who struck a gong to signal to the side-boats.

In the distance, Jaya saw Chams swarm up and over onto one of his boats. The Khmer advance had snarled itself. Sounds flew across the lake like samosan birds scooping up fish: shouts, slams.

The hollow whispering of the wind.

The King calculated quickly. His three boats carried forty men...not enough.

Come on, come on, he told the other boats. Get out of there, come north.

Still no boats broke free from the engagement.

He sighed. This was no doubt only the first disaster on what would be a day of them.

"Turn," said the King. The tillerman thumped once on a gong to signal. The King's boat milled its way round like a waterwheel and the side-boats pushed forward on their oars to slow down.

"Let the side-boats catch up," the King told the tillerman and then walked back to the central pavilion.

Vid asked, "What's the plan now?"

"Cut our boats free and remind our men that the battle will be on the land not on the lake."

The battle swung into view. Ahead, everything had stalled. The vessels of both sides had lashed themselves together into a giant raft of boats.

The King raised his voice only slightly, so that it would not waver. "We head straight into that tangle nose-first. We need four men in the prow. You cut all grapples, even our own. The rest of you, keep the Chams off our sides. As soon as the grapples are cut, I want the paddlers to back us away." The King's hand mimicked a jabbing boat, thrusting its way in, then backing out. "This will take courage. You have it."

Already he heard the men on the hindmost of the Cham vessels shouting to alert each other of his presence. The King stood up in his pavilion, exactly as he would stand on the howdah on an elephant's back. The instant he was in range he began firing his precious arrows.

His first arrow sizzled into the neck of the Cham helmsman. His own men cheered. Good omen, Luckbringer.

What looked like an officer all in armour was stumbling over backs down the length of the Cham boat. Jaya's second arrow drove into the man's mouth, and his forward momentum somersaulted him over the backs of his men.

The mess of boats loomed. The tillerman said one low word and the paddles flashed in sunlight like the tongues of hunting frogs. They accelerated into the heart of the snarl.

Ram.

Rattan crackled. The King's boat listed to the left as if it had been picked up. Jaya was nearly pitched off his feet. Four soldiers stood up, swords raised, and slashed at Cham grapples. A hedge of lances along their sides kept off boarders.

Jaya heard rather than saw the arrows and felt their dim shadows flick across the sun. The pitching of his boat made it easy to fling himself behind the scant defences of his mid-deck pavilion. The wooden floor sprouted the shafts of arrows. The backs of his men grew barley.

But already grapples had been cut; already his paddlers were backing them out of the snarl.

The King stood up and shouted in Khmer to his boats, "Pull out! Pull out now!"

He looked round to Vid. Vid was fine. So was the tillerman. Damage to the men on the right was extensive, but Jaya saw one of his other boats shrug its way out of the mess.

The soldiers went to work, hauling wounded paddlers into the center of the deck. The King danced towards the wounded, to help ease them clear. Other paddlers replaced them, scuttling from the row on the right.

Five would probably die, three more were useless but would survive. One of the wounded grinned and gave a hand symbol for good luck.

The King pointed to another narrow bay between boats. Steer there! "There, there, there," he shouted, pointing.

And he began to whisper the names of the wounded men, remembering their stories to tell their wives and children.

The King's boat gathered speed again and rammed its way between Cham vessels. His men raised their paddles as the Chams shouted to get their own oars up in time. Some snapped and crackled, shards of wood scything through the air.

With a rumble and a judder their boat collided with both a Cham and a Khmer boat. The Chams were faster this time and hooked lines were flung over the figurehead and stern of Jaya's own boat.

The three ships were locked in one embrace. Jayavarman drew his sword. So did Vid.

"You are the son of my friend who protected me," said Jayavarman. "I will not let them take you."

"Nor I you," replied the Cham prince.

The Chams swarmed, pouring onto their confined deck. Pointed paddles jabbed at their faces and the soldiers in crouching phalanx drove spears up at them. But a wall of Cham troops, covered in metal armour, knocked aside the lances and spilled over the paddlers' backs.

Soon it was messy hand-to-hand. Pressed close together, the Khmers could hardly lift up their homemade weapons without whacking their comrades. But the Chams had no experience of defending themselves against these long spears with blades at both ends.

One Khmer soldier successfully swept his lance up and round into a Cham gut and then levered his victim over the side.

Jaya glanced behind him and saw the Cham bleeding as he swam.

The front end of a Khmer spear drove forward into another Cham throat while another tripped and flicked the same man over the top of the low rattan screen.

Two Chams had climbed over the backs of Jaya's men, swatting lances aside and lunging towards the King.

Vid swung, protecting Jayavarman as his father Jaya-Harideva had done.

A Cham charged Vid, and Jaya aimed a blow at the throat left exposed by the lotus helmet.

The Chams tried to grasp the naked, oiled, sweaty Khmers, who slipped out of their arms like greased locks. The Khmers turned and surged onto the Chams' backs. The lotus helmets provided a perfect hold. One Khmer seized and held a head, another opened up the voice box.

Lances were thrust between legs and then levered upwards.

The rattan screens were low, to make it easier to fling boarders over the side. Top-heavy in armour, the Chams fell over backwards into the milky brown lake. They cast off armour too late. They kicked and splashed their way back towards their boats. By now the water all around the boat boiled with crocodiles and asura-fish that could take whole deer.

"Now pull! Pull!" shouted the tillerman.

The paddlers, their faces struck by urgency and fear, dug swift and deep into the water.

Jayavarman nodded thanks to Vidyanandana. Vid's sturdy face beamed back at him. In a flash, Jaya calculated. A Buddhist adopted crown prince over a Hindu one? This Cham over a Khmer?

The soldiers jumped forward, killing any wounded Cham and harvesting armour and weapons. They flung the dead and dying over into the water.

The helmsman shouted something. Jaya didn't understand, but the men did. They swept the prow of their boat through an arc and used it like a lever to push another Khmer boat around.

His boat sprung another Khmer vessel free. Unbidden, his paddlers then shoved their way out backwards.

The King steadied himself for balance and saw that the lead Cham vessel was just in range of his arrows, and that, in its pavilion, the Cham Admiral stood firm and brave and bannered.

With a whisper of hope, the King drew back his arrow. The bow sung, the arrow leapt. Like an angry bull, the arrow charged into the Admiral's neck. A Cham officer cried aloud and a moan of alarm spread through the Cham vessels.

"Down!" Jaya shouted and dropped, rolling off his raised deck. The King's men dived for the shadow of the rattan screens.

The air sizzled like kebabed fish. Arrows applauded all across the deck and the sides of the boat.

Before Jaya could give any other order, the tillerman screamed, "Get the King onward!" Another Khmer barque sliced through the water past them.

Jaya leapt to his feet and saw behind him grappling hooks being thrown free. Eight or nine boats free now? Enough.

Jaya nodded thanks to his helmsman. He had given the right order. The King's boat backed away from the mêlée.

Dead weight had to be cast off. Soldiers had already hammocked up a limp, grey man.

"Let me see their faces!" the King shouted and strode forward.

Mulberry from his own city. Fox from Big Pier.

He saw them, and rehearsed their names and how they had died. So many names he would have to remember with gifts and honor. So many widows to comfort.

Then they were thrown to the fish and crocodiles.

And the King counted ships. Eleven, twelve…more.

"We're through," Jayavarman said to Vidyanandana. "Now the battle can really begin."

The King's nerves crackled as his men dug their paddles swift and hard into the canal water.

Category people raced ahead of the boats along the banks of the canal. They swung the long arms of their irrigation pumps out of the path of the boats. They skidded down the slopes into the water, to seize their buffaloes by the horns and coax them to one side of the canal. From the buffaloes' backs, they waved at the boats that swept past them.

For months the songs had been telling them: the White Rabbit wants to swim. For months they had been dredging the canal. All along the tops of its banks, clumps of weed and black soil still crispened in the dry air.

Swift-footed boys ran barefoot alongside the boats calling, White Rabbit! White Rabbit goes boating!

The King laughed with them, flowering out his arms and chest as if he had already won. Daughters waved from elevated porches. Old men rocked back and forth on their haunches with excitement, laughing toothlessly.

Behind him, all along the straight, deep canal, thirty or forty boats rowed, all the way back to the white glare of the Great Lake, a bubble of reflected light on the horizon. The strategy was that half the boats would turn to guard the canal entrance. Could he hear, even from here, the dim sounds of the lake battle?

The King, standing proud on the poop, could see that on the banks there were barricades of sharpened tree trunks.

The King called, "You roll those in after we pass?"

The boys jumped up and down with excitement and yelped. "Yes, those Chams will not get past us!"

They had the faces of slaves set free.

It worked, thought Jayavarman. Calling on my peasant people. It worked.

Beyond the rows of houses, scrubland bristled.

Where, the King asked himself, are the houses?

Yashodharapura had once housed a million people. In the days of Yashovarman, these fields surrounded villages. Jaya's heart rose to his mouth. What have they done with all the Khmer people?

The Cham King had burned the City in order to take it, and it had been the houses of the categories that had burned, along with their tiny vegetable gardens, their one-tree orchards and the small flowery borders they planted for the spirits. Had the people not been allowed back? Had they all died?

The backs of his paddlers swelled and clenched and swelled again with the pumping motion of hearts.

I always took the main road into the City. I didn't see this. If I'd known this I would have strangled Jaya-Indravarman where he sat.

The silky water slithered past, reflecting sky.

So now we take revenge.

The wide fields, once crammed with children, dogs, cisterns, and ovens—empty. Who supports the temples, who grows rice for the devotees? Do the robes hang grey and tattered on statues in empty temples?

We will have to rebuild. First, conquer all the little kings, then rebuild. Make all the little kings pay for the rebuilding.

The King cried to the people on the bank, "Where are all the houses?"

The people smiled in shame, and shrugged and blinked. All gone.

That is why they have joined with me.

His paddlers beat the water like an egret's wings skimming a lake. Suddenly they came to a clot of people standing and waiting at the mouth of another canal opening to their left. Already?

The King called, "The canal to the Vishnuloka?" The waterway along which all those giant stones were floated.

The people's faces flared as they recognized him. "Yes! Yes!" they shouted. "This is the canal!"

"You make good time!" one man shouted in joy.

The King cried back, "We will kill the tyrant!"

As the boats neared the canal, it snowed petals—white and purple and indigo. The people were throwing them. The flowers fell over the soldiers' backs and swirled on the water in the currents of the swift boats.

A glimpse of sky-blue water, running straight into the heart of the towers, the giant lotuses of stone.

Vidyanandana's face fell in wonder at the size of the temple.

"This was all city, all people, all around here," the King shouted. "It's all been burned."

More people stood on the other side of the Vishnuloka canal. The King called to them, "Help us! Run and see what the Chams are doing!"

The men gaped, sompiahed, and pushed a boy's shoulders. He sprinted off. A team of boys pelted after him, jumping over thorns and thistles.

Vidyanandana's eyes gaped. "Burned?"

Jaya nodded yes in answer. He scanned the wide-open flat plains. Somewhere to the south and west he would expect to see some sign of General Namasivaya's land forces. They would have come from the north, round the western reservoir, and been joined by the rest of the army landing on the north shore.

Jaya turned to face forward. Ahead of them, the great road to the old capital Hariharalaya would cross the canal.

Finally, he could see a village, to the west, shaded by a clump of young trees that looked like a tuft of marsh grass.

Out of it bounded a Cham horseman. His horse bounced to a halt, feathers of dust hanging in the air, swords of sunlight reflecting from his armour.

"We've been seen," said Jaya.

The horseman wrenched on the reins and the horse danced around, back towards the village. The Cham defenders would soon know that they were coming.

The King demanded, "One last sprint." The tillerman sang out to the side-boats ahead. Together the boats surged forward like crocodiles.

At last they saw the bridge, blackened in streaks. The fires.

The King explained, "We need to get past the bridge before they defend it." Dust billowed from the west. "And they're coming."

People crowded the top of the bridge. The King's eyes pulled them closer to him. His own bare-shouldered people. They started to wave. The King waved too, towards the west, to warn them: flee or defend.

"Faster, if we can, faster!" He snatched up one of his banners from the back of his boat, orange, yellow, and shaped like flames. He waved it like a torch to the boats behind, to warn them—the Chams were coming for the bridge.

He turned back and saw about six of the peasants staggering forward, carrying one of the canal barriers of sharpened trunks. Not now! he thought. Then he saw category people, men and women, reaching down towards it from the road embankment.

They were going to blockade the bridge.

My people are made of fire. Fire and flowers combined.

The square mouth of the bridge yawned towards the boats.

The paddlers lowered their blades, and everyone in the boat ducked. Like a gasp of cold air, shadowed stone passed over their heads.

The King looked up and suddenly, ahead of them, in clumsy blocks, the Unfinished Temple baked squarely in sunlight.

They were in the City.

So, now we sail on past all the temples to the tyrant's palace.

To the west, dust rose, a discoloration in the sky, orange, almost as if there were a fire.

"Your general meets the defenders," Vid said.

Jaya tried to avoid calling the enemy the Chams in Vidyanandana's presence. "Our main hope now is that most of the tyrant's troops went charging out to meet him."

"Some," advised Vid. "But not perhaps those of the King's own guard. They'll be there in the palace to protect Jaya-Indravarman." Vid smiled. "Don't underestimate my people, even here."

Wisdom. The Chams would be smart, hard, cruel, and swift. "They will wait at the docks," Vid said.

Jaya breathed deeply as if to suck in courage and intelligence. He said to the tillerman, "Dock at the Unfinished Temple instead. That should leave space for the other boats to get through the bridge. Then we disembark."

From the bridge behind them came a thundering of hooves, a whinnying of horses and women's screams. Jaya saw his people fleeing east across the dark platform of the bridge. Arrows shot up from his boats on the canal. The King saw no Cham horsemen on the bridge itself—the barriers had evidently blocked their crossing. From under the bridge, one of his boats glided, oars up, wooden shields turtle-backed over the heads of his men.

All their cavalry needs to do is ride along the top of the canal banks and rain arrows down on us.

Change of plan again.

"Get us out of the boats now. Trumpet! Signal!" the King shouted. The tillerman blinked. They had agreed that there would be no musical signals inside the City in order to take the tyrant by surprise. The King kept his temper. "They know we're here, man! Signal!"

The musicians sounded the trumpet, meaning dock or retreat. The blaring sound was taken up along the line of boats. "Out, out now!"

"Racing march," the King told his tillerman, and the man began to beat his drum in a running rhythm. The King seized his fire-banner from the deck, gathering up its folds. His boat veered into the bank, settling against it with a thump. Before it had steadied itself, the King flung himself from the poop onto the bank. The grass was patchy, parched grey in places, and though he was pitched onto his hands, he found a footing. He scrambled up onto the top of the dike and waved the orange-red banner and roared to the men below, "Racing march! Racing march!" He ran ahead to the lead of his sword-boats. "Shields in front!"

The platoon leader of the sword-boats jumped, but landed in a buffalo wallow. He hauled himself up, laughing and kicking mud from his feet. Back along the canal, the last of the boats nosed into the bank, men in the water pulling it in sideways. With a rustle like a flock of birds taking wing, soldiers and oarsmen stood up. The rattan screens were lowered, and, as if released from a pen, the men streamed onto the bank, their commanders bellowing, "Run, run, run!"

The King shoved his banner at his platoon leader to hold up, scanned the wave of men to find Vidyanandana, and grabbed his shoulder. "Stick by me," Jaya told him.

Barefoot, over scorching white dust, they all launched themselves forward, jostling each other into position as they ran. Shield bearers thrust themselves to the front or to the side, raising protective walls. The drums beat and the dry ground shivered underfoot.

Like egg in soup, the navy coalesced into a land army.

Khmers! You have sat still and waited long enough. Run free now, like the wild bull. Peasants, charge like the wild boar. Princes, fight like tigers.

It felt good to run at last, good to run to the foreign house and expel the conquerors, good to avenge the deaths of so many, good to take action against the murder of Vidyanandana's father.

Above all, it felt good to be done with dissembling. My banner is raised against you, Jaya-Indravarman.

Boys tumbled out of the bankside houses, or ran towards them out of hamlets to the west. Jaya looked behind him. All along the bank two hundred or more of his men ran, with women and boys running alongside them and cheering. Their young smiles cut through the distance like knives.

On the other side of the canal, the Unfinished Temple loomed over them, its raw, uncarved blocks looking like something piled up by a child.

Ahead on this side was the last of the Yashodharapura forest. The giant green trees rose up like thunderclouds.

A wall of forest around the tyrant's palace. It was a good defence—burn all the ground around so you can see who approaches, and then waylay them with high trees and dense undergrowth.

The Chams were forest warriors. No matter, thought Jayavarman, so are we.

The trees would break up their formation. Like a sieve, the forest would strain them. The King's eyes flicked towards the canal; the bank had been dug all the way to the roots of the trees.

"Push on, push on through the trees."

Their formation broke apart, spreading out among the trees. The Khmers darted like shadows, swift and dark, ducking the branches that sprang back into their faces. They jumped over logs that could conceal traps, making no more noise than a natural falling of leaves.

The band of forest was not wide, a hundred yards at most. Through the trees, the King saw searing daylight on white ground.

A bursting rustle of leaves made him spin around. From out of a hide, a Cham warrior whirligigged towards him, swords spinning.

Jaya thrust his lance; something clanged against his breastplate; he swirled out of the way and heard something sliced, cloth and flesh. His platoon leader fell. Vid swiped his sword at neck level, and the Cham attacker rolled, tumbling across the ground like an empty suit of armour.

A blur of bronze spun out from the left. Jaya caught up the banner as it fell out of the platoon leader's grasp and swiped the air with it, making a curtain to hide behind. He ducked to the side and a sword cut through the banner. Jaya shoved his lance where the hand behind it should be, lodging it between plates of metal.

Vid pushed him on ... go, go, go, out of the trees!

Footsoldiers and shield bearers clenched around Jaya like a protective fist. Another Cham tried to scramble up and over them. They seized him by his helmet, opened up his throat, and cast him aside.

Ringed round with men, Jayavarman ducked out of the forest into the palace parkland.

Elephants cried and like huge rumbling boulders jogged into formation. Beyond them stood the new palace that Yashovarman had built.

Jaya caught Vid's eye. Their plan of reaching the palace was setting like the sun. They had been too slow; they had not realized how little the tyrant cared about defending the City.

Something shot like a serpent across the ground—arrows, aimed at their feet. Ahead of them was a reservoir; Jaya knew it from his visits. It was small with steep stone steps leading down to the water. Archers were lying flat against those steps, concealed and shooting low.

Something made a noise like a giant hornet. More arrows, from high up in the trees. Concealed platforms on the branches, hard to spot, hard to aim at. Jaya blinked southward into the sun when the sky seemed to open its mouth and spit something at him.

An arrow slammed against Jayavarman's forehead. He dropped to his knees before realising the arrow must have glanced off his bronze diadem. Blood dripped onto the white sand.

"King, you are hit!" wailed a solider.

"Shut up, you idiot!" Jaya heard another arrow sizzle into a wooden shield. He heard more elephant cries. Jaya scooped up dust, wiped the blood away with it, scooped up more and caked it on the wound to staunch and hide it.

Vid held his arm and hauled him to his feet. The ground itself seemed to have gone woozy from the blow.

Arrows purred like cats into warm flesh all around them.

"Where are my archers?" the King demanded.

Archers were nobles in flowered cloth and were usually safe in the rear. Currently they were still being cut to pieces in the trees.

The Cham elephant-handlers shouted orders. Necklaces of bronze leaves jingled around the elephants' necks as the beasts advanced, heads down.

A day of disasters.

"Right. Get out of here," the King said. "We head west, west and south to General Namasivaya."

Sergeants, ordinary men at arms, took up the cry. "South and west. To Namasivaya!"

Conches sounded for retreat, the long horns blaring out the instruction: west. Messenger boys hopped like sparrows to carry orders, some cut down by arrows. Men cried and clutched their heels.

Slowly, like grain stirred by wind, the Khmers began to move.

The King stumbled forward, his whole head ringing, blood seeping into his eyes. But he was still able to run, supported by Vid, who held him by the arm.

Drums beat out the racing march. "Go, go, go, go!" sergeants shouted.

Finally some of the Khmer archers fought their way out of the trees. Finally, Khmer arrows arced upwards to rain down on to the pond or into the trees.

Their retreat covered, the Khmers ran, leaving behind bodies fallen in the dust.

Ahead of them lay parkland. Pathways wound across the grass and under the few shade trees, leading to the City.

It did not feel like a retreat. They seemed to be running not for their lives, but for joy.

It was their City.

The paths had been worn by generations of their people. The dust that billowed up into the air had been milled from the bodies of their ancestors, their ash and their dried faeces. The poor shaggy houses that loomed ahead were unmistakably Khmer homes. It was as if the City were joining them in the battle.

The King's troops charged unimpeded into the familiar chaos of home. The sociable huts crowded together, the narrow trails between them were covered with haphazard timbers. The hammocks on the raised porches still swung. Hens fluttered inside fallen cages. People had recently fled out of the path of the battle.

Ahead of them a glaring white mist of dust hid the towers and the trees. Dimly they heard the cries of men and elephants, and the drums, gongs and trumpets of battle music.

The King's troops pounded on towards the sound, understanding now. They were to form a second front, to close on the backs of the Chams. They ran into clouds of dust and covered their faces. Their columns poured between the houses into a market square. Everything was grey, in silhouette as if in fog.

They ran full-pelt into the back of the Cham lines.

The round bottoms of the Cham elephants shrugged their way backwards. Footsoldiers stumbled over abandoned hoes, buckets, and unstable timber. Something half-seen in the clouds of dust was pushing the entire Cham force into retreat. Glancing behind them the Chams finally saw the other Khmer force closing in behind them. Before they could cry out, the King's arrows flung themselves into their backs.

The King turned and waved towards the rooftops.

His troops understood and laughed.

Jaya laughed too. They all knew what they were to do. As boys they had all climbed up onto the tops of houses. They had all thrown fruit or stones at each another, and then ducked down behind the crests of the sloping roofs.

Vid looked confused and shook his head at Jaya. What?

Jaya hauled himself up and then pulled Vid up after him. The Khmers scampered up onto the tops of the houses.

Like smoke from a thousand fires, dust trailed around the Chams on the ground. They heard laughter all around them, invisible. They squinted, blinked, and rubbed their eyes—more laughter.

Reserving so many of his forces to defend the palace had cost the Cham King dearly. From the vantage point of the rooftops, Jaya could see that the Cham elephants were being forced backwards, unable to turn in the narrow streets. The feet of the giant beasts slipped sideways off the narrow, unsteady timbers of the walkways. Oxcarts had been left deserted, blocking the tracks. An aggressive buffalo, still tethered to a house, lowered his horns towards them. The houses seemed to press around them like curious, shaggy animals.

An arrow sang through the air from over the edge of a rooftop. Then another, and another. Like a gathering thunderstorm, the arrows rained down with increasing strength, leaping into hands, throats, anything the Cham armour left exposed. Arrows bit into the sides of the elephants, into their sensitive ears and trunks.

The elephants bellowed and thrashed their way around to face the other direction. They kicked Cham foot soldiers out of their path, or staggered over them. Arrows plunged into the animals' jowls and foreheads. On their backs, Cham officers in howdahs ducked or found arrows in their cheekbones or throats. Beneath them, the panicked elephants began to rock, to toss the howdahs off their backs.

One fall of arrows came after another, dropping like layers of mosquito nets. The elephants screamed. Finally, one of them broke free and ran directly at one of the houses. Khmers leapt down from its roof and rolled away. The elephant twisted the house sideways, splintering the porch-frame, and the house tipped, settling out of the elephant's way.

The elephants stampeded, thundering over the backs of their own troops, pushing over the houses, or breaking through them. Arms windmilling, the Khmers on the rooftops jumped free, and then ran.

A seething flotsam of Cham infantry was left behind, out of formation, wreckage after the passage of a storm.

Another curtain of arrows fell over them, thinner this time, but just as sharp.

The dust, flinty in eyes, throat, and nostrils, wafted over them all. The Cham troops began to run as well.

From his rooftop, it looked to the King like a battle in the clouds. Out of the mist, looming at first only as huge shadows, came Khmer elephants with fire banners. They charged the Cham troops, trampling them. From the ground, from the rooftops, the King's troops cheered them.

Rout.

Namasivaya's elephants and infantry pursued the Chams through the haphazard streets. The last of the Khmer arrows gusted over Cham backs as they all emerged from the City, back onto open ground.

An elephant surrounded by parasols strolled up next to the King's roof. A friendly voice chuckled. In the howdah, blooming with confidence, was General Namasivaya. "White Rabbit, why are you on a roof?"

"To bounce up and down on the heads of my enemies!"

The smile faded as Namasivaya glanced at the King's head. "Someone's been bouncing on yours."

Vid nodded and helped the unsteady King onto the General's howdah.

Namasivaya asked both of them, "What lies ahead?"

"Open ground to the palace. Another wall of elephants around it. There's a band of forest on the right, full of teeth."

A Cham elephant, unmanned, stumbled blindly back across their path, its sides streaming with blood.

Jaya found his footing in the howdah. "We need to regroup. It will be a traditional battle now."

The General nodded, and called. A dull regular thudding signalled: classic formation. Their driver backed the General's elephant calmly away from the house and Khmer footsoldiers nearby slipped into rows around it. A Khmer cavalryman rode up beside it, the first to arrive.

Ahead of them, somewhere beyond the trails of dust, a new sound tumbled towards them, like an avalanche of loose stones.

Jaya had time to mutter, "Cavalry."

Out of the dust, a wave of Cham horsemen surfed up and over the heads of the infantry. Dust thrashed behind the horses like spume. Jaya turned his head away, but even so, grit clogged and stung his eyes.

His own horsemen jerked round, wrestling with the reins to keep their horses in formation. Dust blanketed everything, but the Khmers could follow the sound of the Cham cavalry as it swept back around them in a wide arc, gathering for another charge.

The Khmer infantry was still coalescing around the elephants.

A sound like a breaking wave advanced through the dust towards them.

The Khmer cavalry gathered, with a slapping of harnesses, feet, lances, and arrows. With a sudden spurt of hooves, the Khmer horsemen lurched forward to meet the charge.

The two waves of horses met, breaking around the feet of the Khmer elephants. A Cham horse was up-ended like a boat by the impact of colliding at full gallop. The Cham was thrown headfirst, and from where Jaya balanced, he heard the crack of the fallen cavalryman's neck. Khmer infantry squatted around the elephants' feet with axes. They chopped the legs of the passing horses as if they were birch trees. A horse rolled to the ground, splintered white bone rupturing its shins. The charge passed thundering back towards the City.

Jaya peered ahead, still blinking dust out of his eyes. The avalanche of hooves encircled them once more.

There was no strategy now, just raw battle. The formations held; the disciplines were arrayed. This is what it had been for, all those boyhood years in training.

The training taught this wisdom—that you would die anyway. So die joyously; die well; die with acceptance, in the heat of battle as a hero, not as some tired old man with bad joints.

Jaya laughed and tossed his head like any wild animal. Oh! I am sliding back down samsara from buck-ape to serpent. Hee hee! I feel as hot and as roaring as fire. All this dust is me smoking.

General Namasivaya caught his mood and laughed as well and shook the King by the muscles of his neck. Both men laughed and the troops looked up to see them, the King bloodied but still with them in the thick of the fight.

The King bellowed at them, "Come on! We will win." He felt buoyed up, supported by the power of the earth. "Hammer them! Cut them down like saplings in your pasture. Harvest their heads like rice. Pluck their balls like cotton. Fall into your formations as if into your mother's arms!"

The men flicked their heads back and grinned.

Jaya clapped his hands and did a dance on the howdah that would have been daring in a peaceful ramble let alone the lurch and upset of battle.

The General, the troops, the shield bearers, the archers, the foot-soldiers all roared at him. Inspired, a cavalryman stood up on the bare back of his horse and he danced as well.

Jayavarman clapped again. "Your mother commands, your father commands, your little sister commands! Onward, Khmers! Onward!"

His General clapped his back as if they had always been the best of friends. Jaya scanned the eyes of his men. They glowed like a bush-fire. He was the spark. Flame seemed to leap from head to head.

He howled, and waved them on. They howled back. And together they swept ahead.

They charged the palace elephants and battle was joined.

Great rolling boulders of Khmer elephants avalanched into the ready Cham lines. Arrows hurtled through the air trailing blood behind them. It was a broil of combat.

Headlocks, grappling on the ground, axes rising and falling in waves, the creaking of the ropes of crossbows, the sudden singing of arrows, the sweeping passes of horsemen against horsemen.

They trampled blood-red mud. They slipped and lost their foot-ing. They stumbled over the lubricated dead.

They seemed to be pressed together, bursting from the pressure. They were an explosion of overripe fruit, spurting blood and souls like white dandelion fluff spiralling up into the air.

Floods of blood, blood in puddles, blood oiling the surface of the ground, blood in fountains gushing out of the chests or mouths of elephants. The great beasts collapsed onto their knees as if worship-ping Kali, bowing to death, Yama.

The terrible, fiery smell of human insides—the blood, the mucous, the shit all opened up—presented a spicy dish that overturned the senses and made the head buzz and ache.

The very air had teeth, spears and arrows. The ground roiled, a treacherous mass of red serpents. Holy fathers of all, the battle would mill them all to paste!

Formation? Horses mixed with men who mixed with elephants.

They were a swirling fog of flesh and flailing arms, pushing, jamming, jabbing until the whole motion was not one of pushing forward, or retreating, but a rhythmic, helpless juddering that was most like a coughing fit.

Juddering to a halt.

Unable to move, unable to lift an arm or a shield, unable to reach the enemy or to duck their blows, the soldiers could see the men who aimed arrows at their heads. But they could not duck or raise a shield. Their eyes met before the arrows flew.

Live bodies, dead bodies, both were held upright in place by weight of numbers.

In the front line, men were pushed onto a bristling of weapons as if being fed to sharks. Swords tore them apart in a moment. They were husked, rendered from their bodily integrity, scattered in trails.

God, how could human beings smell so foul inside! Blood and flesh must be putrescent to stink so.

The horses stared like mad things, their eyes strained white. Their mouths drooled froth. They trod flesh like water, mad only to escape. The elephants shook like whole planets about to tumble out of the heavens.

Animal panic whipped them—get away, get away, get away! One of the elephants was mired in blood, sinking into a marsh of it.

Panic found a voice. The elephants made a sound like pigs caught under an oxcart wheel. The horses cawed like old ladies, or snorted like oil lamps exploding.

The two sides ground each other like rice for noodles. Neither could move. This was unendurable.

Then Jaya saw movement, through the dust, sweeping around the forest.

It was like a damburst he had once seen rushing down a gully. The current had borne trees and oxcarts. Jaya blinked. This current of people bore:

Shovels.

Picks.

Saws for cutting stone.

The slaves were coming. The nia were fighting for them. His eyes watered, sluicing away dust, and the King saw the people: old, stooped, young, thin, the enduring people of the fields.

Jaya felt his heart swell like clouds. His heart rose up.

"The nia!" the King wailed. "The nia have joined us! The pual have joined us. They fight with shovels! They fight with hand ploughs! Press on! Press on!"

There was an answering roar. All his men, pressed so tightly together they could not move as individuals, all stepped forward in unison. They were a great wall, a great weight.

The Chams shuddered all together. They strained like a giant bolted door of slate.

Air, soil, breastplates, bones, flesh—all of it shook in waves. Then broke.

The slate door splintered. The ranks of the Chams were shot backwards, scattering.

Flailing, slipping, thrusting, the Khmer pushed on.

The footmen hauled their feet out of the slough of blood. They wore slippers of blood, blood that upholstered their feet and stitched dust into soles.

Peasants and flowered nobles, arrows and peasant axes pressed on, gained speed and gave chase together. The Khmer cavalry, finally given space, charged, sweeping down onto the Chams.

Jaya turned to Vid and said, "We are avenged."

"Yes," said Vidyanandana. But his eyes were full of pain. Lotus helmets were sunk in mud and the ground was burnished with blood.

The dead lay everywhere, up and down the whole trail of battle, like the pathway of a giant snail, its underside torn to pieces on ash.

Silence descended. From somewhere in the direction of the palace, smoke trailed up in thin wisps.

Then, shrill and tuneful at the same time, came the songs of the camp women. They flitted among the dead to gather up arrows or lances. The cheerful wives of horse-keepers and musicians and cooks pressed arrows running with blood into the hands of the messenger boys.

The King's elephant strode on towards the palace. The pavilions were burning, varnish flowering into red, the dark smoke reeking of sap. Jaya saw the heavy, crude carvings of their shared deities. The Chams had not even used Khmer craftsmen. The deities glowed red and orange.

The chases continued as the sun set. The smoke from the palace was dark, as if thousands of crows rose in the sky. Chams of rank were pulled forward to be inspected. None of them was the Cham King. Had he escaped? More likely he was a broken, shorn body, somewhere in the morass.

To appease his Cham allies, Jaya put Vidyanandana in charge of taking prisoner those Chams who were left alive.

The General sniffed in distaste. "We can't camp here. The ground. It's all blood."

The earth smelled of death. All around the burning palace a moat of something dank and dark like oil reflected the flames.

"A lake," said the King. "A lake of blood."

His jaw thrust out. "Come on," he said. "Let us see what is left of our City."

LEAF 85

I called to the brave soldiers, the courageous men. I said to them, all the reservoirs are stained with blood. We have little sweet water. First we will wash with the water and then we will drink it. We will drink each other, but then we have shared so much already. The deserving warriors plunged their elbows into the cisterns and poured the water over their heads into their mouths. I said to the women, prepare a feast, a feast from nothing, boil rice flour into dumplings, bake the dried fish on skewers. Nia and pual came with herbs and other good things. The women brought bowls of food, singing. The hungry men ate. Come, Comrades, I said, let us have games of fighting with blunted lances. Let no one be injured, let all enjoy. They fought each other in quilted jackets and they smiled. The musicians beat gongs and drums and blew the conch shell. The sons of Kambu danced beside the lake of blood. They had won. They were home.

LEAF 86

I thought of Suryavarman who left no heirs. I had a fierce and noble son who was incomplete, and a Kumara who was strong but a devotee of Siva. So I called for the noble Vidyanandana without parallel, the son of Jaya-Harideva. I asked him to climb up beside me and I said to all my warriors, look at this great prince and ally who today saved my life once on water and once on land. Look at the brave soldier and noble prince. Does anyone doubt that this is a man of wisdom and spirit? Does anyone doubt that he is our ally? The assembled gave assent, cheering Vidyanandana. It was then that I first thought I might make a Cham my heir, to join the Kingdoms in peace. A year later, after his service in Malyang, I gave Vidyanandana the title of Yuvaraja, another form of Crown Prince. I made a Cham my son.

Leaf 87

I walked through my dead city, burned years before. The Aerial Palace stared through charred foundations like the sockets of a skull. I heard the echoing laughter of childhood friends. I saw my beautiful Cat as a child slave polishing floors. I heard the giggling of Jayarajadevi as a girl. I saw a plump little fellow run and wondered: who is that? In the upper floor, made of stars and spider webs, sat Yashovarman, King. His hands crawled over his face, thinking of betrayal and of his own weakness. In the lower floors towered Suryavarman. Like a giant mantis he lifted up his arms in blue moonlight, speaking in a voice like dust. You have come home, my son. Our City has been burned and you are fifty years old, and I never thought you would be King, though I loved you. This is why I made myself a god, so I could go on learning.

Leaf 88

I saw the faces of my burnt people wandering through their burnt streets. They could only rustle like leaves in the wind. They could only stare as they have always stared: hungry, bewildered, and angry. Poor homeless spirits! Boys in the trees who threw mangoes, fathers in the streets, mothers selling flour from stalls, all of you whose homes, names, hopes, and loves were destroyed by the foolishness of kings, I mourn for you. I promise you that everything will be restored. I see a golden window in a new hall. All people, no categories enforced, will come and make their cases, demanding justice. The making of justice will be my main work. I felt the world turn about me for I had spoken to the past, and made a promise to the future. I saw both laid out before me like shadows on the forest floor. I felt the moon turn around the earth, the sun move through the sky and stars. They all joined hands to hold the universe together. In this way, in moonlight, I was at the center of the world.

Geoff Ryman

LEAF 89

The fires smouldered; the dawn came quietly. Over the tops of the trees I saw the great Vishnuloka, the eternal prayer of stone. I saw Mount Meru, and the royal mountain. It was then that I said, all this is past. Now there will be a new beginning. I will make a new city here. I will rebuild the wooden pavilions. I will build new temples on new models and I will encircle Yashodharapura, all of it, with a great wall so that none may overwhelm it again. I began in a slow way to be joyful. I gave praise to the Gods and I counted the time I had left. I realized that this happens to all men. We all visit the ruined palace of our face, our friends, our youth, and start again.

It was my people who did the starting.

Season of Drought and Sweating

Map loves prison.

They live four to a cell and are locked in with a bucket behind an iron door. It's hot and it stinks. The tiny window is blocked by their clothes, which they wash in the same bucket and hang out to dry. The food regime is brutal: rice if you're lucky, and soup if you're not. Everything that Map likes.

Map is scared of no one. He enjoys a good fight and gives back whatever anyone gives him four times over with a gleaming smile. He's one of the scariest guys in the place, but he's also sane. Doesn't start fights, but ends them.

It's April again, New Year, and Sinn Rith comes to visit Map.

Rith's not sure why he keeps coming. When someone bears injustice with such equanimity, you have to respect them.

It was a hard story to believe. An old woman comes walking out of the rain and hands you a translation of the *Kraing Meas*. You don't know her name or address, and she can't be found.

If only the translation had been wildly inaccurate. But it matched the photographs of the Book. You or someone must have had the *Kraing Meas*. Where is it? they kept asking. And you just laughed.

"We're going to get nowhere," you said, as if it were all some kind of celestial joke.

Visitors and prisoners mingle in the big hot concrete courtyard. In one corner, some of the guys play *saprak takwa*, kicking a badminton cock. Some of the kids practice sounding like beatboxes and rapping. Rith and Map stroll together round and round the yard as if on Sivutha Street.

Rith is dismayed by Map's appearance. His long fingernails are starting to curl round on themselves, and the red thread on his wrist has turned into a kind of beaded amulet. His hair is long, matted, and held by hair grips, and there are all kinds of paraphernalia dangling from his neck, including a pigeon feather and a beer-bottle cap.

"Map, you look like a crazy man," says Rith.

"Yep. Good crazy," says Map, and holds out his arms and smiles, as if welcoming the sun, the dry concrete, and the smell of sweat. "Do those idiots still think Professor Luc Andrade stole the Book?"

"Oh. His colleagues go all quiet when he is mentioned. He is dead, after all. I think they have decided not to decide. The police? Well, they have all the convictions they can use." Rith laughs and shakes his head. "They arrested everybody. Motoboys, people on the docks, half of Clean Hen, Saom Pich's wife! They were so scared of losing the tourists. They just wanted to show everybody how safe Siem Reap is."

"How quiet it is, with all those people in prison."

"William asked how you were. I said I didn't know, but I'd see you and let him know."

Map laughs, and imitates Rith. "Map's gone crazy! All the pressure has driven him mad."

Rith persists. "Do you have anything you want me to say to him?"

Map pauses and tries to think of something emotional to say and dissolves into giggles. "Tell him I wish he was here! No, no, no, don't say that!" Map's voice goes quiet and businesslike. "How is he?"

"He got married. Did you hear? To a cousin of his. He found an Australian university that does degree courses on the Internet. The UN dig team helps him a lot, they let him use their computers. So he's going to university at last." Rith shakes his head. "I've asked him to talk to my layabout son."

Map's eyes are dim but his smile is thin as if satisfied and his head rocks from side to side. "I told him. I said, he would have all kinds of good luck, just so long as he stayed away from me."

"Why is that?" There is something Rith doesn't understand. William asks after Map, but doesn't come to see him. All the time Rith talks to him about Map, William looks edgy and unquiet, trapped in his own house. "Are you bad luck for everybody, or just him?"

Map tells him, almost serenely. "I killed his parents."

Rith's eyes sag shut. He has to hide them with his hand. "I didn't know that."

"Neither did he for a while." Map looks cheerful. "So it's pretty good going that he can even talk about me without hatred. William," says Map with finality, "is an advanced spirit."

With a twinge, Rith realizes that Map has been able to say that with absolute authority.

They will kill him eventually, when they think nobody's looking.

Which is another reason for Rith coming to visit, in his army uniform. Some respectable people are watching.

Map leads Rith sauntering towards the shady wall. Some of the guys are terrible-looking fellows with deep creases in their cheeks, broken teeth, stained shorts, missing hands, knife wounds, faces as immobile as pig's behinds. They shift very slightly to let Map pass.

Rith has to control a little tremor of fear.

"Has the Book been published yet? Did that printer I gave it to do anything with it?"

Rith shrugs. "I don't know about books."

Map's eyebrows wiggle. "I do. Books aren't necessary when you have a people. Books grow out of people, and if you have the people first, the books will trail after them."

They make their way to a small group of men sitting on the ground. They do not look nearly as threatening as some of the others. Skinny little guys, here for drug offences probably, or pimping. They all wear red threads around their wrists. Map squats down to talk, and tugs at Rith's trousers.

"Okay, roostershits, listen up. This is my good friend Sinn Rith. He fought in the wars; he told people at the trial that I was a good man, full of remorse. But despite that, he's clever." The men chuckle. Most of them have lost teeth, and there is a kind of self-protective air about them. They're a group, Rith thinks. Map's little band.

"If anybody hurts him, I promise you, I'll make him eat his own testicles." Map makes a slitting gesture with his fingernails. The men chuckle again. "Then I'll make him eat yours!" More laughter. Map's voice goes husky and insinuating. "Only gently, so you like it." They hoot with shock.

These are the guys who can't rely on brawn or sheer cruelty. These are the guys who make bad drawings to pass the time, or act in plays or weave cloth.

Around them, the courtyard plays on, huddled around cards or dice, or doing push-ups. One of the rap guys is strolling over, handkerchief tied over his head, blue football shirt in his hand.

"Okay," says Map. "Yesterday we got near the end. Last two. I go first?" A murmur of assent. In a low, slow voice, sounding like he's playing a game of dominoes for money, Map starts to talk.

> *There's an aspect of the Buddha that can't be carved in stone. An image of him would need to be carved in the wind, because he is always moving, sweeping his arms over the heads of the grain. This is Bhaishajyaguru who heals. The smile of the Healing Buddha is not distant and calm, but crumples into weeping. His eyes are not closed in meditation, but are startled open, thick along the lower edge with tears.*

Map mimes it, the crumpled lower lip that still smiles, the wide stare. It's a look that Rith recognizes. From knowing Map.

> *The Healing Buddha is small. He is the pattern on the wings of a butterfly. He is the scales on the gecko's feet. Children work in the fields hammered by heat and they hear him. He whispers to the gleaners who sift the straw. He shivers in the April flowers. Bhaishajyaguru reminds us of the variety and sweetness of the world, as it was in the past and will be again, even when men have made it stink of charred wood and drying blood.*

Total silence for the count of five.

"Okay, who wants to do 150?" asks Map.

"I do," says the rap kid. He talks Khmer like a foreigner. He's Khmer-American, Rith realizes. He got into trouble there, so they deported him to Cambodia, and now he's in trouble here.

The kid starts to bounce up and down and makes a kind of whooshing noise. Once he's going, he starts to drawl the words.

> *Bhaishajyaguru is NOT Buddha as Balual the horse who rescues sailors. He is NOT Buddha as Lokesvara, the creator.*

He makes it sound dark and scary. He has an appetite for darkness that most Cambodians do not have.

> *This is the Buddha of the burned earth, the Buddha of the red land, the Buddha of the rain that turns to blood.*

"A Buddha for us," the boy interjects.

> *This is the Buddha of Forced Seeing who does not close his eyes and who is not serene. The Healing Buddha sits with his people through all their sufferings. He even sits with men who've committed the worst crimes, who no other aspect can help, for whom no hell is far enough away from heaven.*

Even Rith can feel how close that shaves.

> *When everything else fails, Bhaishajyaguru is there.*

"And this is Jayavarman Seven talking," says the boy and makes a fist.

> *For I have lived beyond my time into my eightieth year and I have seen great temples rise from dust and great men fall into dust.*

Some of the sitting skinny guys have their eyes closed. Their mouths move in time to the words. They know them too.

> *I have seen enemies become friends and then enemies again. Through all the waste and confusion, the motion is always onward, like wind over the heads of grain. With motion comes healing, which is acceptance.*

Oh, Map is smart. He grins at Rith and says, "They know it. Some of them know the whole Book." Map sighs. "I won't get out of here. But they will."

APRIL 1191

Over the trees and the smoke and noise of the City, the five great towers rose, covered in gilt: finished.

At the top of the temple of the royal palace gold curtains billowed; breezes stroked the forehead; there was a sound of birdsong. From here, looking out over the walls of the palace, the life of the City could be seen.

Princess Indradevi described it to her sister, who lay on a hammock. "The baby is still tugging at its mother's skirts. She wants that sticky rice. Oh, the mother is a nice lady. She's kneeling down now to talk to her. She's stroking the baby's hair and smiling, but Mother's child is not to be placated. The little one is still crying. She is pushing a fist into her eyes."

Indradevi turned and looked at her sister, who lay still and shrunken, with many layers of cloth wrapped around her. "Can you hear me, Sister?" asked Princess Indra.

Queen Jayarajadevi was able to flick her tongue. Yes. Go on.

It is a great sadness to see a younger sister die. Especially when you have lived with her until your own old age. When you have seen her coltish, gawky, and wayward. When you have seen her grow beautiful, strong, and graceful. Saddest of all when you have seen her flower into someone who is absolutely exceptional in her intellectual accomplishments. When you have led her extreme soul back onto a true Path and watched her help make an empire, becoming its leader in spirit.

You watch as the petals fall. As naturally as a beautiful orchid, the body grows sad and starts to drop away.

"Oh! The mother and child have gone on. I fear we will never know now if the child ever got her sticky rice."

The story goes on after us, and we never know the end. If there ever is an end.

"Two Chinese traders have come up to the stall owner. Devils! They don't want sticky rice; they want to talk to her because she is pretty. She is pretending interest. She smiles. She leans forward. She is not afraid of them. Oh! One of them is stroking his goatee!"

There was a sarika bird in the top of a silk-cotton tree, looking at them sideways.

But oh, Sister, you are not falling like fruit, naturally ripe.

You are dying of a broken heart.

"Oh, 'Sri, our City is so beautiful. The King's new central temple is already rising over the trees, and the City itself is restored. The birds are back, and the homes are all new and strong, and the park is full of monks, meditating among the horses."

Indradevi searched her sister's crumpled, yellow face. "We did so much."

The sarika bird called, as if asking a question.

"Did you hear the bird, Sister? Such a beautiful bird. It is singing to us."

It is singing you to your death.

The anger came again, and Princess Indradevi bunched her fists to fight it. That man, that stupid, stupid man. In the end he is just a man; it is not for us to judge; he is a king and falls victim to the vices of kings, the things they must do. We must not hate, we must not let the world hold sway. Life, death, self, all of them are a willed illusion.

But he must have known that you were delicate. He must have had to consider what it would do to you.

And your stupid son should have given consideration too.

Indradevi spoke of other things. "Oh, and the monkeys are back too. They're sitting under the new trees and they have got hold of a monk's alms bowl. 'Sri! They look like they are asking for alms. People have seen them and are laughing. They keep licking their fingers, to see if there is any food on them. Oh! Now one of them is eating the bowl. Ha ha! He's cracking it with his teeth."

Men. Something happens to people when they pass into male bodies.

"One of the temple boys has seen them, and he's coming with a long cane to chase them away. Oh! 'Sri! One of the monkeys has snatched his cane!"

I want to say something to ease my sister's heart. All I can think of are the small things that she can no longer see. I want to say something that will make her open her eyes, smile, eat, and recover.

I suppose I should be joyful, for I am sure that at the very least she will pass on to a higher life even than this one. Even if she has never achieved her great goal, to reach Nibbana, to clear her mind of self. She came nearer than anyone else I know.

I should be joyful, I should be mindful, but I am flawed and the world is flawed. And so I suffer.

I may as well speak what is in my heart.

"I am angry, 'Sri. I am so angry it floods my heart and my mind. I lose all concentration and mindfulness, even the beauty of the City is not enough to restore me. I am so angry at your husband, I cannot speak of it without sputtering with rage!"

With less strength than the breeze through the temple-top pavilion, the Queen's hand squeezed hers.

"I'm sorry. I am being selfish, but oh, Sister, this is the worst thing I have ever had to bear!"

The Queen's reply was absolute stillness. Nothing. It means nothing. Her stillness seemed to say: *It is how life is, 'Sru. Along with the wind through the leaves, the sounds of birds, the warming hand of the sun. Just life.*

Her cheeks were a terrible shade of yellow, her eyes shadowed, her mouth a string of muscle. Queen Jayarajadevi seemed to say: *it did not start with injustice.*

Indradevi thought: You will always defend him, but yes. He made many great actions, such as no other Universal King had ever before made.

The King had named his enemy his heir. He made the Cham prince his Crown Prince. A very great good, but the King's son Suryakumara turned against his father. He left the Path, and announced he would be a Hindu king.

And the King did what Kings do with troublesome princes. He sent his own son to war crowded round with gold parasols, to draw arrows.

It was not the death of your son that did this to you, Queen. It was the death of your King, the King you thought you had created, a King like no other. He turned out to be just like all the others. He arranged for the death of your son. And then turned his back on the Cham prince as well. Policy.

And so you turned towards Nibbana. You turned away from this world, towards death. The fate that had been awaiting you all your life swallowed you up. You starved yourself.

And that is not the Path.

And so you die losing even Nibbana.

But you were great, my sister. You ruled as much as the King did and with far more wisdom and far more vision. Now he's made Rajendradevi his First Queen. Well, he had to as she is mother of the heir, but everyone knows, all the people, what you accomplished in this world. And as for the next, even if you do not join God, you will be celestial. His mother, his father, oh they are all made aspects of the Buddha. You, what honor will he do you? In death.

Indradevi said aloud, "Oh, my sister, I will build houses for the poor and I will dedicate all that merit to you. I shall write great inscriptions, I shall tell the world of your virtues and your holy actions. I will make sure that you are remembered!"

I hope merit will keep you from sinking in the samsara for having starved yourself to death.

And Sister, oh Kansri, where will I be in this life without you? You have always been here. The whole world will go silent without you. And I will be an old spinster lady, with shadows under her eyes, and a shadow in her womb, some aunty trying to hold us all on the Path.

Listening to the birds and the wind in the leaves for comfort.

Why am I making you hold on? For myself? I will have to be brave and alone sooner or later.

Indradevi said, "Kansri? You have my permission to die. If your heart is broken and you are alone and we are not enough to keep you, if you yearn for your next life. Then go. Go on. We will remember you. We will always love you. Your spirit flies like a bird."

On the ground, in the City, the stall owner was still teasing one of the Chinese merchants. Who had evidently charmed her. Oxcarts full of onions and herbs arrived for the market.

Princess Indradevi said, just to keep talking, just to give herself comfort, "The university is being consecrated today."

The King had finally found his Crown Prince.

It was one of his sons. This was a late surprise to the various generals, allies, war-mates, and fellow seekers after the truth.

It was his son, little Chubby, now with the full kingly honorific of Indravarman. No halfway "kumara" for him.

And Indravarman was beautiful.

He was tall and straight, but had his father's bulk; and in low sunlight, he was the color of a perfect, smooth-skinned apricot. Golden. He loved talking to people; he was good at fighting; he was smart but not so clever that he made things anguished or complicated. He was like the rising sun. His father Jayavarman looked at him long and gratefully, smiling with pride.

Rajapati looked at Prince Indravarman with an ache in his heart.

Only fourteen and certain of kingship. From their glances and approving nods, the people love him too. Only fourteen and able to speak to them like his father, at a moment's notice, eloquently, from the heart.

Rajapati had long ago given up talking to people at all. It only caused trouble.

Able to run, able to fall in love, able to attract people, and hold them. They loved looking at him. Even Rajapati loved looking at him, but with yearning and a sense of loss from which he knew he would never escape. He would have to learn to accept.

Even now, the Crown Prince was rowing the barge, chatting quietly to the rower in front of him. Learning boatcraft? His shoulders, which were already taking on the outline of a fully grown man's, swelled and contracted with a simplicity that made Rajapati want to write an ode to the perfection of the human body. Some human bodies.

Oh, what did I do in a previous life to deserve this?

Perhaps you were a perfect prince who was cruel to cripples.

The boat eased up to the dock. Today was the consecration day of yet another grandiose complex made of stone and other people's sweat. Jayavarman the magnificent flung up his arms to welcome the sight, the men, their arrival. Had he grown taller? Father, you look as big as the moon.

Jayavarman spun and held out his hand towards his son, the only son there who counted. The King's whole face beamed hope and love. The boy grinned back and slipped neatly like a dancer through the rowers down to his father, who seized his hand and held it up.

Look at this boy, isn't he the picture of a king?

The rowers chuckled. The boy beamed back.

He's like a horse being inspected. Perfect teeth, good strong haunches.

Don't try to be humorous, Rajapati. Everybody else gave up listening thirty years ago.

Oh, look, the little dear can laugh. Cheerful, aren't you, Indra? It isn't your mother who's dying, is it, Chubby? Oh no, your mother has done her job properly. Just like a sow. Multiple piglets. And she's First Queen now, it says so on that inscription stone. Queen Rajendradevi, mother to the future king.

Oh God, she'll probably want to teach just like Jayarajadevi. It will be like a pig talking.

Ho, ho, endless amusement. Alone inside your head, Rajapati.

The King sighed in satisfaction with his prince and shook the boy's shoulder, looking at his perfect head with love.

Oh, oh, oh, thought Rajapati, to have had even a glimmer of that from you, Father. I suppose that was what I've wanted all these years.

Rajapati was trapped in a kind of palanquin, scaled down to his size. It looked like a toy. For form's sake, two people carried it, though it was so light one bearer would have done. But two were better at keeping the twisted little bundle inside it quiet.

God, I am so sick of sitting curled up here with my own thoughts. Everybody speedily glancing away to avoid looking at me.

Well, put me away then. Don't drag me out on these occasions; I don't like being gawked at. I didn't ask to be born like this. I didn't ask to be clever, just so that I could fully appreciate how wasted my life is. I didn't ask to be put on public display so that everyone could say: oh, look how generous the King is to that half-human bundle in the box.

Shut up, 'Pati.

You're envious that's all. And you have so very much to be envious about. In addition to looking like a lump of driftwood, you're bitter and mean-minded. You're not even a pleasant person.

In addition to being an affront to very nearly every sense except the olfactory...

...or maybe even that since the maids douse me in so much perfume. They assume I'm this way because I'm diseased, like a leper, and so I must smell.

Just shut up.

Oh good, my box is moving. Something is happening. To me. Don't cheer all at once, grateful population.

The beautiful Indravarman rocked and rolled his way down the plank onto the landing. He walked next to the King as an equal, talking fervently about something.

Watch out, little Chubby. That man next to you? He looks nice.

But he kills crown princes. He might kill you too.

Don't you just wish, Rajapati?

The various dignitaries stood with their studious backs towards Rajapati and his deformities, waiting their turn to follow the King down the gangplank.

With a weariness of the soul, Rajapati realized that he quite sincerely wanted to die.

Really. It would be a kindness, and so easy. Just drop me over the side, like a bird pooping. Plop! Into the water and two minutes later it will all be over.

Silence. Simplicity. Dark. Quiet. I've accumulated not a feather's weight of merit, but at least I don't think I've done enough harm to burn in hell for ever.

As the palanquin bounced down the gangplank, Rajapati promised to kill himself.

We can have a double funeral, me and the Queen. Save on expenses.

No, no, why diminish the Queen? Nice lady and she's had a bad enough time of it lately. Even my shrivelled little heart feels sorry for her.

No, 'Pati, you'll just have to hang on a few days longer.

In which case, I might as well have it out with the King.

Yes.

I'll finally make that scheming old roostershit talk to me. And then I'll die.

Now will you just shut up and enjoy the show?

At the end of the dock, the King turned and said, "We'll wait for the workmen to come."

All the lords, *mratlans*, and the monks and princes had to stand in place. Wind stirred their garments. Some of the Brahmins gave each other meaningful looks. They disapproved of this continual mingling of categories. In silence.

From within the new complex, the sparkling sound of chisels ended.

The workers came lumbering down towards the dock as if to see one of their fellows. They were burned black by the sun, polished like driftwood by toil. They came wiping their hands and faces. The King strode forth to greet them as if they were ambassadors from China. He smiled and called them by name. The men bowed and bowed again. Indravarman was presented to them, and they bowed even lower.

The little dear asked them if they were tired, working so hard.

One of the men chuckled, gap-toothed. "We are so happy to do this! It is another great labour!"

Could that possibly be true? That they were happy to labour on temple after temple? And on that great surrounding wall? On the new university, library, and administration block that rose behind them?

They chatted with the King and then with easy grace remembered their manners and the occasion. They bowed and strolled into the lake, to purify themselves. They poured water over their heads.

The King's face crumpled with love. He announced to the lords, "When we won the battle, the men washed their faces too. They poured water over themselves. It was like this. Just like this."

Another barge with a carved Naga on the prow raised its oars and settled next to the landing.

Again the King mixed formal with informal. Honored generals, Brahmins, and little princes hopped, relaxed, out of the barge. The King strode back up the dock to meet them. With his implacable smile, he looked like one of the guardian statues.

The King greeted the new arrivals, and then, when he was sure the workmen had bathed, he marched all the superior people across the churned earth of the banks, and through a mist of rock dust.

Rajapati's tiny toy palanquin lurched forward towards the build-ing site. In front of the scaffolding, palace women were setting pots of noodles on low tables. Embroidered cloth had been laid out beside them over the ground.

One single gateway had been finished. On its lintel were freshly carved words.

The King stood in front of it, and sighed.

"I am a soldier and an ascetic. I find words desert me. I have never written anything worth reading in my entire life. But this inscription was written by my son, Virakumara."

Who hates you in his heart.

The King blinked and looked down, and said quietly. "My other fine son Indravarman will read it to you."

What does an older brother feel to be overtaken by a younger? How does it feel to have your older brother killed? Poor Virakumara. His shoulders were rounded from too much reading and his ribs too obvious from continued abstinence. He'd grown a Brahmin's beard. What happens when old men have young men's occupations.

Indravarman looked like an athlete who had just won a wrestling match. He grinned at the workers, at the guests.

He turned and said, "It's a very long inscription, Father. And a very hot sun."

"My son wishes to spare you." Flicker. "And it is not an altogether happy day." Pause. Think of your dying queen. Whisper. "Thank you, Son."

Rajapati smiled at the theatrical skill. One might almost think you had a heart, Father.

With graceful ease, Indravarman summarized.

"This stone consecrates the City of Holy Victory, *Nagara Jayasri*. It will be a new kind of place. It will be where monks can come to learn and live and study. It will be a place of administration. All the people who make the City work will find their houses here. The badges of authority, such as the Sacred Sword, will be housed here. Above all else it will be a temple to all religions, and all the Kings. This palace temple will be dedicated to my grandfather, who was compassionate. The *Rajavihara* was dedicated to my grandmother, who was wise. There will be a new hospital here, and a great library and a hall of music and dancing. In this way we establish that the Path is a marriage of Wisdom and Compassion."

He summarized the Sanskrit text, and gave examples from the Khmer list of donations made by Queen Jayarajadevi. Indravarman looked sad and dignified. Finally he finished.

There was a long silence, filled with the sounds of wind and water from the reservoir.

The King spoke next, his voice shaking. "The real spirit of this temple is that of my beloved wife, Holy Victory Queen. The stone tells it." He flicked his hand towards it. "It tells how many bolts of cloth, and gold this and gold that she gave to this foundation and other places. But that is not what she really gave. She gave the ideas that live behind these things. She showed all of us the Path, on which we now walk as a people." His voice went as thin as a child's. "Without her, this building would be uninhabited stone."

How do you get away with it? Rajapati wondered. From anyone else such displays of emotion would be unseemly.

"Across that lake, there is an island, and that island is her idea. On that island will be a new temple."

Another new temple, what a surprise. And just what we needed.

"This new temple will be open to people of all categories. The humblest will be able to go there to wash away sin. No linga, no yoni, no high king giving rites and rituals. Families, babies, old men, the sick, those who have laboured all their lives or who survived these horrible, terrible, dreadful wars. They will go there to wash, to hear birds, to listen to music, and to be in a state of peace."

He's crying. You can't have a king who cries.

You can if the people know his wife is dying. What a great heart he has, they will say, truly he is the King of Compassion, the King of Love, but I know you, Father, and I know you are the reason why Aunty is dying. Which is why Indradevi isn't here, nor even Rajendradevi. You are lucky that three of your remaining sons have come. And your old Cham Crown Prince, he's causing trouble now, isn't he?

Jayavarman breathed in the world again. "So. This new city is consecrated. It is consecrated by the sweat of the people who build it, and the ideas and love that come from those who thought of it. It is consecrated by what it is. Follow the Path." He blew out. "Now, let the labourers eat."

No one moved. The spirits moved in the wind. The dust moved. Everything else, even the birds and crickets seemed to be stilled.

"Eat," beckoned the King again, and held out his hands towards the men. With a sound like the pattering of light rain, the labourers began to move. They walked towards the steaming reed bowls and the folding tables and the smell of rice and cardamom.

Indravarman talked urgently to the King. The King's eyes closed and he smiled in gratitude.

Indravarman turned and ran back to the tables. He was so happy to eat with the workers, to share the meal with them.

Every inch the worthy heir.

The visitors returned to their boats.

The King stomped along the landing towards his barge. Rajapati thought: my father always walks as if he's trying to punch holes in the ground, or stamp his words permanently into the earth. The King's back was turned towards him and it was the back of a man who wanted to be alone, who wanted to be in the prow of the boat by himself, with sun, water, breeze, and lake birds. Instead he sat cross-legged in the shade of the middle deck, facing the procession filing onto the boat with his eyes closed and a smile imposed.

The King meditated. He was always doing that in public. It was how he wanted to be seen. But this time, his face did not glow with serenity. This time it was puffed out with unhappiness and struggle. The eyebrows were wrenched and twisted with grief and hurt.

The things you have done, Father. Sometimes they show.

The boat glided from Victory Lake to the huge and ancient ten-kilometre artificial Lake of Yashodhara.

Sunlight danced on the artificial lake. The boat swung around, and there, ranged before them, was the great sight of Yashodharapura.

The biggest city on the planet, now enclosed in a wall of laterite. What stuff it is. Laterite cuts like wet clay when it first comes out of the earth. But it hardens in air to lightweight, enduring stone. Red-grey laterite, honey-colored now with the sun on it. A perfect wall of stone, extending along most of the horizon. Like a saw blade, the top was arranged with niche stones, thousands of them. And inside the sheltering hood of each was an image of the Buddha.

Thousands upon thousands of images of the Buddha.

On far banks, boys fished, skimming nets on poles over the surface of the water.

Women in groups squatted, washing their clothing.

Boys had driven their oxen down the earthen banks into the lake to drink. You could see the mud-colored swirls where the beasts had trod. The boys were jumping off the backs of the beasts into the deeper water.

Far out towards the first island temple behind them, little fishing skiffs plied their way. Over it all, in scintillating patterns, white water-birds rose and fell.

This is your doing too, Father. This happy kingdom, this place of peace, this giant among nations. You gave it back to us.

Did you have to make yourself inhuman to do it? To make all the Khmers your children, did you have to kill your real ones?

The King's back still did not move.

The barges glided up to the landing beside the Victory Road. Elephants and giant parasols waited for them, men and animals shifting from one foot to another. Prince Rajapati's little bier, with its tiny pointed cupola in the shape of a house, was hoisted up and he was borne up the steps to the elephant platform.

The King rode on alone.

Children ran screaming and laughing. The King was back before his public. The King called down to the children. He knew some of their names.

Their beautiful mothers sauntered next to their children, hushing them and beaming up at their King.

Everything was new. New wooden houses stood on polished green poles, with new palm-frond or wood-tile roofs. Grannies spun new cloth. Young mothers nursed new babies. Tiny plots of ground sprouted fruit from new trees. Everything smelled of wood smoke, cardamom, hot greenery, rice paper drying in the sun, and syrup boiling in vats. Even the smells of fish from the lake were new, delicious, invoking the scents of barbecuing to come later in the day.

The happiest place on earth.

The great elephants lumbered along Victory Road. Stalls sold heaps of grain, valuable tree barks, medicines, or embroidered cloth. People whose religion allowed them to kill offered pork and the fruits of the forest hunt.

A skinny man with broken brown teeth and the moustache of a Brahmin ran out of his stall holding up a reed bowl. "My Lord, my King, Jaya, Jaya!" The man laughed at his own daring. "Oh, Universal King, my food is especially good this morning. Fresh fish, lemon grass, noodles. Oh so fragrant! Please, King, please stop and eat!"

The King did. The elephant was pulled around. The King's boy swung down from the side basket and took up the reed bowl.

The stall owner was overjoyed. He bowed and bowed and laughed and bowed again. The King pressed the dish between his fingers and ate, and then offered some to his boy.

"It's good, it's good!" the King called down. He then ate again from the bowl the boy had touched. "You have saved me the trouble of having lunch."

The man was gleeful and grinned and bowed, and the women under the screens leaned against the posts, arms around each other. These were not attitudes of disrespect, but attitudes of ease, as if they were among their own family. All their faces beamed.

This, thought Rajapati, is how every king would wish to be seen.

You have to acknowledge. He does it through fearlessness. The fearlessness comes from pure thinking. Because he emphasizes that the King is always a man, he is not afraid of looking human. This humility wins hearts.

The King is not afraid of being poisoned, because he knows his people love him. He is not in any case afraid of dying, for he can explain death, and gives death no power over his actions.

Oh King, you know that stall owner would now do anything in his power for you. His family will tease him, but they will also say: we have a good king. That man will save the reed bowl as a souvenir and say: the King ate from my bowl. He will say to customers: see how good my food is.

And his sons will die for you.

The procession walked up the Victory Road towards the eastern gate.

In the old days, you would have think carefully about the symbolic meanings of the gate you used. Coming through the east gate would symbolize something or other, say the King coming from the direction of Life.

This King would say, I always come from the direction of Life, even if I come from the west or the south. With this King, you come in the Eastern Gate simply because that is the most direct way to come.

That was the most annoying thing of all—to be wounded by a man who is perfect in every other way. Who would be interested in hearing your complaints against such a man, such a King? They whisper that he is a Boddhisattva.

The procession passed through the gate. The Gods on one side, holding the Naga serpent, the demons on the other, churning the Sea of Milk. If you were a Hindu, that was auspicious. If you were Buddhist, the Naga was the Rainbow Bridge that connects the worlds. You were entering a holy, Universal City.

The four faces of the Buddharaja stared down. If you were Hindu, these would be the faces of the three gods, the fourth being Buddha. If you were Buddhist, it would be the Four Noble Truths or the four cardinal directions or the four great rivers.

Oh King, you mean everything and nothing at the same time.

Once through those gates, you were in the core of the new City, the Indrapattha.

Here, the red wood buildings housed palace slaves, officials, and children. They were noble structures, carved with Naga serpents on the lintels.

Ahead loomed the towers of justice, where criminals were kept, and just above the rooftops of the houses, the upper storey of the Flying Palace. In front of that, the half-mile long terrace was carved to look as if it were borne up by flying beasts, garudas. The earth-bound palace was an image of the celestial dwelling that flew in the skies, amid cloud fields, and cloud-flowers.

Over that the private family temple gleamed like a golden bell.

The elephants passed through the gates, and the families of the court began to dismount. Rajapati's bier was carried on. The King continued alone, up the steps of the temple.

"Take me to join my father in the temple," said Rajapati.

"You are to go the palace and rest and eat," said his servants. They looked embarrassed, poor fellows.

"Your instructions were to carry the bier to palace?"

"Yes, Prince."

"Then do so," said Rajapati. And he belly-flopped himself out of the bier.

"Lord!" they cried.

"Go on, the King can't punish you. You did what you were told. I'll tell him that. Now go on!"

And the Prince bat-crawled on his arms, hobbling after his father, one step at a time. Undignified? Oh, yes.

Frankly, that's the problem of the people who look at me.

The unfinished man hauled himself like a tree frog up the steep staircase. The stucco was gilded and glowing. The statues had gold leaf pressed over them. Around the base, plates of gold had been drilled into the stone. All these things were the gifts of the Holy Victory Queen. How fitting then, that she should rest here.

Since she evidently no longer wished to rest beside her husband.

On the top of the temple stood a simple red pavilion. Rajapati hauled himself into it.

The King stood over Jayarajadevi's hammock, rocking it gently. He looked up. "Oh God," he croaked in utter despair. "Not you. Of all times."

"Thank you for that sincere greeting."

"I don't want you now, go away."

"No change there, then."

The King looked at him searchingly, with a sadness that could be mistaken for affection. "You know, you have a fine head. If only something kindly or wise ever came out of it."

"Again, Father, it is your complete sincerity of expression that has made you the King you are."

"You're right."

"Then at least we agree on something."

"The Queen is dead, 'Pati. Leave me in peace."

"No, Father." Rajapati's voice skipped. "I'm here to torment you."

The King's jaw dropped and he turned. He almost chuckled. "You're even worse than I thought."

"No, I just can't resist a singeing reply. Words are all that is left to me. My dancing tongue, my gouging steel pen."

The King groaned and hid his head.

"Right, to business. It'll be over with soon, and you will get your wish. I'll leave you, finally and permanently. But first, a little hymn of my own composition. You, Father are Mara. Mara who came and tempted the Buddha with Kingship. Buddha turned him down. You,

Father, are war. You are war and power and ruthlessness. You are oppression and enslavement and falsehood. And the summit of your falseness is that people love you for it. You are evil."

The King's face was bleary with misery and, more amusingly, boredom. "People aren't evil. They sometimes do evil things."

"Such as killing their son because he left the Path?"

Silence. Then the King nodded. "Yes. We could cavil a bit. The person who killed Suryakumara was the man who shot the arrow, but I know what you mean. I did send him to his death."

"And killed your once First Queen in the process. I trust that her death was unintended, but with you ... I ... can't ... be ... sure." Rajapati let the last words drip out slowly.

The King turned his bulk like a wounded elephant. "I grieve, 'Pati. I grieve."

Rajapati felt pity tremble. "I know you do, Father."

"She was so beautiful. She had such a mind, so full of light and kindness and love ..."

"You didn't deserve her."

"No, I didn't." He took up her hand and squeezed it, then pressed it to his face.

"I wish you wouldn't keep agreeing with me, Father. It makes it difficult to tell you off."

The King looked up again. "What do you want?"

Rajapati's eyes boggled. "Now. *That* was a surprise. First time you've ever asked me. Let's see. First and foremost, I want to die. Desperately and really and finally. I'll be finished here in just a moment, since you as always need me out of the way, and then I'll ... I don't know ... fire, water, a great height, something will turn up. It will hurt, but only briefly."

The King wiped his face, calmed himself, and then looked down at Rajapati on the floor. "Can you talk seriously?"

"I try and avoid it whenever possible."

"I know." Slowly, as if in pain, the King shuffled forward, and lowered himself onto the stone.

"But I'll make an exception if it hurts you."

The King took Rajapati's hand and held it, and looked into his face and said again, "What do you want?"

"I just said ..."

"No, no, no. You're not used to winning, so you don't recognize it. But you just won. I'm asking. What do want?"

Rajapati tried to pull his hand away. What he wanted was too big to say, and too small.

The King spoke in a low voice, looking at the hand. "I'd say first and foremost you want to hide. And I've been forcing you to go out in public. I thought that was a way of making you feel part of things."

Rajapati went cold. "It was a way of demonstrating your ideology."

The King paused, swallowed, made himself be patient. "Since my ideology is to be compassionate, you're right, it was." He sniffed. "No one's looking now."

Jayavarman stroked Rajapati's hair. His eyes were staring, but the smile was about to crumple into weeping. "You want to be king. You would have been a very good king. But you never can be. Many people think what happened to you is the result of sin in a previous life…"

Rajapati was alarmed to hear his own voice shaking and see the world around him dissolve in water. "What they say, what they say is that I'm the result of what happens when categories get out of order, and that what happened is like a mongrel dog mating with a civet and being shat out…" Rajapati couldn't finish.

"I can't change that."

"You could look at me."

"Don't I?" The King sounded small and fragile.

"No."

The King rocked back and forth. He looked at Rajapati's hand again. "When you were born, your mother and I were living in a Wat by the sea, and neither of us have ever been as happy again. And when you were born we looked at your face and said what a beautiful baby."

Rajapati managed to speak. "I hate emotion."

The King chuckled. "It's pretty generally a bad thing." He breathed in again, and was calm. "I need your help. I have a task for you."

Rajapati hissed. "I knew we'd get around to what you need reasonably quickly."

"You are good with words. And I need to tell the world that the Queen is dead. Could you write the letters for me? No, Rajapati, please understand. These letters have to come from someone high up and they must be written swiftly and Vira..."The King sighed. "Vira is excessively formal. He'd compose an ode. You write like I would write if I could. I know that you write letters to everyone. It was one way you tried to make yourself king."

"Don't worry. It failed."

"It would fail as soon as they saw you."

It really was that simple. "Yes, it did."

"So write to them all. Well and truthfully and simply. Tell them I grieve."

He stroked Rajapati's hair and, damn him, it worked. Rajapati was moved.

"I could do that, Father, yes."

"I have another long task, that I never thought could be done. I have a long story to tell, Rajapativarman."

Their eyes met finally. The King said, "Could you tell it for me?"

The park in front of the terrace was full of people and candles and prayers.

The King walked to the edge of the platform to acknowledge them.

On the deck, before a statue of Yama, the pyre burned. Silken banners danced alongside the flames. The people chanted her name.

Jayarajadevi! Holy! Holy! Holy!

Cremation was a long process. The royal household sat on the deck, quiet and respectful in the hammering sun. Heat from the fire billowed over their faces. All of the King's many sons and daughters were on the terrace. As First Queen, Rajendradevi sat in the very first rank and had the satisfaction of seeing her son and the King sitting in meditation together by the fire.

Even Fishing Cat was there, disguised as the handmaiden of the Queen-elect.

"I don't know if I can bear it," Princess Indradevi murmured to Cat. Her face was both plump and collapsed. "Why couldn't he just leave the situation as it was and let Rajendradevi stay First Queen?"

Cat answered, "He wishes to reward you. And his kingship depends on him having a holy wife. The people know you. They will be reassured that they have another Jayarajadevi. It will do good for the Kingdom."

Indradevi's shoulders seemed to dip under a heavy weight. "Policy, policy. It leaves no space for people."

Fishing Cat regarded her. She had never been as close to Indradevi as she had to Queen Jaya. But over time, they had become allies. "This policy allows you to fulfil a royal destiny. It allows you to continue to lead your people along the Path."

Indradevi looked up at her, her eyes dead. "I loved him for years. Now finally he has offered, and I find it is the last thing in the world I want. He is not the young man I knew."

"It is not for me to advise, but Princess, I would say: marry him. Become Queen. There will be no need to look happy; quite the reverse. If you looked happy, people might say: see how she rejoices in her sister's death. Look sad, and no one will begrudge you. They'll say: thank God she was there to take over."

Out in the park, the chanting had changed.

Indradevi! Indradevi! Indradevi!

Cat smiled. "You see? You are beloved. Your people need to know you are still here."

The King turned around, smiling, and held out a hand towards his sister-in-law. The hot air wavered, as if from uncertainty.

Indradevi said wistfully, "If I go, it will mean I have accepted him."

Cat considered. "Yes. But think. You are not one to starve yourself to death."

The Princess's eyes flicked back at her. "You are right there," she said. She took in a deep breath. "All right, Sister." She squeezed Cat's hand and stood up.

Oh! thought Fishing Cat. Indradevi has been trained since birth for something like this and does not even know it! The way she casts her eyes down, the way her feet take tiny, delightful, rustling steps. Her unfeigned modesty, the way she cannot help looking gracious, reaching out for the King's hand.

He held hers aloft. Yes! The people jumped up and danced and waved. Oh, they loved it; they would love this marriage; they would love this stability, this restoration, and this seeming victory over death. Their voices came in waves.

The King took the hand of Prince Indravarman on his other side, and the sound of the crowd redoubled.

The air shivered, the flames were hauled straight up into the air.

The revelation in the heat of the fire, in the collapsing logs, was that the pyre already contained nothing. Everything had already been burned.

Finally, as dusk descended, the King signalled that it was seemly for them to leave.

The household stood, making soft, suppressed cries as stiff joints straightened. They all went separate ways. Prince Indravarman was taken to a meeting of ministers and officials. Prince Rajapati was borne away on his bier to the library. Cat got herself to the kitchens to make sure there was food. The Queen-elect sat until the end, staring into the cooling grey pile of ash, already being stirred by evening breezes. Her skin felt stretched from sunburn, and was greasy and gritty from ash. She wanted to wash; she wanted to sleep; she wanted to break out into a run. All her wants cancelled each other out. She sat.

Stars came out. Insects and lizards made night noises. Just as they had done when she and her beloved sister were children, and had slipped out in the evenings. The stages of life: childhood, beautiful adolescence, then the wonderful task, building the City of the Eastern Buddha. Their real home.

How like a fire was life. It started small, with just a spark. It fanned to a mighty flame. Then it greyed to ash and cooled.

The night grew chilly and damp. Finally, Indradevi stood.

She retreated to the upper floor of the palace, where all was polished, bathed, and scented. The musicians made idle tinklings like waterfalls or bird cries. A cousin from Mahidharapura came to offer condolences, and tried to settle on the cushions for a long session of family grief. Indra made it plain she wished to be alone. From down below came the scent of roasted meat. Food! Who could eat? The day was ending like any other.

It was not enough.

With sudden determination, the Queen-elect spun around on her cushion and stood up with a sweep. She scooped up the taper and shuffled through the darkness to a library area. The gold curtains were lowered against insects. She held the taper up, found an oil lamp and lit it.

Prince Rajapati was also scratching away at palm leaves. He had a job at last. Indradevi thought of his mother, and whispered a friendly greeting to him. She got a pleasant smile back. My goodness. Everything was changing.

Dropping down into a lotus position, she snatched up a steel quill. She patted surfaces, trying to find palm leaves ready for writing. She only found an old letter. She flipped the hardened strip of leaf onto its back and began to write.

She wrote with an uncharacteristic gouging motion of determination. She wrote in the high holy language of the Brahmins.

He had for his First Queen Sri Jayarajadevi...

They will not forget you, Sister...

By the rivers of her house, the Queen would walk, practising asceticism...

I will make a new thing. It will look like it honors the King, but it will honor you, it will tell your story.

Her beauty was burned by asceticism, but it was not destroyed or diminished, but made instead a thing of wonder, like a temple hidden in a forest...

I will have this carved in stone and set up in the temple of the Aerial Palace. It will be longer than any other inscription. And more truthful.

She planted the eminent seeds of the spirit, and waited for the opportune rain of the spirit, and the husbandly act of the gardener of the soul. She obtained the fruit of wisdom and grace.

For what is the self but words? And what are words when they are set in stone? They become a kind of eternal self. Oh, Kansri, my sister, your star will shine bright for ever. The words will burn.

The cripple Rajapativarman worked as well.

He had gathered up all the treated palm leaves to himself. He was writing letters to minor officials now, people for whom getting any kind of personal communication at all, even after the cremation, would leave them indebted. Sweet-voiced, skilled Rajapati cut and carved.

> *I write to your grace on the King's behalf as he is stricken with grief. He asked me to make sure you had been informed person-ally by the family of the death of the matchless Sri Jayarajadevi and the observances that were made of it . . .*

At last I am getting towards the end of them, Rajapati thought. There have been hundreds of letters. And each one of them bore my name too. I have my princely head and my thin active hands, and I will be known for something even yet.

That very morning, in the midst of all the funeral plans and acts of statecraft, the King had taken time to sit with him beside the small family reservoir. To begin their secret project.

"I have no idea how to begin," the King had said.

"I should say who you are and what you intend to do," said Rajapati.

"I want to bring the past to life."

"Then that's what we'll say."

And they began their new adventure. The words were beautiful.

There was a cough behind him. Rajapati turned. There was the boy, smiling, looking a little uncertain. "Am I disturbing you?"

Rajapati wanted to say something like: no, I only have twenty-five letters to write; you do know how to write, don't you?

Then he thought: it might be wiser to play the kindly uncle.

"Not at all," he said to the boy, and patted a cushion. "Sit here."

Fishing Cat chatted with the other slaves, collecting up the reed bowls and the enormous urns in which the noodles were carried to the tables.

One of the old kitchen maids, who had followed the young Jayarajadevi from their old home, broke down in tears and hid her face in her shawl.

Fishing Cat comforted her. "She was a good, good woman."

"Yes, indeed, Lady. It has been a long story, Lady."

"Indeed," said Fishing Cat. "Indeed it has."

Cat and the woman collected up a tray of dirty bowls and shuffled with them back to the reservoir. There weren't many vessels to wash. Grieving people don't eat. This had not been the usual sociable funeral feast. There had been little exchange of gossip and connections, and no need to excuse laughter by saying, oh, she would have wanted us to carry on with life.

Cat and the woman climbed down the stone steps to the water and began to scrub.

How grateful I am for simple chores. Indradevi sits and frets and worries. I clean bowls. Somehow that puts everything in place. Crickets chirp. Stars glow. The world comes and says: here I am.

"You go on, Cat, there's not much else to do," said the other slave.

"It will all be there to do again tomorrow." Cat said it with anticipation.

"Oh, yes, we can always rely on our work," said the slave.

"I'll start on the upper floors. I'll take these clean things with me," said Cat, carrying one last burden into the kitchens.

Then she climbed the stairs up into the royal house. She could hear the entire family writing, scratching away behind lowered curtains.

Cat didn't disturb them. She knelt and dusted the floors. Top floors first, then the lower floors. The lamps drew moths, but the smoke discouraged mosquitoes. She looked out over the City, most of it blocked by the terrace, but even so, the sky swelled with light from many fires. In the distance, the canals were outlined with thousands of tiny fires, reflected on water. How large and grand it is, how many people live here, countless people.

See, Sister, she said to the spirit of Jayarajadevi, how many people come here to live in the kingdom you inspired? Can you see what you achieved?

Cat went downstairs to the cisterns to rinse her cloths to dust again. She stepped back into a long corridor on the ground floor. Night sky was reflected on its polished surface.

And Cat remembered. A little naughty running prince, sliding across her floors. Long gone. That house had long ago been abandoned and then burnt, and all her polishing wasted. But a new floor had taken its place. And this one does look like the surface of a lake.

Cat looked around, and threw the cloth down on the floor. She stepped back and ran and jumped and skated again across the palace floor, skirts fluttering. She grinned.

Cat walked on to her little ground-floor slave's room. She whisked back the curtain. The King, round-faced, exhausted, looked up at her in silent need, eyes ringed with concentric ripples, fanned with lines. His wife had died. He was an old man who had a kingdom to run, wars to fight, a new religion to drive into the hearts of his people. He was bereft, a failure, a god.

Cat lowered the oil lamp to the floor and silently took the man into her arms.

LEAF 151

My father, whose name in death is Parama Saugatapada, lay himself down to die by the fountain of Rajayasri (Neak Pean). An orchestra of wounded soldiers, lame or blind, played music that freshened the air and made the water dance. The old soldiers wept, playing last songs for the King. The people came to Rajayasri, the temple my father had made for them so that they could wash away their sins. The people formed a line to say farewell to him who was still Universal King. Chakravartin they called him, bowing. Prince Nia they called him, or Catch-Him-to-Call-Him. I tell you this line extended from Rajayashri to Nagara Jayasri. This line of people extended all across the perfect city, from the Eastern Gate and all the way beyond the western reservoir. All categories mingled within it, united in grief. It was a line of one million people.

LEAF 152

Love is invisible, but it turns the sky and mills the rain and holds up the mountains. The people came to say farewell to their King, whom they loved. This was not a ceremony, prescribed in ritual. It was not a thing to be repeated. It was like the flocking of birds. It was like the rising of the waters. It was like the clouds at dawn. It was like the turning of the cloud-flowers, always spinning, sensed but never seen. The mourning of the people was like a mother setting eyes on her child. It was a recognition. No text directed it. No banners preceded it. There were no elephants or candles or gongs. The people whispered their love and covered their faces and King Jayavarman raised a hand in blessing for each of them. There never was a more beautiful thing in all the history of the City.

LEAF 153

Father, I read these leaves and you are restored to me. I see you by the reservoir walking back and forth with your heavy tread and telling me simple and undeniable things that I turned into swirling cloud-flowers of words.

Oh, Father, I wish you were here. I wish it in the dawn. I wish it at high noon. I wish it in the evening when colors swirl like fire on the lake. I wish you and my slave mother were here to do simple things and reveal their importance. I wish you and your wives were here to make sense of the world and destroy sin. For I love you, Father, Saint, King. As your people will love you forever. I sit with my brother Indravarman in the candlelight and we talk about the old days. Indravarman has been my last and final lesson, Father. Can you read these leaves?

LEAF 154

The beautiful Indravarman started to drag his feet. Hard, unhealing sores appeared. One day he cut his thumb and did not notice and I realized the appalling thing that had happened. A king had become a leper. His hands twisted into useless curls. He did not once complain. He did not make one bitter or angry joke. His words were soft and kindly and healing. You have been the best of all to me, Rajapativarman, he said, for you understand. I wept two whole days afterwards in remorse. I sent him to Ceylon for prayer, for a cure. He came back unable to walk, his skin looking like lichen on stone. I help him rule. I do not do it badly. I write letters.

Geoff Ryman

LEAF 155

*Father, there are people who use us against you. Sri Jaya Mahapranjana
says our misfortunes are the wrath of untended gods, the result of cross-
category marriage. My brother and I are alone. They have started to cut
your thousand Buddhas down from the City walls, and I fear for your
images, and all your inscriptions. So I copy these leaves onto gold, which
knows no decay and which no animal devours. I will wrap the golden
words in orange cloth and seal them in pitch. Like a good farmer, plant-
ing the seed, I will put these words in your name into the earth. They will
bear fruit. The words will come again, when your people need them most.
When they cry out, tormented and disrespected, this book will flourish to
shade them from the sun. But more than that, to love them.*

Love, which is acceptance.

A Reality Check on
The King's Last Song

People who have enjoyed this book might like to know how much of it is fact and how much fiction. Jayavarman VII holds such a central place in Cambodian culture that failing to differentiate historical fact from my own (Western) imaginings would be disrespectful. I also owe it to readers and to the Cambodians themselves to show where some of my information for the modern story comes from.

My Fictional Jayavarman

There is no doubt that King Jayavarman VII retook the city of Yashodharapura from a Cham conqueror in 1181. We know from an inscription on the Phimeanakas temple that he had an ascetic and religious wife called Jayarajadevi, that he spent some time in Champa, and that he waited a long time before becoming king. We also know that he married his wife's sister after her death, and that she is the credited author of that inscription on which much of our knowledge of him is based.

We know that after retaking the city, he inspired or forced a massive building program. Many of the most spectacular Angkor-precinct monuments were built under his patronage—among them Ta Prohm, dedicated to his mother; Preah Kahn, dedicated to his father; the Bayon, Neak Pean, and Angkor Thom itself, the restructured city center that he enclosed for the first time within a defensive wall. The four faces on the famous gates are thought to be portraits of him. We know he built or repaired hundreds of what are now

417

called hospitals. The inscriptions on those buildings honoring his compassion have gone a long way toward creating our modern view of him.

He was the second king in Cambodian history to be a Buddhist, but he was the first to make Buddhism so central to its religious buildings. The entire length of the city wall was topped with niches, each one of which had an image of the Buddha. It is hard not to see this as being to some undefined degree a reaction against Hinduism after worship of its gods failed to protect the city from conquest.

We can see from his great temple the Bayon that to some degree he must have been a religious innovator. The bas-reliefs not only record his victorious battles in detail, but preserve the celebrations of the ordinary soldiers. Almost uniquely in Angkor-era art, the bas-reliefs show scenes from everyday life. A woman merchant, her friend's arm around her shoulders, measures out her stock for Chinese customers. A woman in one of the hospitals gives birth. A family either flees the army or is following it, walking beside their oxcart with a little girl riding on her father's shoulders. It's hard not to feel that this impulse to record everyday life shows a new interest in all of the Khmer people. The beautiful Neak Pean, a fountain that stood on an island in the middle of the giant reservoir, the Jayatataka, was built for all classes of Khmers to wash away sin.

History is a whispering gallery, in which some things are clearly heard and others not. Because the ancient Khmers used the saka dating system we know the year, the day, and the hour that Jayavarman's temples were consecrated. We know one of those temples alone, Ta Phrom, had 80,000 people dedicated to its rites, upkeep, and the feeding of all those tens of thousands of temple staff.

But.

We don't know the date of Jayavarman's birth or of his death.

We don't know why he appears to have built the temple now called Banteay Chmaar in the far northwest of the country.

We don't know why he spent so much time among the neighboring Cham people in what is now Vietnam. We don't know why the Bayon bas-reliefs show Chams fighting alongside Khmer troops against a Cham monarch.

It's difficult for us to keep track of all of his sons, or at least people whose titles bear the suffix "kumara," translated as Crown Prince. We don't know why the illustrious queen Jayarajadevi was *not* his number one, most honored wife. We don't know who his successor Indravarman was or why there are so few inscriptions about Indravarman, and none that honor or praise him.

We do know that after Indravarman, there was vandalism against Buddhist decoration. All the images around the top of the city walls were smashed or recarved to resemble Hindu Brahmins, and that Buddhist images in Preah Khan were also retooled to support Hinduism. A famous statue of Jayavarman was found by archaeologists, evidently thrown down a well. A Hindu backlash?

Jayavarman VII is not the man who made Cambodia a Buddhist nation. That came later, and the vehicle of Buddhism that triumphed was Theravada Buddhism. Jayavarman was a Mahayana Buddhist.

We also know that he had been virtually forgotten by the Cambodian people until he was unearthed by French scholars, who perhaps out of kindness, or perhaps out of colonial politics, drew attention to his great works and the unusually moving (to them, to us) inscriptions. But there is no doubting now the centrality of Jayavarman VII for modern Cambodians' own view of their history.

In 2004, at a talk that set up a writers' workshop in Cambodia, a civil servant stood up in the audience and begin to say something that got an odd reaction and then drew prolonged applause. What he said was afterwards translated for me. He had asked that if I was writing about Jayavarman, could I use him as a model to show to Cambodia's current leaders how badly they were misleading the country.

I talked to Chhay Bora, a trained dramatist who had written and got produced (no mean feat in Cambodia) a spectacular 100-cast-member version of the life of Jayavarman VII. He told me that he would spend hours just staring at Jayavarman monuments, to appreciate what the King had done for his people.

But I also spoke to one famous scholar of Cambodia (who insisted on not being acknowledged) who said that the highly metaphorical inscriptions in his honor might be translated to mean that Jayavarman was the Usurper. I was left with the impression that all stories are fiction.

I'm a novelist, not a scholar. My job at the time was to be inspired by the history, and to build up a coherent picture of a life. To my regret, I didn't take bibliographic references or footnotes. I'm embarrassed that I can't always give references. But I can sort out for readers what is attested, from what I had to create by guesswork, and to give as many of my sources as I can.

Throughout I had to find interesting stories to tell about parts of Jayavarman's life that are hidden from us. I had to decide which authority to believe, or sometimes invent a dramatic new explanation for the few things we do know.

I go through the ancient story chapter by chapter.

Leaf 1 and Leaf 2

No golden books from the Angkor now exist. I spent a lot of time trying to find ways that a palm-leaf book could have survived from the time. In the end I am grateful to Peter Skilling for the suggestions that the book might have been written on gold as in Indonesia. At the very last moment of writing, I read a translation by Saveros Pou of an inscription that commissioned a history to be written on gold.

I am grateful to my Khmer language teacher, Mr. Bun Ny Chea, for the subtitle. Originally I wanted something that meant the Golden Book. His more subtle *Kraing Meas* means something closer to Golden Treasure Manuscript.

Jayavarman is more like a title than a personal name. Parama Saugatapada is the King's attested death-name. All the other personal names I give him are made up.

Place names: I first ran across a systematic use for the ancient real names of temples in Charles Higham's *The Civilization of Angkor.* For example, Indrapattha is Angkor Thom, Madhyadri is the Bayon. Some names I had to make up for consistency. These are noted.

1136

Alexandra Haendel kindly read a draft and objected to my choice of Jayavarman's age. I followed the tradition that he did not become king until age fifty. Her studies have convinced her that he must have been much younger.

Giving him an earlier birthdate had storytelling advantages. For example it allowed this Jayavarman to see the building of Angkor Wat and become a trusted follower of Suryavarman II.

The names for various categories of slaves such as *kamlaa, khnom,* and *nia* are real, drawn from a number of sources. I have to confess, I never got a handle on the great number of different social categories in ancient Angkor. I sometimes got the impression that those classes with Sanskrit names such as *sujati* were an attempt to impose a traditionally Hindu social structure on Khmer society. It's also not clear that the word "slave" is the right translation. In a highly structured society almost everyone may have been tied down to a social role.

Of some help with this complex and changing vocabulary was *Studies in Sanskrit Inscriptions of Ancient Cambodia (on the basis of first three volumes of Dr. R. C. Majumdar's edition),* ed. Mahesh Kumar Sharan, Abhinav Publications, New Delhi, 1974. It helpfully reviewed whole categories of language from religion to administration to social life and dress.

The description of the slave girl's dress is as accurate as I could make it, drawn on many sources, including bas-reliefs.

The name Cap-Pi-Hau is an attested ancient Khmer name, and it does mean Catch-Him-to-Call-Him, but there's nothing factual to link it to Jayavarman. It is highly unlikely than any nobleman's son would allow himself to be called Nia, Hereditary Slave. Cmâ-kančus does mean Fishing Cat, but I made the name up, as I made up the character. "Mulberry" is an attested personal name for a slave.

The royal palace as described is based on the bas-reliefs on Angkor Wat itself, and on artifacts in museums.

There is no evidence that children of lesser kings or noblemen were held prisoner in quite this way. We don't know where Jayavarman grew up or the kind of role his nobly named parents may have played. His mother appears to have been highly connected. Though historians once listed his father as being a universal king, there is no evidence for this. I had to make a novelist's choice, and showed this Jayavarman as a child who had been sent away for schooling and surveillance.

The description of the parade is modeled on one described by a Chinese visitor to Cambodia in 1297, Chou Ta-Kuan. His account, sometimes called *The Customs of Cambodia,* is colorful and unreliable. It tells you where gay men gathered in the City and reads like

Geoff Ryman

traveler's hearsay. His description of the King appearing at a palace window to dispense justice inspired the leaves that follow Chapter 1181, when Jayavarman envisages his future as king.

The description of how Angkor Wat was constructed is drawn at least in part from the tour of monuments given to a group by Roland Fletcher, particularly his description of what we can learn from Ta Keo, the unfinished temple.

Alexandra Haendel objected to the lead roof tiles. I would not have made this up, but I never could refind the reference to the discovery of the lead tiles.

The future king Yashovarman makes his first appearance here. He was indeed the son of the King's nephew, but his character as a bully is pure fiction.

The name Meru for the contemporary Baphuon is a made-up name, to match the other names used for the temples at the time.

The totemic topknots worn by the troops are visible in Angkor Wat bas-reliefs. More on my sources for descriptions of Khmer armies will follow.

1142

I make no apologies for showing the future Jayavarman as being a religious and social radical from an early age.

We do know that the Hindu-ised culture of the Angkor era held Brahmins in high regard, honoring them with high office. Their portrayal on bas-reliefs, with beards and topknots tied up in cloth, gives the impression of a stereotyped ethnic identity.

Steu Rau, the Master of the King's Fly Whisk, was a real person.

There is absolutely no evidence that my Jayavarman ever befriended the great old King Suryavarman II in this way.

It is true that Suryavarman never had children of his own. The tradition that he slept alone on top of the private royal temple comes from legends recounted by Chou Ta-Kuan. Suryavarman II was himself an outstanding and unusual figure, a warlike conqueror and the patron of Angkor Wat. He was a Vishnuite when most kings were followers of Siva, and unusually did not claim descent from any previous Khmer king. In my fictional history, Suryavarman II is also religiously innovative, in an era that was already beginning to doubt the efficacy of the *devarajas*, the god-kings.

A blood tie between Jayavarman and Suryavarman? We do know that Jayavarman's mother was related to the ruling dynasty. Of his father Dharanindravaraman, we know almost nothing. I decided to assign a small, distant fealty. I don't think it unlikely that Suryavarman would have thought of him as a very distant relative…thus the "cousin."

Yashovarman did indeed marry Suryavarman's niece.

The nagahead torque worn by soldiers is everywhere visible on bas-reliefs. As the Naga is the traditional protector of the Buddha himself, it was a small leap in imagination to think that this torque might have some protective, good-luck function for soldiers.

1147

My portrait of Jayarajadevi comes mostly from the Phimeanakas Inscription, the long and startlingly beautiful tribute credited to her sister, Indradevi. I was also inspired by the statue of her in the Musée Guimet, Paris. It shows a physically frail, not conventionally beautiful woman. The face to me is alive with delighted acceptance.

The Dhuli Jeng, Divakarapandita, was a real person and he did live long enough to consecrate three kings. There is no evidence that he took such a special interest in Jayarajadevi or Jayavarman.

The name Jayarajadevi is more like a title. As with the King himself, I had to think about what my characters would be called in their everyday lives. I decided to give even nobles personal names in Old Khmer, not Sanskrit. Getting my hands on Old Khmer dictionaries was a challenge. I did find them in the Center for Khmer Studies, Wat Damnak, Siem Reap, including the French-English Old Khmer dictionary edited by Saveros Pou. But I had to hastily scan it letter by letter in the library. This sadly is why so many of my Khmer names begin with K. The two sisters are called Kansri and Kansru, similar names for sisters, shortened by them to 'Sri and 'Sru. My job was made much easier when I found many Sanskrit and Old Khmer dictionaries in the British Library, London. Some of the words I use come from Judith Jacob's *Cambodian Linguistics, Literature and History*, ed. David A. Smyth. I was never able to find a copy of an Old Khmer dictionary to buy.

Jayavarman's moustache comes from portrait busts of him.

It amused me to draw parallels between my ancient characters and modern Cambodians. The account of Jayavarman's courtship is based on that of Hun Sen and his future wife as recounted in *Hun Sen: Strongman of Cambodia,* by Harish C. Mehta and Julie B. Mehta.

Rajaindravarman, the presiding general at the wedding, was a real person.

I could find no evidence of how an ancient wedding service might have been conducted, so I modeled this one on a Hindu wedding I witnessed in London.

There is no evidence whatsoever that Jayavarman modeled his title on that of his wife. The likelihood is very much the other way around. However, I wanted to dramatize the future king's capacity to turn things upside-down. This anachronistic feminism is somewhat in keeping with the traditional view that Jayavarman's wives were of enormous importance in formulating his approach to Buddhism. Cambodians are proud that their traditions allow women greater freedom than in some other cultures. The bas-reliefs on the Bayon, for example, show Cambodian businesswomen.

The City of the Eastern Buddha is mentioned in inscriptions, but I couldn't find a location for it. The name alone, honoring the Buddha, is unusual. I adopted it as the ancient name for Preah Kahn at Kompong Svay. This is the Jayavarman-style city complex in the east of the country in which I decided to have the fictional Jayavarman establish a small kingdom before becoming universal king. The famous and very beautiful small head of Jayavarman as a young man was found there, and the buildings are instantly recognizable as Jayavarman-era. One of the most exciting of my research days was driving to this temple in a pickup truck on a dirt road surrounded by land-mine warning signs. This truck inspired the character of Ea and his pickup truck in the modern story.

The Old Khmer personal name for Jayavarman, Kráy, is another letter-K fiction. But "Huge, Powerful, Exceeding" does pack a certain prophetic punch if applied to Jayavarman VII.

1151

Jayavarman VII being held as an enslaved prisoner of war is not impossible, but it is complete fiction. We do know that Jayavarman had a complex relationship with the neighboring Chams and that the armies of Suryavarman fought there. This story has many dramatic advantages. It also reflects some of the modern story, not only Luc's kidnapping, but the harsher treatment of the Muslim Cham minority by the Khmer Rouge and the confusing factional wars of the 1980s.

Scholars such as Claude Jacques are confident that Suryavarman II died sometime around 1150 in the middle of a disastrous campaign against Vietnam. The last inscription bearing his name is dated 1145. In that year, he installed Harideva on the throne of one Cham kingdom, Vijaya, some say having killed his own Cham brother-in-law first. In 1149 another Cham, Jaya-Harivarman I, killed Harideva and declared himself King of the Chams. It is this new universal king who is shown as having good reason to find out what the prisoner Jayavarman knows about Yashovarman. This means that, without a clear consecration date, my fictional Yashovarman becomes king in 1151.

This is the first chapter set in my fictionalized Preah Khan/City of the Eastern Buddha. Suryakumara is only one of Jayavarman's historically attested sons.

1152

This chapter was meant to account for the alliances that Jayavarman seems to have had with some Chams. The son he has by Fishing Cat in the first drafts was meant to be Indravarman, the successor King.

Rajapativarman, the author of my utterly fictional royal memoir, is also a complete invention. He is the result of a research disaster that overtook the final draft. Flying back from Cambodia, I picked up a copy of David Chandler's *Facing the Cambodian Past* (Silkworm Books, Bangkok, 1996). His article "The Legend of the Leper King" pleased me. Chandler felt, as I did, that Indravarman might be the leper king of tradition, the *sdach komlong*. So far, so good...except that the article also told me that the real Indravarman died sometime around 1243. This made him far too young to be my fictional character, who was born in 1152. A major character had disappeared from the novel.

A friend, knowing of my bootless quest to buy a copy of Saveros Pou's Old Khmer dictionary, bought me a two-volume collection of Pou's articles. In those I found a translation of a very short text,

"The Stele of Nadun." This records the commission of three different people, all named Rajapativarman, to write for a Sri Jayavarmadeva a history in gold.

I had a new name and a new character. In my fictional universe, all three Rajapativarmans are one person, named three times with different titles because he is the king's son.

But most importantly for me, it was the only reference I had seen to Old Khmers writing on gold. Until then, there was no historical basis for my fictional golden book. I was charmed that the translation describes the commissioned text as "the property of God."

In earlier drafts of this novel, I believed that the Chams were more Buddhist than the Khmers in this era. I was set right by *Cham Art*, by Emmanuel Guillon.

The portrait bust that the stone mason makes, inspired by Jayavarman in meditation, is indeed meant to be the small head on display at the National Museum, Phnom Penh.

1160

One of the most difficult problems I had to solve was: what is Banteay Chmaar?

This temple in the far west of modern Cambodia is another Jayavarman-style complex with battle reliefs reminiscent of those on the Bayon. But the battle honored is not the retaking of Angkor Wat. Instead it shows Jayavarman-era troops battling what look like legendary monsters called Bharata-Rahu. What on earth could those have been?

I found my personal solution in "The Religions of Ancient Cambodia," by Kamaleswar Bhattacharya (published in *Sculpture of Angkor and Ancient Cambodia: Millenium of Glory*, ed. Helen Ibbitson Jessup and Theirry Zephir, National Gallery of Art, Washington, Réunion des musées nationaux, Paris, Thames and Hudson, 1997).

The article discusses a chthonic religion which focused on mountain gods and which may have merged with worship of Siva, also identified with mountains. Ba Phnom southeast of Phnom Penh and other temples were identified with human sacrifice, but a sacrifice intended to allow the God "a human vehicle through which the community can communicate via an intermediary."

My somewhat fanciful solution was a peasant revolt against the

Hindu religion and the role it played in validating kingship. My Bharata-Rahu became a suitably demonised false prophet. In this fictional universe, Jayavarman fought against a peasant revolt led by masked priests. This at least accounted for the images of contemporary soldiers battling with what look like monsters from mythology.

But what was Jayavarman's role in the battle? When did it take place? Inscriptions honor four great heroes who died in the battle, and three of them have the title *kumara*, often translated as Crown Prince. Was Banteay Chmaar built in honor of Jayavarman's sons killed in battle? That would make sense.

But why were these sons not listed in other inscriptions? If they were not his crown princes, whose sons might they be?

My fictional solution was to make them the noble sons of Yashovarman, also known to Jayavarman and honored by him. This of course meant the battle had to happen before the overthrow of Yashovarman, thus giving me a fictional date and a chance to make a character, the Usurper, later called Tribhuvanadityavarman.

1165

The relationship of Root and Rajapativarman echoes the Cambodian folktale *A Khaavk A Khvin*, "The Blind Man and the Cripple."

There is general consensus that Yashovarman was killed in a campaign about the time that the Usurper took power. The Phimeanakas Inscription baffles me at this point. Jayavarman seems to have gone to the Cham Kingdom of Vijaya "to support the king." How would going to Vijaya help the king? Was Jayavarman fleeing the victorious Usurper? That's likely but not the stuff of heroic legend.

My solution was to have Jayavarman forge an alliance with the Cham to remove the Usurper with loyal Cham troops. The battle in this section is not historically attested.

1177

There is no confusion over the date when the Cham deposed the Usurper and took possession of Yasodharapura themselves.

There is confusion over the number and names of Jayavarman's sons and wives. With the exception of Rajapativarman, any name I use for his wives or sons is attested, though the real situation is probably more

Geoff Ryman

complex than I show (or know). Rajendradevi is listed as the King's main wife: my fictional reason for this is that she gave birth to the King's chosen heir, Indravarman. In fact, we don't know for certain that Indravarman was Jayavarman's son. We also don't have a birth date for him. Bringing his birth and the date of the Cham conquest together meant I had a fast-paced dramatic chapter that ends with Jayavarman's decision, finally, to make himself the Chakravartin, universal king.

Jayavarman lived in an age of warfare and treason. He would on occasion have had to be ruthless. The entirely fictional murder of the Brahmin here is one of the few times my fictional Jayavarman shows a ruthless streak.

April 1181

The use Jayavarman makes of a white rabbit is fictional, but the idea is not unlike traditional Khmer stories about Subha Dansay, a rabbit, often Judge Rabbit.

The idea that Jayavarman's Cham allies were the sons of his friend Jaya-Harivarman is a fictional solution to the problem of placing Chams fighting with the Khmer against another Chams.

The scene between Jayavarman and the Cham King is entirely imaginary, though at least the Cham's name is accurate: Jayaindravarman. The Cham, like the Khmer, were Hindu-ized and like them used Sanskrit for things like official titles, so the similarity of the two men's names is without much significance.

The two battles on the lake and on land are as accurate as I could make them. Indeed, inspiration for this book came the moment that Roland Fletcher mentioned that Jayavarman had described the site where Preah Khan was to be built as a Lake of Blood.

I spent a lot of time staring at and drawing the bas-reliefs at the Bayon which show both the lake and land battles. In depicting the kinds of boats and their use in battle, and the ways in which elephants, infantry, and cavalry worked at the time, I made extensive use of *L'Armement et l'Organisation de l'Armée Khmère: aux XIIe et XIIIe Siècles* by Michel Jacq-Hergoualc'h (Presses Universitaires de France).

Jayavarman VII did indeed make the Cham Vidyanadana a *yuvaraja*, crown prince, but after the taking of Yashodharapura. I took some dramatic licence in placing him alongside Jayavarman at the battle for the city. His being one of Jaya-Harideva's sons is entirely fictional.

The celebrations described in the following leaves draw on the bas-reliefs on the Bayon.

1191

We know that the consecration ceremony for Preah Khan (Nagara Jayasri) was held in 1191 and that the foundation stone was written by Jayavarman's son Virakumara. However I have no evidence of the date of Jayarajadevi's death. To make it simultaneous with the foundation ceremony of Preah Khan is pure dramatic license. The Phimeanakas Inscription makes plain that Preah Khan was built or being built at the time of its writing. I took my cue from that.

Some Cambodians who otherwise enjoy the book feel that I have idealised Jayavarman VII. For me the challenge was trying to imagine someone who is worthy of veneration. His dispatch of a wayward Crown Prince by placing him in danger is entirely fictional, as is its contribution to the death of Jayarajadevi. That is sufficient feet of clay for me.

We do know that Jayavarman married Indradevi after the death of Jayarajadevi. The poem she begins to write in this chapter quotes from the real Phimeanakas Inscription.

LEAVES 151-155

According to Chandler, the Brahmin Sri Jaya Mahapranjana served Jayavarman VII and also his two successors. Tellingly, an inscription devoted to this Brahmin is one of the few that also mention King Indravarman only in passing, establishing his death sometime around 1243. The inscription contains not a word of praise for the King, and his death-name is not given, all of which can be read as meaning that this king was not venerated. I imagined this high-ranking Mahapranjana as being a leader of the revolt against Buddhism. There is some evidence of a visit by either Jayavarman or one of his sons to Ceylon, and in this fictional universe it was a visit in search of a cure. To be clear, there is no direct evidence that Indravarman was either Jayavarman's son or a leper.

The farewell to the King at Neak Pean described in these leaves is purely fictional. But it was an easy farewell to imagine, standing in that holy site with an orchestra of disabled men playing traditional music.

THE MODERN STORY

The modern story is also based on informal sources; just visiting, just talking.

My most recent experience of Cambodia is of increasing wealth in both Siem Reap and Phnom Penh. A whole generation, the majority of the population, has grown up since the 1980s. For them the Pol Pot era and the Communist society and civil wars of the 1980s are not even memories. Urban young people are cool, averse to both the curiosity and sympathy of foreigners. They no longer smile so readily, which might be a good thing. Some of them don't believe that the depredations of the Pol Pot era are anything other than propaganda. They want to have fun; they want a voice; they are bored by the past. Though their parents might be depressed, alcoholic, or dead; though the rape of karaoke girls is not thought worth investigating by police; though the numbers of ethnic Vietnamese are still one-fifth of what they were in the 1970s, they think that Cambodia is now normal. They move through the dust of the wars without knowing. The sadness is that that dust is merely tiresome, boring. Cambodia yearns.

AWAKENING

The story of how William got a western name is based on the life of a motorcycle driver I met in Battambang. The way his family died, with the Khmer Rouge murdering volunteer fisherman on the grounds they must be Vietnamese, is based on the memoir by Ronnie Yimsut, "The Tonle Sap Lake Massacre."

The description of William's home life is based on my stay with Mr. Kot Ker and his family.

Mr. Son Soubert, in reviewing parts of this manuscript, told me that the high-school diplomas given to refugees in Thailand were not recognized by the Hun Sen government, creating the kind of educational problems William faced.

Map's name comes from the name of a family member in

When Broken Glass Floats, by Chanrithy Him (W. W. Norton and Company, New York, 2000). I was charmed that it meant Chubby.

Mr. Leam Ran is a Patrimony Policeman who met me many times in the police village by Angkor Wat. He also accepted money from tourists for overnight stays in the Wat, though I never stayed there. He did lead this particular tourist up a staircase at Angkor Wat that disappeared at the top just as a joke. The five hundred dollar bribe to a land-mine clearance agency happened to a friend of his.

It was Mr. Leam who gave me mental permission to paint a darker Cambodia than I had in earlier drafts and to imagine a political, rather than financially motivated, theft of the *kraing meas,* when he outlined his fears that bandits would hold tourists hostage in Angkor Wat...and he'd be the guy to be shot.

April 1967

The description of Phnom Penh in 1967 owes some details and much of its spirit to *Cambodian Witness* by Someth May. There is no chapter set in the Pol Pot era because of the wealth of excellent writing about that time by Cambodians in translation. Please go and read them.

April 13, April 14, 2004

The description of panic in Siem Reap after the fictional kidnapping is a touch overdone for 2004. It's based on the panic in Phnom Penh caused by the violence of the 1997 coup.

The description of how the Patrimony Police celebrate New Year in the temple is based on a quiet party I had with them in 2001. The description of the old Army HQ in Siem Reap is based on my own visit there.

April 14, 2004

The lines about the garment industry came from a casual conversation with a returning Sino-Khmer refugee who owned garment factories. The giant radar photographs are based on those shown to me by Roland Fletcher in 2000.

Geoff Ryman

April 1988, April 1989, April 1990

This long chapter has many sources. In an interview Helen Jarvis provided details of where Mliss might live, the Calmette Hospital, and the orphanage near the Samarki hotel. Specific details of life in the 1980s come from two volumes of journalism by Jacques Bekaert: *Cambodian Diary: Tales of a Divided Nation 1983-1986* and *Cambodian Diary: A Long Road to Peace 1987-1993* (White Lotus, Bangkok, 1997; 1998). For example, the detailed description of the New Year celebrations, from the crowded stalls in the Central Market to the festive horse race, come from his book.

The song Map and Veasna sing was taught to me by my London Khmer-language teacher, Mr. Bun Ny Chea. He also contributed the meaning of Luc's name when heard in Khmer.

Hun Sen: Strongman of Cambodia contributed the scene in which Map burns his old family farmhouse.

Avoir 20 ans à Phnom Penh, photographs by John Vink, texts by Kong Sothanrith and Frédéric Amat (Editions Charles Leopold Mayer), provided inspiration for the photo of Map's wedding and the description of Veasna in Siem Reap hospital after a landmine explosion.

September 1960

Saom Pich is an entirely fictional character. There was not a show-case Brother Number One. Otherwise, all named people are real and were likely to be there.

I first heard of the September 1960 train-station meeting that founded the Workers Party of Kampuchea in Evan Gottesman's *Cambodia after the Khmer Rouge* (Yale University Press, New Haven and London, 2003). David Chandler provided more information on the meeting and on Pol Pot's career in his *Brother Number One, a Political Biography of Pol Pot* (Westview Press, 1999).

April 15, 2004 part two

The visit to the farm at Leung Dai is based on a visit with Mr. Leam to a farm owned by his relatives. The scenes on the lake result from

432

trips from Battambang by boat and a visit to the Vietnamese village with Mr. Kot Ker.

APRIL 16 AND APRIL 16, NIGHT

The visit to the warehouses of APSARA in Siem Reap (and the certainty that much of the statuary in the monuments are in fact copies—including the statue of Jayavarman) happened entirely because of the skills and determination of Mr. Leam.

Rith's home is based on the home of someone who rented cars to tourists that I visited in 2001. The exorcism that Sinn Rith sees Map perform is based on a description in *Cambodian Witness*, by Someth May.

THE SEASON OF RAIN AND FLOODING, SWEAT AND DROUGHT

The description of a severe case of malaria was contributed to by medical student Trent Walters.

Saom Pich's hysterical summary of Cambodia's recent history owes something to so many sources: Gottesman, Baekaert, Chandler, also Henry Kramm's *Cambodia: Report from a Stricken Land*.

The final leaves and their reference to Bhaishjyaguru, the healing Buddha, were inspired by the well-known inscriptions on the houses of the sick that were built or repaired by Jayavarman. The slight presence of a rapper during Map's prisoner term results in part from an impromptu recorded interview with the rapper Sdey recorded in Phnom Penh in 2004.

2004

Cambodia changes so quickly that there is no "present day" to write about. The British publishers wanted the modern story to be dateless, but I persuaded them we needed to be clear at what stage of development the story was happening. The year 2004 was the last possible moment the story would have happened like this.

The Siem Reap I describe in this book has disappeared. The novel would have been more aptly set in 2002. Then it was still a sleepy country town with as much in it for Cambodians as for tourists. Now the smoky roadside food stalls have gone, and there are modern gas stations, not immaculately dressed women selling gasoline in plastic bottles. Even some of the old colonial town has been demolished for modern buildings. Manicured, lawned, and air-conditioned, Siem Reap is a more comfortable experience for people wishing to visit the monuments.

You would not find William living on a farm anymore, though ravenous motoboys will still cluster around you as you arrive.

William's house would be sold for redevelopment to business people or NGOs for, say, $12,000. Since families, not individuals, own houses, the money would have been divided up among most of the family and rapidly spent on new motorcycles, electronics, or the rent for tiny concrete flats, which is where William will have ended up living with a young family. Perhaps he would have been able to finish his degree, but I doubt it. If lucky he will be working in the tourist industry. If not, his sole elevation will have been from motorcycle to duk-duk. If Map ever gets out of jail, and his spirit remains unbroken, he will not stay in Cambodia. He will get out by hook or by crook, to Thailand or the palm-oil forests of Malaysia.

A Note on Spelling

There are many systems for transcribing Khmer into English but every Khmer language course or dictionary seems to use a different one. In practice, this lack of a single system produces many different spellings of Khmer words in everyday English language texts. This is true even of well-known people's names—for example the singer Sin Sisamuth or Sisamouth. A search on Google will produce numerous websites that spell the same name in either way. This is even true of many common words. The rule for this book is simply to spell a Khmer word in the English transcription in which I first encountered it. I champion no one system and my transcriptions are not consistent, though this may cause concern for people who love the country and its language.

Acknowledgments

Special thanks for John Weeks for organizing a range of meetings for me in Cambodia. Other people who were extremely helpful during that visit include Jane Martin, Terry Yamada of the *Nou Hach Literary Journal*, You Bo of the Khmer Writers Association; Amrita Arts Association—especially Sal, Hang Sreang, Kho Tararith of the Sower's Association, and Yim Luoth. That particular visit was made possible by a grant from the Author's Foundation.

People who read early drafts and provided comments are hereby noted: Alexandra Haendel tried to correct my many misconceptions of life in the Angkor era; John Marston commented on contemporary cultural issues; Mr. Son Soubert took time out of a crowded schedule to comment on the section dealing with the 1980s.

People who worked hard to make the drafts they read better: Tudor Parfitt and Anna Davis; people who kept my pecker up: Paul Brazier, Leslie Howle, and Kim Stanley Robinson.

Many people helped me work through issues of the survival of the Book. I am very grateful to the Wellcome Foundation and Nigel Allan for a tour of their palm-leaf manuscript collection. Advisors on palm-leaf manuscripts or people who directed me to them include Jinah Kim, Elizabeth Pye, Alison McKay, Ann Bodley, and U Be Thein. Especial thanks to Peter Skilling, who suggested in a letter that the Book might be written on gold.

The novel was inspired by a tour of Angkor Wat given by Roland Fletcher of the University of Sydney.

Thanks to Bun Ny Chea for lessons in Khmer and cultural advice and Sambath Phalla of CASUNIK. Others who gave advice on contemporary culture, historical issues or archaeological practice include

Dougald O'Reilly, Christophe Pottier, Thina Ollier, Yin Luoth, Chhay Bora, Chat Pier Sath, Sam Player, Hang Sreang, Helen Jarvis, Leam Ran and Kot Ker. Tom Chandler shared his visualizations of ancient Angkor with me. Laurence Festal checked my French.

All these people struggled to relieve me of my ignorance and misconceptions. The errors are mine.

About the Author

Geoff Ryman is a Canadian living in the United Kingdom. His first book based on events in Cambodia was published in 1985, the award-winning *The Unconquered Country*. *The King's Last Song* was inspired by a visit to an Australian archaeological dig at Angkor Wat in 2000. He has been a regular visitor since, teaching writing workshops in Phnom Penh and Siem Reap twice, and publishing three further novellas set in Cambodia. In Britain he produced documentaries for Resonance FM, London, on Cambodian Arts. He has published nine other books and won fourteen awards. He teaches creative writing at the University of Manchester.

Since 2001, Small Beer Press, an independent publishing house, has published satisfying and surreal novels and short story collections by award-winning writers and exciting talents whose names you may never have heard, but whose work you'll never be able to forget.

JOHN CROWLEY, *Endless Things: A Part of Ægypt*
ALAN DENIRO, *Skinny Dipping in the Lake of the Dead: Stories*
CAROL EMSHWILLER, *The Mount; Report to the Men's Club and Other Stories*
ANGÉLICA GORODISCHER, *Kalpa Imperial: a novel* (TRANS. URSULA K. LE GUIN)
ELIZABETH HAND, *Generation Loss: a novel*
JOHN KESSEL, *The Baum Plan for Financial Independence and Other Stories*
ELLEN KUSHNER, *The Privilege of the Sword: a novel*
KELLY LINK, *Magic for Beginners; Stranger Things Happen; Trampoline* (Editor)
LAURIE J. MARKS, *Water Logic: An Elemental Logic Novel*
MAUREEN F. McHUGH, *Mothers & Other Monsters: Stories*
BENJAMIN PARZYBOK, *Couch: a novel*
BENJAMIN ROSENBAUM, *The Ant King and Other Stories*
DELIA SHERMAN & THEODORA GOSS (EDS.), *Interfictions*
JENNIFER STEVENSON, *Trash Sex Magic: a novel*
SEAN STEWART, *Perfect Circle; Mockingbird*
RAY VUKCEVICH, *Meet Me in the Moon Room: Stories*
KATE WILHELM, *Storyteller*

PEAPOD CLASSIC REPRINTS

CAROL EMSHWILLER, *Carmen Dog*
NAOMI MITCHISON, *Travel Light*
HOWARD WALDROP, *Howard Who?*

BIG MOUTH HOUSE (FOR READERS OF ALL AGES)

JOAN AIKEN, *The Serial Garden: The Complete Armitage Family Stories*

LADY CHURCHILL'S ROSEBUD WRISTLET

A twice-yearly fiction &c. zine ("Tiny, but celebrated"—*The Washington Post*) edited by Kelly Link and Gavin J. Grant publishing writers such as Carol Emshwiller, Karen Joy Fowler, David J. Schwartz, Molly Gloss, and many others. (*The Best of LCRW* is available from Del Rey.) A multitude of subscription options—including chocolate—are available on our website.

www.smallbeerpress.com